P9-EMQ-045

Praise for
DEPTH PERCEPTION

"A tightly written novel of romantic suspense by an author at the top of her game." —*All About Romance*

FADE TO RED

"Castillo is pushing the envelope. And she is doing a very convincing and, yes, disturbingly good job . . . This is not a book for the fainthearted . . . If you like nothing better than an adrenaline rush and a hero and heroine possessing multiple character layers, then be assured that *Fade to Red* will be exactly what you are looking for and so much more."
—*A Romance Review*

"A throwback to the old days of romantic suspense . . . chilling . . . Great character development, an ability to totally immerse the reader into the sleazy underbelly of porn and cause a shiver or two." —*Romance Reviews Today*

"Enlightening and original." —*The Romance Reader*

"Chillingly graphic—romantic suspense at its best."
—*The Best Reviews*

THE SHADOW SIDE

"An electrifying chiller rife with action and passion . . . splendid." —*The Dallas Morning News*

continued . . .

THE PERFECT VICTIM

DEAD RECKONING

Linda Castillo

BERKLEY SENSATION, NEW YORK

THE BERKLEY PUBLISHING GROUP
Published by the Penguin Group
Penguin Group (USA) Inc.
375 Hudson Street, New York, New York 10014, USA
Penguin Group (Canada), 90 Eglinton Avenue East, Suite 700, Toronto, Ontario M4P 2Y3, Canada
(a division of Pearson Penguin Canada Inc.)
Penguin Books Ltd., 80 Strand, London WC2R 0RL, England
Penguin Group Ireland, 25 St. Stephen's Green, Dublin 2, Ireland (a division of Penguin Books Ltd.)
Penguin Group (Australia), 250 Camberwell Road, Camberwell, Victoria 3124, Australia
(a division of Pearson Australia Group Pty. Ltd.)
Penguin Books India Pvt. Ltd., 11 Community Centre, Panchsheel Park, New Delhi—110 017, India
Penguin Group (NZ), Cnr. Airborne and Rosedale Roads, Albany, Auckland 1310, New Zealand
(a division of Pearson New Zealand Ltd.)
Penguin Books (South Africa) (Pty.) Ltd., 24 Sturdee Avenue, Rosebank, Johannesburg 2196, South
Africa

Penguin Books Ltd., Registered Offices: 80 Strand, London WC2R 0RL, England

This is a work of fiction. Names, characters, places, and incidents either are the product of the author's imagination or are used fictitiously, and any resemblance to actual persons, living or dead, business establishments, events, or locales is entirely coincidental. The publisher does not have any control over and does not assume any responsibility for author or third-party websites or their content.

DEAD RECKONING

A Berkley Sensation Book / published by arrangement with the author

PRINTING HISTORY
Berkley Sensation edition / December 2005

Copyright © 2005 by Linda Castillo.
Excerpt from *A Whisper at Midnight* copyright © 2005 by Linda Castillo.
Cover design by Pyrographx.
Interior text design by Stacy Irwin.

ISBN: 0-425-20720-X

BERKLEY® SENSATION
Berkley Sensation Books are published by The Berkley Publishing Group,
a division of Penguin Group (USA) Inc.,
375 Hudson Street, New York, New York 10014.
BERKLEY SENSATION and the "B" design are trademarks belonging to Penguin Group (USA) Inc.

PRINTED IN THE UNITED STATES OF AMERICA

10 9 8 7 6 5 4 3 2 1

ACKNOWLEDGMENTS

Special thanks to former state prosecutor Debbie Benko for so patiently and expertly answering my questions about the inner workings of the district attorney's office.

A huge thank-you to insurance compliance officer and fellow writer Susan Jarnagin for helping me through the complex world of the insurance industry.

I would also like to thank Scott Garland, former assistant district attorney, for sharing your knowledge and taking the time to answer all of my crazy questions.

Any and all mistakes contained in the book are from my own lack of understanding or my taking literary license to make the story and plot work.

"The prince of darkness is a gentleman."

—WILLIAM SHAKESPEARE

PROLOGUE

Cashiering at the Snack and Gas wasn't the dream job Evangeline Worth had always imagined, but then she'd always had big dreams. When she was fifteen she'd wanted to be a Las Vegas showgirl. At seventeen she'd had her heart set on becoming a soap opera actress in New York City. Her mama had wanted her to go to college to become a veterinarian because Evangeline had always had a way with animals.

But time and circumstance had a way of chipping away at dreams. Like a thousand other young women, Evangeline had slowly learned to settle for less and make do with what she had. Now, at the age of thirty-six, twice divorced and the mother of four, Evangeline figured she was lucky to have a job at all.

Honestly, working at the Snack and Gas wasn't so bad. Mama complained about the hours, which were midnight to eight A.M., and the neighborhood, which had been on the decline for too many years to count. But Evangeline didn't mind the hours or the neighborhood. The cops stopped by for coffee at least once during her shift. And she'd never felt the least bit scared, even though the coffee shop down the street had been robbed twice in the last six months.

The real pleasure of working at the Snack and Gas was her coworker. Irma Trevino might be sixty-two years old and as crazy as the day was long, but she knew how to have fun. With Irma around, the eight hours Evangeline spent selling beer and gas didn't seem quite so mundane.

"You going to stand there staring into space all night or are you going to help me stock these sandwiches?"

Evangeline looked at her coworker over the top of the cash register and smiled at her scolding tone. "Oh, don't be so prickly, Irma. I told you I'd help."

"Telling me you're going to help and doing the work are two different things."

Shaking her head in feigned exasperation, Evangeline started for the sandwich display cooler at the rear where Irma stood. As she rounded the counter, she glanced through the front window, saw the blue pickup truck idle slowly past the pumps and park near the door. "You're going to have to wait another minute while I ring up this customer."

"Oh, for Pete's sake." Irma glared at her over the display of Powder Puff doughnut boxes, but Evangeline knew that mean-grandma look was an act. Irma was about as mean as a Labrador pup. One that liked to growl a lot.

The bell on the front door jingled, and a thin young man with a day's growth of beard and scraggly brown hair entered the store. You never knew who you were going to get at three o'clock in the morning, so Evangeline always made it a point to look. She and Irma had once talked about what they would do if they ever got robbed. Irma had said, "Give them the money like it was on fire, then get on the floor. Decent robber ain't going to shoot no woman."

Evangeline had never reconciled the word *decent* with *robber,* but she'd thought that maybe even amongst Dallas's criminal element there must be some slapdash code of honor.

But the young man who'd entered didn't look like a robber. Just a regular guy out for beer and cigarettes. There were a lot of those in this neighborhood. People just trying to get by. As long as he wasn't drunk, he wouldn't give them any problems.

Head down, he huddled in his coat as he passed the candy display. His boots thudded against the tile as he walked to the cooler at the back of the store and grabbed a six-pack of Budweiser. Evangeline glanced at the television where a *Seinfeld* rerun blinked in and out of focus. One of these days they were going to have to put an antenna on that thing. Or else shoot it and put it out of its misery.

The man walked to the checkout and set the beer on the counter.

"Evenin'." Evangeline gave him only half of her attention as she punched the sku number into the cash register from memory. "That be all?"

"Yup."

She heard Seinfeld say something funny and smiled as she reached for a bag. Vaguely, she was aware of the man reaching for his wallet. Laughter on the television behind her. The crackle of cellophane from where Irma was stocking sandwiches.

She'd just hit the Total key when in her peripheral vision she saw the man pull something long and dark from beneath his coat. For an instant, Evangeline thought it was a baseball bat. Then she looked up and saw the sawed-off shotgun.

Adrenaline slammed into her with the force of a speeding bus. He raised the gun. The ensuing blast deafened her, and the security camera mounted above the TV exploded into a million pieces. Evangeline yelped like a hurt dog when he cocked his head and looked at her.

"I'll get you the money," she said, her heart rolling into a hard pound.

She wasn't *that* afraid. She didn't like the looks of that shotgun, but she didn't think he was going to hurt them. Still, her hands were shaking when she punched in the code to open the register. "I can't get the safe open," she said.

"I don't give a fuck about the safe," he snarled, glancing out the window toward the pumps. "Just get on the floor like a good bitch."

She thought that was an odd thing for him to say about the safe. There was barely two hundred dollars in the register. It was company policy for them to drop the twenties into the safe at least twice during the shift. Irma had made the drop fifteen minutes ago. She hoped he wasn't pissed when he found out he was risking prison time for two hundred bucks.

She glanced at Irma, hoping the other woman would stay out of sight. A cold finger of dread scraped up Evangeline's spine when she saw Irma walking toward them, her face stern and unafraid. *Too unafraid,* Evangeline thought. She tried to catch the other woman's gaze, but Irma either didn't see her or chose to ignore her.

"What the hell do you think you're doing?" Irma demanded.

The man spun. The second blast rocked the store. Evangeline saw Irma fly backward, her arms flailing, her face a mosaic of horror and shock. Red bloomed like a bloody rose on her white blouse. Then her small body crashed through the beef jerky display and lay motionless on the floor.

Evangeline heard a scream. A scream that was shrill and terrified and seemed to go on and on. Then she realized the sound was coming from her. She couldn't catch her breath. Her heart was pounding so hard she thought her ribs might break. Terror was a violent tornado inside her, pulsing and spinning out of control.

Her eyes met the man's. He had a pale complexion. Blue eyes. Whiskers on pitted skin. *"Why did you do that?"* she screamed. "I gave you the money! Why did you do that?"

"Shut the fuck up!"

But she was already rushing toward her friend. "Irma!"

Behind her, she heard the sound of steel sliding against steel, and it suddenly dawned on her that he was going to shoot her. Oh, God, no! Please!

Another layer of terror enveloped her when she looked over her shoulder and saw him raise the shotgun. "No!" she screamed, thinking of her children. "I have babies!"

Arms outstretched, she pivoted, changed direction, and sprinted toward the rear exit. Out of the corner of her eye, she saw Irma. Her small white face surrounded by a pool of blood the size of an ocean.

Evangeline didn't hear the shot. But the blast hit her in the back like a baseball bat slamming in a home run. Her breath left her lungs in a rush. A terrible sound tore from her throat. Pain exploded between her shoulder blades. When she looked down she saw blood and for an instant wondered how she could bleed in the front when she'd been shot in the back.

And then she was falling.

She tried to break her fall, but her arms refused the command. An instant later the floor rushed up. Her head slammed against the tile. Black and white stars exploded behind her eyes. The world went still.

The knowledge that she'd been shot registered in her brain. She wanted to move, to run. If she could get out the back door, she might be able to get away. But her arms and legs refused the command. Oh, God, why couldn't she move?

She opened her eyes, realized she was lying on her stomach. She saw a pale hand speckled with blood and tissue. The hand was twitching. Shock rippled through her when she realized it was hers.

Vaguely, she was aware of the thud of boots against tile. She wanted to see if the man had gone but couldn't move. But deep inside she knew he hadn't left. That he wasn't finished with her. That maybe the worse was yet to come.

"Turn over," he said.

Evangeline tried to speak. She opened her mouth to form the words, tasted the metallic tang of blood and realized the bullet had paralyzed her. She couldn't run. Couldn't move. Helplessness and horror exploded inside her. And she thought, *Oh, dear God, take me now. . . .*

The sound of his zipper being yanked down registered in her brain, and she wondered what had happened to this man to make him so depraved.

She could hear his boots shuffling against the floor. He cursed as he yanked at her skirt and panties. She closed her eyes when the fabric ripped. It was unreal, lying on the floor, shot and bleeding and unable to feel any of it. She was aware of her body being jostled, but her nerves were dead to sensation. Then he was on top of her. His body against hers, moving, rocking her back and forth. She could see his hand braced against the floor a few inches from her face. He was grunting like an animal. Cursing her . . .

The assault was over quickly. Evangeline lay there, paralyzed and helpless and wondering if he was going to let her live.

"You got blood all over me, you bitch," he said, jerking up his zipper.

When she opened her eyes, he was standing over her. Pale eyes staring at her with the cold blankness of a mannequin. The shotgun muzzle was less than a foot from her right temple.

Take care of my babies, she prayed.

And then the world exploded.

ONE

The city of Dallas rose early on Monday morning. By six thirty A.M., Central Expressway, the Dallas North Tollway, and LBJ Freeway were packed with tens of thousands of commuters, each determined to get to work on time despite the miles of construction, the endless congestion, and the simple fact that there were more cars than roads.

Part southern belle, part cosmopolitan metropolis with a little bit of the Wild West thrown in, Dallas was a city of stark contrasts. A city caught in a perpetual identity crisis. It was a place where gracious old mansions battled for space among the glass and steel skyscrapers that had been born during the oil boom of the 1980s. A city where the slow pace of the Old South clashed with the high-tech scramble of urban America. A place where lush southern magnolia trees shivered in the wicked winds that whipped down from the high plains during the short, cold winters.

But despite its quirks and growing pains, Dallas was home and Kate Megason loved it with a passion. She loved the excitement of big-city living. The restaurants and shopping, parks and cultural events. She loved the interesting mix of cultures that made Dallas one of the most diverse cities in the United States.

But like all big cities, Dallas had a dark side and more than its share of violent crime. Averaging over two hundred murders a year, the city was one of the nation's most violent. As a Dallas County assistant district attorney, Kate took those statistics as a personal affront.

She'd graduated magna cum laude from the University of Texas at Austin. For her law degree she'd chosen Southern Methodist University over Northwestern. And at the ripe age of twenty-six, she'd passed the Texas State Bar exam and become a lawyer. That same year she landed a job with the Dallas County district attorney's office and became one of the youngest ADAs in the county's one-hundred-and-fifty-year history.

Kate believed staunchly in the criminal justice system. She believed just as staunchly in the judicial system to which she had devoted her professional life. She enjoyed the challenge of her work. She craved the satisfaction that came with knowing she'd put a dangerous criminal behind bars where he couldn't hurt anyone else. She liked knowing she made a difference. Maybe even helped make the world a better place to live.

It was almost seven-thirty when she turned off Industrial Boulevard and swung her BMW into the parking garage of the Frank Crowley Courts Building in downtown Dallas. She entered the building and flashed her ID badge at the police officer stationed at the front entrance the way she had every day for the last two years.

"Morning Ms. Megason."

"How's it going, Sam?" she asked as she set her briefcase on the belt and walked through the metal detector. "LaShonda have that baby yet?"

He grinned. "Going to be any day now."

Kate smiled back, liking both the routine and the man. "Number three?"

"Four."

"Give her my best, will you?"

"Sure will. You have a nice day now."

She picked up her briefcase. "You, too, Sam."

Her Italian boots clicked smartly against the tile floor as she crossed to the bank of elevators and rode to the eleventh floor. The doors opened to a wide hall with tiled floors and walls covered with an industrial blue fabric some well-meaning interior designer had installed the year before when the offices were remodeled. Next to two double glass doors, a bronze wall plaque proclaimed the office of Mike Shelley, Dallas County district attorney.

Kate swiped her security card and stepped into the outer office. The familiar smells of paper dust, old books, and new carpeting greeted her as she passed through the main lobby. Even though the operator didn't come in until eight, the switchboard was already lit up like a Christmas tree. It was going to be another wild day at the DA's office.

Just the way she liked it.

Kate turned left and entered the small break room. After setting her briefcase on the table, she quickly made a pot of coffee, then picked up her briefcase and headed toward her own cubbyhole office at the end of the hall. She unlocked the door, shoved it open with a booted foot, and went directly to her desk. Pulling out her Palm Pilot, she checked her schedule for the day. Conference call at ten o'clock. Lunch at noon with one of her paralegals, who would be expecting a positive review and a raise and was going to get both. Court at two o'clock, where she would give her opening statement on a felony assault case. Back to the office in time to meet with a potential witness in a vehicular homicide case. By then it would be well after six o'clock. If her phone wasn't ringing, she might just be able to get some work done.

Kate was a creature of habit and thrived on routine and the fast pace of her job. A workaholic by nature, she lived by her schedule and drove herself relentlessly. She was up before dawn and at the office until long after dark six days a week. Aside from the occasional dinner or lunch or happy hour with coworkers—or the occasional duty visit at her parents' Highland Park home—she didn't have much of a personal life. Kate preferred it that way.

The smell of dark roast wafted into her office, telling her the coffee had brewed. To save time, she dug out the case file she was working on and skimmed the first page as she headed for the break room. Ricky Joe Paulsen was a repeat offender with a cocaine habit and a penchant for violence. He'd gotten off easy twice in the past. Probation for possession of marijuana six years ago. Then a five-year sentence on a burglary conviction. He'd been released after only eighteen months due to prison overcrowding. A week after his release, he beat his girlfriend to within an inch of her life. Kate was going to do her utmost to make sure the son of a bitch didn't kill someone the next time he lost his temper.

She poured coffee into a Lawyers Do It Better mug and carried it to her desk. She would outline her strategy this morning while her mind was fresh, then try to squeeze in the rest of her caseload between court and meetings.

Pulling a legal pad from her drawer, she scribbled the points she wanted to make in her opening statement. Repeat offender. Violent. Potential for extreme violence. No deals.

"Kate?"

She looked up to see District Attorney Mike Shelley standing at her office door, watching her as if she were his favorite child and had just ridden her bicycle without training wheels for the first time. The image made her smile. "You're in early this morning," she said.

"Says one workaholic to another."

"I prefer to think of it as dedicated."

"Sounds healthier if you put it that way. But if you're angling for a raise . . ."

"I already got my raise." Kate jotted a final note on the pad and set down her Mont Blanc. "And it was a good one. Thank you."

"Make it last. Both the mayor and city manager are screaming about budget again." Mike Shelley was a large man with direct, square features and a mouth that was too big for his face. He wore a custom black suit and the requisite conservative tie over a crisp white shirt. His graying hair gave him a distinguished air without making him look older. His forthright expression revealed little of what he was thinking. A trait Kate admired even though it made her just a little bit nervous.

"Can I see you in my office for a moment?"

Surprise rippled through her at the request, and it was quickly followed by curiosity tinged with a low-grade uneasiness. In the two years she'd been working for Mike, she'd learned his habits and preferences. Lunch meant a raise. Dinner meant a promotion. The conference room adjacent to his office was usually reserved for ass-chewings. The only time an ADA was called into the DA's office was when something big was going down.

She wondered if this was something big.

"Of course." Closing the legal pad, she rose.

He smiled as if trying to put her at ease, but it didn't work. Mike Shelley might have the teddy bear face of someone's favorite uncle, but Kate knew a shark with very big teeth resided beneath his benevolent facade. He hadn't gotten where he was by being a nice guy. At least not all the time.

"Sorry for the short notice," he added. "I know you're busy."

"No problem." After plucking a fresh legal pad from her drawer, she rounded her desk.

They walked side by side toward his office. "This shouldn't take long."

Several paralegals and administrative assistants had arrived to start their day, and Kate was keenly aware of the eyes following them as they passed by the break room and cubicles. The district attorney's office was no different from other offices and had a healthy grapevine; it didn't take much to get the tongues wagging.

Mike's corner office was the largest on the eleventh floor and offered a stunning view of downtown Dallas. His rosewood desk was huge and as glossy as a new car hot off the showroom floor. It was stacked with the requisite expanding legal folders and a smattering of photographs of his wife and three children. Kate knew most of what he did was political in nature. But she'd always thought Mike Shelley was too good an attorney to spend so much of his time smoothing feathers.

There were three other people already seated. Barbara Pasquale was a high-level ADA who'd been with the DA's office for going on twenty years. Kate guessed her to be in her mid-fifties. She was attractive in a red power suit and conservative strand of pearls. She was sitting on Mike's black leather sofa, a legal pad in her lap, her legs crossed. She made eye contact with Kate and gave a small nod in greeting.

The man sitting on the opposite end of the sofa was Alan Rosenberg, who was also a high-level ADA. Thin and balding, he had a boisterous personality and was one of the best lawyers Kate had ever met. Every time she heard him argue before a jury, she was invariably relieved that he worked for the DA and not the private sector because there would be a hell of a lot more felons on the street if he did.

"Alan," she said with a nod. "Haven't gone over to the Dark Side yet?"

He grinned. "The thought of facing you in court keeps me here."

She snorted just enough to let him know she didn't buy a word of it, and her gaze went to the third man sitting at the small conference table. Kate knew immediately he wasn't a lawyer. He wore a store-bought suit that was too tight in the shoulders and a hideous tie with a stain in the center. He had steel-gray hair and jowls that hung like strips of meat off his face. But it was his direct stare that gave him away. She'd been a prosecutor long enough to spot a cop on sight, and this man had *detective* written all over him.

"Kate, thank you for meeting with us on such short notice." Mike motioned toward the two ADAs seated on the sofa. "You know Alan and Barbara."

"Of course."

He motioned toward the man sitting at the table. "This is Detective Howard Bates with the Dallas PD."

Kate nodded at the detective. "Hello."

"Ms. Megason."

"Okay." Mike rubbed his hands together as if he were

about to dig in to a hearty meal, then motioned toward the table. "Have a seat and we'll get started."

Kate wasn't easily intimidated, but she didn't like surprises, especially when it came to her job. She didn't like the idea of walking into a high-level meeting without knowing the agenda. She had a sinking feeling she *was* the agenda.

Mike slid behind his desk, slipped his bifocals onto his nose, and picked up a file. "I'm sure you're aware of the Bruton Ellis case."

Kate took the chair opposite the detective. "The convenience store double murder."

"The grand jury indicted on Friday. It's an open-and-shut case. Two women gunned down. A mother of four and a grandmother with her first great-grandchild on the way. Two nice people with families just trying to make a living." Mike looked at her over the tops of his glasses. "One of the women was sexually assaulted *after* she'd been shot in the back."

Kate wasn't exactly sure why he was telling her all of that. She'd heard of the case, but hadn't followed it closely. She didn't know the particulars. She hadn't known about the sexual assault. But at some point her heart had begun to pound.

The DA continued. "Ellis is a repeat offender. Robbery. Drugs. Assault. He had enough crystal meth in his system at the time of his arrest to send an elephant to the moon. Shot out the security camera, but he didn't know there was a second camera, so the entire crime was caught on video."

"That will definitely help convict," Kate said, her lawyer's perspective coming automatically.

"We're counting on it." Mike took off his glasses. "I want you to prosecute the case."

Excitement hit her blood like a mainlined drug, but she didn't let herself react. Most cases with a true bill of indictment handed down from the grand jury were randomly put on the docket. Prosecutors were assigned according to district. Occasionally a prosecutor would be handpicked to handle a specific case, but the practice was unusual.

"Why me?"

"Several reasons, actually. First and foremost you're a

damn good prosecutor. You're thorough. Low-key. Juries love you." He smiled. "Defense attorneys want to marry you. Judges want to adopt you as their child. I think this will be good experience for you, Kate. And I think you'll be able to get a conviction."

She was flattered. But there was more coming. She could see it in his eyes. She could see it in the faces of the other people in the room. That she didn't know what it was gave her a prickly sensation on the back of her neck.

"This defendant is a repeat offender, Kate. He committed a double murder and a rape while in the commission of a felony."

Realization flashed. The quiver of nerves that followed was powerful enough to make her hands shake. "You want me to try it as a capital case?"

Mike nodded, then looked at each of the other people in the room. "The three of us met over the weekend and discussed the case at length. We've got legal sufficiency and adherence to statutes any way you cut it." He looked at the detective. "We looked at the evidence. The statutes of the State of Texas are clear. We believe the cold brutality of this crime calls for the most severe punishment applicable by law."

Kate didn't know what to say. It would be her first capital case. The kind of case most young prosecutors would give their right hand to try. It was the kind of case up-and-coming ADAs dreamed of. The kind of case that could make a career. Or put a young prosecutor on the fast track to a promotion down the road.

But while the challenge of prosecuting her first capital case appealed to her immensely, she couldn't help but wonder why Mike had hand picked her when there were a half dozen other prosecutors in his office with more experience.

Leaning back in his black leather chair, Mike Shelley fiddled with his glasses, but his gaze never left hers. "Next year is an election year. A win would look good on my record. And it could help your own career immensely."

Kate had never been one to talk about her dreams. She liked to keep them close to her chest, in case she fell flat on her face. But she was ambitious, and Mike knew it.

"I can give you until tomorrow morning to make up your mind," he added.

"That won't be necessary," she said. "I'll take the case."

MONDAY, JANUARY 23, 8:58 A.M.

The sun warmed his back as he sat at the bistro table and waited for her to arrive. The aromas of smoked fish and grilling vegetables filled the air. The café was crowded with the noontime business crowd, couples having lunch, students laughing over hafuch, the local version of cappuccino. The leaves of the olive trees that grew along the boulevard shimmered silver and green in the breeze coming in off the sea.

It had been two days since they'd been together, and he couldn't wait to see her. He couldn't wait to see her smile. To touch her skin. To hear her voice and the music of her laughter.

Setting his hand over the tiny velvet box in his pocket, he grinned like an idiot. The diamond wasn't much—less than half a karat and flawed to boot—but he knew it wouldn't matter. She was going to say yes. And when she did, he was going to be the happiest man in the world.

His heart swelled with pleasure and anticipation when he spotted her on the other side of the café. Smiling, he waved and motioned her over. "Gittel!"

She met his smile with a dazzling one of her own and waved back. He couldn't take his eyes off of her as she worked her way around the smattering of tables and colorful umbrellas. She was wearing a pale blue dress with matching sandals. Her legs were bare and sexy, and she was so lovely it hurt just to look at her. And he wondered what he'd done to deserve her in his life.

He'd already told his parents he was going to marry her. It didn't matter that she was from a wealthy Israeli family and he was a hell-raising Catholic boy from Texas. They were in love and he knew with an optimism he'd never before experienced that everything would work out as long as they were together.

"Frank!" Waving her arms, she laughed as the crowd jostled her about. "Sorry I'm late!"

He couldn't wait to get his hands on her. A need that was part emotional, part sexual sent him to his feet. He wanted to cross to her, put his arms around her, and take her down right there on the cobblestone walk.

For an instant time stood still. He watched her approach, liking the way the fabric swept over her body. He felt the warmth of the sun on his back. He heard the din of voices punctuated by the traffic that ran along the thoroughfare. Anticipation pumped through him with every step she took, with every beat of his heart. So much to look forward to . . .

The blast struck him like a speeding, burning car. One moment he was standing, the next he was airborne and careening through space. Agony ripped through his lower body as a thousand missiles penetrated skin and muscle and bone. Pain tore through the right side of his head as his eardrum burst. His world went silent and white, and he was tumbling in a kaleidoscope of shock and pain and confusion.

The next thing he knew he was lying on the ground. He saw black smoke billowing into a perfect blue sky. Around him, people were running, their faces covered with blood and soot, their eyes filled with horror. Raising his head, he looked around for Gittel, but all he saw was the twisted remains of a table and umbrella. He called out her name, but he couldn't hear his own voice, and he realized the blast had deafened him.

Gittel! Gittel!

He didn't know if he was screaming her name or if he was only thinking it. Panic and horror swept through him as realization settled into his brain, as the amount of damage registered in his brain. And he knew people had died.

Oh, dear God, no . . .

Pain zinged up his left leg all the way to his hip as he struggled to his hands and knees. When he looked down he saw that his jeans were soaked with blood. His stomach pitched when he saw the shrapnel jutting from his thigh. His leg was broken; he could see the bone fragments in the blood. But he was alive. He could move. He had to find Gittel.

He looked around wildly. A patch of blue snagged his eye. He recognized the fabric. Gittel, he thought, and his heart began to hammer when he realized she wasn't moving. Groaning in pain, choking on smoke, he began to crawl toward her, dragging his injured leg.

Please, God, let her be all right. . . .

It was as if he were crawling through a tunnel that was devoid of sound and light. He saw mangled bodies and parts of bodies and twisted heaps of metal and blood. He'd never seen so much blood. The cobblestone was slick with it. A red river that ran like death into the street. He could smell it, sickly sweet and mingling with the stench of the dead and dying.

The wail of an ambulance sounded in the distance. Hope bubbled up from somewhere deep inside him. The paramedics would arrive quickly. Gittel would be taken to the hospital, and everything would be all right.

But he knew the instant he saw her that nothing would ever be all right again. She was lying on her back in a pool of blood that glimmered like red ice. Her eyes were open as if she were looking up at the sky. Even torn and bleeding, she was beautiful. So innocent and decent and good.

"Gittel." He reached her, ran his hands over her torso. "Aw, God. Honey, it's me. Wake up."

Her dress was blood soaked, burned in places, and had been nearly torn from her body. Shoving a fallen chair out of the way, he tried to assess her injuries. The world crumbled beneath him when he saw her legs. Both had been severed from the knee down. . . .

Denial and rage rose in a violent tide inside him. "Aw, God, no." He pushed himself onto his elbows and put his arm around her, shook her gently. "Gittel. Oh, God. Oh, baby, no."

No!

No!

Frank Matrone sat up abruptly, his heart pounding, his mind raging at the horrors trapped inside it. He could hear himself breathing hard. Feel the cold slick of sweat covering his body. The scream in his throat receding back into its deep, black hole where a thousand more lay in waiting.

He jolted when a knock sounded at the door. Rubbing his hand over a day's growth of beard, he threw his legs over the side of his bed and stood. Pain streaked up his left leg and exploded brilliant and red inside his head.

"Goddamn it." Face contorted, he sat down hard on the bed and waited for the muscle cramp to pass.

The bell rang four times in quick succession, an annoying buzz that drilled a hole straight to his brain, and he wanted to kill the bastard standing in the hall, gleefully pressing the button.

"Can it, damn it. I'm coming."

Hefting himself off the bed, he limped to the doorway, trying hard to shake off the dark press of the nightmare, knowing that was the one thing that would never really leave him no matter how many shrinks he saw or how many pills he took. God knew he'd had his share of both in the last year.

He glanced at the clock as he crossed through the living room. "Shit," he muttered, wondering who the hell would be dragging him out of bed at nine o'clock on a Sunday morning.

Twisting the knob, he swung open the door. "This had better be good," he growled.

"I guess that's going to depend on your perspective." Sergeant Rick Slater didn't bother with niceties as he brushed past Frank and entered the dimly lit living room. "You look like shit."

"Thanks." Frank closed the door, cringing when the sound slammed into his brain. For the first time he realized how shaky he felt. That his head was fuzzy. To top things off his leg was hurting like a son of a bitch.

Rick crossed to the patio door and pulled the cord to open the drapes. Frank lifted his hand to shield his eyes from the sudden light. Christ, he felt like a vampire. Like the light was going to send him up in flames.

Shaking his head, Rick looked around the cluttered living room. "This place looks like a freaking pigsty."

"You should see it on a bad day." Scrubbing his hand over his face, Frank started toward the kitchen, trying hard not to favor his leg. "What the hell are you doing here this early on a Sunday morning, anyway?"

Rick looked to the heavens as if to ask for patience. He looked military neat in his blue uniform and spit-shined shoes. It was a uniform Frank himself had worn a lifetime ago. But he'd sell his soul before ever admitting he missed being a cop.

"It's Monday, you asshole," Rick said.

That surprised him, and for an uneasy moment Frank tried to remember what had happened to Sunday. Or maybe it was Saturday he'd lost. . . .

"You were supposed to be at Mike Shelley's office at seven-thirty this morning."

The words stopped him cold. Frank was well aware that he'd been on a downward spiral for the last year. He'd been pretty sure he'd hit rock bottom a couple of months ago. Now he wasn't so sure because he'd hit a new low this morning. Missing a job interview, for chrissake.

"Aw, Christ," he said. "Sorry . . ."

"Don't apologize to me, partner. I don't want to hear any more of your excuses. I've done what I can and the rest is up to you. If you want to fuck up what's left of your lousy life, go for it. Just don't expect me to stand around and watch. I can't stomach it."

"I'll call him."

"If I were Shelley, I'd tell you to get screwed."

"Maybe he will."

"I doubt he'll make it that easy for you, partner. You're going to have to do some creative fucking up to get out of this one." Rick stood in the middle of the living room looking exasperated and more than a little angry. "Shelley's a sap. Somehow he got the idea that you're some kind of a goddamn war hero."

"I don't know where he got that idea," Frank said dryly. But for the first time in a long time, he was ashamed. Ashamed for what he had done. For what he had become.

"The ball's in your court, buddy. If you want the job, you're going to have to do some damage control and see if you can salvage the offer."

Frank didn't know what to say.

Rick made a sound of disgust. "I watched you throw away twelve years with the police department. Don't expect me to watch you throw away another opportunity—"

"I didn't throw away those years," Frank snapped with sudden anger. "The department tossed me and you know it."

"They offered you a desk job when you came back, but your ego wouldn't let you take it." He looked around the littered living room. "You'd rather wallow in this shit hole like some kind of a drunken pig. I've had it with you and your bingeing and self-pity."

Self-pity. Jesus.

Furious because it was true, Frank spun away and limped to the patio door and looked out at the gray morning beyond. But he could feel his friend's words crawling inside him, like a bundle of worms in his gut, taunting him with a truth he didn't want to face.

"So you got a rough deal. We both know it could have been a hell of a lot worse. Some of our guys came back in body bags, partner."

The image of Gittel's torn and bleeding body flashed grotesquely in his mind, and Frank could feel the old rage building into a storm he wasn't certain he could contain if it broke free. "Shut the fuck up about that," he said darkly.

Rick didn't look away. "You could have been one of them. Think about that next time you pop a pill."

Frank's hands curled into fists, but he didn't move. Rick was his best friend. They'd been rookies together some twelve years ago. It didn't matter. Frank didn't trust himself not to knock the other man flat, even though he knew everything the other man had said was true. And he would never reveal that there had been times in the last year when he'd thought coming home in a body bag would have been better than coming home alone and torn to pieces inside and out.

Behind him he heard Rick walk to the door and yank it open. "Pull yourself together, Frank. I'm sick of watching you self-destruct." He waited a beat, as if expecting a rebuff. But Frank didn't have a rebuttal. There were no words left inside him. Nothing left to say. Nothing left to feel.

Just a big black hole that had blown through him that day in Jerusalem.

TWO

A hundred questions descended on Kate in the span of a nanosecond, and for an instant she was overwhelmed. She was aware that the room had gone silent. That all eyes were upon her. That her heart was pounding. And that she was excited. Too excited. She needed to calm down. Logical decisions weren't made when there were emotions or ego involved. In this case there was a good bit of both.

When she could find her voice she pursed her lips and met her boss's gaze. "What about the rest of my caseload? It's extensive."

"I want your full focus on the Bruton Ellis case, so I'll reassign most of your other cases to another ADA."

She was so flustered she couldn't even remember her other cases at the moment, but it didn't matter. She would give up all of them for the case she was being handed. She thought about her court date that afternoon. "I'm scheduled to give my opening argument on the Ricky Joe Paulsen case at two."

"You'll need to see that one through to the end. Judge Reinhardt doesn't like surprises, so we had better not switch prosecutors this late in the game." He scribbled a note into the appointment book that lay open on his desk. "How long do you expect the trial to last?"

"A week at most."

"Then it shouldn't be a problem."

She looked around the room, her mind already jumping ahead and prioritizing all the things that needed to be done. "I want to handpick my team."

"I anticipated that."

"I want two paralegals. Two administrative assistants. And three investigators."

One side of his mouth twitched. "One paralegal. One admin. Two investigators."

This is too easy, she thought, and something began to niggle at the back of her mind. Mike Shelley had a reputation for being tough on crime. It was an election year; he would be running as incumbent. And it suddenly dawned on her how important this case was not only to her career but to his.

Not sure how she felt about being used for political gain, she looked down at the legal pad and scribbled. *Three investigators.* If he wanted her to win, he was damn well going to give her the tools to do it.

"What kind of evidence do we have?" she asked.

Shelley motioned at the detective. "Detective Bates?"

The detective slid a small cardboard box toward Kate. "We've got him cold. He had the two hundred dollars on him when he was pulled over for speeding ten minutes after he hit the store. We've got at least one witness who put him at the scene. We've got physical evidence. The murder weapon. We've got ballistics. Latent prints. DNA—"

"DNA?" she asked. "You mean blood?"

"Semen."

"That will help."

"We've also got the videotape from the security camera." The detective motioned toward the box. "I can have a copy made for you. The documents in the box are copies, so they're yours to keep. The Dallas PD has maintained the chain of evidence and will continue to do so. Everything we've got is in the evidence room. It can be signed out, but, as you well know, I highly recommend that if you want to see any of it, you go to Evidence and have a look. Once that chain of custody is broken"—he shrugged—"I'm sure I don't have to tell you that some yahoo defense attorney will start screaming that the evidence has been contaminated."

"When can I get my hands on the tape?"

"I can have it couriered over tomorrow."

"This afternoon would be better." Kate looked from the detective to Mike. "What kind of time frame are we looking at?"

"I want this case tied up yesterday, Kate. Arraignment is the day after tomorrow. Preliminary hearing is probably going to be sometime in March. Motions to suppress evidence sometime in April. We expect the trial to be on the docket in early fall."

Just in time for the election . . . "That's a fast timeline for a capital case."

"You can handle it."

She and her team would have to work quickly. She would have to clear her schedule and start working weekends again. Mentally she reviewed her long-term calendar and realized she would have to cancel the cruise she'd had planned with her parents. She didn't want to disappoint them, but she knew they would understand. When it came to her job, Peter and Isobel Megason understood all too well.

"Does Ellis have a defense attorney yet?" Kate asked.

Alan Rosenberg grinned. "Aaron Napier."

"He's good," Kate said.

"You're better," Mike put in.

She shot him her best cocky smile. But she didn't feel very cocky inside. She felt as if she'd just stepped off a cliff and that someone below had moved the safety net. "Anything else I need to know before I jump into this?"

"I'm sure you're well aware that this will more than likely become a high-profile case," Mike said. "It's a capital case. Brutal and sensational. Once the media catch wind of it, they're going to be all over it. And they're going to be all over you."

"I can handle the media."

"Another reason I chose you." Mike Shelley rubbed his hands together, and Kate knew he was ready to adjourn the meeting. That was one of the things she liked about her boss; he didn't call meetings for the sake of hearing his own voice. He was quick and to the point. Just the way she liked it.

"All right then." Rising, Mike rounded his desk and extended his hand as he approached Kate. "Thanks for taking the case. I know you'll do a good job."

She took his meaty hand in hers and met his gaze as she gave it a firm shake. "I'll do my best."

MONDAY, JANUARY 23, 12:25 P.M.

Three hours later Kate sat at a bistro table with her paralegal, Liz Gordon. Kate had hired her a year earlier, and after a bumpy start and a little bit of head butting, the two women had become friends.

"I don't know what was better," Liz commented, "the coconut shrimp or that nine percent raise."

"You earned it."

"The shrimp?"

Kate smiled, but her mind was no longer on the food. "You can thank Mike Shelley for both."

"I'm sure you had absolutely nothing to do with it."

Kate rolled her shoulder. "He knows you're worth it." She smiled. "So do I."

"Maybe I should have held out for fifteen percent. . . ."

"Don't push your luck."

The waiter delivered two cappuccinos, their frothy tops sprinkled with cocoa powder and cinnamon, then hustled away. Kate picked up her cup and sipped. "Mike offered me the Bruton Ellis case this morning."

Liz's cup froze midway to her mouth. Her gray eyes latched on to Kate's. "What?"

"I said—"

"I heard you the first time. I'm just . . ." She set down the cup. "You didn't take it, did you?"

"Why wouldn't I? This is the case of a lifetime."

"This is a case that's going to have you working eighty hours a week for the next ten months."

"What's wrong with that?"

Liz rolled her eyes in exasperation. "God! You're such a workaholic."

Raising her cup, Kate sipped, eyeing her friend over the rim. "I thought you'd be happy for me."

"Of course I'm happy for you, Kate. I'm just . . . exasperated because I thought we were making some headway with regard to your social life."

Kate snorted. "Who needs a social life when they have a terrific job like mine?"

"That job isn't going to keep you warm at night."

"So I'll buy an electric blanket."

Liz shook her head. "How am I supposed to set you up with the most beautiful man in the world when you spend every frigging moment of every frigging day working?"

Kate laughed, truly amused. Liz had been trying to fix her up on a blind date with her brother's best friend for the last six months. Up until now, Kate had been scrambling for excuses. "Look, I'm going to have to put Thad on a back burner for now."

"Oh, that is so rich. You're virtually glowing because you now have a legitimate excuse not to go out with him. God, Kate, you are sick!"

Kate chuckled.

"It's not funny."

She pursed her lips. "Sorry."

"I'm starting to think you don't like men."

"I like men just fine. It just so happens that I'm focused on my career right now."

Liz pouted for a moment, then shook her head. "Thad Armitage is a dream, Kate. He's Harvard educated. Old-money family. Investment banker. Sexy as sin. Straight. And available. What more can a girl ask for?"

Having heard all too much about the illustrious Thad Armitage III, Kate started to change the subject, but Liz was just getting warmed up. "You need to meet someone while you're still pretty, Kate."

"I plan to be pretty when I'm sixty."

"You know what I mean. I'm telling you, one look at you and Thad will be drooling."

"If I want drool I'll adopt a dog."

"Come on, Kate. You're young and pretty and talented as hell. There's no reason why—"

"I'm also ambitious," Kate cut in. "Some men can't handle that."

"This guy doesn't have a fragile ego."

"That's good to know, Liz, but honestly I just can't spare the time or the energy right now."

Eyeing her the way a mother would a recalcitrant teenager, Liz leaned back in her chair and folded her arms. "I've known you for over a year now, and I've never seen you go out on a date. You're not an alien, are you?"

"Dating is overrated."

"I've never even *seen* you with a man."

"Maybe I just don't broadcast my personal life."

"At the end of the day, don't you want someone to come home to?"

"I have a cat."

"You do not." Liz leaned forward and lowered her voice. "How can you go for months at a time without sex?"

Kate resisted the need to squirm. Instead, she rolled her eyes and tried to look annoyed. But she could feel the heat creeping into her cheeks. The bump of her heart against her breastbone. The little voice inside her head told her to calm down. Reminded her that this was just a friendly chat between friends. Liz couldn't possibly realize what she was prying into.

"Stop playing matchmaker, Liz. It's not going to work. At least not until the Bruton Ellis case is over. I need to stay focused." She forced a smile. "And I need for you to stay focused, too. On the case, that is."

Liz set her cappuccino down with a resonant thud. "Me?"

Kate grinned. "I haven't told Mike yet, but I want you on my team."

"Oh, Kate." Liz practically squealed. "Wow, I'm incredibly flattered. Thank you." Then her eyes narrowed. "Wait a minute. Does this mean we have to start working Saturdays?"

Kate laughed, glad she had Liz to help her keep things in perspective. "Sundays, too, probably."

Making a face of extreme angst, Liz looked to the heavens. "What have you gotten us into?"

"The case of a lifetime." Kate pulled the ever-present legal pad from her purse and uncapped her Mont Blanc. "I've got an hour before I have to be in court. I thought we'd spend a few minutes putting together the rest of the team."

"God help us all," Liz muttered and looked down at the legal pad. "Just promise me that when this is over, you'll agree to go out with Thad."

"If I survive this case, I'm sure I can survive a blind date."

"Good, because I'm going to hold you to it."

MONDAY, JANUARY 23, 8:21 P.M.

It was nearly eight P.M. when Kate left her office. She'd spent the afternoon in court, given her opening argument, and the Paulsen case had begun as scheduled. She'd connected well with the jury, and even though the trial had barely begun, Kate thought she would get a conviction.

But for the first time in her career, her mind hadn't been on the case she was prosecuting. Her thoughts had already jumped ahead to the Bruton Ellis case. She knew it was going to be one of those cases that consumed her life for months on end. The kind of case that would call upon every skill and instinct she'd acquired in the three years she'd been with the DA's office. The kind of case that took a lot of emotional energy and mental stamina. But Kate was ready for it. She felt as if she'd been waiting her entire life for a case like this. It was her chance to prove herself. Her chance to make a difference.

Traffic was light when she pulled onto the Dallas North Tollway. But instead of proceeding north toward home, she took the Mockingbird Lane exit and found herself heading toward the Turtle Creek Convalescent Home, a place she visited at least twice a week no matter how busy her schedule.

She'd been thinking of Kirsten on and off all day, and it wasn't until she turned into the parking lot that she realized the case was something she wanted to share with her sister.

Kate parked and started toward the front portico at a brisk clip. The wind sent dry leaves scurrying across the asphalt, the cold cutting through her coat with the proficiency of a knife. Shivering, she pulled her coat more tightly about her and took the front steps two at a time.

Shoving open the front door, she entered the main foyer. The Turtle Creek Convalescent Home was one of the best in the state of Texas. With its high ceilings, expensive artwork, and tropical plants, the place looked more like a five-star hotel than a convalescent home. The staff and attendants were professional and friendly and wore trim navy scrubs. The on-call doctors were the best in the world. None of those amenities made it any easier to come here.

"Hello, Kate. How are you this evening?"

She looked up to see the home director approach. Nancy Martin was a robust woman with silver hair coiffed into a smooth bob that made her look both elegant and sophisticated.

Kate smiled. "How is she today?"

"She's the same. Your mom and dad were in earlier. Your mom put up some new curtains in her room. Not sure if I like the yellow, but I didn't say anything."

"Yellow? Hmm . . . I'll have to talk to Mom about that." Kate looked toward the hall where her sister's room was. She could see that the door was open. Had been every day for the last eleven years . . .

"I'll just go in to see her," Kate said.

"Sure, honey. Take your time." The director smiled. "Let me know what you think of those curtains."

"Sure." Turning away a little too abruptly, Kate started down the hall, her heels clicking sharply against the marble tiled floor. Most of the residents had already retired for the night, and the hall was so quiet Kate could hear the wind whispering against the windows. Official visiting hours had ended at eight o'clock, but the staff always made an exception for Kate and her parents, especially since Peter Megason had donated money for the new wing they'd added four years earlier.

A stainless-steel handrail lined the tiled wall to her right. A young woman in a pink housecoat sat motionless in a motorized wheelchair, her head drooping, a skeletal hand gripping the armrest. Kate smiled, but it felt tight on her face. The woman didn't acknowledge her, but her hollowed eyes followed Kate as she moved down the hall.

At the end of the hall Kate paused outside her sister's door, pasted a smile to her face, and walked into the room.

In the years she'd been coming here the scene never changed. She saw crisp white sheets on a bed that had the head end raised slightly. An IV bag hung from a chrome stand, a single tube running into her sister's left hand. A catheter bag half full of bodily fluids hung at the side of the bed. Fresh-cut yellow roses from the florist in the gift shop sat on the food table that Kristen had never used. A purple stuffed hippo Kirsten had had since she was six years old sat at the foot of the bed, looking lonely and a little sad. Classical music floated from tiny Bose speakers positioned on the tiled windowsill. A small color television gave off just enough light for Kate to see the outline of her sister's form.

"Hi, sweetie. How are you today?" Kate crossed to the bed and looked down at her twin. "I hear Mom and Dad were here earlier." She smiled, envisioning for a moment the pretty young girl who'd once been so vibrant and full of life. At twenty-eight, Kirsten Megason looked nothing like that girl now. Hair that had once been glossy and brown was now as dry and lifeless as the winter dead leaves outside, even though Kate's mother, Isobel, had her hairdresser come in once a week and give her a shampoo and style. A face that had once been soft and lovely was sunken and contorted, the mottled skin lying like old leather over facial bones that had once been model perfect. A body that had once been healthy and strong was atrophied and frail from disuse.

"I can't believe Mom put up those ugly curtains." Crossing to the embroidered, pale yellow curtains on the single window, Kate reached out and ran her hands over them. "I guess it's a good thing she has a decorator for the house."

She walked to the radio and twisted the dial to a local rock-and-roll station. A smile whispered across her face when she thought of how her mother would react the next day when she arrived to hold vigil and realized Kirsten had been listening to the Red Hot Chili Peppers and 3 Doors Down all night. Kate didn't think the music mattered, but she wished like hell it did.

"I got some good news at work today." Kate dragged the wingback chair to the bed and sat down. Out of habit, she took her sister's hand. The skin was dry and cold to the touch. She could feel the hand trembling and spasming within hers. But Kate had long since grown used to the sensation. Taking it between hers, she rubbed it briskly.

She looked into her sister's eyes then. No matter how many years passed, she always found herself looking for a spark of recognition. A flash of understanding. Anything that would tell her there was still a tiny part of Kirsten that was inside this shell. But the blue eyes that had once been so full of life rolled back white. A mouth that had once smiled so readily opened and closed soundlessly. Hands that had once played the piano with such utter beauty now clenched and unclenched mindlessly.

"I got my first big case today," Kate began. "It's going to be a capital case, Kirs. A man killed two women. Shot them down in a convenience store as if their lives didn't matter. I'm going to make sure everyone knows they did matter. I'm going to make sure those two women get the justice they deserve."

The only answer she received was the whipping of the wind against the window. The old rock-and-roll ballad playing from a radio that had never reached her sister's ears. The dim light from the color television that had never been watched.

"I met with Jack Gamble again last week." Kate lowered her voice. "You'd like him, Kirs. He's good. Tough. Discreet. I think he's honest. He's exactly what we need." She squeezed her sister's hand. "I just want you to know I haven't given up, sweetie. I haven't forgotten."

Kate plucked a moist towelette from the container on the dinner tray and used it to dab the saliva from her sister's chin. "I'm going to find them, Kirs," she said. "And if it's the last thing I do, I swear to God I'm going to make them pay for what they did."

Tossing the towelette into the trash container, Kate closed her eyes, lowered her face into her hands, and wept.

THREE

By the time her team had assembled in the main conference room at nine o'clock, Kate had already been at the office for two hours. She'd worked into the wee hours the night before, formulating strategy and finessing team assignments. At six A.M., she'd dressed, packed a workout bag, and headed to the gym for a rigorous swim to clear her head.

But despite her careful preparations, her heart was beating a little too fast when she entered the conference room. Her newly assembled team sat at the glossy oval table with legal pads and appointment books spread out in front of them, watching her expectantly.

"Good morning." She took her seat at the head of the table, snapped opened her slender briefcase, and removed her notes. Scanning her meticulous handwriting, she looked up and studied the team she had handpicked.

Liz Gordon stood at the VCR rack, her face set in concentration as she studied the operating buttons. Her no-nonsense style and ten years of paralegal and research experience would be priceless during a case like this. Since she and Kate were friends, Liz would be not only good moral support but also a liaison of sorts between Kate and the rest of the group if any personnel problems cropped up in the course of the case, which invariably they did.

Her administrative assistant, Sandra Hopkins, was paging through the folder Kate had put together for each of them. She was in her forties with a grown family. The consummate professional, Sandra was efficient and didn't mind putting in the hours. A good thing, considering the case was going to be a demanding one.

Junior ADA Marissa Riley, who'd begun with the DA's office the summer before as an intern from SMU, sat across from Sandra in her Banana Republic suit and Nordstrom shoes. Ambitious and smart, Marissa's fresh perspective and youthful energy would be an asset to the team.

Investigator David Perrine sat slumped in his chair, a Starbucks coffee and crumpled napkin in front of him. He was in his early thirties, single and ambitious. A tad too cocky, in Kate's opinion, but he had good instincts and kept his cool under pressure. Kate had worked with him several times in the last few years. Because he was a good investigator, she was able to tolerate his other not-so-desirable traits.

She'd spent half the night preparing for this initial meeting. The rest of the night tossing and turning with a bad case of nerves. Standing before her team, she felt those nerves settling. It was the waiting that always got her. Once she could dig in and get things moving, she was usually fine.

She looked around the room and frowned. "Where's my second investigator?" She glanced at the legal pad in front of her where she'd jotted names and titles and personal contact information, then at the group. "Frank Matrone."

The rest of the team looked around the room, shrugging and shaking their heads. Annoyance rose inside Kate. At Frank Matrone for being late for this vital first meeting. And at Mike Shelley for recommending an unproven investigator—a man she'd never met—for the job. Kate had zero tolerance for tardiness. As far as that went, Kate had zero tolerance for any bad work habit. Period.

This meeting was important. It would set the dynamics of

the way the team would work together, and was a prime opportunity for her to let her philosophies be known and lay down her expectations, which were high. From here on out, each member of the prosecution team would work independently and have to rely on good communication to keep other team members apprised of developments.

Kate put a line through his name, then looked at her team. "We've got a lot to go over this morning, so I'll catch Mr. Matrone up on things later."

"That's code for he's toast," David said under his breath.

Several people snickered. Kate shot David a pointed frown, then looked down at her notes. "Ellis allegedly committed a double murder and sexual assault while in the commission of an armed robbery." She removed four neat folders from her briefcase and passed them out as she spoke. "The grand jury has already handed down a true bill of indictment. Arraignment is tomorrow."

She looked around the room. "We will be trying this as a capital case, so if any of you receive any inquiries from the media—no matter how casual that inquiry may appear—you are to refer them to our public information office. I've prepared a folder for each of you containing an agenda for this morning's meeting, contact information for all of us, including the number and e-mail address of the lead detective working the case. Also enclosed is the timeline set forth for the case by District Attorney Mike Shelley. I'd like to adhere to this timeline as closely as possible. I've also included copies of police reports, crime scene photographs, and a manifest of evidence at DPD."

Once again seating herself at the table, she reached into her briefcase and put on her reading glasses. "Regarding evidence, Dallas PD has maintained a chain of custody. No evidence will come to this office. If we need to see something, we will drive over to the evidence cage and sign in, making sure we have a police officer with us at all times. We don't want some defense attorney trying to get evidence tossed because one of us contaminated it. We're going to prosecute this case by the book. And we're going to get our conviction."

"Do we know yet who the defense is going to be?"

Kate nodded. "Aaron Napier."

David made a dramatic sound and reacted as if he'd been punched. "He's good."

"So are we," Kate countered. "We've got a solid case and the evidence to back it up." She looked around the room. "This was a brutal, cold-blooded crime. It's important to remember that the two victims were people. Two women who were mothers with children and grandchildren. They had lives and people who loved them. They didn't deserve to get gunned down like animals."

Kate picked up the videotape. She'd wanted to view it in the privacy of her office before watching it with her team. But Detective Bates hadn't gotten it to her until just a few minutes ago. She was anxious to see it.

"The video we are about to watch is from the Snack and Gas security camera." She passed the tape to Liz.

Liz Gordon inserted the tape, dimmed the lights, then hit a button on the VCR. The room went silent as the grainy black-and-white video brought the pull-down screen to life. Like most security-camera video, the quality was poor. One of the victims was off camera. But Evangeline Worth was standing behind the counter when Bruton Ellis walked into the store. Watching her, it was clear the young mother of four had had no idea that these were the last moments of her life.

Kate had seen plenty of violence in the years she'd worked in the DA's office. She was no stranger to crime scenes or crime-scene photographs or witness accounts of violence. She no longer outwardly flinched at the inhumanities mankind could inflict upon itself. But deep inside, she recoiled with aversion when Ellis gunned down first Irma Trevino, then Evangeline Worth. That aversion augmented into revulsion when he unzipped his fly, got down on his knees, and took her from behind like an animal.

Vaguely Kate was aware of her team members shifting uncomfortably in their chairs, and she was suddenly very glad the lights had been dimmed. She could feel the old rage building inside her, like a tumor festering and swelling until she thought she would burst from the pressure.

She knew what it was like to be a victim. She knew what it was like to have choice and dignity stripped away. She knew what it was like to be hurt and terrified and humiliated. To be the object of another's savage cruelty and helpless to stop it.

Kate jolted when the tape played out. Looking quickly around, she pulled her thoughts back from a place she rarely let them venture. Rising, she turned off the VCR, then turned to her team. "My apologies. I didn't know the tape was quite so graphic."

"It's definitely going to help convict him," David Perrine said.

"There's no jury in the world that won't respond to that," Marissa Riley added.

Kate continued. "The arraignment is this afternoon. Bruton Ellis will be formally charged with two counts of first degree murder, one count of sexual assault, and one count of aggravated robbery. It is our job to prove beyond a reasonable doubt that this man did, indeed, commit these atrocious crimes."

Picking up her legal pad, she began to pace, her mind already leaping ahead to all of the things that needed to be done. "Marissa, I want documents filed this morning. Get us on the docket so we can move forward as quickly as possible after the arraignment. Call the Dallas PD Evidence room and the lead detective and let him know I'll be there this afternoon to review evidence. I'll also want a copy of the interview tape between the detectives and the subject. I want copies of reports from officers on the scene. All by this afternoon."

"You got it," the junior ADA said.

Kate glanced at her investigator. "David, I want a comprehensive background check on Bruton Ellis. I want arrest records. Convictions. Time served. I want to know if he was ever treated for substance abuse or mental illness. I want to know about his friends and family. I want to know what brand of toothpaste he uses. We don't want any surprises. And I want all this information yesterday."

"Hopping into my time machine as we speak." Gathering his coffee cup and notes, he rose.

"Liz, get me everything you can on the convenience store. I want to know if it is corporately owned or a franchise. I want to know if it has been hit before. I want a profile of both the corporation and, if it's a franchise, the franchisee of record—"

Kate bit off the words when the conference room door swung open. The room went silent when a tall man in a nicely cut charcoal suit entered. She knew it was crazy, but for a bizarre instant she felt as if she were in danger. Like maybe this man had snapped and at any moment was going to pull out a gun and start shooting people. He had an edgy, unpredictable look about him. A look that told anyone with a brain to tread carefully.

"Can I help you?" she asked.

A quiver of something she couldn't quite identify went through her when his gaze fastened on hers. His eyes were an unusual shade that wasn't quite brown and not quite green. It was an earthy shade that reminded her of the deep woods of East Texas. Green that faded to black as night descended and the forest became one with the shadows.

Kate had dealt with people of all walks of life in the two years she'd worked in the DA's office. Experience had taught her to recognize certain types of people by the way they looked, their mannerisms, the emotions and thoughts she read on their faces and in their eyes. But nothing had prepared her for what she saw when she peered into the disturbing depths of this man's eyes. He had the look of a person who had seen a lot of things, and she knew instinctively that some of those things had been ugly, that they'd disturbed him in some deep and profound way.

"Sorry I'm late." Looking appropriately repentant, he closed the door silently behind him, limped to the conference table, pulled out a chair, and sat down.

Several seconds ticked by before it dawned on her who he was. Her missing investigator, Frank Matrone. Kate couldn't believe he had the audacity to walk in now, some twenty minutes after the meeting had begun. She'd purposefully moved the sign on the conference room door to the "In Use" position so he wouldn't walk in late. There was an unwritten rule in the DA's office that once that sign was in place, you didn't cross the threshold. Evidently this man didn't do well with rules. That was fine with Kate. She'd never done well with subtle. She sure as hell wasn't shy about getting in someone's face when she needed to.

"Mr. Matrone, I'm afraid this meeting is already in progress.

I'm assuming you didn't see the sign on the conference room door."

Several snickers sounded around the table, but Kate ignored them.

"I saw the sign." He met her gaze levelly, and once again she was reminded of the dark Texas woods. After dark. When the wild animals came out. "Mike Shelley told me I needed to be here."

Kate could tell by the hard sheen in his eyes that the good-old-boy Texas drawl wasn't nearly as friendly as it sounded. She didn't miss the resentment buried in the depths of that hard gaze. She'd done her homework. She knew this man had once been a detective with the Dallas PD. She also knew he'd been a military reservist and that he'd been sent to the Middle East. He'd been badly injured, and when he came back he hadn't been able to resume his career with the Dallas PD. Kate had been around enough to know how to read between the lines. She figured some high-ranking individual within the Dallas PD had pulled some strings and gotten him a job with the DA's office. And she knew this man was not happy about the perceived demotion. She saw bad attitude written all over him in big, bold letters. From the way he sprawled in that chair. To the tardiness of his arrival. The lack of paper and pen. His total disregard of the rules.

Kate admired the men and women who'd put their lives on hold to serve their country. But her admiration didn't extend to vets who took advantage of their status—or had a chip on their shoulders. This was the biggest case of her career, and she wasn't going to tolerate anything less than one hundred and ten percent. If Frank Matrone didn't want to be here, she didn't want him.

"That's all I've got this morning." Kate looked at the rest of her team and motioned toward the door. "My home and cell numbers are in the file along with my e-mail addresses. If you need to talk about the case, please don't hesitate to call me any time. Until this case goes to trial, I am available day or night."

At that, the participants began to gather their materials. Frank Matrone sat sprawled in the chair, staring at her, looking like a bored teenager who'd been asked to stay for detention.

"Mr. Matrone, you can go." She motioned toward David Perrine's retreating form. "I've already been assigned an investigator, but thank you for coming."

Giving him a cool smile, she began stacking her notes into her briefcase. Vaguely she was aware of her team filing from the room. Of Frank Matrone scooting his chair back, rising slowly, and starting toward her. She didn't look at him when he reached her and hoped he would realize he'd been dismissed. But Frank Matrone evidently wasn't ready to be dismissed.

Kate could feel the power of his stare on her back as she turned and popped the tape from the VCR. When her meeting notes and files were neatly stowed, she looked up and met his gaze. "Is there something on your mind?"

"Mike Shelley assigned me to this case," he said. "This is where I need to be. Maybe you could fill me in on what was covered in the meeting."

Feeling the initial fingers of anger pressing into her, she snapped her briefcase closed and rose. "Since you don't do well with subtle, Mr. Matrone, I'll just come right out and say it. You were late. You didn't call. You didn't offer a reasonable excuse. You came to the meeting totally unprepared. I already have an investigator. Therefore, I do not need you. Is that clear enough for you?"

"Look, if this is about my being late—"

She added dense to the list of things she didn't like about him. Where the hell did Mike Shelley find this guy? "This is about your attitude."

"There's nothing wrong with my attitude."

Kate laughed, but she could feel her temper winding up. Taking a deep breath, she pulled herself back, but only a little. There were times when honest emotion spoke better than calm. Particularly when dealing with thick-skulled ex-cops. "You skulk in here like some kind of angry tenth grader and expect me to fall all over myself accommodating you because you decided to grace us with your presence. Well, I'm sorry if this comes as a surprise to you, but I don't operate that way. This is my case, and I plan to win it. Nothing personal, but I don't think you have anything to offer this team. You can tell Mike Shelley that or I will. Do you have any questions?"

FOUR

TUESDAY, JANUARY 24, 9:25 A.M.

Frank might've only been with the DA's office for two days, but he'd heard all about the infamous Kate Megason. She was a favorite topic among the male attorneys during happy hour when the booze was flowing and tongues were dangerously loose. He knew she was a pushy, uptight, type-A personality with a capital letter and double underscore on every single one of those adjectives. He'd even heard her name mentioned a few times back when he'd been a cop. Only cops weren't quite so politically correct and called her things like hard-driving, big-mouthed, ball-breaking bitch.

Frank had figured he could deal with that, since many of those same adjectives could be used to describe him. Well, except for the bitch part, anyway. Frank's personality flaws went far beyond bitch. Just ask his former boss, Dallas PD Chief of Detectives Manolo Blanco.

But while his attitude sucked and his life was totally fucked at the moment, Frank still considered himself a professional, even if he was hanging on to that belief by the skin of his teeth. When Mike Shelley had told him he would be working for Kate Megason, Frank hadn't even blinked. He might have a short fuse these days, but he wasn't so wigged out that he was going to blow the best opportunity he'd had since returning from the Middle East. Having spent the last year in his own private hell, dealing with some mean-spirited, self-absorbed, ambitious, she-bitch lawyer would be a walk in the park.

Or so he'd thought. Having just received a thorough verbal trouncing that would put any drill sergeant to shame, he wasn't so sure.

She was staring at him, her gaze direct, her nostrils flaring slightly. He stared back, his own temper stirring up all sorts of nasty comments. "Look," he began, "I got caught in traffic." It was a lie, but Frank was getting good at lying, especially to himself. "There's construction on—"

"Everyone gets caught in traffic in Dallas, Mr. Matrone, including me. That excuse doesn't wash."

"I was fifteen minutes late, for chrissake."

"Twenty."

"Whatever the case, a few minutes is no cause to have someone removed from an assignment."

"I guess that depends on expectations and whether or not the person doing the removing is willing to settle for less. In case you haven't figured it out yet, I don't ever settle for less than what I expect." She shot him a pointed look over the tops of her glasses. "This meeting is concluded."

He stared at her in disbelief, aware that his heart rate was up. That his temper was revving. That he disliked her. Intensely. It was one hell of a time for him to notice her eyes. They were the color of a deep mountain lake reflecting a cloudless sky and so blue he thought they had to be contact lenses.

All that blue was fringed with lashes that were long and thick and very black. Her brows were thin and dark and delicately arched. A stark contrast to skin that was the pale ivory of fresh buttermilk. Her lips were as pink as a Texas grapefruit. No power lipstick for Kate Megason. But then she didn't need facades. The hard edges of her personality more than made up for the softness of her face.

She wore an uptight suit with uptight shoes, and Frank figured if she got any more uptight, the woman would be in a knot. Her espresso brown hair was cut short, barely longer than his own, but it had the shiny gloss of a raven's breast. He hated boy-cut hair on a woman. He hated bitchy women with holier-than-thou attitudes. But even through the layers of dislike, he couldn't help but notice that beneath that uptight suit and I'll-kick-your-ass expression she had one hell of a body. The kind of body a man would risk bodily harm for just one touch.

Frank figured it was a good thing he wasn't in the market for a woman, to-die-for body or not.

"I don't report to you," he said. "I report to Mike Shelley."

"I think this situation will be best resolved if you walk away and let it go."

"Not a chance, sweetheart." He smiled when she stiffened, and Frank knew he'd scored a direct hit. Bingo. She didn't like being called sweetheart. He wondered how she would react if he told her what he really thought of her. "If you have a problem with my working on this case, I suggest you take it to him."

"I plan to." Snapping her briefcase closed, she turned and walked away without looking back.

TUESDAY, JANUARY 24, 5:24 P.M.

"I don't want him."

"Kate, come on."

"He's got a bad attitude. He disrupted my team meeting this morning. He's inexperienced. I could go on."

"Don't, because it's out of my hands." Mike Shelley leaned back in his leather executive chair and tried to look diplomatic.

Kate knew him well enough to know he was about as diplomatic as Hitler had been. "Why is it out of your hands? You're the DA, for chrissake."

"I agreed to do this."

"Do what exactly? Sabotage my case?"

Looking pained, he leaned forward and frowned. "Look, it's political, okay? I owed the assistant chief a favor."

"Assistant chief of police?"

"He and I go back a ways."

"So you dump Matrone on me? If you owed someone a favor, why the hell didn't you give him symphony tickets or something?"

"He was a good detective, Kate."

"If he was such a good detective, why isn't he still a detective?"

"He was in the military. Reserve, I think. Got called to duty and sent to the Middle East. He got hurt when he was over there and has had a rough time of it, so give him a break, will you?"

Kate knew she wasn't being nice about this, but she couldn't help it. An investigator's role was crucial. This case was important. And she didn't like Frank Matrone one iota. "What's wrong with him?" she asked without sympathy.

Mike Shelley laughed. "You're a hard case, Kate."

"I have a hard job to do."

"I'm really glad you're on my team."

"You're trying to flatter me because you don't want to deal with this."

"Look, I'm not going to change my mind, so you're just going to have to work it out."

"Why do you have to repay this favor on my watch? At my expense?"

"From what I hear, Matrone was a good cop, Kate. Give him a chance to do his job. He might surprise you."

If Kate had learned anything in the course of her career, it was that she didn't like surprises. Particularly when it came to her job.

TUESDAY, JANUARY 24, 11:13 P.M.

"Ellis is going to talk."

"You don't know that."

"I know enough about that sleazy little son of a bitch to know he'll do anything to save his neck, including sell us out."

The man in the Italian-made suit leaned back in his leather chair and contemplated the woman sitting across from him.

She'd poured herself a cognac before sitting down, but he could tell by the way she was gripping the crystal tumbler that the alcohol wasn't helping. She was usually unshakable. It worried him that she was letting this get to her.

"Even if he talks, how much damage can he do?" he asked calmly. "He's a piece of scum. No one will listen to him."

"Don't be naive," she said. "He knows too much. If the wrong person listens, he'll blow this entire operation right out of the water."

She had a point, but he would be a fool to admit it. They had good reason to be uneasy about Bruton Ellis sitting in a jail cell surrounded by two hundred and fifty cops. If he started talking and someone started putting two and two together, the situation could get ugly.

"Bruton Ellis has a record as long as my arm," he said. "He's a junkie and a thug. The police have the robbery and murder on tape. There's not a cop on this sweet earth who will believe him if he tells some story about his being a hired gun."

The woman nearly came out of her chair. "Are you willing to stake this entire operation on that assumption? Are you willing to risk your life? My life? Do you have any idea what will happen if someone figures this out?"

"It's not going to do us any good if we panic."

"I'm not suggesting we panic," she snapped. "I'm concerned. We need to do something."

"Like what?"

It was so quiet for a moment he could hear the overhead fluorescent lights buzzing. The hiss of traffic on the street sixteen stories down. Then the woman in the Ellen Tracy suit leaned forward and pressed her fingers to her temples. "I don't know," she whispered. "I'm scared. This wasn't part of the plan."

"For God's sake, pull yourself together." Realizing his annoyance with her was showing, he reached out and touched her arm. "We're going to be all right."

"Ellis took out the wrong camera. He murdered two people in cold blood. He left DNA behind when he raped that woman. None of that was supposed to happen."

The man sighed, wondering how well she would hold up if

the situation took a turn for the worse. If he had learned anything in his lifetime, it was that fear and panic invariably caused rash behavior. Rash behavior never did anything but get people caught. He'd decided long before he'd committed himself to this that he would not get caught.

"What we need to get through this are level heads and some clear thinking." He gave her arm a final squeeze, then folded his hands and set them on the desktop in front of him. "I don't want you falling apart on me."

She raised her head, her eyes seeking his. "Have you talked to Ellis?"

"No."

"He's been in jail for three weeks. This is Texas, for chrissake. He knows he's facing the death penalty. He has nothing to lose. He'll do anything to save his neck, including implicate us."

"Even if someone does listen to him, he doesn't know enough to point anyone in our direction."

"He knows enough to cause problems."

The man in the custom suit said nothing.

She visibly struggled to calm herself, folding her hands in front of her, then pursing her lips. "Maybe we could contact his lawyer. Anonymously, of course. Pay his legal bills. See if we can help him get a deal."

"I'll see what I can do. Third party, maybe. Napier is protected by attorney-client privilege."

"Not that Napier has any morals."

He contemplated her for a moment, wondering how he'd ever thought she was strong enough to do this. "You know I will not let anything happen to jeopardize everything we've worked for, don't you?" he asked.

She nodded, but he could see she was, indeed, scared. He wondered if she had any idea the lengths he would go to avoid prison.

"There are two ways we can approach this," he said after a moment.

"I've been wracking my brain for weeks, and I—"

He cut her off by slicing his hand through the air. "We ride this thing out and see what happens."

"By the time we realize he's talked, it's going to be too late."

"Or you can let me handle it my way."

Her eyes widened. "What are you talking about?"

She looked so damn innocent. The image she made looking at him with those wide eyes almost made him laugh. He wondered if she was so deep into denial that she hadn't yet accepted what they had been doing for the last four years.

"I'm talking about taking care of the problem."

"Ellis?" she asked.

"For starters."

Some of the tension seemed to leave her, but she still didn't look appeased. "I don't care how you do it. Just keep this situation from getting any worse."

"Let me make some calls," he said and picked up the phone.

WEDNESDAY, JANUARY 25, 9:43 A.M.

Give him a chance. . . . He might surprise you.

Mike Shelley's words echoed inside Kate's head as she headed toward Frank Matrone's office, which was just down the hall from hers. She'd been putting off approaching him, hoping Mike would change his mind and let her remove Matrone from the Bruton Ellis case. No such luck.

She reached Matrone's office to find the door closed. Puzzled and annoyed, she put her hands on her hips and leaned toward the door to listen. Not hearing a phone conversation, she twisted the knob and entered without knocking. Surprise rippled through her when she found the office vacant, the lights off. The computer off. And the message light on the phone blinking wildly.

"I don't believe it," she said, realizing he hadn't yet come in. She glanced at her watch. Almost ten o'clock. Unbelievable.

Spotting a sticky pad next to his keyboard, Kate walked to the desk and snatched it up. She would also send him an e-mail—for the sake of documentation when it came time to fire him. She looked around for a pen. "Why would he need a pen, silly?" she muttered. "He's never here." She tried the pencil drawer and to her surprise it opened. He didn't even lock his desk. What an idiot.

Picking up the pen, she began to write the note, all the while her temper simmering. This was exactly the sort of thing she wanted to avoid. She had a ton of work to do, yet she'd spent the better part of her morning dealing with an AWOL investigator. She had witnesses to talk to. Evidence to review.

"And one asshole to rake over the coals," she said beneath her breath.

"If I'm the asshole you're referring to, we can go ahead and get the raking out of the way now."

Kate actually started at the sound of his voice. She stopped writing mid-word and looked up to see Frank Matrone standing just inside the doorway, watching her with an expression that was at once amused and irritated. He was wearing a black leather bomber jacket and dark slacks. The jacket was open just enough for her to see that his shirt was wrinkled, his tie askew.

Despite the fact that she was his boss and was in the process of leaving him a note because he was almost two hours late, she felt heat creep into her cheeks. She knew what this might look like to him. That she had been ransacking his desk.

"I was just leaving you a note." Setting down the pen, she rounded the desk.

"Yeah? What does it say?"

"You're two hours late."

"I had an appointment."

"You were twenty minutes late yesterday."

He said nothing, his expression inscrutable.

"You need to keep me apprised of your schedule and account for your personal time."

"Does this mean I'm still on the case?"

Annoyance flared, but Kate stomped it down. "It means that for some reason unbeknownst to me, Mike Shelley wants you on this case."

He had the gall to smile. "So we're going to be working together after all."

"It means you're going to be working for me."

He nodded, sobering, but his eyes were amused. He knew she was pissed, and he was enjoying it. Damn him. And damn Mike Shelley for putting her in this position.

"Great." He rubbed his hands together. "So what's first on the agenda?"

"First, I guess we need to discuss the hours you're expected to be here, since you don't appear to have that clear in your mind."

"I'm clear."

"The hours are eight to five with mandatory overtime."

"Got it." He smiled. "About that agenda . . ."

He crossed to the desk and stopped. Kate had never noticed the way a man smelled before, but she did now. Frank Matrone smelled like a subtle mix of pine and soap and healthy man. He was standing three feet from her, close enough for her to see that even though he was clean shaven, he had a heavy beard. He must have shaved hurriedly because he had a nick on this chin. The leather jacket he wore was expensive, but the tie was cheap. He might have looked nice if it hadn't been for the cowboy boots. She hated cowboy boots. . . .

"I'm going to run over to Dallas PD and take a look at the evidence," she said, steering her gaze away from details she didn't care to notice.

"I'll go with you."

She didn't want him to go with her. "Look, Mr. Matrone—"

"Since we're going to be working together, the least you can do is call me Frank." He smiled, but she knew he was trying to disarm her. Fat chance. "It's shorter than Matrone. Less syllables. You can yell faster that way."

She sighed. "Frank, I'd like you to stay here and catch up on what you missed yesterday. I want you to take a look at the security camera video. Review the file I put together for you. I'll meet with you and David Perrine later this afternoon. I'm probably going to have you doing background checks on witnesses."

He had the most penetrating stare of any person she'd ever encountered. Kate was good at reading people. It bothered her tremendously that she couldn't read this man. That she couldn't figure out what was going on behind that shadowed gaze.

"I know my way around the police department," he said.

"So do I."

"No offense, but the cops down in evidence like to make you jump through hoops."

Kate felt a ripple of uneasiness. Surely he wasn't saying what it sounded like he was saying. "They have procedures for evidence."

"For you, maybe." He smiled. "For the most part, they just like to yank your chain."

She didn't like the sound of that. "Me personally?" she asked, not liking the way the question felt coming out of her mouth. It made her sound insecure.

"They get a kick out of pissing you off and watching you stomp and snort." His smile was deceptively charming. "In case you hadn't noticed, cops are jerks."

"I've noticed." She stared at him, not sure whether to believe him. Maybe *he* was the one yanking her chain. But she felt a little embarrassed because she'd always suspected the cops she dealt with didn't much care for her. She felt a little bit like a fool because this man knew it.

"I can help you cut through the bullshit," he added. "Could end up saving you some time and effort."

Kate had planned on giving him the grunt work involved with the case. Background checks. Delivering files. Anything to keep him out of her hair. But if he could help her cut through some of the red tape getting into the police evidence room, it might be worth taking him to police headquarters with her. "All right," she said.

"I'd like to have a look at that security camera video first."

Impatience swept through her. "If you had been on time yesterday morning, you would already know there's nothing more to glean from that tape. This is a straightforward robbery, sexual assault, and double murder."

"I'd still like to see it. Just take a few minutes."

Frustrated because she'd wanted to get started, Kate turned and crossed to the door. "Conference Room B is open. They've got AV in there."

Once in the hall, she didn't wait for him, but started toward her office to get the tape. She was aware of Matrone moving behind her. One of the administrative assistants passed them in the hall. A young woman Kate had seen a hundred times before but had never spoken to. She passed by Kate without so much as making eye contact. Then Kate heard the young woman speak to Matrone. "Hey, Frank." He called her by name, then said something beneath his breath that made her laugh. Kate rolled her eyes, but it didn't elude her that he'd only been around a few days and already knew the woman's name when she did not.

Kate retrieved the tape from her office and met Matrone in the conference room. He was standing at the window, looking out at the Dallas skyline and a slate sky that was threatening rain. He'd removed his leather coat. She got the impression of a tall man—well over six feet—wide shoulders, narrow hips, and legs slightly bowed with muscle. She felt herself hesitate as her eyes took in the length of him and an unfamiliar sensation that was both pleasant and uncomfortable went through her.

She was keenly aware of his eyes following her as she crossed to the VCR. She inserted the tape and hit the Power button. "Here we go," she said.

Rather than sitting, he leaned against the edge of the table, folded his arms and watched the video in silence. Kate stood a few feet away and watched the crime unfold, trying hard not to let it affect her.

When the tape had played out, she turned back to the VCR and started to hit the Eject button. Frank stopped her by putting his hand on hers.

She jolted with the contact and jerked her hand away before she could stop herself.

"I want to see it again," he said.

She felt herself flush, but within seconds she'd regained her composure. "Any particular reason?"

"I just want to see it again." Touching his head with his index finger, he hit the Rewind button. "Cops are slow. Sometimes we have to do things twice before we get it."

Not believing it for a second, she rolled her eyes and hit the Play button. The chilling scene unfolded again. Only this time Kate found herself watching Frank. Even though she had no idea what he was thinking, she didn't miss the narrowing of those dark eyes when Bruton Ellis entered the store. The tightening of his jaw when he pulled the trigger. The flex of his jaw when Evangeline Worth was shot in the back and then brutally raped as she lay paralyzed on the floor.

When the tape finished, Frank leaned over, ejected the tape, and handed it to her. "Okay. You ready to go?"

Kate blinked at him. "Aren't you going to tell me what you think?"

"I haven't decided what I think yet." One side of his mouth curved. "I need to mull it over. Could take a while. It's that slow thing."

She shook her head. "Now that we've pissed away half the morning, maybe we should get over to evidence."

Frank laughed. "Kate, I think we're going to get along just fine."

It was the first time he'd called her by name, and for some reason it seemed too personal. "As long as you come in on time and do your job, there shouldn't be any problems."

He was still smiling when he walked to the conference room door and opened it for her. "After you."

FIVE

The Dallas Police Department was located on Lamar Street just south of downtown. Kate had wanted to drive, but Frank overruled her and they piled into his Chevy pickup truck—which was closer because it had been parked illegally—and headed south. Ten minutes later they entered the Jack Evans Police Headquarters building. They showed their identification and were issued visitor badges, and after a quick security check the elevator whooshed them to the fifth floor where homicide was located.

The division was large and consisted of mostly cubicles with a few offices along the outside wall. Even though the new building was a designated no smoking building, Kate was pretty sure she smelled cigarette smoke. Cops. Jesus.

Frank crossed to a Plexiglas window and tapped with his knuckles. A large African American woman was working two phones, one on each ear. When she looked up and spotted Frank, she snapped, "Hold on," put both phones on hold, and came out of her chair like a tank climbing out of a gully.

"Well if it ain't Frank Matrone in the flesh," she drawled,

opening the door to her office and coming around to meet them. "I'll be damned."

"Cora."

He'd barely gotten out the name when she stood on her tiptoes and threw her arms around him. "Didn't think I'd ever lay eyes on you again. How you been, Sugar?"

Sugar? Frank Matrone was a lot of things, but sugar wasn't one of them. Kate watched the exchange in stunned silence. In the two years she'd been coming to the police department evidence room, the woman Frank had called Cora hadn't uttered a single kind word.

"I'm good." Pulling back slightly, he grinned at her. "I look good, don't I?"

"Good enough to eat. If I was ten years younger and a hundred pounds lighter I'd be all over your ass." She frowned at Kate. "What you doing wit' her?"

"I work for the DA's office now. Investigator."

"Nice title."

"I thought so." Frank motioned to Kate. "This is ADA Kate Megason."

Feeling left out, Kate stuck out her hand. "Hello."

Cora all but sneered, but accepted the handshake. "You looking to get into evidence?"

Kate nodded. "Yes, can you call the sergeant for us, please?"

"Oh, hell, I don't need to call the sergeant when you got Frank wit' you." Waving them off, Cora turned and went back to her office. "Just sign in and I'll buzz you through."

Kate couldn't believe it. For the past two years every time she'd come to the police department to review evidence for a case, she'd had to fill out forms. Plus, wait on the sergeant in charge of evidence to arrive so he could accompany her into the room. She considered that as she signed her name and title.

"Which case you lookin' at today?" Cora asked Frank.

"Bruton Ellis," Frank replied.

"You going to be looking for box number 5335B," the clerk said. "Item 5335A is in a bag on the shelf next to it. Let me know if you need any help."

"I think we got it covered," Frank said.

The buzzer sounded. The lock clicked. Frowning, Kate reached for the knob.

"You be sure to say goodbye when you leave," Cora called out to Frank. "I want to show you a picture of my new grandbaby."

He shot her a smile over his shoulder. "Wouldn't dream of walking out of here and not seeing you again."

She threw her head back and laughed. "Oh, bull. Matrone, you're so full of it!"

Rolling her eyes, Kate shoved open the door and walked in. The evidence room was huge and windowless and filled with rows of industrial-steel shelving with particleboard shelves that ran from floor to ceiling. She heard Frank behind her, but she proceeded down the narrow aisle until she found the numbered box she was looking for. "Here we go."

"Let me get that for you." Nudging her aside, Frank lifted the box from the shelf. Kate stood on her tiptoes and, on the shelf next to where the box had been, found item number 5335A wrapped in plastic. It was the shotgun Bruton Ellis had used to murder Evangeline Worth and Irma Trevino.

She pulled the gun off the shelf. "So how did you manage that?" she asked as they carried both items to the table.

"It wasn't that heavy. . . ."

"Not the box," she snapped before realizing he was messing with her. She pursed her lips. "I meant getting in here without having to jump through hoops."

"Cora and I go way back." When Kate only continued to look at him, he shrugged and added, "They know me."

"They know me, too."

He carried the box to a beat-up wooden table in the back corner. She followed with the bagged shotgun and set it on the table. "Why do they make me jump through hoops and not you?"

"She wants my body."

"I'm serious," she said.

"I'm not kidding. If I didn't like being groped by women so much, I would have filed—"

"Matrone," she cut in firmly.

Frank cleared his throat and sobered. "You sure you want to know?"

"If I didn't want to know, I wouldn't have asked."

"The cops don't much care for you," he said.

Kate knew better than to let that get to her. She knew she wasn't always a nice person. But over the years she'd learned that nice didn't always get the job done. She didn't come here to win personality points or make friends. Her job required her to get things done. In order to be effective, most of the time she had to be firm.

He removed the lid from the box. "Not much here," he said, pulling a large plastic bag from the box. "Looks like the M.E. hasn't sent the clothing over yet."

"Clothing went to the Institute of Forensic Sciences lab."

"DNA?"

"They've got semen." She frowned. "The lab has had plenty of time. Give the M.E.'s office a call when you get back." Kate plucked a small bag containing one shotgun shell from the box. "Latent prints have been done. We should have had the report already." She made a mental note to call them when she got back to her office.

Frank tugged a ladder-back wood chair from beneath the table and sat down. Kate sat opposite him and pulled a legal pad from her briefcase. "What makes you think the cops don't like me?" she asked, plucking a pen from her appointment book.

He looked over at her and smiled. "Don't tell me you're worried about that."

"Of course not," she lied. "I just . . . want to know why I can't seem to get things done here."

He picked up the bag containing the shotgun shell and studied it as if it were the most fascinating piece of evidence he'd ever seen.

She set down her pen. "Matrone."

"Kate, come on. I told you cops are jerks."

"Would you just clue me in, please?"

"You don't want to know."

"I want to know."

"It will only piss you off. You really don't want to know."

"Oh, for God's sake, would you just tell—"

"They call you Megabitch."

Kate struggled not to wince, but wasn't sure if she succeeded. "Megabitch?"

"You know, it's a play on words. Megason. Megabitch."

"I get the connection," she snapped.

"Cops can be real assholes about stupid shit."

"Like calling an ADA Megabitch."

He managed to look contrite. "I told you it would piss you off."

"I'm not pissed off."

"Yeah, that's why you're yelling."

"I'm not yelling." Realizing her voice had gone up a decibel or two, she took a deep breath. "Oh, good grief."

One side of his mouth curved. "See? You're a sweetheart. The cops got it all wrong."

Kate knew it was stupid to let something like that get to her. She had thicker skin than that. Damn it, she knew she wouldn't win any personality contests at Dallas PD. But she couldn't believe the cops she worked with on an almost daily basis called her Megabitch behind her back. On a professional level, it was important for an ADA to have a good working relationship with the police department. On a personal level, knowing the cops made fun of her bothered her more than she wanted to admit.

For several minutes they went through each piece of evidence. Kate listed each item on her legal pad, scribbling notes as she went. Three shotgun shells. One sawed-off shotgun. The six-pack of beer Bruton Ellis had carried to the counter. Kate made a conscious effort to concentrate on the case, but the nickname niggled at her like a stinging insect bite. Was she so driven that she didn't notice that people didn't like her?

She came to a bag filled with what looked like shattered pieces of black plastic. "What's this?" she asked, holding it up.

Frank took the bag from her and studied its contents. "Looks like what's left of the security camera."

"But we've got video. He couldn't have shot out the camera."

He pointed to a piece of glass that was rounded on one side. "That's part of a lens right there."

"He did fire a single shot toward the ceiling." She bit her lip. "You think there could have been two cameras?"

"I'll make a note to check with the store manager." Frank leaned back in his chair and regarded her for a moment. "If he had the forethought to shoot the camera, that means he scoped the place."

"That makes this premeditated," Kate said. "I think the sexual assault was an afterthought."

"Bad medicine." Frank grimaced. "Necrophilia?"

"The M.E.'s report says she was still alive."

"Sick bastard." He sighed. "Do you have the urinalysis?"

"He had traces of cocaine, methamphetamines, and alcohol in his bloodstream."

"Drug use would explain the depravity of what he did to Evangeline Worth." Frank tossed the bag containing a shotgun casing into the plastic box. "How many times did you watch the video?"

"Four times." Kate had been in the process of sliding the legal pad into her briefcase, when she realized he was about to pull some problem out of his hat and toss it in her face. "If you've got something to say, say it."

"All right." He cut her a hard look. "If Bruton Ellis walked into that store to rob it, why didn't he ask for the money?"

Kate blinked, her mind flicking back to the tape. "The clerk saw the shotgun and made the obvious assumption."

"Maybe." But the look he gave her was rich with doubt. "How much did he get?"

"Two hundred dollars." She shook her head. "I don't know what you're getting at, but this case is cut-and-dried."

"Something doesn't feel right," he said.

"Is that a scientific assessment?"

"It's almost as if the money was . . . I don't know . . . secondary. Like an afterthought."

Kate stared at him, weighing everything she knew about the case against everything she knew about Frank Matrone. Her instincts were telling her he was more than a little off base. "Come on, Frank. You take away the money angle, and Ellis didn't have a motive to walk into a convenience store and gun down two women."

His expression didn't change. "So then, why didn't he ask for the cash?"

"I don't know. A guy walks into a convenience store with a sawed-off shotgun, and any rational person is going to assume he's robbing the place."

"True. But there were a couple of other things he either did or didn't do that bothered me, too."

"Like what?"

"He didn't ask about the safe. Any self-respecting robber, even a low-life, dumb-shit junkie like Ellis, is going to know there's cash in the safe."

"Maybe he didn't know about it."

"How is it that he knew about the security camera, but not the safe?"

"Maybe he spotted the camera when he walked in and took it out on impulse without any prior planning."

"So, he sees the camera. Doesn't ask for the money. Doesn't ask about the safe. Murders two women. Rapes one of them as she's bleeding out on the floor. But doesn't take the gold chain she's wearing around her neck? Doesn't ask for purses? I don't know about you, Kate, but my gut isn't buying it."

Kate looked at the plastic bag in Frank's hand and noticed the gold chain and cross that had been removed from Evangeline Worth's body by the medical examiner's office. She felt foolish for not having noticed the jewelry before.

Frank contemplated her for several uncomfortable seconds. "I've worked a lot of robberies over the years," he said. "Most times the shooter goes in with one mission: get the money and get out. The last thing they want to do is pop someone. Sure, sometimes you get some sadistic son of a bitch who likes to kill or rape or whatever. Sometimes the perp will panic and get stupid and start shooting. Bruton Ellis didn't panic. He was high, but he wasn't stoned out of his mind. He walked in and popped those two women without even blinking. As if that's what he went in there to do in the first place."

"I think the second clerk surprised him. He panicked and shot her."

"That old woman didn't surprise him. He knew she was there from the moment he walked in the door."

"How do you know?"

"Because he was looking for her. Watch the tape again. You'll see his eyes scan the rear of the store. A second later she's lying in pieces on the floor."

Kate suppressed a shudder at the scenario. "You think he went in to kill those two women?"

"Looks that way to me."

"What's his motive?"

He lifted a shoulder, let it fall. "That's what we have to find out."

Kate was reluctantly impressed with his eye for detail even though she disagreed with his assessment. "My job is to prosecute him. I leave the investigating to the police. They'll give us motive." Because she didn't want her investigator getting sidetracked because he missed police work, she added, "For all intents and purposes where the district attorney's office is concerned, our responsibility is to prove he did it beyond a reasonable doubt."

"Yeah, well, I've found that once you answer the why, the rest usually follows suit."

"Not on my time." Closing her legal pad, she began putting the plastic bags back into the box. "I've got to get back to the office."

"What's your hurry?"

"I've got to be in court at two o'clock."

He glanced at his watch. "That gives us time to make one more stop."

Kate stomped annoyance. She wanted to grab a salad and review her notes before court. "Where?"

"The scene of the crime. Where else?"

SIX

The Snack and Gas where Evangeline Worth and Irma Trevino were gunned down was located in a downtrodden neighborhood in Southeast Dallas. Frank turned the truck onto Ft. Worth Avenue, oblivious to the potholes that marred the asphalt street.

"Here we go," he said, pulling into the parking lot and parking next to a handicapped space near the front door.

"I don't know what you hope to accomplish by coming here," Kate said.

"You'd be amazed at what you can learn by visiting a crime scene." He grinned at her over his shoulder as he opened the door and slid from the vehicle. "Besides, they have great hot dogs."

"Hot dogs?" Kate swung open the door and was met with a brutal north wind that cut through her coat and went all the way to her skin. The temperature had dropped throughout the day, and if she wasn't mistaken, the clouds on the western horizon held something a whole lot nastier than rain.

Shivering, she crossed to the front door. Frank held it open for her and they walked inside. The convenience store had re-opened just two days after the shootings, but there was no trace of the brutality that had occurred at this very spot just three weeks earlier. A snazzy cardboard dump displaying a new energy drink stood where Evangeline Worth had fallen. But Kate could see that the floor was cleaner there. As if someone had taken bleach to the ancient tiles in an effort to clean what must have been a horrific stain. . . .

A man in a denim jacket and cowboy hat stood at the cof-fee station, pouring black sludge into a cup. A young Hispanic man with a ponytail that reached halfway down his back paid for a six-pack of beer and a pack of Marlboro Lights. A heavyset woman with thinning brown hair and hit-or-miss teeth stood behind the counter. A soap opera blinked silently on a tiny black-and-white television set behind her.

Kate wasn't sure exactly what they were looking for, so she spent a few minutes familiarizing herself with the layout of the store. The cooler where the beer and soft drinks were stored was at the rear. An "Employees Only" sign identified the door next to the cooler. The aisles were narrow and crowded with merchandise. She thought about what it would be like to work here and felt a hard pang of sympathy for the two women who'd died.

Frank went to the hot-dog display and proceeded to make two hot dogs and pour two cups of coffee, which he then put in a cardboard tray and carried to the counter. The clerk didn't greet him and barely spared him a glance as she rang up the sale.

Frank dug into his wallet to pay and flashed his badge. "I'm an investigator with the Dallas County DA's office," he said. "We'd like to ask you a few questions."

Kate pulled a Diet Coke from the cooler, a protein bar from the shelf, and joined Frank at the counter.

The clerk's eyes widened and went from Frank to Kate and back to Frank. "I already talked to the cops."

"We're with the DA's office," Kate said.

The woman looked at them with mistrust in her eyes. "Whaddya wanna know?"

"We're investigating the murders of the two clerks who were killed here three weeks ago," Kate said.

The woman shook her head so hard her jowls shook. "God-awful thing. Those two gals was sweet as could be."

"You knew them?" Frank's eyes flicked to her name badge. "Teresa Sue?"

"I knew 'em. 'Specially Irma. She was a hoot. We got to talking a couple of times at crew meetings and what not. I seen Evangeline once or twice when I was coming on a shift and she was going off. She was quiet. Kept to herself for the most part. They was decent folk, you know? I can't believe they're dead. Took damn near a week to get the bloodstains out from 'tween the tiles." Her gaze shot to the energy drink display. "I sure am glad the police got the bastard who done it."

"Cops did a hell of a job on this one," Frank said, his Texas drawl coming out a little more strongly as he slipped into good-ole-boy mode.

Putting the clerk at ease, Kate thought. Letting her know he was just like her, a working-class citizen just trying to get by. Kate had underestimated him, she realized. Because she knew how it felt to be underestimated, she vowed not to do it again. Even if he did annoy her.

"I see the suits replaced the security camera." He pointed at the small camera mounted to the ceiling above the cigarette display.

"Oh, no." Teresa Sue shook her head hard. "That's the old one."

"The old one?" Frank nudged. "What do you mean?"

"There was two cameras. Some security guy installed a new one about a month ago after that coffee shop down the street was robbed. Some kind of high-tech thingie. He kept bragging that it was so small it fit in that tiny little hole the size of a quarter up in the tile. It wasn't working yet."

"It was hidden from sight?" Kate asked, confused.

"Dang thing was so small, you couldn't even see it."

"So where is it?" Frank asked.

"Well, that's the one that son of a bitch with the gun shot out." Looking vindicated, she nodded her head and laughed. "Old camera is the one that got him on tape."

The hairs at Kate's nape prickled as understanding dawned. Frank looked at her, and she saw the same understanding in his eyes. How had Bruton Ellis known about the new camera? A *hidden* camera he couldn't possibly have seen? Unless he'd known about it before ever walking into the store.

The clerk shook her head. "Musta been a god-awful thing to see."

Kate nodded. "It was."

"Thanks for your help." Frank picked up the cardboard carry tray containing the hot dogs and coffees.

Kate followed him through the door and met him on the sidewalk. "How did Bruton Ellis know about that new camera?"

"Tells me it was an inside job." He opened the passenger-side door for her.

"I want background checks on every employee in that store," Kate said, sliding onto the seat. "I want background checks on any employee terminated in the last year."

"You got it." Frank slammed the door.

She watched as he crossed in front of the truck, then got inside. "Is the store owned by a corporation or a franchisee?" he asked.

"Franchisee, I think." Kate got a whiff of the hot dogs and coffee and her stomach growled. "I'll double-check when I get back."

He set the cardboard tray on the seat between them and reached for one of the hot dogs. "One of these is for you. Mustard. Relish. Light on the onions."

"You eat like a cop."

"Builds character."

Kate looked down at the protein bar in her hand. "This is fine. Thanks."

"Hot dog's going to be a hell of a lot better than whatever's in that bar." Studying her, he added, "Coffee's hot and strong."

She unwrapped the bar and took a bite. But it was the hot dog she really wanted. It smelled heavenly in the confines of the cab. She couldn't remember the last time she'd had a hot dog.

"Don't you ever loosen up?" he asked, taking half the hot dog in a single bite. "You know, break the rules? Eat junk food. Have fun?"

"Just because I don't like hot dogs doesn't mean I don't like to have fun," she said, wondering why the hell she suddenly felt defensive. Wondering even harder why they were having this ridiculous conversation in the first place.

"I think there's hope for you yet, Kate."

"Do you think we could continue this stupid conversation while driving? I've got to be in court by two."

Smiling, Frank started the engine, put the truck in gear, and pulled onto the street. "That gives us time to swing by the PD and talk to the lead detective."

"Look, not everyone can afford to be late the way you are," she snapped.

He cut her a sharp look. "Aren't you the least bit curious how Ellis knew that hidden camera was there?"

"Of course I am. But not at the expense of blowing a case because I don't show up for court on time."

"I'll get you there on time," he said and hit the gas.

WEDNESDAY, JANUARY 25, 1:02 P.M.

Frank wasn't sure why he was dragging Kate along. He suspected it had something to do with the way she wore that suit. Or maybe the way that skirt crept up her thighs when she sat down and crossed those long, shapely legs. Maybe it was the way her scent filled the cab of the truck. Or maybe he had a point to prove, and he wanted her to be there when he did it.

He parked in the rear lot, where the cops parked, and they entered the Jack Evans Police Headquarters building through a rear door.

"I've never come in this way before," Kate said.

"Faster to avoid the security checks."

"Aren't there rules?"

"Rules usually just slow things down."

He'd called Detective Bates on his cell during the ride over to let him know they were on the way. Bates wasn't happy about a last-minute meeting, but Frank had never put too much emphasis on making other people happy. Especially when it came to a territorial detective and sloppy police work.

Frank knew his way around the police department, but it wasn't easy being back. He'd rather swallow his tongue than admit it, but he missed being a cop. The surprised expressions and uncomfortable greetings didn't elude him as he wound through the CAPERS unit toward homicide.

"You know a lot of people," Kate commented as they entered the homicide division.

"Yeah, I'm a regular social butterfly."

"They usually make me wait."

"It's that Megabitch thing." He softened the words with a smile.

"Oh, terrific," she muttered.

They found Detective Bates on the phone at his desk. He was wearing a gray suit that matched his hair to a T. At some point he'd loosened his tie and it hung askew at his neck. He'd removed his jacket and rolled up the sleeves of a shirt that looked as if he'd been wearing it for a week. Knowing Bates, Frank thought, he probably had.

The detective glared at Frank a moment, then dropped the phone into its cradle. "What the hell is so urgent I had to cancel lunch with my wife?" he asked crossly. "Is this about the Ellis case?"

"Since Ms. Megason has to be in court at two, I'll cut right to the chase," Frank said. "We want to know why it wasn't in the police report that Bruton Ellis knew about the new security camera that had been installed at the Snack and Gas."

Bates stared blankly at him for a moment, and Frank knew immediately the other man didn't have a clue what he was talking about. Jesus. He hadn't been lying when he'd told Kate that cops could be dense at times.

"What security camera?" Bates asked. "We got the whole thing on video."

"The hidden camera Ellis took out with the shotgun," Frank said.

"As far as you know that was a random shot to the ceiling and he got the camera by accident," Bates said.

"That might be funny if you weren't serious."

Bates's left eyelid began to twitch.

"He knew the camera was there," Frank said. "A *hidden* camera behind a hole in one of the acoustic tiles. He shot it out thinking it would keep his face off the six o'clock news. Do you have any idea how he knew it was there?"

"If Ellis had inside help, then he would have shot out the other tape—the one that was working."

"Unless his partner in crime wasn't quite up on things."

"Sounds like bullshit." But Bates's face tinged red. "If it'll get the DA's office off my back, I'll have another look at the video."

Kate stepped up to Bates's desk. "We were just at the Snack and Gas, Detective. I'll double-check with the security company the Snack and Gas headquarters uses, but the clerk told us a new security camera had just been installed. It was hidden from view, so without prior knowledge, Bruton Ellis couldn't have just walked in and seen it."

"You telling me you think this was some kind of a botched inside job?" Bates asked, but he was starting to look more intrigued than annoyed.

"I'm telling you Ellis knew about that camera," Frank said. "I'd sure as hell like to know how, wouldn't you?"

"So if some employee helped, why did Ellis get caught on tape? Why did he hit the place right after the cash was dropped into the box and walk away with only two hundred bucks? It doesn't make sense."

"Or maybe Ellis is just a dumb shit and screwed it up. Either way I'd like to know."

"I hate to shoot holes in your sail, Matrone, but in the scope of things it doesn't matter. We got Ellis doing the deed on video. Whether he knew about the camera isn't an issue because he's going down."

"And his accomplice gets off scott-free." Frank laughed, but it was an unpleasant sound. "Who says the criminal justice system doesn't work?"

Bates looked like he wanted to leap over the desk. Frank almost wished he would. He was still pissed at the PD for forcing him to retire, and he'd like nothing better than to take his anger out on some smart-ass detective.

"Or maybe your new job with the DA's office is a little too boring for you, Matrone. Maybe you've turned into one of those wannabe, rent-a-cop types."

"Fuck you." Despite his efforts to keep a handle on his temper, Frank could feel a vein pulsing at his temple, his hands curling into fists at his sides. In the twelve years he'd been with the Dallas PD, he'd never worked with Bates. But the two men had crossed paths enough times for Frank to know he didn't like him.

"Frank."

Kate's voice came to him as if from a great distance. Giving himself a hard mental shake, he hauled himself back from a place he knew better than to venture.

"Ellis knew about that camera and you missed it," Frank said.

"We got him on tape. He's in jail. The rest doesn't matter."

"It matters if there's someone else involved."

"So what did they do? Split the two hundred bucks? Give me a fucking break."

"Someone told Ellis about the camera, damn it."

"Maybe Ellis was in the store the day it was installed, for chrissake! Maybe he talked to the guy who installed the camera." Bates smiled. "Or maybe the CIA is involved and this is some kind of a conspiracy theory to make you look like a fucking idiot. From what I hear, it doesn't take much."

"Frank."

Vaguely he was aware of Kate's voice, but it was her hand on his arm that brought him back. Stepping back, he looked down at her, saw the look in her eyes and realized he was making a very big impression. A bad one. Without saying a word, he turned and strode toward the door.

Kate came up beside him, matching his pace stride for stride. "That wasn't very helpful."

"Fun, though, wasn't it?"

"Not at all." She had to trot to keep up with him. "You got a problem with Bates?"

"You mean aside from his being a smug asshole?"

"This isn't a pissing contest, Frank. I don't need you rushing in like some loose cannon."

He gave her a look that had many a man shrinking back. "Back off, Kate."

But Kate Megason didn't shrink away. She didn't even blink. "I don't care about Bates. What I do care about is this case. We need a good working relationship with the PD to win this."

"Don't tell me how to do my job."

"If you can't control your temper, you'll be more of a handicap than an asset, ex-detective or not."

They reached the elevator. "I'll take that under advisement," he said and slapped his hand against the Down button.

SEVEN

The north wind shook the windows and howled around the eaves like a drove of keening ghosts in search of shelter from the cold. But Kate was only vaguely aware of the wind as she sat at her desk in the study of her north Dallas home and stared fixedly at her laptop screen. Her father had once told her a tornado could go right over the house and she wouldn't notice—as long as it didn't mess up her papers. That much was true. It wasn't unusual for her to become so engaged in her work that she would lose hours at a time and not even realize it.

As her fingers flew over the keyboard, she was only vaguely aware that her neck and shoulders were stiff. She was working on the Bruton Ellis case. Spread out on the desk were his background report, arrest record, conviction record, and the police report Detective Bates had faxed earlier. Investigator David Perrine had been thorough, and Kate had everything right down to Ellis's kindergarten report card. The one that plainly noted that he did not play well with others.

Three years ago, when she'd been an intern at the Dallas

County DA's office, her mentor had told her: "The jury wants to hear a motive. Give them a solid motive, and they will convict." Kate had never forgotten that priceless advice, and to this day it was her first line of attack.

Ellis's motive was clear. He'd walked into that convenience store because he needed money to feed his drug habit. When the two clerks had threatened his goal, he'd cold-bloodedly eliminated them. The rape had been a crime of opportunity. The evidence and motive combined were powerful and would most likely win her a conviction.

Still, Kate couldn't shake a tiny, niggling feeling that something wasn't right. She wanted to attribute that uneasy feeling to Frank Matrone's assertion that Bruton Ellis had known about the camera and that the robbery might have been an inside job. Kate wasn't so sure. And from all appearances, neither was Detective Bates. The only question that remained was whether it was enough for her to proceed and prosecute as planned.

Matrone seemed to be one of those cops who worked as much off gut instinct as he did evidence and facts. Kate, on the other hand, worked strictly off of facts and tangible evidence. She didn't put much value in hunches. Not when it came to the cases she prosecuted. Justice was far too important to her to risk it on something so capricious. Give her solid, tangible evidence and she could turn it into a conviction.

She recalled the way he'd approached the store clerk that afternoon, and she knew immediately he had once been a good interrogator. Some people had the gift of getting others to talk. Frank Matrone might be a little rough around the edges, but after spending the morning with him she amended her initial assessment that he would not be a benefit to the team. It would be up to her to make sure she used his skills wisely.

Realizing it wasn't the first time she'd found herself thinking about her new investigator, Kate steered her thoughts back to the case. Absently she rubbed the back of her neck. A look at the clock on the mantel confirmed that she'd been at the computer too long.

She saved the file she'd been working on and closed it. The search engine she'd been using earlier remained on her screen, the curser blinking on the blank line that put so much information at her fingertips. She stared at it for an instant, not allowing her fingers to type what her brain was telling them to. After a long hesitation, she typed in "Frank Matrone" and hit Enter.

The search engine returned sixteen results. She clicked on the first one, and a story that had appeared in the *Dallas Morning News* some four years earlier materialized. It was a small piece about the promotion of four police officers who'd recently passed their detective examinations. A photograph showed all four men standing in front of a police cruiser. Frank Matrone stood at the end of the group, looking like a naughty kid who'd just emptied the cookie jar without getting caught. Even though the picture was only four years old, he seemed much younger. A tad heavier, as if he'd recently lost weight. His smile was deep and genuine, as if someone had said something tasteless and he'd enjoyed the hell out of it.

Kate mentally compared the image with the man she'd spent the afternoon with, and she instinctively knew something had profoundly changed in the four years since that photograph was taken. She was usually good at reading people, but she hadn't been able to get a handle on Frank. She thought he was probably good at locking people out and wondered what he didn't want anyone to see.

She felt like a sneaky teenager as she right-clicked on the picture and used her photo imaging software to enlarge it. The images of the four police officers filled her screen. But it was Frank Matrone who drew her eye. The image of him grinning with his arms folded at his chest commanded her full attention—and then some. He was attractive in a rough-around-the-edges sort of way. Dark hair. Dark eyes. An expression that could go from charming to cutting in an instant. She wanted badly to believe she was snooping because it was her business to know the people who worked for her. But Kate was honest enough with herself to admit her curiosity about Frank Matrone went deeper than professional interest.

Kate was not some flighty teen girl. She was a mature woman and knew well the dangers of entertaining inappropriate thoughts about a man who was working for her. But she wanted to know more about Frank Matrone. He was funny and unpredictable with an air of mystery that intrigued her a lot more than she wanted to admit. Mike Shelley had mentioned that Frank had been injured while overseas. She wondered if that was why he'd left the police department. If that was why he walked with a limp.

Realizing that she was ogling a photograph of a man she had no intention of getting involved with, she clicked the mouse and closed the image without saving it. Her screen blinked back to her search results page. The second link was also a story from the *Dallas Morning News*. "Police Detective Earns Purple Heart at Great Personal Sacrifice."

Kate stared at the link, her finger hovering over the mouse an instant before she clicked. The article appeared replete with photos. Frank lying in a bed, covered with a white sheet from the hips down. His chest was muscular and covered with a thatch of black hair. He was smiling for the camera, his right hand raised in a thumbs-up.

Army reservist Frank Matrone gives a thumbs-up as he arrived at Ft. Hood yesterday morning after spending seven weeks at a military base hospital in Germany. He was one of two American soldiers critically injured in a suicide bombing on March 20 while on leave in Jerusalem. A parade celebrating the safe return home of one hundred and fourteen other soldiers stationed at Ft. Hood is scheduled for Saturday.

Kate read the story twice. She'd known he'd gone overseas, but her knowledge of what had happened ended with that. When Mike had told her he'd been injured, she hadn't cared. All she'd cared about was getting a good investigator for her case. Someone who could get the job done. For the first time it dawned on her that Frank might be more vulnerable than he let on. That he might be more human than she'd anticipated. That rough-around-the-edges ex-detective might have some issues to work through.

"Do it on your own time, Matrone," she muttered as she shut down the computer.

But as she turned out the study light and headed toward her bedroom, she found herself wondering why he looked so damn sad sometimes. So . . . disconnected. She wondered if any of those things had to do with the time he'd spent in the Middle East.

THURSDAY, JANUARY 26, 12:13 A.M.

A sense of freedom overwhelmed her seventeen-year-old mind as she sat behind the wheel of her mother's 1991 Gold Lexus and grinned out at the open road ahead. The windows were rolled down and REM was cranked up as high as the stereo would go. Michael Stipe was belting out a tune about losing his religion. Kate didn't know exactly what those lyrics meant. All she knew was that she wanted to lose hers, too.

Next to her, Kirsten was sipping a Corona and slapping her palm against the door in time with the drum. The night was sweltering—typical for Houston in July—but neither girl cared about the heat. After days of planning, they'd finally done it. They'd sneaked out of the house while their parents slept. They had Mom's car, a six-pack of beer, and a party to go to. Life just didn't get any better when you were seventeen and as wild as the summer days were long.

Kate and Kirsten weren't going to just any party. They were going to a frat party. A party Kate had been hearing about for weeks now. It was at a big house with a pool not far from the Woodlands. The parents were in Portugal. Mark Preston, a freshman at Texas A&M, had told her there was going to be a keg and plenty of hard liquor. Maybe even marijuana. Not that Kate planned on doing drugs; she drew the line at alcohol. But breaking the rules was so exciting!

She felt so grown-up. As if she were already in college and not some dumb high school senior and too young to matter. She couldn't wait to get to the party. She'd never been to a frat party, and the thought of hanging out with an older crowd excited her until she thought she would burst. She'd worn her tightest jeans and heels that showed off her long legs. Beneath her snug T-shirt, she was wearing a push-up bra with a little bit of padding. She looked older than seventeen. She hoped nobody would hassle them once they arrived.

"Give me one of those Coronas, will you?" she asked.

Kirsten giggled as she pulled a beer from the six-pack and passed it to Kate. *"Just make sure you hide it if you see a cop."*

"We're not going to see a cop."

They were sitting at a stoplight in a quiet industrial area. It was just after eleven P.M. and the streets were deserted. Kate glanced at her watch. If she pushed it, they could be there in twenty minutes. She and Kirsten had agreed to stay for an hour. Then they would leave, sneak back into the house—and no one would ever be the wiser.

Smiling, she took a sip of beer. Michael Stipe was now singing about shining, happy people. She sang along, knowing the words by heart. The beer was just starting to go to her head and she felt wonderful. They had the whole night ahead of them. She wondered if Justin Riley was going to be at the party. She'd met him last year when he'd been a senior, and she would never forget the way he'd looked at her. . . .

The car jolted violently, yanking her from her thoughts. *"What the—"*

"Some bozo hit us!" Kirsten blurted, turning in her seat to look behind them.

But even before looking in her rearview mirror, Kate knew they'd been hit from behind. She saw the headlights in her rearview mirror. Damn. Damn. Damn! Of all the bad luck!

"I told you we shouldn't do this!" Kirsten exclaimed.

"Just shut up and stay calm," Kate snapped. *"And hide the beer."*

"How are we going to explain a dent to Mom and Dad?"

"I don't know. We'll think of something." Kate bit her lip. She was gripping the wheel so hard her knuckles hurt. *"I'm going to see how bad the damage is."*

Putting the car in Park, she swung open the door and stepped into the sultry night. She squinted, trying to see, but the headlights blinded her. She could make out the outline of a man. He was tall and thin with long hair. She hoped he was nice.

"Hello," she said, trying to make her voice strong.

As she drew nearer she could see that he wasn't too old. Maybe in his twenties. He wore a dark T-shirt with the sleeves cut off and blue jeans. He was tall and wiry, but the muscles in his arms were big. He wore a blue bandanna over the top of his head.

"Sorry 'bout hitting you," he drawled.

"How bad is the damage?" she asked.

"I don't think it's too bad."

Kate walked to the rear of her mom's car, careful to keep her distance, and looked at the bumper. He'd left his headlights on, and she could see that there was a dent in the shiny chrome. *Shit,* she thought, and felt a small flare of anger. That anger was smothered by something else when a second man got out of the car. This guy was big, and he didn't look nearly as nice as the first man.

"I figure we can just exchange insurance information and get on down the road," the first man said. "What's your name?"

"Katie," she said without thinking.

"Well, Katie, don't you worry. I got good insurance that'll pay for everything."

He didn't look like he'd have very good insurance.

"Good," Kate said, but she was watching the large man walk toward the passenger-side door where Kirsten sat. Kate's parents had taught her to be careful around strangers, and she was starting to get an uneasy sensation.

"We're kind of in a hurry," she said. "Let me get my purse."

She was aware of the second man standing at the passenger-side window, bent at the hip and talking to Kirsten. Kate didn't know why, but she didn't want him there. She wanted him someplace where she could keep an eye on him.

She walked back to the driver's-side door and spoke to Kirsten through the open window. "Hand me my purse, will you?"

"Sure." Kirsten turned and grabbed the bag from the back seat. When she handed Kate her bag, Kate could see that her sister was nervous. "Hurry," Kirsten whispered, leaning close. "This guy is creeping me out."

"What are you girls doing out this late?" The fat man straightened and looked at Kate over the roof of the car.

"We're going to a—" Kirsten began, but Kate cut her off.

"We're meeting our parents." Kate gave him her toughest look. "And we're late."

"Is that so?"

She jolted when the other man's voice sounded directly behind her. She hadn't seen him approach. For the first time it dawned on her that there wasn't a soul around. That they were totally alone with two strangers in a desolate part of town and nobody knew where they were. In that instant Kate began to tremble inside. She knew something was wrong. She sensed danger. And she knew something bad was going to happen.

She turned to face the scraggly-haired man behind her. The initial fingers of adrenaline ripped through her when she realized he was standing too close. That he was looking at her funny. The way men did sometimes. A way that excited her and scared her at once. And suddenly sneaking out of the house to go to this party seemed like a very bad idea.

"What are you doing?" she asked, but her voice was breathless with fear.

The man laughed. "We're going to have us a little party, Kay-tee."

"We have to go." Kate went with her instincts. Whirling, she grabbed for the door handle. But two strong hands wrapped around her and jerked her violently back. She started to scream, but the next thing she knew she was slammed against the car door hard enough to dent it. Pain radiated up her spine. Then the man with the scraggly hair was against her, pushing and grunting. She smelled body odor and cigarettes and breath that was tinged with alcohol. She felt the slick dampness of sweat against her skin.

Vaguely she was aware of the fat man pulling Kirsten from the car. Kirsten screaming. They can't do this, she thought and screamed. "Run!"

The man tried to put his hands beneath her shirt. Wiry fingers tearing at her bra. Outrage and terror exploded inside her. Kate lashed out with both fists, hitting him on the head and shoulders.

The first blow hit her squarely in the forehead. Her head snapped back and hit the roof of the car. White light exploded *behind her eyes. Another blow just above her left ear shocked her system. Like a stick of dynamite going off inside her head.*

She must have blacked out then because the next thing she knew she was lying facedown on the ground. Her mouth was open and full of dirt and grass. She spat mud and tried to roll over, but his knee was in the small of her back. She saw the bandanna in his hand and then he was using it to tie her hands behind her.

This isn't happening, *she thought*. No. No. No!

"No!"

Kate woke to her own scream. For an instant she was seventeen years old and so filled with horror and revulsion that she wanted to die. Sweat slicked her body and dampened her pajamas, but she was shivering with cold. A cold that came from a place inside her that knew of unspeakable horrors.

It had been a long time since she'd had the nightmare. She didn't know why it had come rushing back tonight. Maybe the pressures of her caseload were taking more of a toll than she'd thought. Kate tried hard to keep her past out of the cases she tried, but she wasn't always successful. She knew that for better or worse, she would always be a product of her past.

Throwing back the down comforter, she got out of bed, pulled off her damp pajamas, and wrapped herself in her robe. A glance at the clock told her it was almost one A.M. Even though she was exhausted, she knew sleep wouldn't come again. In the bathroom she opened the medicine cabinet and picked up the bottle of prescription sleeping pills. It had been over a year since she'd taken one. She didn't want to take one now, and slid the bottle back onto the shelf.

But she could still feel the dark press of the nightmare, hanging on like a leech, sucking the lifeblood from her. Eleven years had passed since that terrible night. But some wounds never healed. The key, she'd realized, was learning to live with them.

The truth of the matter was she was lucky to be alive, but some days Kate didn't feel lucky. She felt damaged and tainted. She thought of Kirsten lying in her bed in her overdecorated room at the Turtle Creek Convalescent Home and felt the old pain slash her with spindly claws. Her sister hadn't deserved to have her life taken away.

Goddamn those sons of bitches who did this to us, she thought with a vicious anger she was all too familiar with.

Giving up on the hope of going back to sleep, Kate crossed to her closet, pulled out a pair of jeans and a navy turtleneck sweater. Quickly she dressed and stepped into her boots. She ran her fingers through her hair, shrugged into her leather jacket, and grabbed her keys. She may not be able to sleep, but that didn't mean she had to stay home and bounce off the walls.

There was plenty she could do tonight.

For what she had in mind, the wee hours of morning were the perfect time to do it.

THURSDAY, JANUARY 26, 1:56 A.M.

The wipers slapped rain mixed with sleet from the windshield as Kate parked on a narrow side street in a nasty part of South Dallas. Not bothering with her umbrella, she opened the door and stepped into the cold night. She took the cracked sidewalk to a three-story brick building bedecked with gang graffiti. A single bullet hole marred the storefront window of the long vacant furniture shop next door. She was keenly aware of a car idling slowly down the street and knew the driver was eye-balling her, wondering what a nice white lady was doing in that part of town at two in the morning.

If only he knew.

The wooden door creaked like old bones when she opened it and stepped into the dark foyer. Her boots thudded in perfect time with her heart as she crossed to the narrow wooden staircase. She took the steps two at a time. The second level smelled of garbage, marijuana, and vomit. Down the hall and to her right, a wino sat slumped against a wall, a bottle of rotgut in his hand, his bloodshot eyes glaring. A mangy cat looked at her from behind a garbage can, a dead rat hanging from its mouth.

Frowning, Kate continued on to the third level and took the darkened hall to a wooden door with an etched glass window. Like a Philip Marlow movie from the 1940s, a printed sign on the glass read: "Jack Gamble, Private Detective." She almost smiled every time she saw it. Almost.

The light was on inside, but Kate didn't need the light to know he was working. Jack Gamble was a night bird. By the time he opened his office for business, most folks were at home and tucked into bed. But then, she supposed Jack's kind of work required the cover of night. That was precisely the reason she'd hired him.

She opened the door to find him sitting behind his desk. He looked up when she entered. Simultaneously his right shoulder moved slightly, and Kate knew he'd put his hand on the gun he had mounted on the underside of his desk. She'd asked him about it once, and in his quiet way he'd told her he'd mounted it there just in case some shady character came calling in the middle of the night. Kate knew all about shady characters, and she didn't begrudge him the gun. She had a legal concealed handgun license herself. But she knew that even in South Dallas, an economically depressed area rife with gangs and crime, nobody fucked with Jack Gamble.

"Kate. What's a pretty lady like you doin' up at this hour?"

"Couldn't sleep," she said, crossing to his desk.

"Well, this ain't no place for no prosecutor. 'Specially after dark."

He'd been saying the same thing every week for the last year. Kate always answered the same way. They were both creatures of habits. Some of them good. Some not so good. But the one thing they both knew was that when she walked into Jack Gamble's office, she was not a Dallas County assistant district attorney. She was a woman on a mission and the only reason she was there was because he could help her reach her goal.

Smiling, she stopped adjacent his desk. "I just can't seem to get through the week without seeing you."

A deep chuckle rumbled up from his barrel chest. "And you got a weakness for ugly stray dogs, too." A man of impeccable Southern manners, he rolled his wheelchair out from behind the desk and motioned to one of two wooden rail-back chairs in front of his desk. "Sit down."

Kate settled into the chair and contemplated the man across from her. In his late forties, he was the size of a woolly mammoth and as black as the west Texas night. But while he might appear to be overweight at first glance, Kate knew the bulk in his upper body was mostly muscle. He was not a handsome man. Once a Dallas narcotics officer, he'd been shot four times during a sting. The first shot had severed his spinal cord just below his waist. The second had hit him in the chest. The third in the stomach. The fourth in the face. The doctors had done what they could, but they hadn't been able to put his face back together the way it had been before the shooting. His forehead was slightly concave on one side. His right eye was higher than his left and slightly sunken. A scar as deep as a man's finger had dug a groove through his right cheekbone.

But his was an interesting face nonetheless. A strong face that spoke of character and intelligence and the kind of courage that was rare and ran deep. He'd come highly recommended by a former ADA who'd used him on a personal matter she'd wanted kept discreet. Within the first five minutes of the initial interview, Kate had known he was the man for the job.

Kate had done her homework before hiring him. She knew he was married with at least seven grown children from two different women, one of whom he'd been married to for the last twelve years. She knew he'd been a good cop with three commendations. She knew he'd been a private detective since leaving the department some six years earlier and that his endeavor into the private sector had been successful and financially rewarding. Above all else, Kate knew Jack Gamble was discreet. That had been the deciding factor for choosing him.

"You must be a mind reader," he said after a moment.

"Why do you say that?"

"I was going to call you in the morning."

Kate sat up straighter. "Did you find something?"

"I been digging around for you going on a year now. 'Bout time I did, don't you think?" Her pulse quickened when he pulled out a tattered brown folder and opened it. "I got a name."

Her heart went into a free fall, like a plane with a stalled engine. She stared at him, and suddenly it was as if she was seeing him at the end of a long tunnel. A name. She couldn't believe it. After eleven unbearable years she would finally have a name.

"Danny Lee Perkins." He passed her the folder.

Kate's hand was shaking when she reached for it. It seemed as if she'd been waiting for this moment her entire life. She took the folder, opened it, found herself staring at a five-by-seven photograph of a middle-aged man with thinning brown hair, pale blue eyes, and a pocked complexion.

Facedown in the grass. Dirt in her mouth. Horror exploding in her brain. Pain ripping through her body. Her innocence shattered. Her life changed forever . . .

She ran her tongue over the bridge where her broken front tooth had been repaired. The old hurt mingled with a fresh wave of hatred. She stared at the photograph, aware that her mouth had gone dry. Her heart was pounding. Eleven years gone. He would be older. Heavier. But she knew he would be the same in one aspect. . . .

Her eyes sought his right cheek, and she had to make a conscious effort to choke back the sound that tried to squeeze from her throat. The birthmark was one of the few details she remembered about his face. Eleven years ago, from her hospital bed, she had described it to the police as a "red mark on his cheek." Later, when she could bear to think of it, when she could force herself to recall his face, she'd realized the man who'd attacked her had had either a port-wine stain or cherry hemangioma birthmark.

This man had the mark.

Slowly she raised her eyes to Jack Gamble. The big man was leaning back in his wheelchair, watching her with eyes that saw more than she wanted him to.

Kate's hand was steady when she set the folder on the desk. "It's him."

"I thought so."

"What do you have on him?"

"Eleven years ago he moved from Houston to Louisville, Kentucky, to live with his aunt. Worked at an auto body shop for the next two years. Kept his nose relatively clean. Then he moved to Knoxville, Tennessee." He flipped the page. "He got into a fight at a bar and did nine months on an assault charge. Two years ago he got busted with a syringe and some crystal meth. Did four months. Kept his nose clean while he was on probation." Scratching his temple, he scanned the file. "Moved back to Texas seven years ago. Lived in Beaumont. Houston. Bay City." He looked up at Kate. "He moved to Ft. Worth last year. That's where I lost track of him."

Kate could feel herself coming apart inside. Staring across the span of desk at a man she'd known for the last year—a man who'd proven himself far too astute—she wondered if he could see the turmoil inside her. The statute of limitations for sexual assault in the state of Texas was seven years. There was an exception for DNA evidence, but eleven years ago that exception hadn't been in place. Which meant the man who'd hurt her so brutally, the man who'd ruined her sister's life, would never be forced to pay for what he did.

Kate was going to make sure he did.

"What about the other man?" she asked, referring to the man who'd nearly killed her sister.

"I have a couple of names. Eddie Calhoun. Ricky Steiner. Ronny Stein. Rick Steinle. He's used a lot of aliases over the years. I'm following up on a couple of leads. Last I heard, he was in federal prison in Terre Haute, Indiana, on a murder one charge. I'm going to make some more inquiries when the offices open in a few hours."

Kate thought prison was too good for the man who'd beaten her sister so brutally she'd suffered irreparable brain damage. Kate wanted him in hell where he belonged. She wanted to be the one to put him there. "How much more time do you need?"

He rolled a shoulder. "Hard to tell at this point. The man sitting pretty in Club Fed might not be our man."

"If it's not him, I want you to keep looking." Digging into her bag, Kate removed a plain white envelope. "There's another five thousand in there."

"Kate . . ."

"I want you to find them, Jack. Both of them." She glanced at the folder on the desk, picked it up. "His last known address in here?" She gave him a pointed look. "I need his last known address."

"I'll have it for you in a couple of days." He gazed levelly at her. "Leave the looking to me, Kate. You hear?"

For the first time since she'd known him, Kate got the impression he hadn't given her everything he had. Maybe because Jack was a good man and had a pretty good idea what she was going to do with the information. But she didn't need a good man. She didn't even need a friend. She needed a PI with a don't-ask-don't-tell philosophy.

She'd made the mistake of letting him see too much over the last year. As unlikely as their friendship seemed, she knew he cared for her. To be perfectly honest, she cared for him, too. But she wouldn't let that deter her from her goal.

He was looking at her as if he thought she might do something rash. But Kate Megason never did anything rash. Sooner or later she would get those two men. Even if it took another year, she would see to it that Danny Lee Perkins and his son-of-a-bitch sidekick paid for what they did.

Rising, she dug into her bag for her keys.

"I'll see you out," Jack said.

He always asked, and Kate's answer was invariably the same. "I can handle it, Jack." Smiling, she patted her Chanel bag where she kept her .22 mini-magnum revolver. "Let me know when you get an address on Danny Lee Perkins."

"Will do."

She started toward the door. "Keep me posted on the other guy."

"I'll do it."

Kate walked through the door without looking back.

EIGHT

"Why don't we have video?"

Kate looked across her desk at David Perrine, who sat in one of two visitor chairs, nursing a double cappuccino. They were in Kate's office because the conference room was being used by another attorney who evidently had more clout than she did.

"Detective Bates said the police interview room camera wasn't working. We're going to have to make do with audio," David said.

She looked at the empty chair next to him and frowned. As usual, Frank was late. Nine-thirty and he hadn't even bothered to show. What was his problem? More importantly, what was she going to do about it?

"So did Matrone survive your meeting with him yesterday?" David asked.

"Mike wants him on the case," was all she said.

David smiled. "But if it were up to you, he'd be toast."

"Burned to a crisp." Leaning forward, she popped the cassette into the tape recorder on her desk. "We can—"

The door to her office swung open. Kate looked up to see Frank Matrone stride in, looking like he'd just stepped out of the shower.

"We're pleased you decided to grace us with your presence," she said.

"Sorry I'm late."

"I hope your job as investigator here at the district attorney's office isn't interfering with your sleep."

He grimaced, looking appropriately contrite. "It's not."

David chuckled. "Oh, brother."

Frowning, Frank pulled out the second visitor chair and sat down. "Did I miss anything?"

"You mean besides points?" David stuck out his hand. "You're not chalking up any, buddy."

"Never do." Frank shook the other man's hand.

He was wearing the same black leather jacket. His hair was still damp from a recent shower. He'd left a tiny piece of tissue paper on a razor cut on the point of his chin. Even though his aftershave was subtle, Kate could smell it from where she sat. Some woodsy, outdoor scent that made her think of pine trees and fresh air. He was wearing black slacks and a white shirt with a red silk tie. Better tie today. He looked nice. Except for the cowboy boots . . .

She looked away before her mind could take the thought any further. "If you two are finished bonding, I'd like to get started." Glaring at Matrone, she added, "What you are about to hear is the initial interview between Detective Bates and Bruton Ellis. I've asked for a transcript, too, but as usual things are backed up over at the PD, so it's going to take a few days."

"Ah . . . they're probably not that backed up," Frank said.

Kate shot him a withering stare. "Don't tell me. This is part of their 'Let's put Megabitch through the hoop' thing."

"Megabitch?" David echoed, looking startled. "They call you that?"

"Never mind," Kate snapped, wishing she hadn't mentioned it.

"I'll make a few calls when we're finished here," Frank said. "I can probably have it over here by this afternoon."

As much as Kate didn't want to, she had to admit he was probably going to be an asset to the team if only to help her cut through all the red tape between the DA's office and the PD.

She hit the Play button on the recorder. The speaker in the center of the table hissed for a moment. Kate turned up the volume. An instant later Detective Howard Bates's gravelly voice recited his name, title, and date, and advised all present that the interview was being recorded. He then Mirandized Bruton Ellis.

"Do you understand these rights?" Bates asked.

"I know what they mean."

"You know why you're here?"

"It ain't to color fuckin' Easter eggs."

"Watch your mouth."

A brief scratchy silence, then Bates continued. "Were you in the Snack and Gas convenience store early this morning?"

Silence hissed for the span of several heartbeats.

"If you want I can stop this interview right now and take you back to your cell."

"It gonna help if I talk to you guys?" Ellis asked.

"Maybe."

Another scratchy silence.

"So fuckin' talk," came another man's voice. "Don't sit there like a stupid shit and waste our fuckin' time."

Classic bad-cop psych-out, Kate thought and looked down at her legal pad. The other detective present was Joe Milkowski. A real badass from what she'd heard.

For several minutes Detective Bates questioned Ellis about what happened in the convenience store. Ellis's answers were short and belligerent. Kate could hear the temper building in Bates's voice, but he was a seasoned detective and kept a handle on it. Pushing just enough to keep Ellis going, trying to rattle him and get him to open up.

"We got you on the security camera tape," Milkowski said after twenty minutes of getting nowhere.

"You're lying!" Ellis snarled. "There ain't no fuckin' tape."

Kate found herself wishing for video. Things were so much clearer when you could see expressions and mannerisms and body language. She could hear Milkowski grumbling and cursing beneath his breath.

"Want to see it?" Bates asked, and a resonant click sounded. "See that stupid shit with the shotgun under his coat? That's you, Einstein. And we got you by the dick."

Ellis made a sound of distress. "No . . ."

"You cooperate with us and we'll do what we can to cut a deal," Bates said. "You keep fucking us around and you're going to death row."

"Death *row*?" Ellis cried.

"Yeah, you know, Huntsville. That's where they strap ruthless motherfuckers like you to the gurney and inject them with enough drugs to kill a fuckin' rhinoceros."

"What do you want from me?"

For the first time Kate heard fear in the other man's voice. Good. He was scared. A scared man was a man who cooperated. A man who would talk to save his neck.

"Why don't you start by telling us what you did," Milkowski said.

Ellis sniffed, and Kate realized he was crying. "Oh, man."

"You give us a confession and we'll do what we can to get you life instead of lethal injection." A pause. "You got thirty seconds or I swear to Christ I'm going to turn off that recorder and walk out of here."

"I didn't—" Ellis's voice broke.

"You did, asshole. We got you on tape."

"I gotta go to the bathroom."

"You can go when I say you can go."

Another sound of distress.

"You went in there to rob the place, didn't you, Ellis."

"No!"

"You lying little shit."

"I'm not. They told me to take the money. To make it look like a robbery."

A pregnant silence ensued. Even though there was no video, Kate envisioned the two detectives exchanging looks. "What the hell are you talking about?" Bates asked after a moment. "Who?"

"A guy. He hired me to go in there and kill those two bitches."

"Did he tell you to rape one of them, too?" Milkowski swore, then came the sound of the legs of his chair screeching across the tile. "Get this piece of shit out of here."

"Wait!" Ellis cried. "I said I'd talk."

"Why would someone hire you to off two women in a friggin' convenience store?" Bates asked.

"I don't know! But he paid me. Five thousand dollars. In cash."

"Cash, huh? That's convenient."

"It's not like he's going to give me his fuckin' Visa number. Christ!"

"You got the cash?"

"No," Ellis muttered. "I spent it."

Another, longer silence ensued, then Bates's gravelly voice broke it. "You know what, Ellis? I think you're a lying shithead. Do you think cops are that stupid? You think you can walk in here, make up some wild story, and get yourself a deal?"

"I didn't make it up! I swear! This guy hired me to go in there and blow away those two broads. He paid me five grand. In cash! I swear!"

"Why would he do that?"

"I don't know, man. I didn't ask."

Bates sighed, an angry impatient sound as it hissed out of the speaker. "Who was the guy?"

"All I know is he goes by Segal."

"Segal, huh?" A hard laugh sounded. "Well, why don't I just look it up in the fuckin' Yellow Pages under Murdering Asshole?"

Curious about his reaction to the tape, Kate glanced at Matrone. Surprise rippled through her when she found his eyes already on her, his expression as hard and unreadable as a block of ice. Even though she'd caught him staring, he didn't look away or try to pretend it hadn't happened. He didn't even look particularly uncomfortable. Just . . . intensely interested. It was a strange moment she didn't quite understand. She wanted to believe he was watching her to gauge her reaction to the audiotape. But something in the depths of his dark green eyes belied the explanation.

Inexplicably her cheeks heated. She felt uncharacteristically flustered. Hoping he didn't notice, she dragged her gaze away from his and to David Perrine. He was slumped in the chair, staring at the floor, listening intently.

"Why did he hire you to kill those two women?" Bates barked.

"I didn't ask," Ellis replied. "I took the money and I did it. End of story."

"Where did you spend the money?"

Ellis groaned. "I needed . . . you know, some coke."

"Of course," Milkowski said dryly.

The interview lasted another twenty minutes. When it was finished, Kate snapped off the recorder and shot David Perrine a pointed look. "What came back on Ellis's background check?"

David set his empty cappuccino cup on the tabletop in front of him and dug around in a brown expanding file, finally pulling out a few pages. "He was arrested for DUI three times before the age of twenty, twice in Texas and once in Oklahoma. Fourth time the State of Texas took his license. He was arrested in 1999 for assault. Case was tossed. He was arrested in 2000 for a burglary in Dallas County. Served sixteen months before being released. He was arrested again in 2001 for a robbery at a gas station in Collin County. Did two years and got out on an early release program." Frowning, David set down the report. "In 2004 he was indicted on a weapons charge, but he beat it."

"He fits the profile." She looked down at her notes. "What do you think of his saying that someone hired him?"

"I think he'd say anything to save his dirty red neck," David shot back.

Kate looked at Frank, who'd been quiet up until now. "Will the cops look into that allegation?"

"They'll look into it, but they've got a dozen other murder cases dogging them. This one's pretty cut-and-dried, so they're going to want to put it to bed. They might do a little digging, but they're not going to put too much weight in what he said." He leaned back in the chair. "There's no doubt Ellis did it. We've got the tape. That's enough for a conviction."

"That's all we need," David added.

Kate contemplated the two men. Even though she didn't know Frank well, she could tell there was more on his mind than he was saying. With a sinking feeling, she knew it had to do with what Ellis had said about someone having hired him. It was weird that Frank had mentioned it even before seeing the interview tape.

"Okay, let's go to work on this." She glanced at her notes. "David, the police questioned a possible witness. A man who'd pulled into the Snack and Gas to fill up. Name is Harry Bunger." She rattled off the witness's contact info and David scribbled. "I want you to talk to him. Get a statement. See if he gives you anything we can use."

"I'm on it," David said.

"I want the hard copy of Ellis's background check."

"I'll have it on your desk this afternoon."

She looked at Frank. "See if you can expedite a transcript of this police interview. If they could courier it over this afternoon, that would be great."

Frank gave her a slow smile that, she felt, was far too intimate for an office environment. Jesus, she wished she could get a handle on him.

"I can have a typed transcript here within the hour," he said.

"That would be a record." David shot Frank a curious look. "You got something on the chief, or what?"

"Assistant chief," Frank said deadpan.

David chuckled, then looked at Kate. "I don't get the megabitch thing."

"I think we've had enough discussion about that." Not sure if she was amused or annoyed, Kate looked down at her notes. "I'm going to go over the ME's report and ballistics." She paged through the thick file she had already accumulated. "Frank, I want you to start contacting family members of the victims. Talk to them. Check any possible ties to Ellis. We probably won't need any of it, but I don't want any surprises hitting us down the road."

She'd barely gotten the words out when the door swung open. Liz Gordon rushed in, her expression harried and apologetic. "Sorry to barge in, Kate, but I thought you might want to see something." She rushed over to the twelve-inch color television on Kate's credenza and switched it on.

Kate swiveled in her chair to see a baby-faced reporter from one of the local news stations gazing steadily into the camera, his voice low. "We now bring you District Attorney Mike Shelley's press conference live from Dallas police headquarters."

The camera panned to Mike Shelley standing outside the glass doors of the Jack Evans Police Headquarters building with Chief of Police Charlie Buchanan. The two men were flanked by an entourage of city politicians and several uniformed police officers looking like they'd drawn the short straw and hadn't had a choice but to show up. A dozen microphones were being shoved at Mike's face, and he looked like he was enjoying every minute of it.

"The Dallas County district attorney's office has carefully reviewed the evidence and interviewed witnesses in the Bruton Ellis case. Taking into consideration the brutal nature of the crimes committed, it has been determined that we will be trying this brutal double murder as a capital case."

A murmur rose from the crowd. Mike raised his hands, asking for silence, and continued. "I have assigned an experienced assistant district attorney to prosecute the case."

A dozen questions sounded at once, but Mike remained calm and pointed to a popular local journalist and called her by her first name. "Nancy?"

"Can you tell us which prosecutor will be trying the case?" she asked.

"The prosecutorial team is still in the process of being assembled. I will send out a press release when the time is appropriate." Mike Shelley paused dramatically. "One thing I can tell you is that the district attorney's office will use every resource to ensure that justice is imposed in this brutal case."

Several journalists asked questions simultaneously. Taking the hubbub in stride, Mike pointed to one of the reporters. "Fredericka?"

"Is it true that Life, Inc., has vowed to very strongly protest any case in which the death penalty is being sought?" The camera panned to a stern-looking woman with dark red hair and matching lips.

"All I'm going to say about possible protests is that we live in a free society, and as free citizens, everyone has the right to protest something he or she doesn't agree with."

"What if those protests are violent?"

Another barrage of questions rose, but Mike stepped away from the podium.

Kate had heard enough. She couldn't believe Mike had agreed to a press conference without at the very least warning her. But then, she'd always known he loved the limelight. He was a media hound and never turned down an opportunity to look good. Even if that opportunity was going to be met with controversy.

"Looks like the cat is out of the bag," David said.

"Let's hope no one shoots the cat," Frank added.

"Thank you for that," Kate said dryly and turned off the TV. "It's only going to be a matter of time before our names are made public."

"What was Mike thinking?" Liz asked.

"I'll make a wild guess and venture to say he's thinking about the election in November," David put in. "Think he used the word *brutal* enough times?"

Kate shot him a warning look. "I'll send an e-mail to everyone on the team, reminding them to refer all media inquiries to our public relations department."

"You might want to put something in that e-mail about Life, Inc., Kate."

All eyes turned to Frank. "They've become more than a little radical in the last couple of years when it comes to capital cases."

A newshound, Kate was all too familiar with the anti-death penalty group and realized with a deepening sense of dismay that the personal safety and security of her team could very well become an issue. "I'm familiar with Life, Inc."

"Then you know the prosecutor who put one of the Texas seven on death row had to send his family to an undisclosed location during the trial because they had been threatened."

"Do you think that might happen with this case?" Liz asked, her expression concerned.

Kate looked at Frank. "What do you think?"

"I think from this point forward, all of us should keep our eyes and ears open," he said. "If anything happens that makes any of us uneasy, even if you feel it may not be important, bring it to either my, David's, or Kate's attention immediately."

Kate nodded in agreement. But her mind was already jumping ahead to the few choice words she had for Mike Shelley. He'd been foolish to hold a press conference so soon. He'd put his office—and her team—in the spotlight weeks before the preliminary hearing.

"That'll be all." Picking up a stack of documents from her in-box, Kate set them in front of her and began to page through them as the three members of her team filed out.

She'd already turned to her computer to draft the e-mail when Frank's voice sounded behind her. "I need to talk to you about something."

"If it's about being late, don't bother." She frowned at him. "It would be a tremendous help if you would just start showing up on time."

"It's about the case."

"What about it?"

"I want to talk to Bruton Ellis," he said.

If he hadn't looked so serious, Kate might have laughed at the absurdity of his request. "You know that in order to do that, Aaron Napier will have to give you permission. You know there's no way in hell he's going to let you do it."

"I've always prescribed to the where-there's-a-will-there's-a-way philosophy."

"That philosophy in the DA's office can get you fired or disbarred or both."

He gave her another slow smile that made her think he knew a hell of a lot more about the DA's office than she gave him credit for. "I'm not a member of the bar. I can't be disbarred. As far as firing me goes . . ." He shrugged. "I have friends in high places."

"That is so inappropriate."

"I'm an inappropriate kind of guy."

Kate wanted to give him a smart comeback, but her mind was already back on the case. "Why do you want to talk to Ellis?"

"Put me in a room with him and I'll know within five minutes whether or not he's lying about someone hiring him."

"What are you going to do? Rough him up?"

He smiled. "Cops don't rough people up."

She didn't smile back. "I don't want you talking to Ellis."

"I could talk to Bates, have him ask Ellis a few questions for me."

"If that gets out and we get slapped with a mistrial, I'll have your job."

"You keep forgetting I have friends in high places."

Kate thought about what Bates had said and wondered if it were true. Maybe Frank missed police work. "You're an investigator for the DA's office now, not a detective."

Ice flickered in his eyes, but was gone in an instant. "With all due respect, I think there's more going on here than meets the eye. I'd like to—"

"I need you as an investigator, not running off on some wild-goose chase."

It was the first time she'd seen him flush. And she knew immediately it was anger that colored his cheeks, that the emotion was powerful and deep and came from a place where there was plenty more.

"It's good to know you have so much faith in cops," he said.

Kate hadn't wanted to pull rank, but she knew men like Frank Matrone didn't do well with subtle. "This has nothing to do with cops or the police department or even the fact that you used to be a cop. It's about your role in this case."

He stared at her for an interminable moment, his expression angry. "How are you going to feel if you're wrong about this?"

Kate had never been one to shrink away from conflict, but she could feel her neck and shoulder muscles tightening, the way they always did when she got into a confrontation. The truth of the matter was she didn't want any problems with Frank. She needed the collective focus of her team on the case. She needed *his* focus on the case. But she could tell by the way he was looking at her that this wasn't over.

"This isn't about my feelings," she said. "This is about the case. It's about evidence. And our ability to prove to twelve people beyond a reasonable doubt that this man is guilty as charged."

"Or maybe you're afraid I'll screw up your winning streak if I dig up something that adds reasonable doubt."

"Look," she snapped, "we have two dead women. We have their murders, a sexual assault, and the commission of an armed robbery on videotape. That's all I need to get my conviction."

"This is all about getting your conviction, isn't it?"

She stared into his eyes, taken aback by the anger she saw there, wondering what she'd done to elicit it. "Yes."

"Let's just hope you got everyone involved and not just the fall guy," he said and walked out.

THURSDAY, JANUARY 26, 5:28 P.M.

Kate knew better than to let Frank's parting shot get to her. There was no doubt Bruton Ellis had done the crimes. They had him on videotape. But as hard as she tried to put her worry aside, a niggling little voice wouldn't let her. By the end of the day the stress had taken its toll in the form of a headache.

She hadn't seen Frank since their heated exchange that morning, which was probably a good thing considering she was still angry with him. Absently she picked up the brown expandable file David had set in her in-box before he left. Trying to decide if she wanted to go through it now or wait until she was home, she leafed through its contents. Her finger stopped on a hard copy of the benefit package from the Snack and Gas franchisee, Quick Stop, Inc. Curious as to what benefits would become available to Evangeline Worth's surviving children, she pulled the stapled bundle from its nest and skimmed.

On the last page there was mention of a life insurance policy. It would pay one thousand dollars for every year of employment upon the death of an employee. Evangeline Worth had been with the Snack and Gas for five years. That meant her beneficiary—in this case her four children, all of whom were minors—would receive a lump sum of five thousand dollars. Not much considering they'd lost not only their mother, but their sole source of income.

Feeling a raw pinch of sympathy for the dead woman and the family she'd left behind, Kate skimmed the rest of the documents. The franchisee of record was Quick Stop, Inc., a corporation based in Oklahoma City. The corporation on the benefits package, however, was listed as Quorum Partners Limited. Kate thought it was odd that the policy owner was a parent company and not the franchisee of record. It was a small thing. Probably insignificant with regard to the case. But Kate was meticulous by nature, a stickler for detail, and downright anal-retentive when it came to being thorough.

A glance at the clock told her it was probably too late in the day to get much done, but at the very least she could get the ball rolling with some calls. Snatching up the phone, she dialed the number of the franchisee.

"Good afternoon, Quick Stop, Inc."

Kate identified herself, asked for the legal department, and was immediately put on hold. She drummed her fingers impatiently for a full minute before someone answered.

"This is Debbie, can I help you?"

"This is Kate Megason with the Dallas County district attorney's office. I'm working on the case related to the murders of Evangeline Worth and Irma Trevino."

"Oh, God, that was so terrible. I was really glad to hear the police got the guy. How can I help you?"

"I have a life insurance policy in front of me for Evangeline Worth."

"I'm glad to hear she had the forethought to buy life insurance. She had four dependents, you know. Kids."

"This policy wasn't initiated by Ms. Worth. The policy was taken out by the company she worked for."

"Hmmm." The woman made a sound of confusion. "We don't administer life insurance from this office."

Kate paged through the policy. "The policy holder is listed as Quorum Partners Limited."

"Oh. That's our parent company."

"Is that where the life insurance policies originate?"

"I'm not sure, to be perfectly honest. I usually deal with worker's compensation issues, OSHA requirements, store accidents, you know, slip-falls, stuff like that."

But Kate's curiosity had been roused. "Can you give me the number for Quorum Partners Limited?"

The woman rattled off the number. Kate thanked her and without hanging up dialed Quorum Partners Limited. A recorded message told her the office closed at five and would be reopening at eight the next morning.

"Crap," Kate muttered and dropped the phone into its cradle.

Turning to her computer, she called up her contact list and dialed Frank Matrone's number. She counted four rings and was about to hang up when he answered with an annoyed "Yeah."

"It's Kate," she said, taken aback by the roughness of his voice. "Are you . . . all right?"

A beat of silence and then a decidedly annoyed, "I'm fine. What's up?"

She wanted to believe the nerves quivering just beneath the surface was because they'd parted on uneasy terms. But that didn't explain why the photo she'd seen of him in the *Dallas Morning News* article flashed in her mind's eye. He'd been lying in a hospital bed, his bare chest covered with a thatch of dark hair. He'd had a heavy five o'clock shadow. A smile that hadn't looked real. A thumbs-up with a hand swathed in bandages . . .

"Don't you ever go home?" he asked after a moment.

"Oh, I was . . ." She didn't know why she was so flustered. Kate *never* got flustered. "I was going through some papers from the Ellis case and I found a life insurance policy."

"Who's the beneficiary?"

"Her four children stand to receive five thousand dollars."

"Not much."

"No, it isn't." Kate looked down at the benefit package. "Quick Stop, Inc., is the franchisee of record. But the policy holder is Quorum Partners Limited."

"Parent company?"

"Right."

"I ran a D & B on Quick Stop. But not Quorum."

"That's why I'm calling."

"And I thought you'd called just to hear my voice."

He was flirting with her. And Kate's heart was beating a little too fast despite her efforts to quell it. "I'd like for you to see what you can find out about Quorum. I'm sure all of this is routine, but since we're dealing with a capital case, we've got to cross the *t*'s and dot the *i*'s."

"Dotting and crossing as we speak. I'll try to have something for you in the next day or so."

"I'm going to do a little poking around. If I find anything on my end, I'll let you know."

Kate wanted to talk to him about their argument that morning, but didn't know how to breach the subject. If she was too soft, Frank would bulldoze right over her. If she came on too strong, she risked alienating him and causing more problems than if she just let it go.

The silence turned uncomfortable. Frank cleared his throat. Kate closed her eyes, annoyed with herself for letting herself get rattled. "I'll see you in the morning."

He disconnected without replying.

THURSDAY, JANUARY 26, 9:34 P.M.

The two men met at the Comedy Club on Beltline Road in Addison. The place was dark and loud and packed with happy-hour revelers and corporate executives out to blow off steam. The comedian was just winding into high gear when the man in the Armani suit found a table at the rear. He sat with his back to the wall so he could watch the door and not have to worry about anyone looking over his shoulder. He'd just blown out the candle centerpiece and set his briefcase on the floor at his feet when the man in blue jeans and an expensive jacket joined him.

"This fuckin' guy is funny as shit," the man in blue jeans said.

A waitress in a low-cut peasant blouse took their drink orders and hustled away. The man in blue jeans watched the show and laughed. The man in the Armani suit didn't think the comedian was particularly talented. But then, he hadn't chosen this place for the entertainment.

Neither man spoke until the waitress returned with their drinks. Finally the man in the blue jeans looked at the man sitting across from him, all traces of laughter gone from his face. "So, what do you have for me this time?"

"Gainful employment, if you're interested."

"I'm always interested in working for you. You have a gift for interesting jobs, and you always pay me what I'm worth."

The man in the Armani suit swirled the ice in his glass. "I pay for discretion."

"Discretion is my specialty. What do I have to do?"

"Screw up someone's life for a little while."

"I'm good at that. Just ask my ex-wife." He glanced at the comedian onstage and chuckled. "Does this person have a name?"

Reaching into the briefcase, the man in the suit removed the folder and slid it across the table. "There's a photo, too."

The other man opened the folder. His eyebrows rose as he paged through the dozen or so documents and the single photograph. "A fucking ADA?"

"She's digging into something that could potentially cause me problems. I want her stopped."

"Permanently?"

"That would be a big mistake at this point in the game."

"I'm talking an accident, of course."

"Too much risk. This woman is a prosecutor. Any whisper of foul play will bring down the wrath of the entire criminal justice system. I do not want attention drawn to this case."

"We're talking high risk, man."

"I know the risks."

"Then you know risk is expensive."

He contemplated the other man. "How much?"

The man in the blue jeans removed a pen from his breast pocket. He wrote a five-digit number on a napkin and slid it across the table. "This kind of work doesn't come cheap."

"Evidently not."

The man in the blue jeans looked interested. "Nice face. Young. But she's got a tough look about her."

"She's a pit bull. But even pit bulls have a weak spot. I want you to find hers."

"You've piqued my interest. When do I start?"

"Right away." The man in the suit motioned toward the file on the table between them. "All the information you'll need is in the file. I'll wire the money to your account like before."

"How far do you want me to take this?"

"For now I want her distracted, not hurt." The man in the Armani suit rose. The comedian and cigarette smoke had given him a headache. "If this doesn't work, then we'll take it to the next level."

FRIDAY, JANUARY 27, 3:15 A.M.

Kirsten's screams echoed inside Kate's head as she ran through the darkness. Screams filled with pain and horror and outrage. At some point Kate had begun to cry. Giant sobs racked her body. She was crying so hard the tears were choking her, blinding her.

"Kirsten! Run!" Ahead, she saw the outline of a stand of trees. A warehouse surrounded by a chain-link fence to her left. If she could reach the trees, she could hide. Get a rock. Maybe the police would come and save them. She headed for the trees at a dangerous speed.

"Shut that bitch up!"

She looked to her left to see the fat man standing over Kirsten. He drew his foot back and kicked her hard. Kate screamed. "Kirsten! Oh, God! Don't hurt her!"

She was nearly to the trees when he caught her in a flying tackle. She went down hard. He came down on top of her, and they hit the ground with bone-crunching force.

Kate felt her front tooth break. She tasted blood at the back of her throat. But every pain that racked her body was made smaller by the fact that she knew the worst was yet to come.

She tried to get to her knees to crawl away, but it was impossible with her hands bound behind her back. "Where do you think you're going, pretty little Katie?" he said in a raspy voice.

Grabbing her shoulder, he forced her onto her back. Kate tried to lash out with her feet, but he drew back and slammed his fist into her left cheekbone. This time the world went silent and still.

It was as if she left her body for a moment. She could still see his face. His lips were pulled back into a snarl. Yellow teeth. Heavy whiskers. Greasy hair. She saw intent in his eyes, and she knew he wasn't going to stop. That she would be hurt tonight, and there was nothing she could do to stop him.

She looked at the man. "Why are you doing this?"

He glanced around, then licked his lips. "I ain't never had me an uppity little cunt before."

The ugly words penetrated her brain like a bullet. The meaning shocked and horrified. She could feel the adrenaline like an electric current, running through her body. Terror leaping like hot fingers.

The sound of tearing fabric snapped her back. He'd torn her T-shirt from her body with his fist. Sick horror spread through her. She wanted to cover herself, but couldn't. Oh, God, please no! "Don't," she heard herself say. But the voice was little more than a moan.

"Shut the fuck up, you little cunt. You're going to like this."

He was breathing hard. Pressing against her. She could feel the hardness of his arousal against her hip and felt a slow rise of nausea. Her arms were pinned behind her at an uncomfortable angle, the weight of their bodies causing great pain. He fisted her bra and yanked violently. Her entire body jolted as the fabric cut into her skin and then snapped. She saw him looking at her breasts, and part of her wanted to die. Oh, dear Lord, she couldn't bear this.

She tried to twist away. She didn't care if he hit her again. Anything would be better than having him touch her.

But her efforts were useless, and in the next instant his hands were on her breasts, squeezing and hurting.

Kate threw her head back and screamed. He hit her again, but she didn't stop screaming. She felt her lip split. Felt her mouth fill with blood.

"Shut up!"

A terrible sound tore from her throat when he rammed his fist into her stomach. The breath left her lungs in a rush. She heard herself retch, tasted vomit at the back of her throat. Then he was stuffing her bra into her mouth. . . .

She lay still as he ripped her jeans from her body. Her panties tore away easily. She couldn't believe this was happening. Couldn't believe he was going to hurt her this way. Rape didn't happen to girls like Kate. It always happened to someone else.

She tried one last time to kick him, but he hit her again. In the stomach. Her left breast. Pain radiated through her entire body. She tried to twist away. But he hit her again, with his fist in the temple, and stars danced in her peripheral vision. She lay there dazed and hurting and terrified. She was keening, moaning, sobbing into her gag like an animal. She couldn't see Kirsten and wondered if the same thing was happening to her. Maybe the fat man wouldn't hurt her, wouldn't let this happen.

"Open up, Katie. Sweet, sweet Katie."

Then he was between her legs. Kate closed her eyes, tried to go someplace else in her mind. She couldn't bear this. The horror of what he was doing to her.

Pain ripped through her as he tried to enter her. She screamed into her gag, but the sound was little more than a whimper. Stop! her mind cried out. Oh, dear God, make him stop!

But he didn't stop. Pain burned like fire between her legs as he forced himself inside her. Shame and humiliation and the horror of what was happening exploded inside her. Then he began to move. He rasped horrible things as he violated her. "Pretty cunt. Tight little whore. Oh, yeah. Oh, Katie . . ."

Kate wanted it to be over. She closed her eyes and cried into the gag. Then he put his mouth on hers. She smelled alcohol and cigarettes and bad teeth. Gagging, she turned her head. Surprise and hope flashed inside her when he withdrew and let her turn away. Then she was on her belly and he was coming at her from behind.

Her seventeen-year-old mind could never have imagined what he did to her next. The pain was like nothing she'd ever experienced. The horror was too much for her mind to absorb.

He wrapped one hand around her neck and crammed her face into the dirt. Then he was pushing into her. Tearing her skin. Pain ignited like fire. She struggled, but he shoved her face harder into the dirt. It was in her eyes, in her mouth. She could feel something sharp cutting the side of her face. She couldn't breathe. . . .

Then he was inside her and she couldn't think of anything except the pain. The horror of what this evil man was doing to her. And for the first time in her young life, Kate wished she was dead. She did not want to survive this. She did not want to carry this experience with her for the rest of her life. She thought about Kirsten and prayed that God would spare her. This was Kate's doing. She'd been the one to suggest they sneak out of the house. This was her fault.

She didn't know how long the violation went on. It seemed like a lifetime. When he finally withdrew and stood, she lay there, her body racked with pain. Her mind too overwhelmed with horror to react. She could feel the warmth of semen and blood between her buttocks. Her mouth was open, the bra hanging out. Blood and saliva forming a puddle. At some point she'd vomited. She could smell it as it wet the dirt. But still she didn't move.

Vaguely she was aware of his boots crunching in the dirt. The two men talking. Then he was standing over her. Groaning, Kate shifted onto her side. Drawing her knees up to her chest, she looked up at him. He was holding a wrench in her right hand, looking down at her, intent clear in his eyes.

"Close your eyes," he said.

She knew he was going to kill her, but she was strangely unafraid and accepted that she would die here and now.

He raised the wrench over his head.

She closed her eyes.

And then the world shattered.

Kate jerked awake abruptly. Groggy and disoriented, she fumbled for the alarm and punched the snooze, but it didn't stop the incessant noise. By the fourth ring she was awake enough to realize it wasn't her alarm drilling into her brain, but the phone.

The first thought that struck her was that something had happened to Kirsten. Kate had had enough tragedy in her life to know phone calls in the middle of the night were never good.

Rolling onto her side, she reached for the phone, "Hello?"

Silence.

"Hello?" she repeated. "Is someone there?"

She could hear the faint hiss of an open line; she sensed someone on the other end. She could hear faint breathing. A slight rustle.

The hairs at her nape prickled. Gooseflesh raced down her arms. "Who's there?"

"Check your front porch, Katie," came a guttural, whispered voice.

Kate sat up straight, adrenaline shooting from her belly to her toes. "Who is this?"

"Are you sure you want to know?"

A click sounded and then the line went dead.

For the span of several seconds, Kate sat there holding the phone, her mind racing in perfect time with her heart. All she could think was that the caller knew her name. He had her phone number, which made her uneasy because her number was unlisted. As an ADA, she dealt with some form of the criminal element on an almost daily basis. Even though the State of Texas kept her abreast of the release dates of prisoners she'd sent to prison, she'd gotten an unlisted number to keep some convict from calling her when he was released.

So how had this guy gotten her number? Who was he? And what had he meant when he'd told her to check the porch?

For an instant she considered calling 911. But with Dallas being one of the most violent cities in the nation, she knew something as minor as a prank call wouldn't warrant sending an officer. What could the police do? The caller hadn't threatened her. All she could do was report the incident to the phone company first thing in the morning and get her number changed.

Slipping into her robe, she opened the night table drawer and pulled out the mini magnum. Easing the hammer back with her thumb, she left the bedroom and padded down the hall and into the living room.

Around her the house was silent and still. Her footsteps were little more than a whisper as she crossed through the living room. At the front door she parted the curtain at the sidelight and peeked out. Her vision was relatively unobscured. The porch was small, and she could see there was no one there. Then she spotted the small object about the size of a wadded-up sock on the welcome mat, and a chill raced through her.

Kate flipped on the porch light. The gun cocked and ready in her hand, she stepped onto the porch and looked around. "Who's there?" she called out in her toughest voice.

The only answer was the hiss of wind through the trees.

Seeing nothing out of the ordinary, she stooped to get a closer look at the object. If some prankster had thrown a used condom or something gross, she was going to . . .

Adrenaline struck her like a fist when she realized the object was a tattered blue bandanna. A bandanna just like the one used to bind her hands on that terrible night eleven years ago . . .

Facedown in the grass. Dirt in her mouth. Horror exploding in her brain. Pain ripping through her body. Her innocence shattered. Her life changed forever . . .

She heard her quick intake of breath. Nausea filled her mouth with the bitter taste of bile. She stared in disbelief. All the while her heart screamed a denial. This couldn't possibly have anything to do with what had happened in Houston all those years ago.

But Kate didn't believe in coincidence. Her logical mind knew the bandanna had not been tossed onto her porch randomly. Someone knew. And they were using that knowledge to frighten her.

The overriding question was who. Who would have something to gain by frightening her? Had some convict been released and decided to exact revenge against the woman who'd sent him to prison? Did it have something to do with the Bruton Ellis case? Or maybe the man who'd raped her and left her for dead had come back to finish the job . . .

Shuddering at the thought, Kate went back inside and locked the door behind her. Flipping on lights as she went, she strode to the kitchen, yanked open the drawer, and removed a plastic freezer bag from its container. At the small desk where she paid her bills, she opened the pencil drawer and removed a letter opener. Then she crossed back through the living room, checked the sidelights again, and opened the door. Kneeling, she used the letter opener to put the bandanna in the freezer bag.

She knew one of the trace evidence analysts at the Institute of Forensic Sciences. She could take it to him, pay for testing herself, and see what came back. But Kate knew that even if the thing was covered with blood or semen, unless a crime had been committed, there was nothing the police could do.

But how could anyone possibly know what had happened? Her parents had gone to great lengths to protect her and Kirsten's privacy. Their names had never been made public. The only people who'd known about the sexual assaults were the police and hospital personnel.

Holding the mini magnum in one hand, the bag containing the bandanna in the other, Kate looked out at the trees surrounding the gravel driveway. "You make one wrong move, you son of a bitch, and I swear to God I'll put a bullet in your heart."

The night responded with a cold gust of wind that chilled her to the bone.

NINE

Frank had had a bad night. He'd had a lot of bad nights in the last year. Nights that were sleepless and black and endless. Judging from the pain zinging up his leg, this morning wasn't going to be any better. Maybe even worse.

The doctor had warned him this could happen. He'd prescribed painkillers, which Frank was all too willing to take. But it was like trying to put out a forest fire with a straw.

The first tinges of pain had wakened him at midnight. At first, it had been a gentle ebb and flow that had lapped at the backwaters of his consciousness like tentative fingertips. But within an hour those waves had augmented to huge undulating monsters that had pulled him from sleep and into a black abyss of torment.

He'd been dreaming of that day at the café in Jerusalem. Of Gittel in her pretty blue dress. A smile so lovely it hurt just to look at her. A need so powerful he could barely bring himself to remember.

Even in sleep his mind could recall the moment with startling clarity. The violence of the blast. The shock of pain when his eardrum had burst. Searing heat that ran from his left buttock to his toes as shrapnel severed muscle and shattered bone. He saw blood against the cobblestone street. Black smoke billowing into a blue sky. He smelled burned flesh and singed hair and the coppery stench of blood. He could feel the heat of the fire burning his skin.

The nightmare was bad enough.

But the pain was worse.

By midnight it had been like death, black and vicious, and Frank thought he died a little more with every minute he endured it. At one A.M. he took the usual dose of muscle relaxers. An hour later he doubled the dose. By two forty-five he was sweating and writhing and cursing the very God who'd spared his life that fateful day one year ago. By four-thirty A.M., desperate and willing to do anything to stop the cycle of pain, he did the one thing he hated most and dug the powerful painkillers out of his medicine cabinet and downed them with vodka and tap water.

But not even the marvels of modern narcotics could ease the pain of a nervous system gone haywire. By the time six A.M. rolled around, Frank was starting to think death was a better alternative than the agonizing existence he'd been relegated to since a piece of shrapnel had shattered his leg. The doctors had saved the leg. With the help of a titanium rod and a small piece of bone from his hip, they'd even managed to keep him out of a wheelchair.

No one had counted on an obscure nerve disorder stepping in eight months later and turning what was left of his life into a living hell. After four doctors and too many misdiagnoses to count, he was ultimately diagnosed with Reflex Sympathetic Dystrophy Syndrome. A chronic condition characterized by severe burning pain, swelling in the afflicted limb, and extreme sensitivity to touch. A terrible disorder that affected the nerves, skin, muscles, blood vessels, and bones. Frank had been in stage two by the time it was diagnosed. By then the disorder had affected every facet of his life, including his job and his frame of mind.

He spent the night in a hazy world of cold sweats, total physical exhaustion, and pain so horrific at times he could hear his own screams echoing inside his head. It hurt to lie on the sofa. It hurt to lie in bed. He tried elevating his leg, but the pain was so bad he couldn't lie still. It was too goddamn cold to get into the pool. A warm shower usually helped, but by then he was so fucked up on painkillers he couldn't stand.

So much for that pain management clinic he'd attended a couple of months back.

Several times he considered calling the emergency room. A couple of times he even reached for the phone. Both times Frank set it back into its cradle. He would never forget the way the paramedics and emergency room personnel had looked at him last time. As if he were some kind of mental case. The doctor had taken one look at his mangled leg and year-old scars and chalked his "discomfort" as psychological in origin. The ordeal had been a humiliation Frank could do without. If it killed him, he was going to wait until his personal physician's office opened at eight-thirty.

He knew he should call Kate. But he knew from experience that no matter how hard he tried to speak normally, the powerful narcotics invariably affected his speech. He could imagine how the conversation would go down if he called in, slurring his words.

Groaning, he reached for the painkillers on the night table beside his bed. He couldn't remember how long it had been since he'd taken one, but he didn't care. If he was lucky, he'd pass out.

An animal sound squeezed from his throat as he twisted the lid off the brown bottle. He could feel his heart pounding madly in his chest, his leg throbbing with every excruciating beat. His hands shook as he tapped out a pill. His fingers were so thick he could barely get the capsule into his mouth. His mouth was so dry he didn't know how he was going to swallow. Then he remembered the vodka.

He tossed back the pill and took a long pull. Setting down the glass, he fell back onto the pillows. Another hot wave of pain rolled up his leg. His quadriceps cramped. Searing heat spread from calf to thigh to buttock to spine.

"Aw, God." Frank saw stars. Felt his eyes roll back in their sockets. He heard that terrible sound again and for a moment thought some wild animal was running loose in his house. Then he realized the sound had come from him. He acknowledged that he was in trouble. That he needed help. That he should have done something about this a long time ago.

Another wave of agony struck him like a tidal wave, burning him with heat so intense he clamped his teeth together to keep himself from screaming. But he didn't have the breath to scream.

Stars exploded black and white in his peripheral vision. The room dipped and spun like a carnival ride. Closing his eyes, Frank cursed and prayed for the darkness to take him.

FRIDAY, JANUARY 27, 5:25 P.M.

"Damn you, Matrone."

Kate set the phone in its cradle and tried hard not to let the anger get the best of her. But she was fuming. It was the third time she'd tried to reach Frank and the third time she'd been forced to leave a message.

He hadn't shown up for work this morning, didn't bother to call, and by the end of the day Kate was ready to drive over to his house and strangle him with her bare hands. She'd spent the morning in court, the afternoon had been divided by meetings and a conference call she hadn't been able to wriggle out of. Every moment in between she'd been unsuccessfully trying to run down her AWOL investigator. Where the hell was he? What was he thinking not showing up for work?

Resigned to picking up the slack herself—at least until she could get the situation resolved—Kate opened the brown expandable file she'd pilfered from Frank's desk and began to page through it, trying to figure out what he'd been working on.

"You look frazzled."

She glanced up to see Liz Gordon at her door and managed a weak smile. "You have no idea."

"Anything I can do to help?"

Kate sighed, wanting to unload, knowing she couldn't. Being an ADA definitely had its advantages. But at times like this—times when she was stressed out and weary to her bones—Kate wished she were one of the girls so she could confide. Maybe even complain a little. "Thanks but I think I'm going to have to deal with this particular problem on my own."

Liz plopped into the visitor chair opposite her desk. "Matrone?"

If Kate hadn't been so surprised, she might have laughed. "Does that mean I'm not the only one who's noticed he doesn't show up for work half the time?"

"Please tell me you're not going to fire him."

Kate didn't respond.

Liz made a sound of exasperation. "Kate, do you have any idea how many hearts you'll break?"

"I have no earthly idea what that means."

"Half the women in this office are in love with him. The other half just wants to sleep with him."

Kate rolled her eyes. "Oh, brother."

Leaning back in her chair, Liz smiled. "Don't tell me you've got your head buried so deep in work that you haven't noticed."

"The only thing I've noticed is that he doesn't show up for work."

"Kate, the man is drop-dead gorgeous. We're talking hot. We're talking melted Belgian chocolate and Godiva dark rolled into a single, mouthwatering piece of man-flesh."

Kate stared at her friend, not sure what to say, painfully aware of the heat creeping up her cheeks. She did not want to think of Frank Matrone in terms of man-flesh or chocolate.

"You're blushing."

"No, I'm not."

"Oh my God!" The paralegal choked out a laugh. "You *have* noticed! Kate Megason *is* human. Break out the champagne!"

Kate glanced uneasily toward her office door. "Would you keep your voice down? I'm trying to maintain a professional image here."

"Oh, Kate, I was starting to get *worried* about you. Like maybe you'd been born without ovaries or something."

"My ovaries are just fine, damn it. Not that it's anybody's business."

"So do you think he's cute?"

"I think my dad's pug is cute."

Liz bit her lip. "I probably shouldn't tell you this."

"Tell me what?"

"Promise you won't get mad."

"The only thing that's going to make me mad is if you don't tell me what you're talking about."

"Someone in accounting started a running bet."

"A bet?"

"You know, like the Super Bowl pool? Everyone puts in five bucks. Winner takes all."

"I know what a pool is, damn it. What I'm wondering is what it's got to do with me."

"The accounting department has you and Frank together by Valentine's Day."

"What?"

"Payroll thinks you'll sleep with him before then. Well, everyone except for Teresa Berg. She thinks you'll blow it before it gets that far. There's almost two hundred and fifty dollars in the pot."

Kate didn't know what to say. She felt foolish and embarrassed and utterly certain that she did *not* want to continue this conversation. "That is the most ridiculous thing I've ever heard."

"You were in on the pot when Steve Wetzel and his admin got together."

"That was different. They were having an affair. They got married, for God's sake." Kate grappled for words. "Don't you people have work to do?"

"There's nothing wrong with having a little fun on the job."

"There's absolutely nothing going on between Frank Matrone and me. We don't even like each other. And I would very much appreciate it if you curtailed the juvenile antics."

Liz only looked at her with mild disbelief. "Don't tell me you haven't noticed the way he looks at you."

"Most of the time he looks at me like he wants to strangle

me." But Kate was not dense; she'd caught Frank's eyes straying. But he wasn't the first man who'd looked at her that way, and she hadn't given it more than a passing thought. She had too much responsibility on her shoulders to put any weight in something as trivial as a lingering look from a male subordinate.

"I don't think strangling you is what he has in mind," Liz said. "Unless he's into that autoerotic asphyxiation."

"I think this particular conversation has run its course."

Liz smirked. "Whatever you say."

Exasperated, Kate looked down at the file in front of her and tried to remember what she'd been doing.

"You know he was hurt overseas, don't you?"

Kate didn't look up. "I'm aware of that."

"Maybe you ought to cut him some slack."

Kate stopped what she was doing and gave her friend a stern look. "We shouldn't be discussing this."

Liz leaned forward and lowered her voice. "I heard from Emily in payroll that he was hurt in a suicide bombing in Israel last year. He was nearly killed."

Remembering his limp, Kate felt a tinge of guilt for not being more sympathetic. She'd seen the carnage on the news. As an ADA, she'd seen enough violence to know that sometimes people didn't recover. Even badass ex-cops like Frank Matrone.

"I know," she admitted, but felt rotten because it hadn't mattered.

"It might be a good reason to give him another chance."

"Liz, look, I don't mean to sound cold, but I need an investigator I can count on."

The silence that followed smarted more than Kate wanted to admit.

After a moment Liz rose. "A few of us are meeting at Martini's for drinks later. There's a standing invitation for you to join us."

"Thanks, but I'll probably spend the rest of the evening slogging through this file. I'll catch you next time."

"I'm going to hold you to that one of these days," Liz said and started toward the door.

FRIDAY, JANUARY 27, 5:55 P.M.

Half an hour later Kate left the Frank Crowley Courts Building, her briefcase jammed with files, her shoulders knotted with tension from what had been a very long day. She wanted to blame the tension on the hours she'd been keeping. But as she wove the BMW through rush-hour traffic, it struck her that Frank was the source.

She understood all too well that there were times when personal problems or health problems interfered with life. That sometimes those things took precedence over work. But experience had taught Kate that life didn't wait for problems to be resolved. The Bruton Ellis case would proceed with or without Frank Matrone.

An investigator played a crucial role in the prosecution of a case. If he were unable to work because of personal or health problems, he needed to be upfront about it and put in for a leave of absence.

"So what the hell am I supposed to do?" she muttered as she sped through the tollbooth at the Wycliffe Plaza. "Let him screw up the case? Not bloody likely."

The way Kate saw it, there was only one way to handle the situation. The way she always handled problems. Confront it head-on and try like hell to avoid a collision. She didn't always succeed, but over the years she'd found that forcing an issue, however difficult, invariably opened the channels of communication.

Slowing to the speed limit, she tugged her Palmtop from her briefcase and called up her contact list. Giving her driving only half of her attention, she picked up her cell phone and dialed Frank Matrone's home number. A busy signal elicited a sigh.

"You can't even make a simple phone call easy for me, can you, Matrone?"

Realizing it would be more expeditious for her to just swing by his house, she hit a few keys on the Palmtop and called up his address. He lived in an older, middle-class neighborhood in northwest Dallas, just north of Love Field. Five minutes away, she thought, and bit her lip.

The clock on the dash told her it wasn't too late for a professional call. The worst thing that could happen would be that she would disturb his dinner.

If Matrone were having personal problems or health problems, it would be best for everyone involved—Frank included—if he took a leave of absence until he could resume full duty. At this point she would even agree to let him stay on part-time. As long as Mike Shelley let her hire a third full-time investigator . . .

Feeling better now that she'd made a decision, she exited the tollway and headed west on Walnut Hill Lane.

TEN

Frank Matrone lived in a small, ranch-style house with a manicured lawn and fenced backyard. Spotting the number painted on the curb, Kate pulled into the driveway and parked next to his truck. The lights were on inside, but the blinds were drawn. From all indications he was home.

She knew it was silly—she had absolutely no reason to be nervous about confronting him—but her palms were wet as she slid from the car and slammed the door. Damn it, Frank was the one who should be sweating this, not her. *He* was the one who hadn't shown up for work.

But the rationalizations did little to calm her nerves as she took the steps to the front door and rang the bell. A minute ticked by and she rang the bell again. When there was still no answer, she leaned forward and put her ear to the door. She could hear music. Country, if she wasn't mistaken. But no Frank.

"Terrific," she muttered and rapped her knuckles hard against the door.

Surprise rippled through her when the door squeaked open.

Kate stared at the three-inch gap, wondering why it hadn't been closed and locked. Dallas had one of the highest crime rates in the nation. Everyone locked their doors.

Except for Frank Matrone, evidently.

For the span of three heartbeats, Kate debated whether or not to enter or turn around and walk away. But because she wanted to get this done, she pushed open the door. "Hello? Frank? Are you home? It's Kate Megason."

The door opened to a comfortable living room with hardwood floors and a tattered Navajo print rug. A brown leather sofa and matching chair were grouped in front of a sandstone hearth. The battered old coffee table was made of dark wood and piled with what looked like bills and magazines. Against the far wall, a large-screen television hulked, its smooth face dark. From the stereo George Strait belted out "Desperately."

A pillow and comforter lay on the floor in front of the television. A tall ficus tree stood near the window. A decent oil reproduction hung on the wall above the sofa. No sign of Frank . . .

"Hello? Is anyone home?"

Vaguely concerned, Kate crossed to the dining area where a glass-top table and four chairs sat beneath a slowly revolving ceiling fan. Beyond, she could see into a galley-style kitchen. The light above the stove was on. A bonsai squatted in the window above the sink. Old appliances. Overripe bananas in a glass bowl on the bar.

"Gittel."

Kate spun at the sound of the guttural male voice behind her. Shock vibrated through her at the sight of Frank. Pale and haggard and glassy-eyed, he looked nothing like the man she'd spent much of the last week with. He was standing less than three feet away. His right hand was on the back of the leather chair, and he was leaning heavily, as if using it for support. He was wearing only drawstring pants that rode low on lean hips.

Her face heated as her eyes flicked over him. She got the impression of taut male flesh, a thatch of dark hair on a wide chest, and a belly as flat and hard as West Texas limestone.

She blinked at him, stunned and ridiculously embarrassed. "Frank? Are you all right?"

It was a stupid question considering he could barely stand upright. But while Kate knew something was wrong, she didn't know what. She sure as hell didn't know how to help him.

"Gittel . . . for God's sake . . ." His voice was rough and so low Kate could barely make out what he was saying.

"It's Kate," she said tentatively, aware that her heart had begun to pound.

"Knew . . . you'd come . . . back." He took a faltering step toward her, his face going taut as if he were in pain.

The initial jab of uneasiness went through her like a mild electrical shock, and for the first time it struck her that he was intoxicated. That he thought she was someone else. And that this was the kind of situation that could get out of control quickly if not handled properly.

Even though he'd once been a cop and was still a certified peace officer licensed to carry a gun, she knew none of those things were a guarantee that he wouldn't cross a line. She found herself wondering if Frank Matrone had a dark side. If she was about to get a glimpse of it.

"Frank, it's Kate.

He blinked at her. "Kate?"

"Look, you're obviously not . . . feeling well, so I'm just going to . . . leave. This was probably a bad idea, anyway. Is there someone I can call for you?"

"Just . . . you . . ." He let go of the back of the chair and stepped toward her.

"Maybe you should sit down."

"Don't . . . wanna . . ." He staggered slightly as he moved toward her. "C'mere . . ."

"You're drunk."

"Just g'ting . . . warmed up."

She tried to get out of his way, but for all his staggering around, his reflexes were quick, and the next thing she knew his hands were on her shoulders, holding her in place. Uneasiness swirled through her, but Kate quickly realized that despite his obvious state of intoxication, his touch was gentle, almost reverent, and she let him lean on her for a moment.

"Matrone, you are *so* going to regret this," she said beneath her breath.

"Already . . . do," he slurred.

She made eye contact with him. The power of his gaze riveted her in place, and for an instant, Kate couldn't look away, couldn't move. A slow thread of awareness rippled through her when his eyes moved slowly down her body. Then his gaze fastened to hers. And within the depths of his eyes, she caught a glimpse of the man inside, and it stunned her.

His eyes reflected a disturbing mix of raw emotions that scraped at her heart like a rasp. She saw grief in its most fundamental form. The kind of sorrow that could shatter a heart. A soul that had been scarred to its core. And all she could do was stand there and wonder what terrible things had happened to him to make him hurt so profoundly.

Shaking off thoughts she didn't want to have, Kate slid his hands from her shoulders. "Let's get you to bed so you can sleep this off, then I'm going to leave."

"Gittel . . ."

The next thing she knew his fingers were wrapped around her upper arms, and he was pushing her backward. Kate yelped when her spine made contact with the wall. "Matrone, you are about to make a very big mistake."

"No . . . m'stake," he slurred and raised his hand to cup her face.

"Cut it out," she snapped and tried to duck to the right.

He prevented her escape by locking her in with his arms. "Don't leave me."

Kate knew what would happen next. It was like watching a tornado barrel toward an unsuspecting town, knowing the result would be disastrous, helpless to prevent it. Anger kicked through her when he leaned close and made an awkward attempt to kiss her. A clever turn of the head and his lips grazed her cheek. Pulling away, he looked at her as if to ask, *How did that happen?*

"Don't try that again," she said and gave him a hard shove.

Without warning his legs buckled. He reached out to break his fall, but didn't succeed and his knees hit the floor with a hollow *thunk!*

She hadn't intended to push him down, just get him away from her. "Frank . . . damn it."

"S'ry . . ."

She was standing with her back against the wall. He was on his knees in front of her. She felt herself go rigid when he leaned forward and put his arms around her hips.

"Gittel," he whispered and laid his head against her.

Kate didn't like any of what was happening. But looking down at this strong, shuttered man, she suddenly knew he wasn't a threat. And in some small corner of her mind, she knew his need to touch her had more to do with grief than lust.

For several uncomfortable seconds, she stood there, not sure what to do. Then, exasperated as much with herself as she was with him, she pried his arms from around her and wriggled away.

"Yo, Matrone! Whassup, man?"

Kate looked toward the door to see a Hispanic man standing just inside the front door, staring at them as if he wasn't sure if he'd walked in on something he shouldn't have or something that needed to be stopped.

"Who are you?" Kate asked.

"I live next door." The man's eyes flicked to Frank. "Everything okay here?"

"Fine," she said. "I just—"

Frank chose that moment to reach for the buttons on her jacket. Grasping his wrists, Kate shoved his hands away and stepped back. "Do you think you could help me get him into the bedroom?"

The man's eyebrows went up. "Whatever you say."

Realizing he'd misinterpreted her words, she sighed. "Before he passes out."

"Gotcha." He crossed to them.

The man was short, but substantial in build. He was wearing a pair of blue jeans with a white muscle shirt. Intricate tattoos decorated his biceps. A gold chain hung from his neck, the attached religious medallion gleaming on his chest.

Kate watched him move in behind Frank. "Up and at 'em, Romeo." Grasping Frank beneath his arms, he proceeded to drag him toward the bedroom.

"Does he always drink like this?" Kate followed him into the bedroom. It was dark, but the light from the hall gave her the impression of a large room, heavy furniture. A king-sized bed, unmade. A dumbbell set in the corner. Some type of wispy palm near the window. She'd never imagined Frank with a green thumb.

"He don't drink." The man grunted as he hefted Frank onto the bed.

Kate turned on the light, then gave him a look that hopefully relayed she hadn't been born yesterday. In the back of her mind she wondered if the two men were drinking buddies. Fellow enablers deep into denial. "He's definitely under the influence."

"Painkillers." The man motioned toward two prescription bottles on the night table.

She picked up one of the bottles and read the label. Oxy-Contin, a powerful narcotic painkiller. The other was a muscle relaxant. "Why does he take these drugs?"

"He got hurt overseas."

"Pain pills shouldn't do *that* to him."

"He hurt too much." The man touched his chest. "Inside, you know? He take too many."

"You've seen him like this before?" Kate asked.

"Sometimes. You know. When it's bad. He don't sleep. Waits too long to take the pills." He mimicked drinking. "Drink with them, too."

Pills and alcohol. Kate almost couldn't believe it. Almost. But prescription drug abuse would explain his erratic attendance. Disappointment was surprisingly strong. All she could do was shake her head.

As if realizing he'd said too much, the man took one last look at Frank and started toward the door. "He have some problems, you know?"

Kate took one more look at Frank. He was lying on his back with one arm thrown over his forehead, the other hung over the side of the bed. His eyes were closed.

Realizing she was staring, that she didn't want to be alone with him in his bedroom, she turned and walked into the living room. The man was standing at the door with his hands on his hips.

"Alcohol and drugs are a dangerous combination," she said.

"Look, lady, Frank's a good man. Smart, too. He know what he's doing."

"It looks like it," she said dryly.

"So, are you two . . ." He did the Groucho Marx thing with his eyebrows.

"Of course not," Kate said quickly. Then, remembering what the scene must have looked like when the other man walked in, added, "He thought I was someone else."

"The woman who die."

Kate looked at him in shock. "What?"

"In Jerusalem. He was there, you know. Had him a woman, too. But she was killed."

Kate stared at him in shock. Remembering the way Frank had looked at her, Kate felt a quiver of compassion. "I didn't know."

"He don't talk about it. Like things private, you know?"

For the first time, Frank's excursion into drugs and alcohol made some sort of sense.

The man stuck out his finger and twirled it next to his head, the sign for crazy. "Made him a little nuts, you know?"

It was then that Kate realized she was in a position she did not want to be in. "Look, he's been drinking. He's probably been taking pills. He shouldn't be left alone."

"He don't need no baby-sitter."

Some friend you are, she thought. "What if he gets into trouble during the night? What if he overdoses?"

"Lady, I got three kids next door." He started toward the door.

"You can't just leave him like this."

The man didn't stop. Didn't even look over his shoulder.

Panic sent her after him. "Does he have a family member I can call to stay with him?"

The man stopped at the door and turned to her. "I think he have a sister in Amarillo."

"Like that's going to help." Kate looked at her watch. Almost seven o'clock. "I have work to do."

"He'll be fine," the man said.

But while Kate did not want to spend the rest of the evening playing nursemaid to an intoxicated Frank Matrone, her conscience would not let her walk away. If he got into trouble during the night, if something happened to him, and she'd been in a position to help and hadn't, she'd never be able to live with herself.

"I'll let him know you were concerned," she said.

"I appreciate that." The man opened the door.

"What's your name?" Kate called out.

"Jesus." He backed through the door and disappeared into the night.

ELEVEN

Frank was no stranger to the unpleasant aftereffects of overindulgence. But the son of a bitch inside his head hammering his brain with the baseball bat was taking things a little too far this morning.

Rolling onto his side, he opened one eye and stared at the alarm clock a full minute before his brain was able to translate the numbers into something meaningful. For an instant he considered going back to sleep and blowing off whatever he'd had planned for the day—not that he remembered what day it was. But he'd already lost at least one day this week. He didn't think his surly boss would tolerate another.

A moan ground in his throat when he sat upright. Dizziness swirled when he swung his feet over the side of the bed and set them on the floor. Nausea churned in his gut, but it wasn't bad enough to send him stumbling to the toilet. That was probably a good thing since he wasn't sure he could make it anyway.

The good news was his leg wasn't hurting. At some point during the night, the mangled nerves that ran from ankle to hip had calmed. The cramps had left his muscles sore, but the pain was gone. Definitely something to be thankful for.

The thought of coffee got him through the door. In the hall he staggered, hit his hip on the jamb, and walked unsteadily into the kitchen. He hit the lights, winced at the sudden brightness, and flicked them quickly off. At the counter he began the ritual of making coffee. Water in the reservoir. Grounds in the filter. Once the coffee was brewing, he went to the bathroom to brush his teeth and splash water on his face.

So far, so good. Frank Matrone had survived the night. Five minutes and he was still standing. No pain. No pills. The day was definitely looking up.

Back in the kitchen, he ran the tap and downed a full glass of water. He was in the process of taking his City of Dallas PD cup from the shelf when the sight of the briefcase and laptop on the dining room table stopped him cold.

What the hell?

Frank stared, baffled. The first thought that registered was that it wasn't his. The second thought that struck him was that he had absolutely no idea how it had gotten there, or who the owner was. He had a sinking feeling he wasn't going to like what he discovered.

Coffee forgotten, he left the kitchen and limped to the dining room table. The laptop was a sleek, top-of-the-line model. A brown expanding legal fold jammed full of paper and manila folders sat on the chair. Briefs and legal documents, if he wasn't mistaken. The slim, black leather briefcase looked vaguely familiar. . . .

He entered the living room. The blinds were closed, casting the room in shadows. He checked the front door, found it locked. He turned to inspect the rest of the house—and got the surprise of his life.

Kate Megason lay curled on the sofa, fast asleep. Frank stared, aware that his heart had begun to pound. All the while his mind scrolled through the black abyss of his memory bank, searching desperately for anything that might explain her presence. Had she come by to see him the night before? Had he let her in? Had they talked? Had she seen him snot-slinging, knuckle-dragging wasted? Why the hell couldn't he remember?

But Frank knew damn good and well why he couldn't remember. He couldn't remember because he'd stepped onto a rocket and taken a trip to the moon courtesy of an array of prescription painkillers and half a bottle of vodka. The official term for it was blackout. In the last year he'd spent more time in that soundless, colorless void than he cared to admit. It was his deep, dark secret. A secret he wasn't proud of. Something he definitely didn't want to share with his boss.

For the first time in a long time, he was embarrassed. Worse, he was ashamed. Ashamed of what he had let himself become. His mind scrambled for an explanation he could offer her, but there was no way she was going to buy some lame justification. Kate Megason might be uptight, but she wasn't stupid.

She looked soft and feminine and somehow vulnerable lying on his sofa with her hand tucked beneath her cheek. Her skin was as flawless and pale as a baby's. Her lashes and brows were black as velvet against her creamy complexion. She was lying on her side with one leg drawn up slightly. At some point, she'd removed her shoes and placed them neatly beside the sofa. They were black leather with high heels and a single thin strap. Frank had never been unduly interested in women's feet, but Kate Megason's were sexy as hell. Through her nylons he could see that her toenails were glossy and red.

She'd removed her suit jacket and draped it over the sofa arm. He'd never seen her without it. That was a shame because she had some very intriguing curves. She was wearing a white silk blouse. Even though only one button had been left open, the collar gaped slightly and he could see the curve of her breast, the white lace of her bra.

Her skirt had ridden up slightly, revealing a slender thigh, and for the span of several heartbeats he couldn't take his eyes off that dangerous stretch of flesh. She was long and slender with just enough flesh to make a man want to put his hands on her. Her legs were long and shapely, and he wondered what it would be like to have them wrapped around his hips. If she would whisper his name as he pumped in and out of her. He wondered if Kate Megason ever lost control. . . .

He scrubbed a hand over his face, aware that his beard was heavy. That his cock was hard as a rock, despite the fact that he had a hangover and was pretty sure the woman he was fantasizing about was going to fire him the instant she woke up.

Frank couldn't blame her. His work ethic hadn't exactly been stellar as of late. Hell, if he were in her shoes, he'd do the same thing. There was no place for a junkie in the DA's office.

Disgusted with himself, he turned and started toward the bedroom.

"Matrone."

Kate's voice stopped him mid-stride. For several long, uncomfortable seconds he stood with his back to her. He didn't want to face her. Not only was he hung over and in no mood for a lecture—or the inevitable end of his short-lived career with the DA's office—but his erection was still at half-staff. Like a lot of other things, he didn't think he could explain it away and still save face.

Knowing he didn't have a choice, he slowly turned to face her. She'd already risen and had bent lightly to tug at her skirt. Her hair was mussed. Her mouth was pale and full. She looked flustered and annoyed and very, very sexy.

"What are you doing here?" he asked, the words coming more harshly than he'd intended.

"In case you don't remember, you didn't show up for work yesterday. I came over last night to find out why."

"Did you find out why?"

"I have a pretty good idea." Her gaze searched his, as if she were seeking some elusive answer in the depths of his eyes.

But Frank knew she wouldn't find any answers by looking at him. He didn't have any answers. Not even for himself. "Look, Kate, I appreciate your concern, but I had some things come up yesterday."

"Had some things come up?" Her expression turned incredulous. "Frank, you were so wasted, you couldn't stand."

"I didn't know you were coming over. I'd had a rough day—"

"You of all people should know how dangerous it is to mix drugs and alcohol."

Surprise speared him that she knew about the pills. How the hell had she found out? "I don't know what you're talking about." Turning away, he started toward the kitchen. But if he thought pouring himself a cup of coffee would garner him a moment to gather his thoughts and come up with a reasonable excuse as to why she'd found him in the condition she had, he was wrong.

"You know exactly what I'm talking about."

In the kitchen he crossed to the coffeemaker and did his best to ignore her while he dumped coffee into a mug. The thought crossed his mind that he should offer her a cup, but the truth of the matter was he didn't want her there. He didn't want to talk about last night or the hundreds of other nights he'd spent in the throes of oblivion because he'd been hurting too badly to face life unanesthetized.

Turning abruptly, she left the kitchen. "Great," he muttered, anticipating the slam of the front door.

He was standing at the counter, gripping his cup of coffee, when she strode back into the room holding the brown prescription bottles like weapons. "Frank, my God. You were a cop. You've seen what this stuff can do to people."

All he could think was that he was living proof of what it could do to people. "They're legal."

"That doesn't matter."

"You don't know the whole story."

"I know what I saw."

"Look, Kate, I'm not some fucking junkie, so don't treat me like one. That prescription was given to me by my doctor."

"I don't think he told you to take them with a bottle of vodka."

Gritting his teeth, Frank took the only route he had left and lied. "I wasn't drinking last night."

"You're lying. Damn it, I smelled it on your breath. Your neighbor told me it's not the first time."

"I guess my secret is out," he said.

Kate just stared at him, shaking her head.

Frank crossed to her, took the prescription from her, and set it on the counter. "Not that it's any of your goddamn business, but I was injured when I was in the military. I suffer from chronic pain. Yesterday was a bad fucking day. I had a couple of drinks, got the dose mixed up. You show up and start jumping to conclusions."

"You want to know what I think?"

"Not particularly." He sipped coffee, trying not to react when he burned his lip.

"I think you're telling the truth about the chronic pain. But I think there are some other things going on that you either don't want to face or don't want me to know."

Frank said nothing. He didn't want to hear what he knew she was going to say next.

"I think this prescription has turned into a problem for you. I think that's why you can't get to work on time. And I think it's why you didn't show up yesterday." She looked at his trembling hands and shook her head. "I think that's why you can barely hold that cup this morning."

"That's bullshit."

"Frank, you're smart enough to know when you're in trouble. If you need help—"

The surge of anger struck him like a tidal wave. He stared at her, aware that his heart was pounding. That she was beautiful and perfect and standing there judging him when she had absolutely no idea what he had been through. He thought she probably couldn't imagine half of what had happened to him in the last year. And it made him furious.

Cursing, he hurled the mug into the sink. Glass shattered. Coffee spewed. Kate gasped and took a quick step back, her eyes wide and shocked.

For several uncomfortable seconds, they stared at each other, both of them too stunned to speak.

Frank couldn't believe he'd done that. That he'd lost his temper when she was only trying to help. He should be thankful someone in this world cared enough to say the things she had said. But there was a small part of him that was furious. A small part of him that was terrified he'd fallen too far to ever claw his way out of the deep, dark hole he was in.

"If you're going to fire me, now is probably a prime opportunity," he said after a moment.

"I'm not going to fire you."

Frank lowered his head and pinched the bridge of his nose. "I'm sorry I lost my temper. You caught me at a bad time."

"If you don't get some help, you're going to be having a lot of bad times." Turning away from him abruptly, she strode briskly into the dining room.

He watched her slide the laptop into its case, and wondered if he would still have a job by the end of the day. The investigator position was the only opportunity he'd had since coming back from the Middle East. He hadn't been very excited by the idea of working with a bunch of lawyers, but he knew there wasn't a whole lot more he could do. There wasn't a real high demand for an ex-cop with a bum leg, a boatload of personal demons, and a drug habit.

"Kate," he began.

She cut him off neatly by snapping her briefcase closed. "I'm leaving," she said crisply. "I suggest you clean up your act."

Frank stood in the doorway and watched her cross to the front door and let herself out.

TWELVE

The woman in the red power suit and Via Spiga pumps didn't bother knocking before entering his office. "Megason is still digging."

The man looked up from his laptop and frowned. "How do you know?"

"I just received a call from Quorum. She's called twice. Asking questions, wanting names."

The man tried to look unaffected by the news, but he didn't like the idea of someone like Kate Megason asking questions. "That's probably routine."

"I still don't like it." Shaking her head, she dropped into the visitor's chair. "If she digs too deep, she's going to find something." The woman's eyes were troubled. "We've got to protect our interests."

He considered her, wondering if she really had the stomach for what he was thinking. "Let me make some calls, and see if I can come up with a fix."

"What kind of fix do you have in mind?"

"The problem will fix itself once we get Megason under control."

"From what I hear, I don't think she's the kind of person who can be controlled."

"Everyone can be controlled with the right tools." He smiled. "Or in this case, information."

"You have something on her?"

"I have something on everyone." He smiled. "Including you."

She laughed, but he didn't miss the flicker of unease in her eyes. Good, he thought. She was wary of him. He would make it a point to keep it that way.

He reached into his briefcase, withdrew a file and passed it to her across the desk. "I've found a big chink in Kate Megason's armor."

The woman looked down at the dossier someone had painstakingly compiled. Her mouth quivered with a smile as she began to read. "My God, are you sure about this? Where did you get this information?"

"Information is my specialty," he said vaguely. "In the right hands information can be more effective than any weapon. In this case I'd say this qualifies as a nuclear blast, don't you think?"

"Why didn't you tell me about this?"

"I didn't think it was necessary." He paused. "Until now, anyway."

"How can we use this?" she asked, shaking the document.

"Leave that to me." Lacing his hands behind his head, he leaned back in his chair and wondered if she had any idea the lengths he would go to in order to protect himself. If she realized those lengths included sacrificing her.

"If she's as tough as everyone says, she's not going to back off," she said.

He considered that for a moment, vaguely impressed by her ability to anticipate problems. And he remembered that was why he had taken her on as his partner. He only hoped her spine proved to be as worthy as her mind. "She'll back off."

"And if she doesn't?"

"Let's suffice it to say I'll do whatever necessary to make sure she does." He smiled at the possibilities.

TUESDAY, JANUARY 31, 9:04 A.M.

For the second time in a week Kate was sitting in Mike Shelley's office wondering why she was wasting time on an unnecessary meeting when her time would be used more effectively if she were working.

After the fiasco at Frank's house on Saturday, she'd called Mike first thing Monday morning and told him everything. When she'd walked out of Mike's office an hour later, she'd felt confident he would remove Frank from the case, urge him to take a leave of absence, and, perhaps, enlist in some type of rehab program.

She should have known politics would get in the way.

The tension in the room was palpable. Mike Shelley sat behind his desk, looking like a disappointed parent as his eyes drifted from Kate to Frank and back to Kate. Matrone sat in the second visitor chair with his ankle crossed over his knee, looking like he'd rather be getting a root canal.

"I'm assuming both of you know why you're here," Mike said.

"I'm getting a pretty good picture," Frank muttered.

"All I want is what's best for the case, Mike. You know that." But judging from the DA's expression, she had the sinking feeling the meeting wasn't going to turn out the way she wanted it to.

Sighing, Mike looked at Kate. "I understand your concerns and I share them."

"Do you?" she asked tightly.

His gaze flicked to Frank. "Frank and I met yesterday afternoon and have discussed the issue at length."

"I wasn't aware that he'd shown up for work yesterday," she said dryly.

"I was working off premises," Frank cut in.

"Children." Mike raised his hands. "Look, we're all professionals here."

"One of us is," Kate muttered.

"Kate—"

"Mike, with all due respect, I have a case to prosecute. I need someone I can count—"

"I have an office to run," Mike cut in. "I suggest you two work it out. I do not want to have this meeting again."

She couldn't believe her request had been dismissed so easily. All she could think was that someone very high on the food chain had saved Frank Matrone's ass and now she was going to pay the price.

Her glare swept from Mike to Frank. "At the very least I need him to show up at the office."

"Mr. Matrone has assured me he will be here."

"Mike—"

"Kate, this meeting is over. I know where you stand. I know where Frank stands. And I've made my decision."

It was difficult, but Kate held her silence. She'd worked with Mike Shelley long enough to know that once he dug in his heels, that was the end of it. Whether she liked it or not, she was going to have to make do with Frank.

As a general rule, Kate made a conscious effort not to waste too much energy on useless emotions. But she was angry when she strode into her office and slid behind her desk. She'd barely sat down when Frank appeared at her door.

"I figured we ought to go ahead and get this over with." He was wearing black trousers with a gunmetal shirt and burgundy tie. The clothes fit well, and Kate couldn't help but notice that while he may have recently lost weight, he was still solidly built with well-defined musculature.

"Come in." Her voice was crisp and calm, belying the fact that her temper was lit.

He entered her office. Tension rose inside her when he closed the door behind him, and she wondered if he was planning on raising his voice. But his expression was inscrutable when he limped to the visitor chair opposite her desk and sat. She thought about the injuries he'd suffered overseas, and she tried hard not to feel guilty for having tried to get him removed from the case.

"This was not personal," she began.

"You told my boss I'm a goddamn drug addict," he said tightly. "That's as personal as it gets."

"I walked into your house Saturday night to find you totally incoherent. You didn't even know who I was." She hadn't told Mike that Frank had made a halfhearted pass at her, but feeling she needed to explain her actions, she laid it out for Frank now. "For God's sake, you thought I was someone else. You made a pass at me."

His jaw flexed and he looked away, and for the first time she saw that he was embarrassed. "It's not like I was expecting you."

"You're on call twenty-four/seven when you work for the DA's office. You know that."

"I have an old injury," he ground out. "It gives me problems sometimes."

"Problems so bad you have to render yourself unconscious?"

He said nothing, but she could tell by the look in his eyes that he wasn't happy with himself. "Frank, this isn't about you. Yes, you need to address your problem. But the reason I went to Mike is because I need to win this case."

"You crossed a line, Kate. You stabbed me in the back without knowing the whole story."

"Maybe you should enlighten me to the story." The moment the question was out, Kate regretted having asked. The truth of the matter was she didn't want to know this man's demons. She didn't want this to turn personal. She didn't want to feel his pain or care too much. She knew that to some people that would make her a coldhearted bitch. But Kate didn't care. The case always came first.

"It doesn't matter." Frank rose unexpectedly, and Kate got the impression that she'd touched on a wound he didn't want prodded. And it was suddenly clear to her that he hadn't yet dealt with whatever had happened to him overseas.

Had him a woman, but she was killed.

Jesus's words came to her unbidden, and an unexpected quiver of sympathy ran through her. Uncomfortable with the intensity of his stare, she looked away. "As an officer of the court, I had to report what I saw."

"You don't know what you saw. You made an incorrect assumption and jumped to conclusions."

Denial, she thought and didn't respond.

A taut silence ensued. Frank stared out the window, his expression annoyed and decidedly unhappy. Kate divided her attention between him and her computer screen.

"It wasn't my intent to hurt you or your career," she said after a moment. "I wouldn't do that."

"*Career* is a pretty generous word at this point, but I sure as hell don't need you telling my boss I'm popping pills."

"Mike Shelley is a fair man."

"Especially when someone above him is looking out for me."

She sighed. "Look, I've got an appointment with Evangeline Worth's mother in half an hour."

His gaze met hers. "What about?"

"Routine. I always make it a point to interview the victim's family." Realizing they'd landed upon common ground that might act as a buffer and get them—and the case—back on track, she sighed. "Do you want to ride along?"

TUESDAY, JANUARY 31, 10:49 A.M.

Evangeline Worth had lived with her mother and four children in a rundown neighborhood in South Dallas. The streets were narrow and riddled with potholes. Most of the small clapboard houses sported sagging porches, peeling paint, and curled roofing shingles. A few of the homeowners had added chain-link fences and steel bars to the windows, giving the neighborhood the feel of a prison yard.

The Worth household was the gem of the block. Neat flowerbeds with red brick edging lined the sidewalk. The house sported a fresh coat of pale yellow paint, and hunter green shutters. Even though the grass was brown, it had been manicured before the first frost hit. A well-cared-for Ford Escort sat in the driveway, the paint as shiny as the day it had been driven off the showroom floor.

Kate took it all in and tried not to let it bother her that Evangeline Worth was no longer around to take pride in the place she had worked so hard to make a home.

"Nice place," Frank said, parking his truck on the street.

"If you don't mind the occasional drive-by shooting." Kate

motioned toward a Cadillac across the street that had been jacked up and set on concrete blocks. A bullet hole the size of her thumb marred the glossy paint of the driver's-side door.

Kate wasn't looking forward to this interview. Talking to the families of murder victims invariably took something out of her. People needed someone to blame when a loved one died, some bad guy to lash out at. On more than one occasion, Kate had found herself the object of a bereaved family member's grief and rage. But no matter how painful, she always showed up. And she always assured them she would do her utmost to see that justice was served.

She and Frank walked together up the crumbling sidewalk to the front porch. The morning was mild for January, with the temperature hovering around sixty degrees. But there were dark clouds piling up on the northern horizon, and Kate thought she'd heard on the news there was a cold front on the way.

Frank knocked. A moment later the door squeaked open and an elderly African American woman peered at them from behind thick wire-rimmed glasses. "Can I help you?"

Kate flashed her identification. "Mrs. Jackson? I'm Kate Megason with the district attorney's office."

"I already told the police everything I know."

"I realize this is a difficult time for you and your family," Kate said. "We just want to talk to you for a few minutes."

"'Bout Evangeline?"

"Yes, ma'am," Frank said.

The frail woman considered him for a moment. Her skin was the color of dark chocolate and lay like fine leather over a face that had once been lovely. Her eyes were an unusual shade of blue. Her hair was white and had been pulled into a neat bun at her nape.

"Come on in," she said and tugged open the door.

The first thing Kate noticed was the enticing aroma of something meaty and delicious. Through the hall she could see into the kitchen and got a glimpse of antiquated appliances and a yellow Formica countertop. The living room was furnished with an overstuffed sofa and two mismatched chairs, one of which had been meticulously patched. On the small television set up on a TV tray, Bob Barker asked a heavyset woman to bid on a car.

"This is a nice place you have here," Frank said.

The old woman gave Kate a look as if to ask, "Where did you find him?" and motioned toward the sofa. "You may as well sit down."

"Thank you." Kate started toward the sofa.

The old woman hobbled to the patched chair, braced herself on the arms, and fell into it. "What's this all about? Haven't you people asked enough questions?"

"I'm going to be prosecuting your daughter's murder, Ms. Worth. I want to ask you some routine questions that might help me build a case."

"Ain't none of this routine for me."

Kate felt Frank's eyes on her, but she didn't look at him. By unspoken mutual agreement, she knew he was going to sit this one out. "I understand."

"Ain't nothing been the same round here since she been gone. Evangeline was always such a good girl. Hardworking. If it wasn't for her we never woulda made it out of the projects, but here I am. Own my own home." The old woman shook her head. "She should be here, not me."

Before even realizing she was going to move, Kate leaned forward and set her hand over the woman's. The older woman looked at her with a measure of surprise in her eyes. Kate didn't look away and hoped her expression relayed that her action was an honest one.

"Have you ever heard the name Bruton Ellis?" Kate asked.

Worth pulled a well-used tissue from her housedress and blotted her eyes. "Not till I heard it on the news that he'd been arrested for killing my baby."

"Evangeline never mentioned him?"

"Lord Almighty no. She don't hang out with no white trash like that."

"Did you ever see a blue truck in the neighborhood? Maybe parked on the street or driving by slowly?" Pulling a police photo of Ellis's truck from her bag, Kate held it out for her to see.

"Never see it before," she said.

"Did Evangeline have a boyfriend?"

The old woman shook her head. "That girl was too good for the men who courted her. Damn crack dealers and gangsters all of them."

Kate tucked the photo back into her bag. She knew the police had already asked all of these same questions and that they were tedious for the elderly woman. Still, Kate always made this visit. And she always asked the questions that needed to be asked. "Evangeline had four children?"

The woman nodded. "God, those babies miss their mama somethin' awful."

"Has their father been notified?"

"We ain't heard from either man in too many years to say."

"Are you their legal guardian?"

"Evangeline wouldn't have had it any other way. Oh, sweet Jesus, she lived for those kids. That was why she was working the way she was. The Lord do work in mysterious ways, but I don't think I'll understand this one till I'm up in heaven myself and ask Him face-to-face. Leaving those poor babies without a mama like that."

Kate heard grief in her voice. She saw it etched into the creases of the woman's face. She felt a shadow of that same grief ebbing and flowing in her own heart. And for an instant it was as if she were looking into a mirror and seeing herself, broken and grief-stricken and left without hope.

Realizing the silence had gone on too long, Kate offered her hand to the woman. "I'm very sorry for your loss, Ms. Worth. Thank you for your time."

"I just hope you lock him up and throw away the key."

Digging into her bag, Kate pulled out one of her cards. "If you think of anything else that might be important, please call me. You can reach me after hours on my cell phone number, which is written on the back."

The old woman took the card and slid it into her apron pocket without looking at it. "Don't know what else I could say that you ain't already heard."

Kate rose without commenting. She was aware of the woman struggling to her feet. Of Frank moving toward the door. Movement in her peripheral vision caught her attention, and she turned to see four children crouched on the stairs, watching her through the rail. They'd been listening, she realized, and at least one of the little brown faces was tear streaked.

"They ain't been back to school since their mama died," Ms. Worth said.

Kate didn't know what to say. Four children left motherless. A frail old woman left to care for them. Nothing she could say seemed fitting.

She started for the door, but the sound of light footsteps turned her around. A little girl no older than four clung to her grandmother's hip, her eyes watchful and cautious.

"Is the white lady going to bring mama back, Grandmimi?" the little girl asked.

The old woman pulled the girl to her, and held her close, her ancient eyes meeting Kate's. "There ain't no one can bring your mama back, baby."

Kate knew it was cowardly, but she turned away and started for the door. She knew facing that child was the one thing that would make the case personal. Better to keep her emotions locked down tight. Her motivations buried in the recesses of her own memory.

Neither she nor Frank spoke as they walked to his truck. Once inside, he buckled his seat belt and pulled onto the street. "Tough scene."

"It's always difficult talking to the family. Especially when there are kids involved."

"Why do you do it?" He glanced away from his driving to meet her gaze. "You could have sent me or David or simply looked at the police reports."

"I prefer a personal visit. Mostly just to make sure there's no relationship between the vic and the susp—"

"Bullshit." He hit her with a hard look. "Why the hell do you put yourself through that?"

"Because it makes me a better prosecutor," she said honestly. "It makes me want to win. It reminds me why I do what I do."

For a moment, he didn't say anything, then he looked at her and nodded. "Damn good answer."

THIRTEEN

Kate spent the rest of the day reading—police reports, the coroner's report, witness statements—and outlining her strategy on the Bruton Ellis case. It wasn't until the office had gone quiet that she realized she hadn't eaten. Hungry and exhausted, she wanted nothing more than to pack her laptop and briefcase and head for home.

But there was one more stop she needed to make. A stop Kate had been dreading all day.

Today was Kirsten's twenty-ninth birthday. She was six minutes older than Kate. But while Kate never missed her sister's birthday, she never celebrated her own. Liz had once brought in a birthday cake, but afterward Kate had asked her not to do it again. Other than the anniversary of that terrible July night eleven years ago, Kirsten's birthday was the most difficult day of the year. It was a day that stood in testimony to what had happened. A stark reminder of what had been lost.

It was dark when Kate left the Frank Crowley Courts Building. She stopped at an upscale pastry shop on McKinney

Avenue and picked up the frivolous cake she'd ordered earlier in the day. German chocolate with fudge lettering that said: *We love you, Kirsten. Happy birthday.*

Ten minutes later she pulled into the parking lot of the Turtle Creek Convalescent Home. A quiver of dread moved through her when she spotted her parents' Lincoln. She knew they visited Kirsten every day; she'd known they would visit today. But there was a small, cowardly part of Kate that had been hoping they'd already come and gone.

The halls were dimly lit when she entered the building, cake in hand. Nancy Martin smiled and waved from the nurse's station as Kate passed.

"I'll only be a few minutes," Kate said.

"Nobody follows the rules around here anyway," the other woman replied, referring to the fact that it was well after visiting hours.

"I'll save some cake for you and the rest of the night shift."

Nancy patted her substantial hip. "Like we need all that sugar."

Outside her sister's room, Kate took a fortifying breath and pushed open the door. Isobel Megason was standing at the window with her back to the room. She turned upon hearing Kate enter. She looked elegant and trim in an understated Nipon pantsuit that was the same cool blue as her eyes.

"Sorry I'm late."

"Katherine." Isobel crossed to her youngest daughter, her suede pumps muted on the tile floor. Chanel whispered around her when she leaned close, set her cheek against Kate's, and kissed air. "We're so glad you finally made it."

Kate looked at her father. "Hi, Dad."

Peter Megason was lounging in the recliner, a hardback book open on his lap, looking at her over the top of the bifocals perched on his nose. He wore a pale yellow cashmere sweater over dark trousers. "I was hoping you'd make it before they kick us out."

Kate smiled at him, felt the tension twisting her neck muscles into knots. "Wouldn't miss it for the world." She looked at Kirsten. "How is she today?"

"Same as she was last year at this time," Isobel said.

Kate crossed to the small table near the window and set down the cake.

"What kind of cake did you bring?" her father asked.

"German chocolate."

"I might just have a piece of that myself." He started to rise.

"Let me get it for you," Kate said quickly, wanting something to do besides sit in this tiny room with her sister and two people who blamed her for her condition.

"I tried to call you today," Isobel said. "You didn't return my call."

"I was busy, Mom." Kate lifted the cake from the box and picked up the plastic knife the pastry chef had left inside.

"I saw on the news that you're going to be prosecuting the Bruton Ellis case," Peter said.

Kate nodded and she began cutting the cake. "I need to talk to you about that."

"You're not going to cancel the cruise, are you?" he asked.

Kate slid the piece of cake onto a paper plate and took it to her father. "I'm sorry, but I'm swamped."

"We've had this planned for months," Isobel said.

"Can't be helped."

"Well, I'm sure you'll do a good job, honey." Her father accepted the piece of cake. "Terrible crime. Makes you wonder about people."

"Not all people," Isobel put in. "Just a select few with evil minds and black hearts." She shot Kate a pointed look. "I don't know how you can stand dealing with those kinds of crimes day in and day out."

"It's my job."

"You could have become an investment banker like your father. Or maybe a broker." She looked at her husband. "She would have made a terrific broker, Peter, don't you think?"

"I think Katie can do anything she sets her mind to," he said diplomatically.

"Katherine, you could be making twice what you're making now and working half as many hours. We'd probably even get to see you more often. Peter was just telling me that if you were to get your license, the firm would make a place for you right away."

"A vice president position," her father added.

"I love my job," Kate said simply.

Isobel snorted haughtily. "How can you love dealing with murderers and rapists and God only knows what else?"

To the outsider looking in, the words wouldn't appear harsh, but Kate felt them like a slap. "I like putting criminals behind bars and getting justice for the victims."

"What about when justice isn't done?" Isobel said.

"Isobel," Peter warned, "leave her be."

Kate looked at her mother. She could tell by the light in the other woman's eyes that she was just getting warmed up. That this wasn't going to be pleasant. And she knew that coming here tonight had been a mistake.

"You're right, Mother. The system isn't perfect and, unfortunately, not every case turns out well." Kate concentrated on putting the cake back into the box and closing the lid. "All I can do is my best."

"And when your best isn't good enough?"

"Isobel, please," Peter said.

"Most of the time my best is enough," Kate said.

Isobel looked at her for a long time before asking, "Why do you do it, Katherine?"

"Because I can make a difference. Because I'm good at what I do."

An unpleasant smile twisted her mother's mouth. "Is that all?"

The old pain twisted inside her. "If you have something to say, Mother, maybe you ought to just say it."

Isobel's eyes went cold. "Maybe you think you have something to atone for."

"Issy, that's enough," Peter said sharply.

Kate's mother ignored the warning and came around the bed to face her daughter. "The head nurse told me you come here almost every day."

"She's my sister," Kate snapped. "Why wouldn't I?"

"You're too busy to visit us, but you're never too busy to stop in and see your sister."

"Kirsten takes a hell of a lot less energy," Kate said levelly.

Isobel's eyes blazed. "Or maybe it's guilt that's driving

you, Kate. Maybe you feel you have an obligation to Kirsten. Did you ever stop to think about that?"

"Isobel!" Closing the book he'd been pretending to read, Peter sprang out of the recliner and glared at his wife. "She has nothing to feel guilty about." He looked at Kate, his expression apologetic. "She had a few drinks before we left the house."

Isobel's laugh was bitter. "Oh, you think you know your daughter so well."

"Of course I do."

Isobel turned cool blue eyes on her daughter. "Why is it that the innocent ones are always the ones to pay for the things we sinners do?"

Kate stared at her mother, her heart pounding, the anger and hurt twisting inside her like a knife. "I'm not going to have this conversation with you."

"That's it, Katherine. Go ahead and walk away. Go put some slimy son of a bitch in jail if that's what it takes for you to live with yourself."

"Isobel, my God!" Peter shouted.

Kate's legs were shaking when she crossed to Kirsten and kissed her forehead. "Good night, kiddo," she whispered.

"It should be you lying in that bed instead of Kirsten," Isobel said.

"That's enough!" Peter strode to his wife and took her arm. "Get a hold of yourself."

But Isobel shook him off, her eyes never leaving Kate. "If you hadn't lured her from the house that night, none of this would have happened and I'd have both of my daughters instead of just one."

At the door Kate turned and met her mother's gaze. "You'd still just have one."

Peter started toward her, but Kate raised her hand to stop him. "I'm fine," she said and fled.

TUESDAY, JANUARY 31, 8:16 P.M.

He watched her from within the shadows of his Lexus.

She didn't even look up as she descended the steps of the convalescent home and started toward the parking lot. Stupid for someone so intimately acquainted with crime not to be more aware of her surroundings.

She'd probably acquired more than a few enemies in the years she'd been working in the district attorney's office. If something were to happen to her, her past cases would be the first place the police would look. The thought of just how many ways he could play the situation pleased him. Talk about red herrings.

He watched her, liking the way her long strides ate up the asphalt as she crossed to her BMW. The wind had picked up, and he could see her long coat flapping about her calves, and he found himself wondering what it would be like to run his hands over those calves. If they were as sleek and pretty as the rest of her . . .

Something hot and uncomfortable jittered low in his gut when he imagined her flesh slick with sweat. The reaction surprised him. It had been a long time since he'd enjoyed an assignment. He knew it was twisted, but the thought of fucking a woman he was probably going to end up killing excited him.

A smile touched his mouth as he watched her dig in her bag for her keys. Preoccupied after visiting her sister, no doubt. Tired after a long day. A crime waiting to happen.

He hit a button and the window slid down in time for him to hear her engine start. The headlights popped on, and an instant later she was pulling from the lot.

He waited a full thirty seconds before starting the Lexus. He was already familiar with her routine and knew she would drive straight home. She always went home after visiting her sister. She was never out past ten o'clock. Never went out on dates. Not a very exciting life for a twenty-eight-year-old looker. He'd had enough women in his life to know they had needs just like men. Even uppity bitches like Kate Megason.

Her car had already disappeared onto Mockingbird Lane by the time he pulled from the lot. She drove like a bat out of hell, but he knew where she was going. The fact that she was a creature of habit was going to make this job a breeze.

He pulled onto the street and followed.

His assignment was to intimidate. Frighten. Terrify. But the man had told him that may change. When and if the time came, he would make it look as if one of her past cases had come back to haunt her. A logical assumption that would take the heat off of him and the people who'd hired him. A single shot to the head, and it would be done.

If all went well, he would be sipping mojitos at some obscure little café in South Beach by the end of the week. Holding that thought, he hit the gas.

TUESDAY, JANUARY 31, 11:58 P.M.

Kate knew she was pushing herself too hard. Working too many hours. Getting up too early. Staying up too late. But pacing herself was the one aspect of her job she'd never quite gotten the hang of.

She'd been staring at her laptop screen for so long the words were starting to blur. Her eyes felt as if someone had tossed sand in them, and the tiny particles grated against her eyeballs every time she blinked. Her neck and back were beginning to ache.

Kate knew she should have indulged in a hot bath and called it a night upon arriving home from the convalescent home. But the scene between her and her mother kept replaying in her mind's eye.

Maybe you think you have something to atone for.

The words echoed uncomfortably inside her head. It was the first time Isobel Megason had spoken them aloud, and even though Kate had always suspected her mother blamed her, it still hurt.

The scene in Kirsten's room was one of many in the last eleven years. In the weeks following the incident, Kate had been too immersed in her own misery to notice the way her mother looked at her. But as the long road to healing began, seventeen-year-old Kate had begun to see things more clearly.

The realization that her mother blamed her for what happened had shattered what was left of Kate's heart. After all, it had been her idea to sneak out of the house that night. Her idea to buy the beer. She'd cajoled until Kirsten had agreed to accompany her. To this day there was still a part of Kate that blamed herself. . . .

"Enough." Pushing away from the desk, she rubbed her eyes. She could tell by the soreness that she'd strained them again. "So much for pacing," she muttered.

She was in the process of saving the file she'd been working on when the screen blinked and Kate found herself plunged into darkness.

Realizing the electricity had gone out, she let out a long sigh. "Crap."

More concerned with the possibility of data loss than the power outage, Kate rose and started for the kitchen. There, she snagged the flashlight from the top of the fridge, used the beam to locate a spare fuse in the drawer, and headed toward the garage. She was nearly to the hall when movement at the window above the sink sent a hot zing of adrenaline through her belly.

Heart pounding, she snapped off the flashlight. Never taking her eyes from the window, she pressed her back flat against the wall and ordered herself to stay calm.

For a full minute Kate stood there, shaking, her breaths coming shallow and fast. Around her the house was so quiet she could hear the wind whipping through the trees. Dead leaves skittering across the driveway. The ticking of the mantel clock in the study. The rhythmic drip of water in the sink a few feet away. Slowly her pulse began to slow. Had she seen someone outside the window? Or had she seen nothing more than the silhouette of the tree branches as they swayed in the wind?

Taking a final look at the window, she switched on the flashlight. "You're jumping at shadows, Megason," she whispered.

But she was thinking about the bandanna that had been left on her porch a few days earlier. Her senses were on high alert when she checked the bolt lock on the back door. Finding it secure, she proceeded through the utility room and into the two-car garage where the fuse box was located. Her stocking feet were silent against the concrete floor as she crossed to the fuse box.

The sight of the folded piece of paper tucked into the seam made her blood run cold. Her hand was shaking when she plucked it out and unfolded it.

I could have had you tonight the same way I had you eleven years ago. Are you still as sweet as you were when you were seventeen, Katie? Do you smell the same? Would you still cry out in pain? Or have you come to like it? I can't wait to find out . . .

Kate couldn't believe what she was reading. Nobody knew what had happened eleven years ago. How could someone have written this?

The realization that someone had been in the garage struck her brain like a bullet. Lowering the paper, she looked toward the pet door that led to the backyard. The family who'd lived in the house before her had had two Newfoundland retrievers. A giant breed that had required a large pet door. Kate had always planned on replacing it, but it was one of those household tasks she'd never gotten around to.

Raising the flashlight, she shone the beam on the pet door. The rubber weather flap swayed in the wind. The opening was large enough for a man to crawl through, which meant someone could have gained access to the garage and tampered with the fuse box. In fact, they could be hiding in the garage. . . .

A sound sent her heart slamming against her ribs. She jerked the light in the direction of the sound, but the car was in the way. And she knew that whomever had placed the note in the fuse box was still in the garage.

She backed toward the door. "The police are on the way," she called out. But her voice was breathless with fear.

Something clattered to the floor to her right. Gasping, she jerked the beam to the corner where a steel-shelving unit was stacked with gardening tools. A hand shovel lay on the concrete floor. She stared at the shovel, certain it hadn't been there that morning when she'd left for work.

Kate was not easily frightened. But standing in the cold silence of her garage with nothing more than a flashlight for protection, she was afraid.

Lunging back, she darted into the house. She slammed the door and threw the deadbolt. Spinning, she ran through the utility and into the kitchen. Her stocking feet were silent against the tile as she darted to the phone, snatched it up, and punched 911.

"I want to report a prowler," she blurted.

Another layer of fear settled over her when she realized the line was dead. "Hello?" She hit the plunger several times, but the line remained silent. *"Hello?"*

Kate couldn't believe this was happening. She could feel the fingers of panic digging into her, stealing her control. "Cell phone," she whispered, trying to remember where she'd left it.

I could have had you tonight the way I had you eleven years ago. . . .

A gasp escaped her when the kitchen doorknob rattled. She spun. A scream tore from her throat when she saw the silhouette of a man through the glass. She'd checked the lock; it was secure. But if he broke the glass he could be inside in a matter of seconds. . . .

Dropping the phone, Kate leapt into a sprint and raced through the living room. Breaths tore raggedly from her throat as she burst into her bedroom in search of her cell phone. "Oh, God. Oh, God. *Where is it?*"

Her heart pounded like thunder in her veins. She could feel the panic encroaching. The terror grabbing her and shaking her like a giant beast.

She spotted her purse on the night table. Dashing to it, she yanked out the phone and punched 911. The operator had barely answered when Kate shouted, "I want to report a prowler! He's trying to get into my house. 3553 Bluffview! *Hurry!*"

Taking the phone with her, she strode to the night table and removed the .22 mini-magnum revolver. Kate had taken the state-required test to qualify for her concealed weapon permit; she went to the range every couple of months. But the tiny revolver felt inadequate in her hands as she wrapped her fingers around the grip and pulled back the hammer with her thumb.

There was no lock on her bedroom door, so she didn't bother closing it. If someone was in the house, she wanted to see him coming. Kate had vowed a long time ago she would never let anyone hurt her again. She would kill to protect herself. Or she would die trying.

Leveling the gun on the doorway, she moved to a corner of the bedroom. She crouched, shaking, listening. But all she heard was the wind in the trees. The frantic beat of her heart. And the echoing whisper of winter-dead leaves.

FOURTEEN

"Congratulations." Mike Shelley handed Kate a copy of the *Dallas Morning News* across his desk. "You're famous."

"What is it?" Dread curdled in her gut as she took the newspaper from her boss.

"A potential problem," he said. "Have a seat."

A ripple of unease moved through her when she saw her name in prominent black and white on the front page of the Metro Section. "Must have been a slow night for news," she muttered, sinking into the chair.

Assistant DA Reports Prowler in North Dallas Home

Last night at just after midnight, police received a 911 call from the North Dallas home of Dallas County Assistant District Attorney Kate Megason. Upon arriving on the scene, police found an armed Megason, who has a legal concealed weapon license, but no sign of the purported prowler.

Megason, who has been with the district attorney's office for two years, has gained a fair amount of media attention because of her tough stance on crime. In a press conference on Wednesday, District Attorney Mike Shelley announced that Megason would be prosecuting Bruton Ellis, the man charged with gunning down two Dallas convenience store clerks. Megason will be seeking the death penalty.

Kate looked up from the newspaper and made eye contact with her boss. "I can't believe this garnered space in the metropolitan newspaper of a city the size of Dallas."

"Were you going to bother telling me about it?"

She took a moment to gather her thoughts, but her heart rate was up. She was perturbed by the story and uneasy because she could tell he was pissed. "This sounds a lot worse than it really was."

"You're about to prosecute a capital case. You reported a prowler last night. Did it cross your mind that those two things could be related?"

"Look," she said, trying to regain control of the conversation. "My electricity went out. I heard a noise in the garage. I got spooked, and I overreacted. There was no prowler."

"Kate, how long have we known each other?"

"Three years."

"Long enough for me to know you don't overreact."

"Mike . . ."

"Tell me what happened," he snapped. "And don't leave anything out."

Quickly Kate recapped the incident from the night before, beginning with her electricity blinking off and ending when the two police cruisers arrived on the scene. She played down how frightened she'd been. She didn't tell him about the note. In fact, she hadn't even told the *police* about the note. She knew omitting pertinent information wasn't a very smart thing to do. But Kate had a terrible feeling that what happened last night hadn't been some random prowler.

There *had* been someone in her garage. But she didn't think it was related to the Bruton Ellis case. Whoever had been in her garage was somehow connected to what happened eleven years ago. That was the one thing she did not want dredged up.

"I'm glad you're all right," Mike said when she finished.

"To be perfectly honest, I didn't think it was important enough to mention to you this morning."

"Or maybe you wanted to see if this would slide by unnoticed because you don't want anything getting in the way of your prosecuting the Bruton Ellis case."

"I thought no such thing because there is no connection between what happened last night and the case."

"You sure about that?"

Kate escaped having to answer when someone knocked on Mike's office door. She glanced over her shoulder to see Frank Matrone enter. His hair was mussed as if he'd just stepped out of the shower, toweled it dry, and hadn't bothered to comb it. He was wearing a nicely cut black suit, a burgundy tie, and cowboy boots.

"Sorry I'm late." He smiled at Kate, then addressed Mike. "You wanted to see me?"

"I wanted to see you twenty minutes ago." Mike motioned toward a second chair. "Have a seat."

Irritation rippled through her when Matrone walked to the chair next to hers and sat down. "Hi, Kate. How's it going?"

Ignoring him, she glared at Mike. "What's he doing here?"

Mike frowned at her. "In case you've forgotten, he works here. He's your investigator."

She shot Frank a withering look. "I know that. I'm asking you what he's doing at this meeting."

"Be nice," Mike said, then shot a look at Frank. "You seen the paper?"

"Not yet. What's up?"

"Give him the paper, Kate."

For an instant she was tempted to roll it up and hit him with it, but decided that wouldn't be very productive and instead passed it to him with a tad too much force. "That story is hardly newsworthy."

Frank took the paper, his heavy brows knitting as he began to read. Kate made eye contact with Mike, but her attention was on the man sitting next to her. His chair was too close to hers. So close she could smell his aftershave. A pleasing scent that spoke of masculinity and the out of doors . . .

Silence reigned for a full minute as he read. Slowly Kate's initial irritation began to give way to uneasiness. She didn't like surprises, but she had a sinking feeling she was about to get one thrown in her face. She could feel her shoulders tightening, her neck muscles following suit.

Frank lowered the paper and gave her an assessing look, and suddenly she knew why she was here. Why Mike was looking at her as if she were a naughty teenager about to be grounded for the rest of her life. Why Frank Matrone had been called to join them.

"You think this has something to do with the Bruton Ellis case?" Frank asked after a moment.

"You're the ex-cop. I was going to ask you the same thing," Mike said.

Frank rolled his shoulder. "Hard to say." He looked at Kate. "Did you see anyone? Did they say anything?"

"No and no," she said.

"Did he call you by name?" Frank asked.

Kate met his gaze, words from the note flashing in her mind's eye. *Are you still as sweet as you were when you were seventeen, Katie?*

"No," she replied.

His gaze lingered on hers for an instant too long before he turned his attention back to Mike. "Life, Inc., has been making noise since you announced the DA's office would be seeking the death penalty."

"Prowling around an ADA's house in the middle of the night isn't their usual modus operandi," Kate interjected.

"Anyone you put away been released from prison recently?" Mike asked.

"I look at the report from TDOJ every month, and there have been no cautions for this office," she said.

"What do you make of it?" Mike asked Frank.

Frank gave Kate an assessing look. The kind of look a cop gave a hostile witness when he wasn't getting the whole story. "Hard to tell on so little information."

Sighing as if he were annoyed, Mike looked at Kate. "You should have brought this to my attention immediately."

"I thought—"

"You thought I wouldn't find out and you wouldn't have to deal with it," he cut in. "Give me a break, Kate, I didn't get to be DA because of my outgoing personality."

"Believe me, I didn't think that for a second," she said under her breath.

Mike didn't smile. "I'm an inch away from assigning you personal protection."

She stared at him, frustrated because that was the last thing she wanted to happen. Angry because he was right and she was coming very close to looking like an irrational fool. But she didn't want anyone in the DA's office to know about what had happened eleven years ago. She especially didn't want anyone to know she'd hired Jack Gamble to track down the men responsible. Or that she planned to take care of the rest on her own.

"I understand your concern," she said. "And I appreciate it, Mike. I really do. But I feel that to assign me personal protection at this juncture is an overreaction and a total waste of manpower and budget."

Mike looked at Frank. "What do you think?"

"Why are you asking him?" she asked.

"Because he's the only one in this room who used to be a cop," Mike snapped.

Kate turned her attention to Frank. He contemplated her steadily, his expression inscrutable. "I could do a security inspection," he said.

"What does that entail?" Mike asked.

"I did them when I was a patrol officer. People have them done mostly to save money on their homeowners insurance. I make sure she has adequate exterior lighting. All exterior locks are in working condition. That sort of thing."

"I have an alarm system," she said.

"Most alarms wouldn't keep out a determined preschooler," Frank returned smoothly.

Kate had been hoping fervently that the entire incident would pass with minimal fanfare. Had she been a private citizen, the newspaper story wouldn't even have been a blip on the media's radar. But because she was a public figure—a somewhat *controversial* public figure who was about to try a capital case—it had become a news item and subsequently an issue with her overprotective boss.

"Do the security inspection," Mike said to Frank.

Kate braced when Mike turned his attention to her. "I expect you to be a professional about this, Kate. If anything unusual happens that you feel could be related to the case or this office, it is your responsibility to keep me informed. I will assign you personal protection if necessary. Are we clear on that?"

"Crystal," she said.

"This meeting is over." Mike looked at his watch. "I'm late for a luncheon."

Kate didn't look at either man as she rose and started toward the door. As she left Mike Shelley's office it struck her that she wasn't nearly as concerned about her personal protection as she was about keeping her secrets.

WEDNESDAY, FEBRUARY 1, 5:46 P.M.

"You wanted to see me?"

Mike Shelley looked up from his desk. "Have a seat."

For the second time that day Frank settled into the wing-back chair opposite the DA's desk and wondered what the hell he was doing there. Kate Megason was conspicuously absent, which told Frank this meeting was going to be a lot less interesting than the one they'd had earlier in the day.

"Thanks for staying late," Mike said, shoving the document he'd been working on into a folder and closing it. "I don't know where the hell the day went."

Had Frank given a damn about the job, it might have crossed his mind that he was about to get fired. But in the last year, life had taught him to keep things in perspective. Getting fired was a long way from the worst thing that could happen to a man.

"You up for a little overtime?" Mike asked.

"Depends on what you want me to do."

Mike leaned back in his leather executive chair and laced his fingers behind his head. "I want you to keep an eye on Kate for a few days."

That was the last thing Frank had been expecting him to say and for a moment wasn't sure how to respond. "I thought you had decided what happened didn't warrant personal protection."

"I had the police report couriered over this afternoon. I didn't like what I read, so I called one of the detectives. He thinks the situation warrants a closer eye." Mike passed a copy of the police report to Frank. "I'm concerned and wanted to get your take on it."

His curiosity piqued, Frank quickly skimmed the report. Two squad cars had responded to Kate's 911 call. One of the officers had noted footprints in a flowerbed beneath the kitchen window as well as at the rear of the house.

Frank made eye contact with the DA. "Peeping Tom?"

"I don't know what to think."

"Interesting detail for her to forget to mention."

"I thought so, too. She downplayed the entire incident."

"Why would she do that?"

Mike shrugged. "The only thing I can think of is that she's afraid this kind of publicity could get in the way of her trying the Bruton Ellis case."

"I don't see how that could happen. Besides, she's too smart to put her personal safety at risk."

"That's true. I've known her since she was a wet-behind-the-ears intern fresh out of SMU. She's talented. Ambitious. Driven. I've watched her grow into the powerhouse she is today. She's tough as nails."

Having already figured most of that out on his own, Frank waited, wondering what he was leading up to.

Mike glanced at the police report and shook his head. "But when she lies to me about something as important as this, it makes me wonder what she's hiding and why."

"So what do you want me to do? Stake out her place?" he asked, only half kidding.

"I know this is out of the usual realm of responsibility for an investigator. But you're the only investigator I've got with law enforcement experience. It would just be for a couple of hours an evening. Low key. Unobtrusive. Just . . . keep an eye on her. Make sure there's nobody skulking around, peeking in her windows, whatever."

"And make sure she doesn't see me."

"That would be a big help since she's a pretty good shot."

Frank laughed, but he wasn't sure Mike was entirely kidding. "How do you propose I keep an eye on her without her knowing it?"

"You worked in narcotics. I assumed you could work out the details."

Frank rolled his shoulder, thinking it was always the details that got a man into trouble. "You think someone's going after her? Someone who's recently been released from prison? Some death penalty opponent? What?"

"I don't know. This just isn't sitting well with me. I like Kate. She's a friend. I don't want to see her get hurt if there's some nutcase out there."

The thought that Mike Shelley's interest in Kate went beyond professional floated through Frank's mind. She was a lovely young woman twenty years his junior. Shelley was a powerful man. The kind of man a woman like Kate would be drawn to. Frank didn't like it that the thought didn't sit well with him.

"If you're up to some overtime, I'll keep you on as her investigator," Mike said. "If you're not, I'll find a way to pull you off the Ellis case so you can make time for the surveillance. Up to you."

Frank thought about that for a moment. "I'll need a car she won't recognize."

"I'll get you something out of impound. Anything else?"

"How about a bulletproof vest for when she finds out?"

Mike made a sound of distress. "Let's hope it doesn't come to that."

"Kate said she checked with TDOJ. I'll check again, just to make sure there's not some parolee out there with a grudge against her."

"Excellent." Standing, Mike extended his head. "I appreciate your doing this on such short notice."

"Let's just hope she doesn't mistake me for a prowler."

FIFTEEN

Kate lived in a classy area of North Dallas known as the Bluffs. The secluded neighborhood was located on a wooded greenbelt overlooking Mustang Creek. The homes were older and set on generous lots with mature trees—both of which went for a premium in Dallas. Her house was a smallish, single-story brick ranch with mullioned windows and glossy black shutters. In some places lush English ivy crept up the brick all the way to the eaves. A leaded-glass door and side-lights graced the front entrance. Dual flickering gas lamps cast warm yellow shadows against the house, giving it a warm and welcoming glow.

Frank didn't feel very welcome. When he'd called her earlier and told her he could do the security inspection tonight, she'd made her displeasure clear. That was fine by Frank. He'd never been good at making people happy. The fact of the matter was he didn't want to be here any more than she wanted him here.

He parked in the driveway and shut down the engine. Grabbing the clipboard and flashlight from the seat, he swung open the door and stepped into the night. The wind slapped him like a rude, cold hand as he started toward the house. His leg was hurting. It felt as if some little son of a bitch was gleefully ramming an ice pick into his shin all the way to the bone. Since he was working tonight, Frank figured he would start with ibuprofen and work his way up from there.

On the front porch he rang the bell. A moment later the door opened and Kate was standing there, looking at him as if he were some mangy dog with a dead rabbit in its mouth. She was wearing snug, faded jeans that revealed nicely curved hips and a flat belly. A cropped SMU sweatshirt offered a peek at the silky flesh of her abdomen and her navel—which was pierced with a tiny gold ring—and his initial irritation quickly yielded to a hefty dose of male interest. The sweatshirt didn't do a thing for her figure, but he saw the faint outline of generous breasts, and he was pretty sure she wasn't wearing a bra.

The night was definitely looking up.

ADA Kate Megason didn't look the least bit uptight braless and in jeans and a sweatshirt. In fact, she looked so good he had a difficult time finding a place to put his eyes that wouldn't get him into trouble. He settled on her face, only to quickly discover that her mouth was every bit as sexy as the rest of her.

"Kate," he croaked, then cleared his throat noisily.

"Oh, Frank. Hi."

"You look surprised to see me."

"Sorry." Touching her temple with her finger, she rolled her eyes. "I forgot about the security inspection."

He was keenly aware of her scent, a musky, mysterious floral that made him want to put his nose to bare flesh and draw the essence of her into his lungs. Or maybe he'd rather run his tongue along her belly until she quivered. . . .

The thoughts took him by surprise. The hot rush of blood to his groin downright shocked him. It had been a long time since he'd felt this kind of raw, physical attraction. Since Gittel. That Kate was the focus of that attraction troubled him. He did not want to have a hard-on for a woman who could barely stand the sight of him.

"I probably should have called on the way over," he managed.

"My bad. You called this afternoon." She looked flustered for a moment. "I guess I should have written it down. Come in."

The house was warm and smelled of lemon polish and sugar cookies. The kind his mother used to make at Christmas a lifetime ago. It was a pleasant, sweet smell that reminded him of coming home. Reminded him of a time when life hadn't been so damn complicated.

He walked into the living room and was immediately taken in by the loveliness of the place. Her taste in furnishings was eclectic, but ran to the contemporary. A soft beige sofa and two huge chairs with sloping arms formed a comfortable grouping opposite an old-fashioned sandstone fireplace. The coffee table was a glossy mahogany and contrasted nicely with the muted furniture and walls. The shelves on either side of the hearth were filled with books. A nice collection ranging from legal volumes to bestselling novels to leather-bound antiques.

"Nice place," he commented.

"Thank you." She was almost a foot shorter than he was, and he amended his earlier estimate of her height and put her at about five feet four inches. She was one of those people whose personality made her seem larger than she really was.

"If this isn't a good time . . ." He let his words trail.

"This is fine." She smiled, and he felt it like a small electrical shock that ran the length of his body and sizzled along his nerve endings. Her eyes were incredibly blue. The kind of blue a man could fall into and get hopelessly lost if he wasn't careful. Frank had never considered himself vulnerable when it came to women. He was discriminating and cautious to the extreme. But Kate Megason was making him feel a little reckless and a whole lot rash. . . .

"I was just catching up on some work in the study," she said.

"Now, there's a surprise."

She blinked, then gave a self-deprecating smile. "My secret's out, huh?"

"Being a workaholic isn't so bad." He looked toward the study, where he saw a wall of books, a glossy desk with a laptop open. "The Bruton Ellis case?"

"I'm just gearing up for the preliminary hearing."

"I'm sure you'll knock 'em dead." He grinned. "No pun."

Her smile widened. "I hope not."

"This shouldn't take long."

"What exactly do you need to do?"

He lifted the clipboard in his hand. "This is the standard home security inspection checklist used by the Dallas PD. What I'm going to do is walk the perimeter of the house. I'll check the locks on your doors and windows. Exterior lighting. Fencing. Then I'll fill out this form and make some recommendations. Pretty routine stuff."

"I really do have an alarm system," she said quickly.

"You get points for that, but I'll check it and make sure it's in good working order." He looked down at the clipboard and checked one of the boxes. "This should save you about twenty percent on your homeowner's insurance."

"That's good." She looked impatient for a moment, and he got the impression that her mind was already back at her laptop. That she wanted to get back to it, and he was interrupting her. That maybe she wasn't quite as enamored with him as he was with her. . . .

Good grief.

"I should be out of your hair in about fifteen minutes," he said.

"Oh, sure. Just do whatever you need to do. I'll be in the study." She started to turn away, then paused. "I can make coffee if you'd like some."

Frank knew she was just being polite. He knew he should say no, if only to let her get back to work. But for the first time in what seemed like forever, he wanted to be with someone, even if it was for some stilted conversation over coffee and a glimpse of that ring in her navel.

"Coffee would be great," he heard himself say.

"I was just about to start a pot brewing when I saw your headlights in the driveway, anyway. Decaf okay?"

It wasn't. Frank liked the leaded stuff and lots of it. But he would drink a mug of nails if it would garner him an opportunity to look at her for another fifteen minutes. "Fine," he said. "I'll go ahead and start the inspection."

His eyes made a final sweep of her as she turned toward the kitchen. Nice ass. The little ring was gold. And she definitely wasn't wearing a bra. . . .

He was sweating beneath his jacket as he stepped onto the front porch and closed the door behind him. His sex felt heavy and full as he took the steps to the yard.

"Cut it out," he muttered.

Frank started around the house, using the time to cool off both mentally and physically. He couldn't remember the last time he'd reacted to a woman this way. For the last year he hadn't so much as *noticed* a female, let alone gotten hot under the collar. He wanted to believe this was merely his body's way of telling him it was time to venture back into the land of the living. That he was one step closer to healing.

On the other hand, maybe he just needed to get laid.

He didn't think Kate Megason was the woman for the job.

Putting thoughts of getting laid out of his mind, he opened the back gate, frowning at the lack of a padlock, and made a note on the form. The back of the house was as pleasing to the eye as the front with lush landscaping and a custom swimming pool. Security wise, however, the place left much to be desired. He skirted the house, making notes and checking boxes on the form as he went.

A cedar plank privacy fence surrounded the backyard, standard fare in the city of Dallas. The fence was good for privacy—which Kate seemed to like—but bad for security. Privacy fences not only protected the homeowner from prying eyes, but if some scumbag were to scale the fence, he wouldn't be seen by neighbors. Frank noted that on the form and continued. He looked out at the greenbelt beyond. The trees that were so coveted in Dallas would make perfect cover for some bozo looking to score some loot. The area was relatively secluded and very dark. Someone could walk along the creek totally unseen, scale the fence or go through the gate, cross the yard unnoticed, and gain access into the house through the pet door or even break a window before Ms. ADA had a clue she was in trouble.

Making notes as he went, Frank walked along the rear of the house. The flagstone patio was small and jammed with vacant terra-cotta pots. The hot tub was covered with a protective tarp for the winter. Everything was neat and in its place. He was stepping past the barbeque and a nice smoker when movement at the back window caught his eye. Even though the mini-blinds were closed, the slats weren't tight and he could see into her bedroom. The glossy wood of a mirrored dresser. The slowly turning ceiling fan above the bed. Warm lighting.

The sight of Kate stopped him dead in his tracks. He knew what was going to happen next. Common decency told him to keep moving. She couldn't possibly know those mini-blinds weren't one hundred percent private. But Frank had never claimed to be decent. And when she reached for the hem of her sweatshirt and drew it over her head, he didn't turn away.

She was standing with her back to the window, but he could see the front of her in the dresser mirror. He could see her face. Her breasts were full and gently sloped. He was standing too far away to see much detail. But his imagination filled in the blanks.

He went hard instantly. Only this time the rush of blood was so powerful, he was dizzy for an instant. It was the kind of arousal that was edgy and uncomfortable and prodded him like a sharp stick, forcing him to a place he didn't want to be.

It seemed like an eternity that he stood there, aching and pulsing and feeling like a goddamn Peeping Tom. But it was only a short moment before she reached into her drawer and quickly slipped into a bra. A second later the sweatshirt was back on. The light went out.

Frank stood there for a full minute, his heart pounding, his erection pressed painfully against his fly. "You're an idiot," he muttered.

He knew he hadn't done anything wrong. He'd just been standing at the wrong place at the wrong time. But a little voice reminded him that he could have looked away. He could have kept moving. But for the life of him he hadn't been able to make himself do it. He hadn't been able to take his eyes off of her. And he could no more prevent his physical reaction to her than he could stop the beating of his heart.

Turning on the flashlight, he shone it on the form and wrote, *Blinds northwest corner of house,* and started for the front.

He was standing on the porch, looking down at the clipboard, making a few final notes when her voice drew him from his concentration.

"So do I pass inspection?" she asked.

For an instant he saw her as she had been without a shirt. A smooth, pretty back. Full breasts that were uptilted. Nipples puckered with cold . . .

"Uh, a couple of things . . ."

"Oh." She bit her lip. "Anything major?"

Frank knew he was acting like an idiot. That he should leave the score sheet with her and get the hell out of there. But he couldn't get the image of her out of his mind. Couldn't get his mind off the notion of what she might look like without the rest of her clothes. What it would be like to put his hands on all that pretty flesh.

He told himself she was out of his league. That he didn't stand a snowball's chance in hell. But his cock didn't care about either of those things, and so he stood there with a hard-on that showed no signs of abating and tried like hell to say something coherent.

"You scored mid-range," he heard himself say. "I made a few recommendations."

"Would you like to come in?" She stepped back and opened the door for him to enter.

"Sure." He stepped into the foyer.

"Are you all right?"

He must have looked at her blankly, because she motioned toward his leg.

"You're limping," she said.

Realizing he'd been favoring his leg, he mentally berated himself. "I'm fine," he said a little too roughly.

"Oh, well . . ." She motioned toward the kitchen. "The coffee's brewed."

Her eyes met his and for an instant he couldn't look away. She might be a pushy, type-A personality at the office, but tonight the dynamics had changed. Take away the power suit and I'll-kick-your-ass pumps, and there was a youthful softness about her he hadn't noticed before. She had a strong mouth, full of sass and damn near as shapely as her body. But her eyes had a fragile quality that called upon his protective instincts.

Breaking eye contact with him, she turned and walked into the kitchen. He knew better than to indulge, but his eyes took on a life of their own and latched on to her backside. Another hot rush of blood to his groin made him glad his coat was long enough to cover his fly. The woman definitely knew how to fill out a pair of jeans.

"Here we go."

He looked up to see her come through the saloon doors holding a tray. Watching her, he suddenly felt optimistic, like maybe the assignment Mike had given him wasn't going to be as bad as he'd thought.

She set the tray on the coffee table and took a seat in one of the chairs. Frank wanted to sit next to her, but decided that would probably cause more problems than it was worth and took the sofa.

"Cream or sugar?" she asked.

You, he thought, with a little bit of cream so he could lap it out of her navel with his tongue. "Black."

She handed him a cup, then picked up her own and leaned back in the chair, contemplating him. "So what are your recommendations?"

Frank drank some of the coffee, then set the cup on the table and tugged the score sheet from the clipboard and passed it to her. "Since you have a privacy fence, I think some exterior lighting is definitely in order. I prefer motion-sensitive lighting."

"Motion detectors?"

He nodded. "Floodlights. They're common and inexpensive. I'd install two at the rear of the house, one on each corner, and two in the front."

"That's an easy enough fix. I can hire that out right away."

"Or I could install it for you." The words were out before he'd even realized he was going to say them.

She looked away from the form and met his gaze. "You don't have to do that. I can hire a handyman or electrician."

"The wiring in the rear is already there. All I'd have to do is swing by the hardware store and pick up the lights and install the fixtures. The front will need some additional wiring, but it's pretty basic stuff." When she continued to look unconvinced, he smiled. "Besides, I'll do a better job than some handyman."

"Oh, well . . . Of course, I'd pay you whatever you deemed necessary."

Like an idiot, he waved the statement away. "I'll do it for cost."

"You'd have to do this after hours." She looked flustered for a moment. "Things are about to spin into high gear with regard to the Bruton Ellis case."

"I ought to be able to knock it out in a couple of hours." He struggled for something to say. "How's the Ellis case coming along?"

She sighed, her eyes flicking toward the den. "Aaron Napier, the defense, is trying to wrangle a deal, but we refused. We're going to win this one hands down. Preliminary hearing has been scheduled for March 1. Motions to suppress evidence will be sometime in April. I expect the trial to be on the docket in early fall."

"That's fast."

"Just in time for the election."

"Mike's a political animal." Frank smiled. "I think he's counting on you to help him win."

He saw the shadow of a smile an instant before she looked at the form. "What's this about the mini-blinds?"

"The ones in the northwest corner of the house aren't totally private."

"I've been meaning to order new ones, but I've been so busy with work. I didn't think it was a big deal since the backyard is private."

Frank rolled his shoulder, aware that he was sweating beneath his coat. That he was uncomfortable because he was hard again. That he couldn't stop thinking of the way she'd looked without her shirt on. . . . "Now might be a good time to get that done," he said easily.

She looked at the checklist. "Trimming back some of the overgrown bushes ought to be an easy fix. I like to putter when I have time."

"It's always a good idea to keep walkways clear. Burglars like the dark. And they like hiding places. You take those two things away, and they'll go elsewhere, where the pickings are easier."

"Okay." She set the paper on the table and her gaze met his. "Thanks for coming out and doing this."

Realizing he'd stayed longer than he should have, Frank rose. "Not a problem. If everyone in Dallas had their homes inspected, the cops would have fewer burglaries to contend with."

She rose and for the span of two heartbeats they were standing face-to-face with a scant two feet separating them. Frank was keenly aware of her scent, titillating his senses, teasing his libido. Her eyes were large and dark against her pale complexion. Even though her mouth was bare of lipstick, her lips were the color of some ripe tropical fruit. He wondered what it would be like to lean close to her and set his mouth against hers.

"I'd better get going." Stepping away from her, he started toward the door. Vaguely he was aware of a phone ringing in the background. Her footsteps against the hardwood floor.

"Excuse me," she said and started for the phone.

"I can see myself out." Frank reached the foyer and swung open the door. Cold night air hit him in the face and he felt some of the tension drain from his shoulders and neck. He'd just stepped onto the porch when he heard Kate speak.

He didn't catch the words but something in her voice made him stop and turn. An alarm trilled in the back of his head when he saw her face. Something protective and male slithered through him when he realized she'd gone pale. That her hand was clutching the phone so hard her knuckles were white.

For a split second he debated whether to keep going or go back inside. But even though Frank didn't necessarily trust himself when it came to Kate Megason, he did trust his instincts. At the moment, those instincts were telling him something was wrong.

SIXTEEN

"How did you like my note, Kay-tee?"

The raspy voice on the other end of the line made the hairs on Kate's neck prickle. She was standing in the hall with the phone pressed to her ear. She could hear her heart beating heavily in her chest. Her breaths coming too hard, too fast. Vaguely she was aware that Frank hadn't yet walked out the door, so she turned her back to him. "Who is this?"

"Don't you remember me? That night in Houston. Me. You. Your sister. You were the best fuck I ever had."

Shock punched her with such violence that for a moment she couldn't think. Couldn't catch her breath. All she could do was stand there and clutch the phone, telling herself it wasn't him.

"Do you ever think of that night, Katie? Do you think of me?"

Kate couldn't find her voice, didn't know what to say, what to feel. There were too many emotions exploding inside her for her to sort through them. Rage. Shock. Horror. Shame so deep she could feel it all the way to her marrow.

"Who the hell is this?" she hissed.

"I'm hurt that you don't recognize my voice. Ah, sweet Katie, how could you forget me? I was your first—"

She slammed down the phone. Setting her hands against the console table, she leaned heavily, aware that her entire body was shaking. The back of her neck was slick with cold sweat. Her heart was pounding, and she couldn't catch her breath.

"Kate?"

She spun at the sound of Frank's voice. He'd walked back into the living room and was standing just a few feet away from her. One look at his face and she knew he'd heard the entire exchange. That she was a wreck. That she probably had some explaining to do. If only she could figure out how.

"You're shaking." His cop's eyes flicked to the phone. "Is everything all right?"

"Fine." But she figured they both knew she was not fine by any stretch of the imagination.

"Who was that on the phone?"

Her gaze snapped to his. Struggling to calm herself, she left the hall and walked into the living room, hoping he didn't notice that her legs were shaking. "Nobody," she said.

"Nobody seems to have you pretty shaken up."

"It was a personal call, Frank."

But she could tell he wasn't buying it. At some point he'd slipped into cop mode. She'd dealt with enough of them to see the suspicion in his eyes, and the hard gleam that told her he wasn't going to let this go. Damn. Damn. *Damn.*

"Look, I didn't walk back in here to pry into your personal business," he said. "But you're obviously upset, and I'd like to know why."

"I'm not upset."

"Really?" Without warning he reached out and took her right wrist in his and held her hand out for both of them to see.

She tried to yank her hand away from his, but he was holding on too tight. When she stopped fighting, she looked at her hand, found it shaking violently within his grasp.

"I guess that's why you're shaking, huh? Because you're not upset?"

Kate had always believed she was good at keeping a handle on her emotions. Many times her job demanded it. The things that had happened to her eleven years ago hadn't made her weak; they'd made her stronger. But hearing the man's voice, knowing she was going to have to deal with this, shook her so badly she couldn't get a grip.

"It was a prank call," she said after a moment.

Without speaking, Frank led her into the living room and guided her to the sofa. "Sit down."

Kate sank into the sofa without a fight.

Never taking his eyes from hers, he took the chair across from her. "What did he say?"

"Just . . . meaningless stuff." She raised her gaze to Frank's, hoping he'd let this go. But she could tell by his determined expression that he was going to press her. A small part of her wanted to tell him everything. But because of the nature of the calls, she couldn't. She didn't want anyone to know what had happened to her eleven years ago.

But Frank wasn't just anyone. He was a cop. And judging from the way he was looking at her, unless she came up with a really good lie pronto, he would not let this go. "He . . . talked dirty," she said. "Heavy breathing. You know what I mean."

"Don't you have an unlisted number?"

"Yes, of course. I don't know how anyone could have gotten it."

"Has this guy called before?"

Feeling like a fool, kicking herself for having not just hung up the phone, Kate gave a reluctant nod.

"How many times?"

"Twice."

"In addition to the prowler." He shook his head. "Kate, you're a smart woman. You know better than to stick your head in the sand. Why didn't you mention this?"

"I didn't think it was an issue." When he only continued to stare at her, she continued, "Come on, Frank. It was a prank call."

"And you're a prosecutor. You've put people in prison, and more than likely picked up some enemies over the years."

"I'm aware of that," she said tightly.

"And you've decided not to do anything about it?"

"Look," she began, "it was some jerk with too much time on his hands. I've been meaning to change my number; I've had it for quite some time. I just haven't gotten around to it yet."

"Do me a favor and make time for it tomorrow, okay?"

"First thing in the morning." Kate paused for a moment, then rose. "I'm sorry, but I really have to get back to work."

As if realizing there was nothing more he could do, Frank rose. Before starting toward the door, he looked at her and Kate got the impression that while he might be walking away now, he wasn't going to let this go. "If anything else happens, you'll tell me, right?"

Kate nodded adamantly. "Of course."

"Right." He stared at her an instant longer, then limped toward the door.

"Thanks for the inspection," she said.

"I'll pick up the floodlights in the morning."

"Don't be late for work." She softened the words with a smile.

He smiled back. "Wouldn't dream of it," he said and went through the door.

WEDNESDAY, FEBRUARY 1, 11:39 P.M.

Bruton Ellis had spent a good bit of his adult life behind bars. He didn't like being in jail, but there was something to be said for three square meals a day and a warm bunk. As far as the rest of life's small pleasures—which in his mind consisted of sex and drugs and not necessarily in that order—they could be had even in prison—for a price.

But his needs were simple. He kept to himself for the most part. He knew how to lay low and stay out of trouble.

They'd put him in the special housing unit, otherwise known as the SHU, pronounced "shoe." You could give the place all the fancy names you wanted, but the ten-by-twelve-foot cell still boiled down to solitary confinement. The place didn't even have bars. Concrete walls. Steel door with a single window and a slot for the food tray. A stainless-steel toilet. Stainless-steel sink. And a lumpy mattress on a double-decker bunk.

Home sweet home.

It was the sociable ones who suffered while in solitary. But Bruton Ellis had never been the most sociable type. In fact, he *liked* being alone. Drugs were harder to get, but once he figured out the flow, he could usually get enough to get by.

It wasn't the solitude keeping him up tonight. He'd been locked up for three weeks now. Plenty of time for him to figure out the big-shot corporate executive who'd hired him to kill those two women wasn't going to ride in on a white horse and hand him a get-out-of-jail-free card. The son of a bitch had cut him loose.

His lawyer had urged him to cut a deal. But Ellis had been certain the corporate fucker was going to come through for him. But he hadn't, and now the DA was going for the death penalty. The thought turned Ellis's bowels to water.

Lethal injection.

Jesus fucking Christ.

That was when the panic had set in. He'd spent two days calling the number the man had given him. For two days he'd listened to the voice on the other end of the line telling him the number had been disconnected.

The motherfucker had cut him loose.

He was on his own and the State of Texas wanted to stick a needle in his arm for what he'd done.

And so Ellis did the only thing he could and talked. He'd told his lawyer everything. The problem was he didn't know enough to incriminate anyone except himself. In the end his lawyer had told him to keep his mouth shut. Ellis could tell the smug little son of a bitch didn't believe him.

He might have been the one to blow away that black girl and that old Mexican bitch. But what about the guy who'd offered him five thousand dollars? For the hundredth time Ellis kicked himself for not getting his name. What had he been thinking?

But Ellis knew what he'd been thinking. He'd been thinking that five thousand dollars bought an awful lot of crystal meth, and at the time, the only thing that mattered was getting high.

He had to find someone who would listen to him. Someone who would believe him. Maybe the DA would cut him a deal.

Ellis didn't relish the idea of spending the rest of his life in prison. But he relished the thought of death row a whole lot less.

Frank had barely sat down behind his desk when Kate rushed into his office.

"Don't get comfortable." She reached for his leather jacket and handed it to him across the desk. "We're leaving."

His leg had kept him up most of the night and he was in a pissy mood. But one look at Kate and his spirits began to lift.

"Your place or mine?" he asked.

A chuckle escaped her before she could frown. "I just got a call from Aaron Napier. Bruton Ellis wants to talk to us."

"About what?"

"Aaron wouldn't say." She looked excited.

"Weren't you just telling me it's irregular for a defendant to want to talk to the prosecution?"

"Very."

His suspicion that there was more to the murders of Evangeline Worth and Irma Trevino than a robbery gone bad spun into high gear. "I'll drive."

"I'll let you."

Fifteen minutes later they parked in the public lot outside the Lew Sterrett Justice Center. After a quick security check, they took the elevator to the second floor. Aaron Napier met them outside the interview room. He was an attractive African American man with the charisma of a Hollywood actor and the physique of a pro football player. He wore a tan silk jacket over a black polo shirt and black trousers.

"Kate." Smiling, he extended his hand. "Thanks for coming. How are you?"

Kate returned his smile. "Are you sure you want us talking to your client?"

Napier shrugged, then shook hands with Frank. "I advised him against this, but he insisted." He glanced at his watch. "This is all kind of last minute. He was frantic when he called at eight o'clock this morning. I've got court in half an hour, so we'll have to make this quick."

Napier crossed to the interview room door and pushed it open. Kate went in first. The room was painted a two-tone institutional gray. Bruton Ellis sat at a scarred, rectangular table. He was a tall, thin man with greasy brown hair and bad skin. His hands were cuffed in front of him. He kept fidgeting, his fingers toying with the cuffs. She could see that his ankles were shackled as well.

She nodded at the police officer standing at the back of the room and took one of the plastic chairs opposite Ellis. Frank took the chair beside her. Napier took the chair next to Ellis.

Kate wasn't sure why they were there, so she directed her first question at Ellis. "Why did you ask for this meeting?"

Ellis tossed a nervous look at Napier, who gave him a subtle nod. "I got information," he blurted. "I wanna cut a deal."

"It's too late to cut a deal," Kate said.

Ice flashed in Ellis's eyes for an instant, then he looked as if he wanted to cry. "It ain't fair for me to take all the blame for what happened to those two chicks, man."

"You pulled the trigger," Frank cut in.

Ellis's eyes flicked from Kate to Frank and back to Kate. "A guy hired me to take out them out. You gotta fuckin' believe me."

"Why would I believe anything you have to say?"

"Because I'm tellin' the fuckin' truth."

"Watch your mouth," Frank snapped.

Ellis blinked at him. "He was some rich dude. A businessman. You know, executive type. He wore suits, man. He paid me five grand. Said I should make it look like a robbery."

"Give us a name," Frank said.

"I don't have his fuckin' name. He never told me."

"You're wasting our time," Kate put in.

Ellis looked desperate. "I can tell you what he looks like."

Frank looked at Napier and shook his head. "He's wasting our time."

Napier shrugged.

Kate frowned at Ellis. "Unless you can give us some new information, this is a waste of time."

Ellis made a choking sound. "I don't want to go to the

death chamber." He looked at his lawyer. "Tell them! I'm telling the fuckin' truth."

Frank got up. "I've heard enough."

Ellis jumped to his feet. "Wait!"

The police officer stepped forward and put his hand on Ellis's shoulder. "Sit down."

Ellis sank back into the chair. He was breathing hard. Even though the room was cold, sweat had popped out on his forehead. "You gotta fuckin' believe me."

Frank shook his head. "We don't have to do shit."

Ellis looked at Kate as if expecting her to rescue him. "I didn't do this by myself. The guy hired me, and now he's going to get off and I get death fuckin' row. It ain't right, man."

"You want a deal?" Rising, Kate picked up her briefcase. "You're going to have to come up with something a hell of a lot more concrete than some phantom corporate executive."

She started toward the door. Vaguely she was aware of the police officer asking Ellis to rise. Of Frank behind her. Of Aaron Napier lagging behind. She was midway to the door when Ellis lunged. "Wait!"

The cop moved in and muscled him back into the chair.

But Ellis's attention was on Kate. "He drives a Jaguar! Black with spoke wheels! I swear!"

Frank opened the door for Kate and they walked into the hall. "You fuckin' bitch! Cunt!" She could hear Ellis choking back sobs, but she felt no compassion.

"Fun guy," Frank said.

She let out a breath. "What do you think?"

"I think he's got a problem with female authority figures."

She snorted as they approached the bank of elevators. "I wonder why Napier allowed it."

"He's got the hots for you."

"Oh brother."

Frank pressed the Down button. "Come to think of it, I think *I* have the hots for you."

"You're a sexual harassment lawsuit waiting to happen, you know that?"

But Frank was grinning when he stepped into the elevator.

"What do you make of Ellis?" she asked when the doors had closed.

Frank punched the button for the lobby. "I don't put much weight in anything he told us in there. He's a lowlife bucket of slime. But something about this case has bothered me from the get-go."

Surprise and something akin to uneasiness moved through her. "Are you telling me you don't think he acted alone?"

"I'm telling you I wouldn't be surprised if another player popped up on the radar if we looked hard enough."

"Why would someone hire him to murder two clerks and ask him to make it look like a robbery? It doesn't make sense."

"Murder rarely makes any sense." Something dark glittered in the depths of his eyes. "Unless someone has something to gain."

"Like what?"

Frank shrugged. "The usual. Monetary gain. Revenge. Power. Take your pick."

Kate was so deep in thought, she barely noticed when the elevator doors chimed open. "Who's your suspect?"

"The man in the suit." He fished keys from his coat pocket and started for the parking garage.

"That certainly narrows it down." Kate had to jog to keep up with him. "Does he only have one arm, too?"

He shot her a dark look.

"Frank, the police have already investigated this crime. They've handed us a suspect. It's our responsibility to prosecute, not get caught up in some wild-goose chase."

She nearly bumped into him when he stopped abruptly and turned to her. For the span of several heartbeats they were nose-to-nose, so close she could feel the warm brush of his breath against her face.

Frank stepped back. "The least we can do is look at the corporation."

"You mean Snack and Gas?"

"The franchisee." Frank rolled his shoulder. "Squeeze a little and see what pops out."

A few short days ago Kate would have thought he was crazy for letting something as nebulous as gut instinct carry any weight. It surprised her to realize that at some point she'd come to trust his judgment.

As they left the Lew Sterrett Justice Center, she wasn't sure if that was good or bad.

THURSDAY, FEBRUARY 2, 3:10 P.M.

It took the remainder of the morning and most of the afternoon for Kate and Frank to decipher the corporate structure of the Snack and Gas where Evangeline Worth and Irma Trevino had been murdered. They were sitting at the small conference table in Kate's office with two boxes of Chinese takeout, two soft drinks, and a stack of files between them.

"If having a complicated corporate structure was a crime, these bastards would be doing time." Sighing, Frank picked up a Dun and Bradstreet report. "The Snack and Gas store number 6911 is owned by franchisee Kirk Jarvis dba Quick Stop, Inc., in Oklahoma City. Quick Stop, Inc., in turn, is owned by Quorum Partners Limited out of Tallahassee, Florida."

Something inside Kate quickened. "Did you say Quorum Partners?"

Frank's gaze sharpened on hers. "You asked me to run a D and B on them a few days ago, which I did, but nothing popped."

Reaching into a manila folder, Kate withdrew the life insurance policy on Evangeline Worth and handed it to him. "This was the reason I asked you for the report the other day."

Frank took the document and began to read. "A life insurance policy on Evangeline Worth." He looked at Kate. "Where did you get this?"

"It was in Evangeline Worth's employee file."

"It says here there are seven pages total. Why do we have only six?"

"I hadn't noticed," she said, feeling a little foolish.

Frank turned to his laptop, his fingers playing quickly over the keys. "Quorum is owned by Ferguson and Rooks, a law firm here in Dallas. Ferguson and Rooks owns several companies. Capricorn Real Estate Investment Company, Endroad Holdings. Those two companies are the parent company of several franchisees."

"Franchisees of what?"

Frank looked over the top of his laptop at Kate. "Java, Inc., is the franchisee of record for a chain of coffee shops in the northeastern United States. Tuscan, Inc., owns pizza parlors in the Midwest. Quick Stop, Inc., owns convenience stores on the West Coast and in Texas. Pretty complicated corporate structure. Wonder why?"

She rolled her shoulder. "Tax breaks. Maybe something to do with insurance. Worker's compensation. Unemployment. Could be any number of things."

"Or maybe they're trying to hide something."

"Did anyone ever tell you that you have a suspicious mind?"

"When dead bodies start showing up, they're usually thankful." He paged through the Dun and Bradstreet report in front of him. "Ferguson and Rooks has offices at The Crescent."

Kate arched a brow. "High rent isn't against the law."

"That's ten minutes from here."

"I think we've spent enough time on this particular wild-goose chase."

"I'll spring for a cappuccino."

Kate sighed.

"I'll drive, too."

"What can you possibly hope to achieve?"

Rising, he reached for both of their coats. "Probably nothing, but I've always liked shaking down lawyers."

"I hate to put a damper on your fun, but you work for lawyers."

Frank grinned. "I want to shake you down, too."

"Oh brother." But Kate was smiling as she grabbed her coat.

THURSDAY, FEBRUARY 2, 4:05 P.M.

The offices of Ferguson and Rooks were located on the nineteenth floor of The Crescent, Dallas's most luxurious office tower. The elevator doors swished open to an opulent lobby with marble tile floors. Nifty pendant lights hung from high, multilevel ceilings. A model-beautiful young woman sat at a mahogany-and-glass desk. On the wall above her, gleaming brass letters signified the law firm of Ferguson and Rooks.

Kate's heels clicked smartly on the marble floor as she and Frank crossed to the receptionist's desk.

"May I help you?" she asked.

Frank flashed his identification. "We'd like to speak to Belinda Ferguson and Jameson Rooks."

"Do you have an appointment?"

"No, but we'd be happy to get a warrant if you prefer." His smile was charming.

Looking as if she wasn't quite sure whether to be charmed or alarmed, the young woman punched numbers on the switchboard.

Kate strolled to the opposite side of the lobby and pretended to study the museum-quality oils adorning the walls.

A moment later Frank came up beside her. "Pretty smooth, don't you think?"

"I think what you just did was an abuse of your position."

"Avoided a lot of phone tag."

Kate rolled her eyes. "This guy's an attorney, Frank. He knows his rights, and he's not going to put up with any crap. If he complains to Mike about the DA's office overstepping bounds, you can bet we'll hear about it."

"May I help you?"

Kate turned to see a tall, distinguished man enter the lobby. He wore an Armani pinstriped suit with a pale yellow shirt, a Hermes tie, and glossy wingtips. He looked to be in his early fifties, his age given away only by the gray at his temples. He had the physique and grace of a man twenty years younger. His eyes were the color of a January sky, icy and cold and gray.

"Mr. Jameson Rooks?"

"Yes."

Kate held up her identification and extended her hand. "Thanks for making time for us. We're with the DA's office. We'd like to ask you a few routine questions about an incident at one of the Snack and Gas stores here in Dallas."

The man grimaced. "The murders. Of course. We're still

reeling over that. Vicious thing." Rooks motioned toward the wide hall. "I've got a few minutes before I have to leave. Why don't you come into my office? I'll help you any way I can."

"Thank you."

He led them down a wide hall. Matted and framed photographs of several Texas city skylines festooned the walls. Dallas. Ft. Worth. Houston. At the end of the hall they entered a large corner office. Two glass walls offered a stunning view of downtown Dallas. The furniture was stark, black leather, stainless steel, and glass. A sago palm as large as a man soaked up light in the far corner.

A woman of about forty years of age sat on a black leather settee. She had light brown eyes and tawny hair. She wore an elegant white suit with matching pumps. Diamonds glinted at her earlobes. She looked like a sleek white cat sitting there, watching them as if they were about to muss the Aubusson rug.

"This is my partner, Belinda Ferguson."

Kate crossed to the woman and shook her hand. "Hello."

"Belinda, this is Kate Megason and Frank Matrone of the Dallas County DA's office."

Ferguson nodded. "You're here about the two clerks?"

"We like to cover all our bases," Frank said.

"Please. Have a seat." Rooks crossed to the wet bar at the back of the room. "Would you like a drink? Soda? Iced tea?" He smiled. "I've got something stronger if you like."

"We're fine," Frank said.

Shrugging, he poured amber liquid into an ice-filled tumbler and carried it to his desk. Kate took the chair across from him. Frank remained standing.

Rooks sipped, regarding them over the rim of the glass. "I obtained a copy of the tape." Shaking his head, he rubbed the back of his neck. "I've never seen anything like it in my life."

Belinda Ferguson rose from the sofa and stood next to the desk. "We've been in contact with the security director of the franchisee," she said. "He's going to use portions of that tape and produce it into a training video. To try to prevent things like this from happening in the future."

"This isn't the kind of crime a training tape could have prevented," Frank said.

Rooks looked at him. "Nonetheless, we wanted to do something. That kind of work . . . late-night convenience stores can be dangerous. If a training video can prevent even one death"—he shrugged—"I feel it's the least we can do for the franchisee."

"You're paying for it?"

Belinda Ferguson nodded. "We've also begun a charitable trust for Evangeline Worth's four children. Our firm is donating twenty-five thousand dollars."

"That's generous of you," Frank said.

"We feel it's the least we can do. Four children losing their mother that way." The lawyer shook his head. "Even as removed as we are here at the firm from the actual store operations, it's a tough thing to deal with."

A heavy silence weighted the room for the span of several seconds.

"In any case." Rooks leaned back in his black leather executive chair and contemplated them. "Tell us how we can help you today."

Kate started to speak, but Frank cut in. "We were wondering about the life insurance policy on Evangeline Worth."

"Life insurance?" Rooks looked from Frank to Kate, then back to Frank. "I'm afraid I'm not aware of any life insurance policy."

"Let me refresh your memory," Frank said. "Ferguson and Rooks owns Quorum Partners Limited. Quorum is the policy holder and partial beneficiary of a life insurance policy on Evangeline Worth."

"All of which is administered by Quorum." Rooks raised his hands. "We're corporate attorneys, Mr. Matrone. We may own a company, but we have little or nothing to do with the running of that company. We don't set policy, either. We certainly don't get involved in insurance issues."

"You just collect the benefit."

Rooks's expression cooled. "And you don't approve of the practice?"

"Home office buys a policy. Clerk kicks the bucket. Home office gets a big chunk of cash. I think they call it dead-peasant insurance," Frank said. "Reminds me of vultures picking over carrion."

"All legal in the State of Texas."

"As long as the company has an insurable interest," Frank finished. "But it reeks of a corporation capitalizing on an hourly clerk's death."

"I know how it might look on the outside looking in, Mr. Matrone. But I can tell you that a company has a right to protect its assets. Our employees, whether hourly or executive, are our greatest asset."

"How much do you get?" Frank asked.

Belinda Ferguson shot him a dark look. "What are you insinuating?"

Frank shot a darker one back at her. "We're just trying to figure out how things work. I think we figured it out."

Rooks frowned. "I'll have to check the policy. I have no idea."

"We'd appreciate that," Frank said.

Sensing the meeting was about to go south, Kate stepped in. "We appreciate your meeting with us on such short notice. We won't take up any more of your time."

Rooks rose. "I'll see you out."

Kate shook hands with Belinda Ferguson, then left the office and started down the hall with Frank and Rooks behind her.

In the reception area Frank paused and looked around. "Nice office."

"My daughter is an interior designer."

"She's good."

"I think so." Rooks smiled like a proud papa. "Ferguson and Rooks will be moving to Providence Tower in the fall, however. My daughter will be designing the penthouse for us."

"Must have to sell a lot of beer and cigarettes to afford that kind of high rent," Frank said.

Rooks's expression chilled. "For a public servant, you have a smart mouth."

Frank met his gaze in kind. "A lot of people think that."

"I can see why." Rooks gave Kate an incredulous look.

Vowing to strangle Frank when they got back to the office,

Kate extended her hand to Rooks. "Thanks again for meeting with us."

He accepted the handshake. "If there's any way we can help, please don't hesitate to call." He brushed his thumb over the top of her hand before releasing it.

Back in the truck, Kate leaned against the seat. "That was real smooth."

"I don't think Rooks thought so."

"What do you think?"

"I'm kind of hungry. I thought we could stop off at—"

"About Jameson Rooks and Belinda Ferguson."

Frank left the visitor parking garage and turned onto Cedar Springs. "I think they reminded me why I don't like lawyers."

"They're corporate lawyers."

"If it walks like a duck . . ."

"As far as our investigation, I think we have everything we need from them."

"Yeah," he conceded. "And maybe one day dead-peasant insurance will be illegal in America."

As they headed back to the office, Kate found herself thinking about Evangeline Worth's four children.

SEVENTEEN

Surveillance was one aspect of police work Frank had never cared for. Back when he'd been a cop, he'd much preferred the adrenaline rush of drug busts and undercover stings over the slow-paced crawl of surveillance. Sitting in his car in some upscale Dallas neighborhood watching the alley cats fuck was not his idea of satisfying work.

But while his moonlighting job left much to be desired in the way of professional satisfaction, he knew it was the chance to see Kate that had him coming back.

He'd been on the job for three nights now, and had managed to fall into a routine that suited him. He put in eight hours at the office, grabbed a sandwich on the way home, changed into jeans, and spent the next two or three hours ogling his attractive boss from the privacy of the impound car Mike had assigned him. Life could be a hell of a lot worse.

"You're pathetic, Matrone," he muttered.

He'd seen her twice at the office today. She'd been wearing black. Black slacks. Black turtleneck. Black boots. All that black made him wonder if her underwear was black. If her bra was lacy or plain. If her panties were practical or sexy. She'd looked good enough to eat in a single bite, and by the end of the day he'd been ravenous.

But Frank knew she wasn't the kind of woman who would be interested in an ex-cop with a bum leg and a prescription drug habit. She was probably sleeping with some Ken-doll lawyer or banker type. Some overeducated pretty boy who bought her expensive jewelry and took her to fancy restaurants. Some rich jackass who gave her polite sex a couple of times a month. If Frank ever got her into his bed, there would be nothing polite about it. . . .

"Don't go there, partner."

Headlights cut through the darkness at the end of the street. He watched the car approach, knowing it was her, and his heart bumped hard against his ribs. The BMW swung into the driveway. Simultaneously the garage door went up, and she parked inside.

He'd learned a lot about her in the last three nights. She was a creature of habit and kept to a relatively strict routine. She was up at five-thirty. On the road by seven. At the office by seven-thirty. She had lunch at her desk or with one of her team. She worked late, usually until seven or seven-thirty. From there she drove straight home. No happy hour. No dates. No visitors. Not even an excursion to the mall. Twice, she'd made a stop at a local convalescent home—probably to visit some elderly relative.

So what made her tick?

He'd just turned on the radio to listen to a Mavericks basketball game when her garage door went up. The BMW backed out of the driveway and headed down the street. Once she was out of sight, Frank started the Camry and followed.

She headed south on the North Dallas Tollway. He followed at an unobtrusive distance, always keeping one or two cars between them. South of downtown she exited the tollway and entered a neighborhood most people wouldn't risk venturing into after dark. The neighborhood was a mix of homes and businesses, most of the windows locked down behind steel bars. She drove through the neighborhood with the speed and adeptness of a woman who was familiar with the area. A woman who knew exactly where she was going. But where the hell was that?

She turned left, then made a quick right onto Bellamy Street. Her brake lights flashed, and she pulled to the curb. The streetlamps had long since been shot out and the neighborhood was very dark. Not wanting her to notice his vehicle, Frank continued past in time to see her get out of the car, look both ways, then continue into a three-story brick building.

His curiosity piqued, he circled the block, killed the lights at the end of Bellamy and parked curbside. What the hell was she doing in a bad part of town this time of night?

"Only one way to find out," Frank muttered and settled in to watch.

Kate hadn't been planning on seeing Jack Gamble tonight. She'd come home from work tired and distracted with more than enough work to keep her busy until the wee hours. She'd barely walked in the door when her cell phone rang. It had been Jack on the line with news she'd been waiting on for eleven long years. She'd changed in record time, and within minutes she was back in the car and heading south.

She found Jack sitting behind his desk. "What you got for me?" she asked without preamble. "Good news?"

"Depends on what you had planned for one of them men you been looking for," he drawled.

Her heart was pounding when she lowered herself into the rail-back chair opposite his desk. "Did you get an address?"

"I got a dead man." He passed her a manila folder. "Signed, sealed, and delivered by Fate."

Kate's hand was shaking when she reached for the file. Keenly aware that Jack's eyes were on her, she opened it and found herself looking at a copy of a State of Arizona death certificate for one Eddie Calhoun. Thirty-eight years old. Cause of death massive trauma from a car accident on Interstate 10.

Beneath the death certificate was a photograph. Even after eleven years, Kate recognized him as the man who'd raped and then beaten Kirsten nearly to death.

At first she didn't know what to feel. Relief because at least part of her mission was finished. Grief because no matter what she did, Kirsten would never get out of that bed. Regret because Kate had always believed she would be the one to kill Eddie Calhoun.

"I guess that part of it's over," she said after a moment.

"All of it can be over if you let it," Jack said.

Kate raised her gaze to his. She'd never told him what happened, but he was a resourceful man. She was pretty sure he'd done some checking and figured it out. Sometimes she thought she saw the knowledge in his eyes.

Because both she and Kirsten had been sexually assaulted, their names had never been released. Kate's father had gone to extreme measures to keep their names out of the media. But there was a record of the crimes, and if anyone dug deep enough, they would find something. Jack Gamble, she thought, could find anything if he set his mind to it.

Kate told herself it didn't matter. Jack Gamble worked for her. He wasn't her friend. All she wanted from him were the names and addresses. The rest was up to her.

"If you're not up to getting that second name for me, just say the word," she said.

"You know I'm up to it."

"Good, because I want this finished." Kate rose on legs that weren't quite steady. "I have to go," she said and started toward the door.

"Kate," he called out after her.

Knowing what he was going to say, she didn't stop until she reached the door.

Jack wheeled his chair back and came around the desk. "The Lord has a way of takin' care of things for folks. Instead of you doing something you are going to be sorry for, maybe you ought to just let Him handle it."

She wanted to tell him that the Lord hadn't been there the night two depraved men had nearly killed her and her sister. Instead, she gave him the coolest smile she could muster. "I never do anything I'll be sorry for later," she said and walked out.

Kate was halfway down the steps when the tears came. She wasn't sure why she was crying. Eddie Calhoun was dead. He was in hell where he belonged. She should be happy because the truth of the matter was she hadn't wanted to kill him. She didn't want to kill anyone.

Pushing through the door, she stepped onto the sidewalk. She could hear her sobs echoing off the building. Her boots clicking against the sidewalk. She was midway to her car when the two men stepped out of the alcove. It was too dark for her to get a good look at them, but she could see that they were looking at her. That one of them was smoking a cigarette. It occurred to her that she should be concerned for her safety. Strangely, she wasn't. The only thing that concerned her was the very real possibility that if anything happened and news got out that a Dallas County ADA was hanging out with a shady private detective, she would have some questions to answer.

She gave the men a wide berth as she walked briskly past them and headed toward her car.

"Hey, baby, whatcha so upset about? You lookin' for a date?"

Laughter sounded. She didn't look at them. Didn't slow down. *Stay the hell away,* she thought.

"I got somethin' for you, mama. Come get it."

Kate was ten feet from her car when she heard the shuffle of shoes against concrete. She glanced over her shoulder to see the two men directly behind her. "Stay away from me," she said.

But the man in a camouflage jacket and shoulder-length dreadlocks darted around her and blocked her path. She tried to go around him, but he quickly stepped in front of her.

"Whas your hurry?" he said.

"Get out of my way," Kate said in the toughest voice she could muster.

"That ain't no way to talk to a nice guy like me." She heard the second man behind her, and at that point Kate knew they weren't going to leave her alone. Damn. Damn. *Damn!*

"What's a nice lady like you doin' in this part of town so late?"

Laughing, the second man grabbed his crotch. "Maybe she's looking for a little bit of dark meat."

The first man sneered. "You looking for something you can't find up in North Dallas?"

Kate's heart had begun to pound. She turned slightly, keeping both men in her direct line of vision. But she was keenly aware that they now stood between her and the car. "You don't want to do this," she said.

"Do what?" the second man said. "We jus' talkin'."

"How 'bout a little touchy feely, baby?" The first man put his hand on her shoulder.

In the year Kate had been coming here, she'd never run into trouble. She'd always figured most of the troublemakers in this neighborhood were too afraid of Jack Gamble to mess with his clientele. But she was a realist; she'd known this day would come. She'd visualized this moment. She knew what she had to do. She just hadn't expected to be so damn terrified.

In a single, smooth motion, Kate ducked. At the same time she reached for the mini magnum beneath her jacket. She brought up the tiny gun and pulled back the hammer with her thumb. "Get away from me, or I swear I'll put a hole in you."

The breathlessness of her voice surprised her. It sounded like someone else's voice. Someone terrified and desperate and very capable of carrying out the threat.

"Easy, mama." The first man raised his hands. "Damn."

"Kate!"

Kate swung around, but she didn't lower the gun. Shock pelted her when she saw Frank Matrone jogging toward her, his expression taut.

The two men turned and ran. Kate stared at Frank, disbelief barreling through her. She couldn't believe he was here. What the hell was going on?

"What the hell do you think you're doing?"

Censure and anger rang clear and hard in his voice. The next thing she knew Frank's hand was around her wrist, and he was forcing her to lower the gun. "Jesus Christ."

She let him take the gun, then watched, numb with shock and the remnants of adrenaline as he eased the hammer back into place. His hands were shaking when he opened the barrel and dropped the five cartridges into his palm.

"Wh-what are you doing here?" she asked.

"Saving your ass, evidently." None too gently, he took her arm and started toward her car. "What the hell are you doing?"

"Hold it right there, my man."

Kate froze at the sound of Jack Gamble's voice. Frank had his hand on her arm. She felt his fingers go rigid at the sound of the slide on Jack's semiauto .380 being jerked back, dropping a bullet into the chamber.

"Nice and slow," Jack cooed. "Get your fuckin' hands off her and drop the piece."

Frank released her. "Whatever you say."

"Jack. It's okay." Kate turned to see the large African American man in a wheelchair, the .380 trained on Frank, his expression as cold as black ice.

"He's okay," she said. "He's . . . with the DA's office."

Jack lowered the .380 a hair, his gaze seeking Kate's. "Looked like he was roughing you up to me."

"He wasn't," she said.

The black man looked down the street where the other two men had disappeared. "What about those other two jokers?"

"They ran." Frank was standing a foot away from her with his hands up, his expression part anger, part disbelief. "Would someone mind telling me what the holy hell is going on?"

Shaking his head, Jack holstered the pistol. "Kate, damn it, I knew somethin' like this would happen sooner or later."

"Nothing happened," she said. "I can take care of myself."

"Sure you can," Jack growled. "Could have turned out a whole lot worse."

The two men exchanged looks, and she sensed a silent communication passing between them. One that said they didn't think she could take care of herself.

Jack withdrew his identification and flashed it at Frank. "Jack Gamble. I'm a licensed private detective."

Frank's questioning gaze went from Jack to Kate. "You a client of his or what?"

Because Kate couldn't answer that without opening a can of worms she didn't want to get into, she answered with a question of her own. "What are you doing here?"

"Trying not to get shot." Bending, Frank scooped up the mini magnum. "Is everyone around here packing heat tonight?"

"Everyone 'cept those two jackasses who took off down the street." A grin spread across Jack Gamble's face when he looked at Kate. "Their eyes just about popped out of their heads when you drew down on 'em."

Frank didn't look amused. "You got a concealed weapon permit for this?" He held up the gun by its grip.

"Of course I do." But her only thought was that she was going to have to do some fast-talking and creative lying to explain why she was here.

She held out her hand for the gun. "I'll take that."

Ignoring her, Frank stuffed it into the waistband of his jeans. But his attention was on Jack. "You look familiar. You ever been arrested?"

"Not that I know of."

"I know you from somewhere," Frank insisted.

"Sure as hell ain't from no rap sheet."

Kate sighed. "He's an ex-cop."

Frank's eyes narrowed. "That true?"

"Retired in ninety-eight," Jack said. "You?"

"Last year."

Kate nearly rolled her eyes as the two men's demeanors changed. If she hadn't been so shaken, she might have smiled at the way they were looking at each other. Cops. Jesus.

"What's your name?" Jack asked.

"Frank Matrone. Northwest substation." He didn't offer his hand for a shake.

"Southeast Division."

"If you two are finished with the male bonding, I have to get going." She gave Frank a cool stare and for the second time she held out her hand. "My pistol."

"I'll keep it for safekeeping."

"I want it," she said. "It's perfectly legal, and I'm leaving."

"I'll follow you back to your place."

"I'm capable of getting home on my own."

Vaguely Kate was aware of Jack wheeling his chair toward the building and rolling toward the door. She wanted to tell him good night, but didn't want to alert Frank to just how familiar she was with Jack Gamble. She was still trying to decide how to lie her way out of this.

"Let's go." Frank motioned toward the street. "You've got some explaining to do."

EIGHTEEN

"You were spying on me." Kate flung her coat over the back of the sofa and spun to face Frank.

"I wasn't spying on you," he said, closing the front door behind him.

The realization had struck her on the drive back to North Dallas from Jack Gamble's office. By the time she'd pulled into the driveway, she was furious.

"What are you, some kind of stalker?"

"Look, Kate, the fact of the matter is something bad might have happened to you if I hadn't been there."

"Something bad *did* happen. You showed up!" Grinding her teeth, she stalked over to him and planted her index finger in his chest. "And now you've got some explaining to do."

"There's nothing to explain. I was in the area. I recognized your car—"

"That's a stupid lie." Shaking her head, she stepped back and took a deep, calming breath. "You had better start talking."

He shrugged. "I was trying to keep you safe."

"Safe from what?"

"In case it's slipped your mind, someone broke into your house the other night. Remember? A frantic 911 call? Flashing red lights? Two cops coming to the rescue?"

"I remember," she snapped. "That still doesn't ex—"

"Not to mention the calls you've been getting."

"One call."

"You told me two."

"Why do you care, anyway? I haven't exactly been nice to you since we've been working—"

Dread rolled slowly over her as realization dawned. And suddenly she *knew* why he'd been there. "Mike Shelley put you up to this."

Frank said nothing.

"That son of a bitch." She couldn't believe it. "Of all the underhanded, ineffectual, unprofessional—"

"He was concerned about your safety and, frankly, so was I."

Kate threw up her hands. "I don't believe this!"

"Calm down."

"Calm down? How can you tell me to calm down when I just found out my boss and one of my staff are spying on me?"

"I wasn't spying on you, damn it. I was keeping you under surveillance in case some pissed-off ex-con tried to get to you."

That stopped her, but only for an instant. Kate didn't like having her privacy invaded. She didn't like her boss going behind her back. She sure as hell didn't relish the idea of Frank Matrone finding out why Jack Gamble was working for her.

She stared at him, aware that her pulse was pounding, that she was angry and troubled and feeling so edgy she thought she might just crawl right out of her skin. "Mike has no right, and neither do you."

"He doesn't want you hurt, damn it." His jaw flexed. "Neither do I."

Kate blinked, not knowing what to say, feeling as if he'd just sucker-punched her. "Who made the decision that I should be followed?"

Frank shifted his weight from one foot to the other. "Kate, he only had your best interest in mind."

"Did it cross either of your minds that maybe I should have been included in the discussion?"

"If I hadn't stepped in when I did, who knows what those two clowns would have done. If you'd stop being angry and think about that for a moment, you might realize it was a good thing I was there."

"That was random, Frank. Those two losers are not ex-cons. They have nothing to do with any of my cases."

"You could have been hurt."

"I could get hurt walking across the street tomorrow."

Frank stared at her for so long, she wanted to fidget. The anger was starting to wear off and she was getting the uneasy feeling that he knew more about her than he was letting on. That maybe he knew what had happened eleven years ago. That Mike knew. That maybe they felt sorry for her. That they knew about the deep, dark secret she'd never told a soul.

"How long have you been spying on me?" she asked when she could find her voice.

"Kate . . ."

"How long, damn it!"

"Less than a week."

She shook her head. "You son of a bitch."

"Maybe you ought to talk to Mike about this."

"Don't worry. I will."

Frank sighed. "What were you doing in that part of town, anyway?"

"That's none of your business."

"If either of those two goons had been armed, one or both of us could be lying on a slab at the morgue about now. I'd say that makes it my business."

But Kate was one step ahead of him. She'd formulated her lie on the drive back to her house. "I was following up on an old case. A *closed* case. The grand jury didn't indict. I thought the guy was guilty. I wanted to follow up, so I hired a private detective to look into a few things."

It was a good lie as far as lies went. She knew Jack Gamble well enough to know that if Frank called him to check up on her, he would never divulge information about a client. She hoped this would be the end of it and Frank would let it go.

"Why didn't you use one of your investigators?"

"Because I have budget constraints."

He was looking at her as if he wasn't buying it. "What case?"

"That's none of your business."

"Mike is going to want to know about what happened tonight."

The thought of her boss finding out about Jack Gamble filled her with dread. Like Frank, Mike would have questions. Questions she could not answer. "This has nothing to do with the DA's office. You have no reason to tell him."

"You just said this was about an old case."

"A case I'm looking into on my own time and on my own dime."

Giving a short, humorless laugh, he lowered his head and pinched the bridge of his nose. "Kate, you're putting me in an awkward position."

"You put yourself in an awkward position."

She jumped when the phone rang, and she was keenly aware that Frank had raised his head, that he was watching her. Even though she'd had her number changed, she suddenly didn't want to answer the phone. Nobody called her this late in the evening.

The phone rang again.

"Aren't you going to get it?" Frank asked.

"They'll call back if it's important. I'd like to finish our conversation so you can leave."

"Do you always get calls this late?"

"It's probably my mother. She always calls around bedtime." She glanced at the phone, then back at him. "I think you'd better go."

He didn't budge. "I think you ought to answer that."

The answering machine clicked on. Never taking her eyes from his, Kate stalked toward the front door, opened it. "We can finish this tomorrow."

But Frank's attention was on the phone.

"You've reached 555-8933," came her voice from the answering machine. "Leave a message and we'll call you back." *Click.*

"*Katie,*" came a whispered male voice. "You changed your number, you little cunt. Do you think that's going to keep me from talking to you? Think again."

Click.

Frank's gaze cut to Kate. She was standing at the door, her back ramrod straight. Her gaze was level on his and slightly defiant. To a less observant person, she might have looked stubborn and mildly annoyed. But Frank was adept at reading facial expressions and body language. He saw the tension in the rigid set of her shoulders. The way her hands tangled in front of her. The way she'd gone pale all the way to her lips.

"This is just a wild guess, but I'd venture to say that wasn't your mother."

"That's not funny."

"Neither is your lying to me." Frowning, he crossed to the door, removed her hand from the knob, and closed it. "Sit down. We need to talk."

Giving him a withering look, she strode to the living room and sank onto the sofa.

Frank held his ground at the door for a moment, not quite sure how to handle the situation. The call had clearly upset her. Cool, unshakable Kate. For the first time he considered the possibility that the stalker was someone she knew. An ex-boyfriend or acquaintance. That would explain why she was being so secretive.

Sensing he needed to tread lightly, he walked to the living room and took the chair opposite the sofa. "Look, if this is something personal—an old boyfriend or whatever—it doesn't matter." He shrugged. "I'm here, okay?"

When she looked at him, Frank thought he saw a flash of something he recognized in the depths of her eyes. An emotion he saw in his own eyes when he looked into the mirror. Pain. Self-reproach. The remnants of old wounds that hadn't healed. That may never heal. And for the first time since he'd known her, he wondered if Kate Megason was keeping secrets. He wondered if those secrets had something to do with her visit to a private detective by the name of Jack Gamble.

"Thank you," she said after a moment.

"Do you know who it is?"

"I'll deal with it."

"Is this related to one of your past cases?"

"No."

"Do you feel as if you're in danger?"

"No."

Frank didn't believe her, and he didn't want to leave. He had a bad feeling about this. Kate was too levelheaded to put up with this kind of nonsense from some ex-boyfriend. So why wouldn't she talk to him?

"Will you do me a favor?" he asked after a moment.

She gave a minute nod.

"If you get into trouble, will you call me? Any time. Day or night. No questions asked. Okay?"

She closed her eyes briefly. It was a small reaction, but one that spoke volumes. "Okay."

Giving her shoulder a final squeeze, he walked to the door and let himself out.

Tuesday, February 7, 12:59 a.m.

It was going to be a bad night.

Frank had had a lot of those in the last year. Nights when he was hurting so badly he wished the doctors had taken his leg when they'd had the chance.

His concern for Kate added a cruel twist to the old pain. He'd told her to call him. A lot of help he was going to be when he was stoned out of his mind on painkillers.

But his leg was hurting like a son of a bitch. It had been giving him problems all day. When he'd arrived home and stepped out of his jeans and saw the swelling and discoloration around the old scars, he knew that in another hour he'd be mindless with pain.

"Damn it," he muttered.

Wearing only his boxer shorts, he went to the medicine cabinet and pulled out the brown prescription bottle of OxyContin.

Take one tablet every twelve hours.

"Yeah, right," he said and downed two with a full glass of water.

He'd wanted to keep a clear head in case Kate needed him. In case she called. Like that was going to happen.

But there was no way he was going to risk a repeat performance of the other night. Once the pain grabbed hold, the cycle was impossible to break. He had no desire to spend the next twelve hours writhing in pain.

After grabbing an ice pack from the refrigerator, he limped to the study, went directly to his desk and flipped on the computer. He elevated the leg on a padded stool and set the ice pack against the hot flesh, hoping it would hold him over until the painkillers kicked in.

He'd been thinking about Kate all evening. He wasn't sure exactly what was going on with her, but his cop's suspicions had been thoroughly roused. Why the hell was she hanging out with some shady private detective in South Dallas? If she was seeing him about an old case, why was she being so secretive? And why had she been so reluctant to admit she'd been receiving prank calls? What was she hiding?

Picking up the phone, he dialed Rick Slater's cell phone from memory. The other man picked up on the second ring.

"How's the graveyard shift treating you?" Frank asked.

"Dandy if I was a freaking vampire. What's up?"

"I was wondering if you could plug a couple of names into the computer and see what comes back."

"This official or what?"

"Unofficial."

"Jesus, Matrone. Everything's always frickin' unofficial with you." The other man sighed. "What names?"

"Kate Megason. Jack Gamble."

A taut silence ensued, then Rick swore. "What the hell are you doing running a goddamn ADA's name through the computer, bro?"

"Mike Shelley asked me to keep an eye on her."

"Yeah? So why aren't you using his computer?"

Normally Frank wouldn't have revealed any more than he had to, but this was one of those times when the truth was better than any lie he could have made up. "Red tape," he said and paused. "Some joker's stalking her and she doesn't want to talk about it."

"Stalker, huh?" Rick made a sound of indecision. "What do you want to know about her?"

"Just plug her in. See if anything pops."

"What about the other name?"

"Jack Gamble. He's a private dick here in Dallas."

"Name sounds familiar."

"He used to be a cop."

"You're going to owe me for this."

"I already owe you."

"You're going to owe me double, then."

"Just run the names for me, okay? Let me know what you come up with."

Frank disconnected. His computer had booted so he launched his Internet browser and pulled up a search engine. Aware that the drugs were beginning to fuzz his brain, he typed in Kate's name and hit Enter.

The search returned ten results. Frank clicked on the first one and began to read. It was a story from the Lifestyle section of the *Dallas Morning News:* "Dallas County ADA Wins First Case. The First of Many to Come, Legal Eagle Promises." The story was mostly fluff, but there was a color photo of Kate, and for an instant Frank couldn't take his eyes off it. Holding a fluted glass, she was smiling at the tall woman standing next to her. Kate looked lovely and elegant in a long blue gown. Frank had seen enough of her through her bedroom window to know the dress didn't do her justice.

The photo had been taken at a charity ball sponsored by her mother, Isobel Megason, to raise money for a local women's shelter. Frank skimmed the article, picking up several unimportant facts he hadn't known about Kate. She and her family, Peter and Isobel, were originally from Houston, where her father had been an investment banker at a Fortune 100 company. She'd never been married. Wasn't looking for a husband. She liked to cook and ski.

"So what makes you tick?" Frank said aloud.

And he clicked on the next link.

NINETEEN

Kate spent the night tossing and turning, her mind grinding with everything that had happened the night before. By the time five A.M. rolled around, she'd given up on the notion of sleep and got up to make coffee.

But two cups of coffee did little to clear her head. Normally, she would have slipped into her sneakers and sweats and gone for a long, brisk run. This morning, she didn't—and she hated the reason why. As much as she didn't want to admit it, it was fear keeping her inside. Kate had sworn she would never let it get the best of her. It was one of the reasons she'd become an ADA. One of the reasons she carried a concealed weapon. But here she was, hiding in her house like some scared little rabbit, afraid to come out of its hole.

Was she going to let some low-life son of a bitch do that to her?

"No, damn it," she muttered.

After slipping into her sweats and sneakers, she zipped her cell phone into her pocket and let herself out through the front door.

The air was moisture laden and so cold she could see her breath. The neighborhood was quiet at this hour. Winter fog swirled within the pre-morning shadows of the woods that ran thick along both sides of the street.

After some light stretching, Kate set off at a slow pace, wondering if she was still in good enough shape to make it to the bridge at Mustang Creek. She waved at her neighbor, Mrs. Beck, as she jogged past her driveway. The retiree waved back as she picked up her copy of the *Dallas Morning News*. "Get some exercise for me, too, Kate!" she yelled.

Laughing, Kate picked up speed and entered the shadows of the woods at a brisk pace. The road was narrow, the asphalt glossy from the drizzle. The trees arced overhead like gnarled fingers, giving the road the feel of a cave. Kate's footfalls echoed off of the trees. She could hear her breaths coming quickly now. Her hands were cold, but her muscles were warm. Her blood was beginning to pump. She felt good and was glad she'd made herself do this.

She passed by a driveway and mailbox at a fast clip. Through the trees she could see the lights of her neighbor's house. The Kimberman family, if she wasn't mistaken. She turned right at the stop sign and picked up her pace. Her arms were pumping. She'd found a good rhythm. She could see the bridge ahead. Deep breaths. Longer stride. Focus, focus, focus . . .

The traffic from Northwest Highway two blocks away was a distant hiss. Her lungs were beginning to burn, but she was going to make the bridge.

Lights flickered off the wet trunk of a live oak to her right. Veering toward the shoulder, she tossed a quick look behind her. She saw headlights. A glimpse of a black hood. Tinted windshield. The car was a little too close.

"Go around, Einstein," she panted.

Even though her sneakers were reflective and her windbreaker was yellow, Kate knew from experience that it was difficult to see pedestrians at this hour, so she veered onto the gravel shoulder and kept running. The bridge was just ahead. She was getting winded. Legs still felt good. Fifty yards to go.

Behind her, the car's engine revved. Too loud. Too close.

Kate glanced over her shoulder in time to see the car heading straight for her. Engine roaring. Drizzle flying in the white glare of the headlights. Adrenaline cut through her like a blade. A dozen thoughts descended at once, and in that instant Kate knew the car wasn't going to stop.

Arms outstretched, she leapt into an all-out run and headed for the ditch. In her peripheral vision she saw one of the tires drop off the asphalt and edge closer. Rubber skidded over gravel. Then it was as if a giant sledgehammer slammed into her hip. A scream tore from her throat. She saw her feet leave the ground. Then she was in the air, brown grass and gravel a blur beneath her.

Her elbow slammed into the windshield. Pain streaked up her arm all the way to her shoulder. The impact sent her into a cartwheel. Her sneaker glanced off the hood. And then she was tumbling end over end.

Kate landed hard in gravel. The breath left her lungs in a rush that was part groan, part scream. Vaguely she was aware of the car speeding away. Pain in her arm. Her hip. Cold water seeping through her clothes. Rain falling on her face.

It was the fear of the car returning to finish the job that had her rolling onto her side. Groaning, she reached for the cell phone and dialed 911.

TUESDAY, FEBRUARY 7, 7:45 A.M.

Frank woke to the intermittent chirp of his cell phone. "Yeah," he muttered in a gravelly voice.

"You awake?"

"What the hell do you think?"

Rick Slater laughed outright. "I think you're damn lucky I called, bro, because you're about to be late for work."

Growling beneath his breath, Frank looked at the alarm next to his bed and cursed. "What do you want?"

"I got a hit on Megason."

"You're kidding." Frank sat up straighter. "What you got for me?"

"It's not the Megason you asked about."

"I'm listening."

"There was a police report made back in July of ninety-four by Isobel and Peter Megason."

Kate's parents, Frank thought. "What kind of report?"

"Got a hit on Harris County and Houston PD. Looks like there was a sexual assault and attempted murder of two seventeen-year-old females. Pseudonyms were used. Case is still open, so it's not a matter of public record."

Kate? he wondered.

"Jesus," Frank said, shocked.

"I couldn't get much. Because there was a sexual assault involved, no names were released. But these were brutal crimes. One of the females was critically injured. The other hospitalized in fair condition. No arrests were ever made."

Frank's mind was reeling. As an ex-cop, he knew that in the State of Texas a victim of sexual assault could be assigned a pseudonym to protect her privacy. At the age of seventeen, a teenager was considered an adult, so the protection of juvenile records would not come into play. Had Kate been one of the minors?

"Hey, my man, if one of these minors was Megabitch, you didn't get this from me. This is some heavy shit."

The thought actually made him nauseous. "That goes both ways, partner."

"Like I'm going to cut my own throat." Rick laughed. "No, thanks."

"Thanks for the info, buddy. I gotta run."

Frank disconnected. He didn't know for certain if the juvenile female Rick had mentioned was Kate, but he had a feeling it was.

Jesus.

He wondered how the stalker fit into the picture.

Turning back to his computer, he pulled up an online directory and typed in "Turtle Creek Convalescent Home" and hit Enter. The search returned four results, one being the home page of the convalescent home where Kate had visited twice in the three days he'd been watching her. The time in the bottom right corner of his monitor was 8:01 A.M. Using his cell phone, he dialed the number.

"Turtle Creek Convalescent Home," a clipped female voice answered.

"This is Burt's Flower Shop Galleria," he said, naming a prominent North Dallas florist shop. "I got a delivery for a patient by the name of Megason. Can you confirm your address for me?"

The woman rattled off the address.

"What's the first name?" he asked. "I can't read it on this form."

"Kirsten," she said.

"Kirsten M-E-G-A-S-O-N?"

"That's correct."

"Thanks." He disconnected, then sat there and stared at the phone. All the while Rick's words rang uncomfortably in his ears.

. . . there was a sexual assault and attempted murder of two seventeen-year-old females.

"Oh, Kate," he whispered. "Damn."

But his cop's mind had already jumped ahead to ponder the question of how an eleven-year-old sexual assault was related to Kate's being stalked and her association with Jack Gamble.

He jumped when his phone rang. Frowning, he snatched it up. "Matrone."

"Frank, it's Mike Shelley. I need for you to get over to Medical City Dallas ASAP."

The hairs on his nape stood up. "What happened?"

"Kate was hit by a car this morning while jogging. I just talked to her, and she thinks someone tried to kill her."

Tuesday, February 7, 8:35 a.m.

Frank had spent too much time in hospitals in the last year to hold anything but disdain for them. He'd spent six weeks in a military hospital in Germany. Two additional weeks in Ft. Hood, Texas. Once he'd been discharged from the military, he'd had months of grueling physical therapy. He swore he'd never walk into another hospital.

He hadn't counted on someone he cared about getting hurt.

She thinks someone tried to kill her.

Mike Shelley's words chilled him as he strode briskly down the hall that would take him to the emergency room. He reached the nurse's station and set his hands on the counter. "I need to see Kate Megason."

A large woman in green scrubs and a nametag that said "Karen" frowned at him, unimpressed. "You and everyone else. Take a number, hotshot."

Frank removed his badge from his wallet and shoved it at her. "Now," he said.

Without speaking, she rounded the counter and led him down the hall. Ahead, Frank saw two uniformed police officers talking to Kate's paralegal, Liz Gordon. He knew one of the cops from his years on the force, a rookie whose name he couldn't recall.

"How is she?" he asked as he approached.

Liz Gordon turned. Her face was red and tear streaked, and he got a sick feeling in the pit of his stomach. "She was hit by a car. The doctor's with her." Liz dabbed at her eyes with a tissue. "They won't let us see her."

Frank tried hard not to react, but the worry ran through him like a thin, hot wire through flesh. A dozen terrible scenarios had run rampant through his mind on the drive over, and now each and every one of them crowded into his brain like a violent mob. He looked at the young cop standing next to her. "Did you talk to her? What happened?"

"I got a couple of minutes with her. Looks like a hit-and-run," the young officer said. "Ms. Megason was jogging. Car hit her, and didn't stop."

"Anyone get a plate or a make?"

Both cops shook their heads.

He looked at Liz. "What's her condition?"

"She was awake. I heard her bitching at the doctor a few minutes ago."

"Bitching is a good sign," Frank said.

Liz choked out a laugh. "I hope she's okay."

All heads turned when the double doors down the hall swung open. A young doctor in wrinkled blue scrubs started toward them, his eyes going from Liz to Frank. "Either of you here for Kate Megason?"

Frank started toward him. "How is she?"

"She's going to be okay. She sustained a few minor lacerations. Some deep bruises. The good news is that there was no concussion and no broken bones. Her blood work looks good. We're waiting for one more X-ray to come back from radiology. If everything looks good, she can go home."

If Frank hadn't known better, he would have sworn his legs went a little weak.

"Thank God," Liz murmured.

"Can I talk to her?" Frank asked.

"We gave her a mild sedative, so she'll be a little drowsy. She'll need someone to drive her home."

Liz shot a pointed look at Frank. "Knowing Kate, she's going to want to go to the office."

"Not on my watch," he heard himself say.

"She'll bulldoze right over you if you're nice."

"I think I can handle it." He smiled, and they shared a moment of understanding.

Liz glanced at her watch, then at the doctor. "Can I see her for a sec? I've got to get back to the office."

"No more than two visitors at a time."

She headed for the double doors. Frank crossed to the two police officers and introduced himself.

"I knew I'd seen your face before," the rookie commented.

"I'm working for the DA's office now," Frank said. "Did you take the report?"

He nodded. "I was in the area when dispatch put out the 911 call, so I responded and was first on the scene."

"What did she say?"

"Car came at her from behind. She didn't see it until it was too late."

"She get a color or make? Anything?"

"She thinks it was a dark sedan with tinted windows. That's all I could get."

"Covers a lot of vehicles in the metroplex." Frank sighed. "Anyone at the scene check for tire treads?"

"We sent an accident team. They'll write it up, put it in the report."

"Can I get a copy of the report when it's finished?"

"This got something to do with a case, or what?"

Frank handed him one of his business cards. "Just routine."

"I'll fax it over as soon as it's written."

Frank watched the two cops walk away. He thought about Kate and something uncomfortable niggled at the back of his neck.

Ms. Megason was out jogging this morning, and the guy didn't stop.

In the city of Dallas, most hit-and-run accidents were alcohol related. Most occurred on major thoroughfares in the evening or late at night. Kate lived in a quiet residential area. Most of the streets were either cul-de-sacs or dead ends; there wasn't much through traffic. Unless the driver lived in the area, it was unlikely he'd been passing through.

Unless Kate had been targeted and run down on purpose.

It wasn't the first time the thought had forced its way into his mind. As much as Frank hated the idea, he was going to have to consider it.

Cursing under his breath, he left the hall and pushed through the double doors that took him into the emergency room holding area. Even this early in the day, the ER was a madhouse. There were a dozen curtained bays and all of them were occupied. A toddler clinging to his mother wailed as she tried to get him onto a gurney for a doctor who barely looked old enough to shave. A nurse in yellow scrubs spoke quietly to a young woman in a wheelchair. A technician jogged through the aisle, a clipboard in one hand and a tray in the other.

Frank spotted Kate at the end of the row and felt a hard tug in the center of his chest. She was wearing a hospital gown and sitting on a gurney with her legs dangling over the side. Even from across the room, he could see that both knees were badly abraded. A bandage the size of Texas covered her left elbow.

Liz was standing next to the gurney, her purse draped over her shoulder. She was talking animatedly. Relief went through him when he saw Kate smile. Damn, even drugged and skinned up she looked sexy as hell.

Her smile fell when she spotted him. Her eyes were dark against her pale complexion, and for a moment she looked vulnerable.

"I'm okay," she said testily.

Frank stopped a foot away from her and let his gaze linger on her knees. "Yeah, the bloody knees are a dead giveaway."

Unaware of the tension running through him, Liz leaned forward and gave Kate a hug. "I've got to get back to the office, kiddo. When I heard what happened, I just ran out and left my phone ringing off the hook."

"I'll be in later," Kate said.

Liz shot Frank a pointed look. "I told you."

Kate's eyes narrowed, going from Liz to Frank. "Told you what?"

She shook her head at Kate. "The doctor said you should go home and get some rest."

"I have back-to-back meetings all after—"

"Reschedule her meetings," Frank said to Liz.

"I'll get right on it," Liz said.

"Don't talk about me as if I wasn't sitting here," Kate said.

"I gotta run, honey. If you need anything, just let me know. I'll be at the office late. I can bring anything you need by your house later, okay?"

"Liz—"

Liz had already turned to Frank. Reaching out, she squeezed his arm. "Thanks for taking her home."

"My pleasure."

"Taking me home?" Kate looked a little alarmed.

Frank felt that same alarm running through him, but it had nothing to do with hit-and-run drivers and everything to do with the way she looked sitting on that gurney wearing nothing but a wrinkled hospital gown and a frown.

Smiling, Liz waved. "Be safe," she said and pushed through the double doors.

"Traitor," Kate muttered.

Frank turned his attention back to Kate. She looked calm and relaxed for a woman who'd been the victim of a hit-and-run. Then he remembered the doctor telling him she'd been sedated.

"Do you feel up to answering a few questions?" he asked.

"I just answered a bunch of questions for the police."

"I'd like to hear what happened while it's still fresh in your mind."

For an instant she looked like she was going to argue. Then she sighed as if in resignation and nodded.

"You always run in the rain?"

"I don't let weather stop me."

"What time did you leave the house?"

"About six-thirty or so. I usually do a couple of miles. I like to run down to the bridge that spans Mustang Creek."

As she spoke, he took a quick visual inventory of her injuries. Skinned knees. Bandage on her elbow. Even her knuckles were abraded. One of her fingernails had been broken to the quick. A powerful wave of male protectiveness washed over him when he thought about all the other places beneath that gown that might be skinned or bruised or both.

"How far did you get?"

"Almost to the bridge. I was in the zone, I guess. Not paying attention to what was going on around me. I heard the vehicle. I moved over to let him pass. The next thing I knew the car was right on top of me. I heard the motor rev. By the time I turned to look, it was too late."

"The motor revved?"

She nodded.

"Did you notice any details about the car? Make? Model? Plate number?"

"All I saw were headlights. It happened fast."

"Did the driver have his high beams on?"

Her brows snapped together, then her gaze went to his. "I think they were."

"Then what happened?"

"At first I thought he was going to pass me. You know, that he'd just gotten too close. I moved onto the shoulder. And the next thing I know the car is so close I could feel the heat coming off the engine." In an unconscious protective gesture, she wrapped her arms around herself. "Bumper hit my left hip. The impact sent me airborne."

A shudder moved through her. He wasn't sure if it was his hormones flaring or his need to protect, but the urge to touch her was powerful. But Frank kept his hands to himself.

"Did he stop? Did you hear him apply brakes? Did you hear the tires lock up in the gravel? Anything like that?"

Her eyes were filled with knowledge when they met his. "No."

Frank didn't like the way this was shaping up. Even a driver who was legally drunk would usually attempt to stop, even if it were only for a few seconds before realizing what he'd done and fleeing the scene. That left only one scenario: Whoever had struck her had done it on purpose.

The thought sent a wave of fury rolling through him. He wondered if she'd drawn the same conclusion. If she would have been so forthcoming without the tongue-loosening effect of the sedative.

"Do you think it was an accident?" he asked.

Her eyes were liquid and very dark when she raised them to his. "A drunk driver, maybe."

Frank didn't buy that for a second. He didn't think she did, either. He couldn't shake the feeling that she wasn't telling him the whole story. The only question that remained was why.

TWENTY

By the time the X ray arrived from radiology, Kate was climbing out of her skin. She didn't like hospitals. Didn't like being poked and prodded. She sure as hell didn't like the idea of some son of a bitch trying to run her down.

One look at Frank, and she knew he was feeling protective. Kate wasn't sure how she was going to handle that. The man was sticking to her like glue.

The doctor gave her a clean bill of health and within minutes they were in Frank's truck and on the way to her house. The doctor had prescribed some mild painkillers, which was a good thing because by the time they pulled into the driveway, every bruise and scrape had come to life with a vengeance.

"Stay put," Frank said as he parked in the driveway. "I'll get the door."

Kate reached for the handle anyway. She was halfway off the seat by the time she realized the doctor hadn't been exaggerating when he'd told her she was going to be hurting. Every muscle in her body felt as if it had been run over by a steamroller.

"I've got you." Putting his hands beneath her arms, Frank eased her to the ground.

"I can do it."

"Yeah, I can tell by the way you're groaning."

"I'm not groaning, damn it."

"Whatever you say." He closed the door and they started for the house.

She pulled mail from the mailbox while he took her keys and unlocked the front door. She walked into the living room and tossed the mail on the coffee table, absurdly happy to be home. She'd been planning on getting rid of Frank, grabbing a quick shower, then heading to the office. But as she crossed to the dining room, her head began to spin and she realized it was going to take a lot more than a shower to get her to the office.

Gingerly she walked to the kitchen, aware that Frank was behind her, watching her. She could hear the prescription bag crackling. Trying to appear unaffected, she pulled a glass from the cupboard and filled it with cold water from the refrigerator. "Thanks for driving me home," she said, keeping a light tone.

"No problem," he said.

Turning to face him, she feigned a yawn. "I think I can take it from here."

One side of his mouth curved. "If I didn't know better, I'd think you were trying to get rid of me."

"I like you, Matrone. Why would I try to get rid of you?"

"Because I'm not going to let you go to the office. Because I'm going to ask you questions about what happened. Because I'm wondering why someone tried to kill you."

Kate had been putting off thinking about that last part. But she knew that at some point she was going to have to face it.

"Why don't you take your shower and I'll whip up some lunch? Then you can answer some questions, crawl into bed, and call it a day."

She blinked at him, not sure if she was annoyed or charmed by his offer. "I'm not hungry."

"You can't take these on an empty stomach." He set the prescription bag on the counter. "Judging from the way you're moving, you need them."

Kate had thought she was doing a pretty good job of hiding the pain, but she was quickly realizing Frank was more observant than she'd given him credit for.

"We need to talk about what happened."

He was watching her closely. Too closely. His scrutiny was beginning to annoy her.

"I already told you everything," she said. "It was a hit-and-run. A drunk driver more than likely. I was at the wrong place at the wrong time." But the explanations sounded lame even to her.

"Kate, has it crossed your mind that maybe this wasn't an accident?"

"Of course I've considered that," she said. "I'm aware of the possibility that I've made some enemies over the years. But I'm diligent about reading the latest prisoner-release reports from TDOJ, and I know there's no one I sent to prison who's been recently released."

"Those reports don't take into consideration the prisoner's pissed-off family members or spouses."

"I think you're jumping to conclusions."

"I can't tell if it's those painkillers making you dense or if you're so deep into denial you don't see what could be happening."

"What I see is an ex-cop overreacting to a hit-and-run accident, reading all sorts of sinister conspiracies into it."

Lowering his head, Frank pinched the bridge of his nose. "They say doctors make the worst patients." He raised his head and scowled at her. "From what I'm seeing here prosecutors make pretty bad victims."

Not liking the way he used the word *victim,* Kate turned away and started toward the living room. For an uncertain instant she stood there, looking around, desperately needing something to do, anything to keep this man from digging into something she did not want uncovered.

"This is the third incident inside two weeks," came his voice from behind her. "For God's sake, you're a prosecutor. You know better than to let things go unresolved."

She turned to face him. "What do you want from me?"

"The truth would be a good start."

"I haven't lied to you."

"Lying by omission. You're keeping something from me."

"I don't know what you want me to say."

"Kate." His voice softened. "I'm not the enemy."

He reached for her arm, but she stepped back. She tried hard not to limp as she strode to the coffee table and picked up the stack of mail. Ignoring Frank as best she could, she carried the mail into the kitchen. Junk mail went into the trash. Bills onto the built-in desk next to the refrigerator, along with an advertisement she wanted to look at later. She liked everything in its place. She was in the process of tossing several pieces into the trash when the plain white envelope caught her attention. There was no return address. Not even a postage stamp.

Curious, she carried the unmarked letter to the bar. The envelope wasn't sealed. She lifted the flap, pulled out the single sheet of paper, unfolded it and began to read.

I could have had you this morning. Just like before, I could have had you on the ground, helpless and whimpering and begging me to stop. Do you remember, Katie? Do you wake up in the middle of night and think of me? Am I in your dreams? Your nightmares? I think of you all the time, sweet Katie. Even after all this time, I long for you. I ache for you. Get ready, because I'm coming for you.

Shock was a violent punch to the solar plexus. For several seconds she couldn't catch her breath. Kate stared at the ominous words, disbelief and dread climbing up her throat to fill her mouth with bile. Vaguely she was aware of the paper shaking in her hands. Of her heart pounding out of control. Of Frank watching her with a quiet intensity that made her want to turn tail and run.

"What is it?"

His voice came to her as if from a great distance. Folding the note, willing her hands to still, Kate tucked it back into the envelope without meeting his gaze. "Nothing."

"Nothing, huh?"

She raised her gaze to his. She'd almost convinced herself

he was going to let this slide. But Frank Matrone didn't let things slide. One look into his eyes and she knew he was going to force open a door she wanted to keep locked down tight.

"You're sheet white." His gaze flicked to the note, then back to her.

"I'm just . . . shaken up from this morning. That's all."

"You're a hell of a lot more than shaken up."

Making a sound of annoyance in an effort to hide the hard churn of emotion, she turned away. "I'm going to take a shower."

"Give me the note."

"No." She started for the hall.

"Kate, damn it, if someone is stalking you . . ." His voice trailed. "You're too smart to ignore this."

That stopped her. As desperately as she didn't want to open the Pandora's box of her past, Kate knew he was right. She could no longer ignore this. She could not sweep it under the rug and hope it would go away. But there was a very large part of her that simply couldn't bear the thought of bringing what had happened to her and Kirsten eleven years ago back into her life.

For a full minute she stood with her back to him. She could feel herself shaking, both inside and out. She could feel Frank's eyes on her, but she didn't turn to face him.

"Let me see the letter," he said.

When she didn't move, he crossed to her. Without speaking, he turned her to him. His face was solemn when he opened her fingers and took the envelope. Kate could feel her emotions burgeoning as he opened it and began to read. For the first time in a long time she wanted to crumple. She wanted to curl into a ball and hide. Shame and outrage and a thousand other feelings she couldn't begin to name overwhelmed her, like a tidal wave swamping a tiny island.

Kate had always considered herself an enlightened and educated woman. She dealt with all types of crimes on a daily basis. She *knew* what had happened to her and Kirsten was not her fault.

But nothing would ever erase the shame. The scars. Nothing would ever ease the terrible weight of guilt for what had happened to her sister.

Hugging herself, she walked to the bar, pulled out a stool, and climbed onto it. Closing her eyes, she lowered her face into her hands and tried not to cry.

TUESDAY, FEBRUARY 7, 11:49 A.M.

Frank had always possessed a sixth sense when it came to lies. He'd known for quite some time that Kate was hiding something. That she was in trouble and needed help. But he'd never expected this.

He stared at the crude lettering, his mind reeling, his heart breaking for her. Simultaneously something primal and male stirred violently inside him at the thought of someone hurting her.

He found her sitting at the bar with her face in her hands. She looked small and vulnerable and somehow broken. The urge to go to her, draw her into his arms, and tell her he was going to make everything all right was strong. But Frank was fresh out of promises. He knew firsthand that sometimes bad things happened to good people. He knew that sometimes the best they could hope for was that they could learn to live with it.

"How many letters have you received?" he asked.

For a moment he thought she wouldn't answer. Then she raised her head. Her spine stiffened, and she looked at him with a directness that had him admiring her strength when he knew her reserves had long since worn thin.

"That one makes two," she said.

"I need to see the first one."

Her eyes skittered away.

He waited.

After a moment she slid from the stool and left the kitchen. He wanted to follow her, but sensed her need for space and so he gave it to her. She crossed through the living room and into the den. A moment later she reappeared with a small plastic storage container in her hand.

She set it on the bar and removed the lid. Inside, Frank saw a legal pad where she'd jotted notes. A folded piece of paper. A blue bandanna.

"I received the first phone call on January twenty-seventh."

"How many calls have you received?"

"Three." She picked up the legal pad. "I started a time line and documented everything."

"Good job."

Her smile was wry. "You can take the lawyer out of the courtroom, but you can't take the lawyer out of the girl."

Frank smiled, but it felt uncomfortable on his face as he reached for the pad. Her handwriting was neat and precise. She'd used black pen with a fine tip. She'd logged dates and times and used quotation marks to indicate what the caller had said. "Have you handled these items much?" he asked. "We might be able to raise some latents."

"I don't want the police involved."

"You can't handle this on your own."

"I mean it, Frank. I don't want this made public."

"Kate, how many times have you seen people refuse to ask for help when they should have? How many times have you seen the results?"

"I know how things work," she snapped. "But damn it, Frank, we're talking about . . ." She couldn't finish the sentence.

"We're talking about your personal safety."

"We're talking about a nightmare I don't want dredged up, damn it!"

Frank understood, as much as he could, anyway. He sympathized. But there was no way he was going to be able to honor her request to keep this quiet and still keep her safe.

Needing time to decide how to proceed, he looked down at the notebook. "It says here that you received the second note the same night you made the 911 call."

"The stalker left the note in the fuse box in the garage."

"You didn't tell the police?"

"I didn't want anyone to see the note."

Using the pen to avoid smudging any potential latent prints or DNA evidence, Frank turned over the note and read.

I could have had you tonight the same way I had you eleven years ago. Are you still as sweet as you were when you were seventeen, Katie? Do you smell the same? Would you still cry out in pain? Or have you come to like it? I can't wait to find out. . . .

Jesus.

Frank looked at the last item in the plastic box. A blue bandanna. The kind he used to put around his neck when he was a kid playing cowboys and Indians. But the bandanna looked somehow ominous lying in that box. Knowing what had happened to Kate, he didn't want to ask about its significance. He knew he wasn't going to like the answer he got.

"What about the bandanna?"

When she didn't answer, he looked at her and was taken aback by the paleness of her complexion. He'd seen corpses with more color. She was staring at the bandanna. He was standing a couple of feet from her, but it was close enough for him to see that she was shaking. That her lips were dry. Her eyes liquid. And it was suddenly painfully clear that she was holding it together by a tattered thread.

"I can't talk about this." Abruptly she reached for the storage container and snapped on the lid, as if closing the box would keep the items inside from hurting her.

"Kate . . ."

Before he could finish, she turned and walked to the living room. Frank let her go. He would give her a few minutes to pull herself together. But he couldn't let this go.

He found a glass in the cupboard and filled it with water from the tap, then took it to the living room. Kate was sitting on the sofa with her legs pulled up, hugging a pillow to her, the way a frightened child might hold a favorite stuffed animal.

Without speaking he handed her the glass of water. "This isn't going to go away," he said. "We've got to deal with it."

Her eyes were dark and knowing and filled with dread when she took it. "I hate this."

"So do I." Grimacing, he took the chair across from the sofa. "Kate, you need to talk to me. Tell me everything that's happened."

When she said nothing, he sighed. "How am I supposed to help you if you won't talk to me?"

Lowering her head, she pinched the bridge of her nose and closed her eyes.

"Kate, you're a prosecutor. You've spent the last two years putting some very bad people in prison. You know what guys like that are capable of."

She raised her head and glared at him. "This has nothing to do with my job."

"How can you be sure? Maybe that's what he wants you to think."

"Read the note. This is about . . . the past."

Frank waited, but his patience was stretched taut. After a moment, he said, "I know what happened eleven years ago."

Myriad emotions flashed in her eyes in an instant. Anger. Pain. Outrage. Shame. But it was shock that stood in the forefront. Her neck and shoulders went rigid. Her hands curled into the pillow. Her nostrils flared, an animal scenting danger. "You can't."

The sharp pang of sympathy went all the way to his bones. "I do," he said. "I'm sorry."

"How did you find out?"

"I was a cop for twelve years."

"That doesn't give you the right to use those resources to dig into my past."

Frank leaned back in the chair and tried to decide how to approach this. He'd broken some rules by running her name through the computer. As far as he was concerned he'd had a good reason. "Kate, someone tried to kill you this morning."

"I'm aware of what happened this morning," she snapped with sudden anger.

"We need to find this bastard who's stalking you," Frank said. "We need to stop him. And in the interim we need to keep you safe."

She looked away. Stubborn. Beautiful. Hurting in a way no human being should ever have to hurt. "I don't want Mike to know about this," she said.

"I know where you're coming from, but—"

"No," she snapped. "You don't know where I'm coming from."

"The police will need to see these notes."

"Frank, damn it, I don't want that nightmare dredged up. For God's sake, I'm a prosecutor. When people look at me, I don't want them to see a victim."

She tossed the word at him like a dirty word. Frank didn't have any platitudes, so he let it go and said what had to be said. "Kate, your being a prosecutor is precisely the reason why we've got to get to the bottom of this. Intimidating a prosecutor in any way, shape, or form threatens our entire criminal justice system. We can't sweep this under the rug because you don't want to deal with it."

"This is not about my job."

Frank sighed, feeling as if he'd stepped into very deep water. "Why don't we start by getting the facts on the table. Once we get the facts laid out, we can decide how to handle it later, okay?"

After a moment she raised her head. When her eyes met his they were dry and she was once again in control of her emotions. "I think this is about what happened eleven years ago. The notes appear to be from one of the perpetrators. Whether or not that's really the case, I don't know."

"Someone could have done some digging, found out what happened. Knowing it might be a sensitive issue for you, they could be trying to use it to intimidate you."

"Why?"

"Let's face it, Kate. Not everyone agrees with capital punishment."

"Maybe," she conceded. "But I think it's a weak angle."

But Frank could feel his mind shifting into cop mode. "Eleven years ago . . . was there an arrest made?"

She shook her head.

"Was there ever a suspect?"

"No."

"What about the voice on the phone? Could it be the same guy?"

"I don't know. The voice is raspy, as if he's trying to disguise it." She bit her lip. "I wasn't struck with a sense of familiarity."

"Has he ever asked for money?"

"No."

"That night eleven years ago . . . Was it one man?"

She closed her eyes briefly, then looked down at the pillow she was hugging against her and relaxed her grip on it. "Two. I was able to give the police a description of both men, but they were never able to come up with a suspect."

He thought about that for a moment, and for the first time he began to understand what drove her. "So the two men got away."

"Scott-free."

Something dark and uncomfortable niggled at the back of his brain. "How does Jack Gamble play into this?"

She had a good poker face, but it wasn't good enough to hide the lie from him. "I told you. Jack Gamble is looking into another case. My relationship with him is totally unrelated to any of this."

Frank wanted to believe her, but he didn't. "I'll double check with the TDOC," Frank said, referring to the alert sent out by the Texas Department of Corrections to all state law enforcement agencies as well as city, state, and county courts notifying the courts and law enforcement when a convicted felon was released from prison.

Kate nodded. "I've already checked the alerts, but maybe someone fell through the cracks."

"Anyone else you can think of who might want to hurt you?" Frank asked. "Any enemies? Neighbors? Disgruntled friends? Ex-boyfriends?"

Kate shook her head. "My life pretty much revolves around work. I know my neighbors well enough to say hello, and that's about it."

"What about family?"

A shadow he couldn't quite read passed over her expression. "There's just my sister, Kirsten, and my parents."

"Do you get along with them?"

"Kirsten suffered permanent brain damage eleven years ago."

Jesus. "I'm sorry," he said.

"My parents never really recovered. Nobody was the same afterward."

Frank knew firsthand how violence could destroy lives. How, like a greedy hand, it could reach out and snatch away happiness and the grand illusion of safety.

"Life, Inc., usually starts making noise about the time the DA's office announces it's going to try a capital case. They've been known to get creative in their tactics."

"What could they possibly hope to gain?"

"Maybe they think if you're distracted you'll lose the case."

"Lawrence Bertrand may be a zealot, but he's a pragmatist. If he wants something to happen, he'll take a more direct route."

Bertrand was the principal of Life, Inc., an anti-death penalty group based in Dallas. He was outspoken and charismatic and thrived on visibility. He loved media attention and played even the most experienced journalists like a finely tuned violin.

"Maybe I ought to pay him a friendly visit," Frank said.

"It probably couldn't hurt at this juncture."

He smiled. "At last we agree on something."

"Probably won't last." She gave him a small smile, and then a breath shuddered out of her. "So now you know my deep, dark secret."

He wasn't expecting her to say that, and for a moment he didn't know how to respond. "We all have secrets."

Her gaze met his. "What are yours?"

Frank didn't answer.

"Off limits?" she asked.

"For too many reasons to count."

"It's not easy having the tables turned, is it?"

"I'm just afraid if you know all my secrets, you'll get bored with me."

She didn't smile. "Or maybe you're like me and you'd rather fight crime than be a victim of it."

"You're not a victim." He held her gaze, but it wasn't easy because he was thinking about Gittel. A lovely young woman who'd been so vital, some days he still couldn't quite believe she was gone. A woman who'd felt passionately about her cause. A cause that, he believed, had ultimately killed her. He stared at Kate, seeing the determination in her eyes, and for the first time saw the parallel between the two women. A parallel that made him feel a little sick . . .

"I want to put a tap on your phone," he said. "Maybe a trace."

"No."

"Why not?"

"Because there are procedures and red tape, and I do not want the DA's office involved."

"Sometimes what we want and what we need are two different things."

"If the situation escalates, we'll deal with it then."

"The situation has already escalated," he said sharply. "Someone tried to kill you this morning, damn it. Next time the son of a bitch might succeed. At the very least, you need protection."

Her expression turned fierce. "I do not want Mike Shelley to know about this."

"Kate, if I keep my mouth shut and something happens to you—"

"Nothing's going to happen to me." Springing to her feet, she flung the pillow at him.

Frank caught the pillow. It didn't elude him that she'd winced upon standing or that she was favoring her right leg. Damn stubborn woman.

"Goddamn it, Kate. Can't you see that you're in danger?"

She spun, crossed to him, and got in his face. "Don't do this to me, Frank. I mean it. I don't want what happened eleven years ago dredged up."

Frank stared at her, wishing he could abide by her wishes, knowing he couldn't. He knew if he went to Shelley, it would cost him something precious. Maybe even the tentative friendship he and Kate had forged. But what was the alternative?

The image of Gittel lying motionless and bloody on the cobblestone flashed in his mind's eye. He could not—would not—let the same thing happen to Kate.

TWENTY-ONE

One look at Mike Shelley's expression and Kate knew why she'd been summoned to his office. She steeled herself against the hot flash of fury that ran the length of her body. This was no time for emotion, either hot or cold. Her credibility was on the line, and no matter what the cost, she would walk out of here with it intact.

Damn Frank Matrone.

She couldn't believe he'd done the one thing she'd asked him not to. Even after she'd opened up and told him the truth, he'd disregarded her wishes and gone to her boss without a single thought as to how it would affect her personally or professionally.

The son of a bitch.

She knew Frank wouldn't see it that way. No, she thought darkly, Mr. Ex-cop evidently felt the need to rush in and save her.

"How are you feeling?"

Mike Shelley's voice jerked Kate from her dark reverie.

She looked across the span of polished wood desk, forced a smile, and lied through her teeth. "I feel fine."

The truth of the matter was it had taken twenty minutes in a hot shower and half a dozen ibuprofen, but she'd made it to work before eight o'clock.

"You look good."

She wanted to tell him to stop beating around the bush and get to the point, but she didn't think snapping at him would help the situation, so she held her silence.

"Do the police have any leads?" he asked.

"I talked to Detective Ruiz this morning. They were able to pick up a partial tread print, but so far it hasn't been much help."

"Let's hope they get this guy. I don't like the idea of one of my prosecutors getting mowed down."

"I don't think this has anything to do with my being a prosecutor."

Mike looked like a stomach cramp hit him. "Kate, let's cut the bullshit. You know why you're here."

"You spoke to Matrone."

"Don't blame him. He's just doing his job."

"What did he tell you?"

"He told me you're being stalked."

That wasn't what she wanted to know. What she needed to know. All she could wonder was if Frank had told her boss about the rape. The thought sent a rise of pain into her chest.

She wasn't sure how she managed, but she laughed. "He has a real knack for melodrama, doesn't he?"

"Kate, you should have come to me with this."

"I don't think a few prank phone calls warrants his talking to you about some mad stalker."

"He thinks you're in danger."

"He's overreacting."

"He's an ex-cop, Kate. I trust his judgment."

"What are you saying, Mike?" she asked, hating the defensive ring in her voice.

"I think your safety takes precedence over everything else."

"You mean over the case?"

He sighed. "I'm assigning the case to someone else."

"What?" She felt the words like a fist to the solar plexus, but she didn't let herself react. "Who?"

"Ricardo Cano. He's good."

"I'm better."

"Kate, this isn't a pissing contest."

"I can win the case, Mike."

"There's no way you can give it your all when some nutcase is stalking you."

"I can't believe you're penalizing me for something I have no control over."

"You are not being penalized."

"Threaten a prosecutor in Dallas and get a new prosecutor. That's not a good precedent."

"Kate—"

"Matrone is wrong. He's out of line."

"He made a recommendation. The decision was mine, and it wasn't an easy one to make."

A slow wave of fury rolled through her. "I don't believe this."

"You can't effectively prosecute this case and deal with a stalker at the same time."

"Stalker?" Another laugh squeezed from her throat, but it had a desperate ring to it. "Come on! I received a couple of phone calls—"

"Someone broke into your house, damn it. He's called you and left notes. For God's sake, this bastard tried to run you down in his car! That goes beyond stalking and you know it."

Frustration burned through her with such force that her hands curled into fists. Kate wanted badly to argue. The words hovered on the tip of her tongue. Cutting words that would win her no points with her boss. But she knew that to debate the issue farther would cost her precious credibility.

"I'm sorry, Kate. But until this stalker is caught, you're off the case and out of the public eye." He tapped the green expanding folder in front of him. A personnel file, she realized. *Her* file. "Do you realize you've accumulated thirty vacation days in three years? You haven't taken a single day off since you started here three years ago."

"I've had a busy caseload."

"Don't think I don't appreciate it, because I do. But I want you to take some time off." His expression softened. "I'll see about getting some off-duty officers to keep an eye on you until they catch this guy."

Alarm swept through her. "That's not necessary."

Mike raised his hands. "Don't argue, Kate. I've already got a headache and the day has barely begun."

WEDNESDAY, FEBRUARY 8, 9:33 A.M.

Kate knew better than to seek out Frank in her current frame of mind. She was dangerously angry. She could feel it pumping through her with every jagged beat of her heart. Adrenaline and negative energy pulsing through in a swift and deadly current.

I'm assigning the case to someone else.

Frank had had no right to tell Mike what she'd told him in confidence. He'd had no right to invade her privacy or interfere with her life. He'd sabotaged the biggest case of her career. She'd lowered her guard, shared something painful and private, and he'd stabbed her in the back.

Heads turned as she strode briskly down the hall toward his office, but Kate refused to let the stares or the whispers stop her. One way or another, she and Matrone were going to have this out.

She could see that the door to Frank's office was closed, but it wasn't going to keep her out. The emotions inside her were ugly. There was a small part of her that hoped she would not find him inside, because at the moment she wasn't sure what she would do when she saw him.

She twisted the knob and shoved open the door. A small ripple of shock went through her when she found Frank at his desk, the phone to his ear. His eyes were on her, and within their depths she saw knowledge and wariness and she wondered if her intent was that clear. She closed the door behind her.

"I'll call you back." Frank set the phone into its cradle and looked at her expectantly. "Kate."

"I just came from Mike Shelley's office." She barely recognized her voice. It was shaking and tight and full of emotion.

It was the voice of a woman on the edge of a very steep cliff and about to fall. "He removed me from the Bruton Ellis case."

"I know you're upset—"

"I'm more than upset, you son of a bitch. I'm furious! I trusted you and you stabbed me in the back. How could you do that?"

Looking uncomfortable, he rose and came around the desk. "I did what I thought was right to keep you safe."

"This was the biggest case of my career and you sabotaged it." She stepped toward him. "You had no right."

"Kate, you need to calm down."

In some far corner of her mind she knew he was right. She knew she was on the verge of doing something she would be sorry for later. But with her temper pumping pure adrenaline, she could no more calm down than she could slow the beat of her heart.

"Don't tell me to calm *down*." She jabbed her index finger into his chest with the last word.

Satisfaction rippled through her when she saw the quick flash of anger in his eyes. But she wanted more. She wanted him angry. She wanted him upset. She wanted him frothing-at-the-mouth furious. Just like her.

Raising his hands as if in surrender, Frank stepped back. "I did not stab you in the back."

"You betrayed a confidence."

"I did what I needed to do to keep you safe."

But Kate was beyond hearing, beyond reason. All she saw before her was a man who'd taken something precious from her. A man she'd trusted with her deepest, darkest secret only to have him use it against her.

"The things you and I discussed were *private*," she said. "I did not want Mike Shelley brought into it."

"I didn't—"

Using the heel of her right hand, Kate shoved him hard enough to send him back a step. "Don't *lie* to me. I just came from his office. He took me off the case."

Frank's jaw flexed. His eyes flicked to the door. Another wave of satisfaction went through her when she realized he wanted out of there. That he did not want to deal with her. Too bad.

"You had no right to tell him what happened to me."

"I didn't tell him about what happened in Houston."

But Kate was too angry for the words to penetrate the black veil of fury. Using her other hand she shoved him back another step.

"Cut it out," he snapped.

"Or what?" She shoved him again. "Are you going to go to Mike Shelley and tell him I'm behaving irrationally?"

"You are, damn it. If you'd just stop and think about what's happened, you'd realize I didn't have a choice."

But the rage inside her had built to unmanageable proportions. Kate was beyond listening. Beyond logic or reason. "Here's a choice for you, *Matrone.*" She slapped her palm against his chest with the last syllable of his name. "Stay away from me. Stay out of my business. And stay the hell out of my life. You got that?"

His jaw flexed. "I got it."

Kate stepped back, feeling light-headed, as if she'd just stepped off a wild carnival ride that had zapped her equilibrium. She blinked at Frank, realized she'd lost control. That she'd made a fool of herself. That she should get out of there before she did any more damage.

Squaring her shoulders, she turned and walked away without saying another word.

WEDNESDAY, FEBRUARY 8, 9:45 A.M.

Frank gave her points for not slamming the door. If he'd been in her shoes, he probably would have for the sheer satisfaction value.

He stood there for a full minute, willing his heart to slow, telling himself he hadn't done anything wrong. He could still feel where she'd jabbed his chest with her finger. He told himself he'd done the right thing by talking to Mike Shelley. But he still felt like hell.

It didn't take a rocket scientist to figure out what drove her. He knew it all boiled down to justice. Eleven years ago she had been the victim of a savage crime. All control had been taken from her. She'd been brutalized and terrorized and humiliated. It was like salt on an open wound that the culprit had never been caught. Every case she prosecuted was personal. Every case was about justice.

"Shit."

Scrubbing a hand over his jaw, Frank walked to his desk and sank into his chair and tried not to feel guilty for the way things had played out. But every time he closed his eyes, he saw Kate. She'd looked at him as if he'd thrust a bayonet into her solar plexus.

He wasn't sure how he was going to handle the situation. The only thing he knew for certain was that somehow he had to make it right.

A knock on the door drew him from his reverie. "It's open."

The door opened and Mike Shelley walked in. "I guess we fucked that up pretty good."

"I guess we did." Frank leaned back in his chair and frowned. "Where is she?"

"In her office. I told her to take the rest of the day off and cool down."

"I can't blame her for being pissed."

"Kate's a professional, Frank. Once she realizes this was done for the sake of her personal safety, she'll be all right."

"I take it you're going to have someone else watching her?"

"I got the budget okayed for a couple of off-duty officers to park outside her house and keep an eye on things for a few days."

"I think that's a good idea." He tried hard to ignore the jolt of disappointment that went through him at the thought of not seeing her on a regular basis. "You want me to stay on the Ellis case?"

Mike nodded. "Ricardo Cano's going to ask for a continuance, but we're still shooting for October. Kate's going to turn over her files and notes tomorrow."

"Good," Frank said, but he didn't mean it. There wasn't anything good about any of this. At least he could take consolation in the fact that Kate would have a couple of Dallas's finest keeping an eye on her.

TWENTY-TWO

Kate was still shaking when she parked the BMW in her driveway and shut down the engine. On the twenty-minute drive to the house, her mind had replayed the scene between her and Frank a dozen times, and each time she felt worse about the way she'd handled it. Control was power, and she'd lost any semblance of it the instant she'd marched into his office like some hotheaded intern and proceeded to make a fool of herself.

She'd learned a long time ago there was no place for emotion when it came to her job. It was those lingering emotions that troubled her now, and for the first time she realized not all of what she was feeling stemmed from losing the case.

Frank had disappointed her on so many levels she didn't know where to begin. She didn't want this to be personal, but it was. Frank had hurt her. He'd betrayed her. Kate didn't want it to matter. But it did.

In the few short days she'd known him, he'd earned her respect. He'd gained her admiration. At some point his opinion had begun to matter. She wanted to deny the rest of what was eating at her. But Kate had always believed in facing the truth, no matter how brutal. The truth of the matter was that for the first time in her adult life, Kate had felt a tiny flicker of feminine interest.

The realization shocked her. Made her feel damningly human and more vulnerable than she'd felt in a very long time.

"Oh God, Megason, don't even go there," she muttered as she unlocked the door and let herself inside. Toeing off her boots, she set her briefcase on the floor.

She was midway to the kitchen to make tea when her cell phone chirped. Thinking it might be Frank or Mike, she unclipped it from her purse and checked the display. A number she didn't recognize popped up in the window. "Hello?"

"Ms. Megason, this is Thelma Jackson. Evangeline's mama?"

"Hello, Ms. Jackson. How can I help you?"

"I just thought someone important should know those folks Evangeline was workin' for keeps callin' and askin' for her death certificate. I ain't got no death certificate. I keeps tellin' them that, but they say they need the 'riginal one and only her next of kin can get it."

"Ms. Jackson, I wish I could help you, but . . ." She floundered for words. "The case was assigned to another ADA."

"You mean you ain't gonna be prosecutin' that man shot my girl?"

Kate closed her eyes. "Ricardo Cano is the new prosecutor. He's quite capable, Ms. Jackson."

"I bet he ain't as capable as you. You a real go-getter, Miz Megason. So far you the only one who seems to give a rat's ass."

Kate didn't know what to say. "I'll make sure Mr. Cano gets your message."

"Y'all are shuffling this case around like it ain't important. You just watch. The man that done this is gonna walk away free as a bird."

"Ms. Jackson, I can promise you the DA's office is going to prosecute this case to the full extent of the law."

"Or mebbe my girl is just another South Dallas statistic they gonna put in some report that no one reads. My girl is gone and now I gots four babies to care fo'. They already askin' me about the bad man. What am I 'spose to tell them?"

Guilt was like the stealthy slash of a blade. In her mind's eye Kate saw the frail old woman standing in the cluttered living room of her little house in a neighborhood where the crime rate was off the scale. She saw four children whose lives had been shattered by violence. She saw a young mother who would not see her kids grow up because her life had been cut short.

Pulling her mind back from a place she didn't want it to go, Kate focused on the only way she knew how to help Thelma Jackson and her four grandchildren. "What were you saying about the death certificate, Ms. Jackson?"

"A secretary from some place called Quorum been callin' me, askin' me for stuff I don't have. I'm just a grievin' old woman. I don't know nothin' about no death certificate." She laughed, but it was a sad, bitter sound. "Come next week, we ain't even gonna have milk and bread."

Quorum Partners Limited.

Kate remembered the name—the company owned by Ferguson and Rooks. "Ms. Jackson, did the person say why they needed the death certificate?"

"Something to do with life insurance. I swear that gal has called me four times. She ain't no lady, either. Got a mouth on her. I tol' her I ain't got no death certificate."

Kate thought about that for a moment, found herself wondering why Quorum Partners would need an original death certificate. Usually, the beneficiary was the party who sent in the death certificate in order to receive benefits.

"I'll give the medical examiner a call and see if I can get the original death certificate mailed directly to you and a copy mailed to Quorum." It was out of her realm of responsibility, but Kate felt compelled to help the elderly woman. It wasn't like she had anything else to do. "I hope it will speed things up so you can collect the life insurance benefit you and the children are entitled to."

After hanging up, Kate picked up her briefcase and carried it to her office. Sliding behind the desk, she tugged out the brown expandable file marked *Bruton Ellis case #BL5335* and set it on the desk. Kate's mother had always told her she had a difficult time letting things go. Kate had never argued the point because it was true. It was true now, she thought as she slid the manila folder marked "life insurance" from a file she should have handed over to Ricardo Cano before leaving the office.

She'd asked Frank to dig up what he could on Quorum Partners Limited. Sure enough, there was another folder with the name typed neatly on a computer-generated label. Tucked inside was a Dun and Bradstreet report with the company's basic information, such as address, phone number, tax ID number, and a list of corporate officers.

She called the Dallas County medical examiner's office. Dick Robey wasn't in, but Kate spoke to his assistant, who promised to put the death certificate in the mail by the end of the day. Kate thanked him and disconnected, but she didn't put down the phone.

I'm just a grievin' old woman. I don't know nothin' about no death certificate. Come next week, we ain't even gonna have milk and bread.

Thelma Jackson's words refused to leave her alone. On impulse, Kate picked up the phone and dialed the number for the Quick Stop, Inc., corporate office in Oklahoma City. A receptionist answered with an enthusiastic "Quick Stop."

"This is Kate Megason with the Dallas County district attorney's office. Can I speak to someone in your benefits department, please?"

"One moment."

She tapped her pencil as her call was transferred.

"Sue Cramer."

"This is Kate Megason with the Dallas County district attorney's office."

There was a surprised silence on the other end of the line and then a wary, "How can I help you?"

"I'm working on the murder case of two of your employees, Evangeline Worth and Irma Trevino."

"Oh, yeah. Terrible thing. Just awful. What can I do for you?"

"I need you to fax me the life insurance policy for Evangeline Worth."

"The life insurance policies are administered out of our parent company, Quorum Partners Limited. I might be able to get you a copy, but it could take a few days . . ."

Kate didn't think Thelma Jackson and those four children had a few days. "I'd hate to have to go to the trouble of getting a subpoena," she said easily.

"A *subpoena*? Oh, well . . . maybe I could call them."

Kate smiled. "My fax number is 214-555-5667. How soon can you send it to me?"

"Is five minutes all right?"

"Perfect." Kate thanked her and hung up.

Less than two minutes later her fax machine began to hum. Kate rose and watched the machine spit paper into a slot. She wasn't sure why she was doing this. She wasn't even on the case anymore. But it beat the alternative of sitting here and feeling sorry for herself. Or God forbid, passing the time thinking about Frank Matrone.

She skimmed the policy. There was nothing amiss. All the signatures were in place. A state of Oklahoma notary had notarized the signatures, including the single witness. She was about to shove the policy into the folder when her eyes landed on the missing page—and an amount she hadn't noticed earlier in the week when she'd read the benefit package. A second amount that was much more significant than five thousand dollars. Kate dropped into her desk chair and squinted at the amount in disbelief. A three followed by five zeroes stared back at her in stark black and white.

"What the hell?"

Slipping on her glasses, she read the small print. *Upon the death of Evangeline Kay Worth a sum in the amount of three hundred thousand dollars and 00 cents will be paid to Quorum Partners Limited.*

"Jesus," she muttered.

Kate recalled the afternoon she and Frank had met with Jameson Rooks and Belinda Ferguson. She thought it interesting that neither lawyer had mentioned the amount of the benefit. It was possible they didn't know, but neither of them seemed like the kind of lawyer who would let so many zeroes go unnoticed.

A company collecting a three hundred thousand dollar death benefit on an employee, while the deceased employee's elderly mother struggled to buy bread and milk for four motherless children, seemed fundamentally wrong. No wonder the practice was referred to as dead-peasant insurance.

Kate was just in a bad enough mood to stir the beehive.

Going back to the information Frank had gathered earlier in the week, she located the phone number for Quorum and dialed. A moment later she was greeted with a terse "Quorum Partners Limited."

Kate quickly identified herself and, looking down at the signature on the life insurance policy, asked for William Blaine.

"I'm sorry, but he isn't in. Would you like voice mail?"

"Give me Amanda Price," she said, going to the next name on the policy.

"I'm sorry, but Ms. Price is no longer with the company."

Kate made a sound of frustration. A sound that wasn't lost on the administrative assistant. "Give me your chief financial officer."

"One moment."

Once again she was put on hold. A moment later a high-pitched voice accosted her with "Mr. McLaughlin's office."

"This is Kate Megason from the Dallas County district attorney's office. I need to speak with Mr. McLaughlin."

"I'm sorry, but he's in a meeting. Can I tell him what this is regarding?"

"This is regarding the deaths of Irma Trevino and Evangeline Worth," Kate said. "Is the chief operating officer available? Any of the directors?"

"Let me try Mr. Adamson."

Kate ground her teeth as she was put on hold again. Absently she paged through the folder, landing on the Dun and Bradstreet from Frank. She skimmed the report, her eyes drawn to the names of Ferguson and Rooks dba Endroad Holdings, Inc. A lot of layers for a chain of convenience stores. Calling up the Dun and Bradstreet software, she logged in to her account and entered Endroad Holdings, Inc. She was surprised to see that Endroad owned several companies, most of them franchisees of convenience stores, lowbrow coffee shops, and a chain of pizza parlors.

"Bill Adamson's office, this is Adrian."

Jerking her attention back to the matter at hand, Kate identified herself. "I need to speak with Mr. Adamson regarding the deaths of the two Snack and Gas employees."

"I'm sorry, but Mr. Adamson is at an off-premise meeting. Is there something I can help you with?"

Kate unclenched her teeth. "Tell Mr. Adamson I need some information for an ongoing investigation. Tell him I'm getting the run-around. And please tell him I don't like it." Kate recited her cell phone number. "If I don't hear from him within the hour, I'll assume he prefers I get a subpoena." It was an idle threat, but she knew from experience that it usually worked. "You got all that?"

"I'll notify him right away."

She hung up without thanking him.

WEDNESDAY, FEBRUARY 8, 7:01 P.M.

Kate spent the rest of the afternoon researching each company that fell under the Ferguson and Rooks corporate umbrella. She wasn't sure what she was looking for. Mostly, she was just trying to feel useful. Maybe she was just trying to keep herself from getting depressed.

She brewed hot tea and made an organizational chart of the corporate structure of the Ferguson and Rooks companies. She cruised several search engines, reading, seeking, filling her print tray with information. Ferguson and Rooks. Endroad Holdings. Quorum Partners Limited. Java, Inc. Tuscan Bread Company. Snack and Gas. It wasn't until she reached the end of the chart that the search engine took her to a story that stopped her in her tracks.

A two-year-old archived newspaper article from the *Times Record News* of Wichita Falls, Texas, read:

Two clerks at the Little Italy pizza parlor west of downtown were gunned down in an apparent robbery late Saturday night. Forty-three-year-old Kimberly Getz and twenty-six-year-old

Darren Chaney were victims of an apparent robbery gone bad, says Detective Rick Wetzel of the Wichita Falls Police Department. In an interview Monday, Detective Wetzel stated the robbery may have been an inside job because the robber shot out a hidden security camera. . . .

The parallels between the Wichita murders and the murders of Evangeline Worth and Irma Trevino chilled her.

Kate flipped through the file she had compiled and pulled out the Dun and Bradstreet report. Sure enough, twenty-nine Little Italy stores were owned by the Tuscan Bread Company, out of Kansas City, Kansas. The Tuscan Bread Company was owned by Endroad Holdings, which was owned by none other than the Dallas law firm of Ferguson and Rooks.

"Gotta be a coincidence," she muttered to herself.

Kate expanded her search, seeking similar crimes committed in the last five years. There were two additional murders at Little Italy stores. More digging revealed similar crimes at Java the Cup coffee shops. In the last five years Quick Stop, Inc., the franchisee of over two hundred Snack and Gas convenience stores, had reported six robberies. Five of those robberies had a fatal outcome. Five had had the hidden camera shot out.

Kate was shaking when she finally pushed away from her computer and stood. What the hell had she stumbled onto? Was it coincidental that there had been so many robberies with fatal outcomes? That the shootings were so eerily similar? Were these crimes somehow linked?

As an ADA, Kate knew the importance of motive when it came to prosecuting a case. Who would have something to gain by robbing and murdering clerks? Had she stumbled upon some sort of organized robbery/murder ring? But why would someone risk so much when such a small amount of money was actually stolen?

She considered calling Mike Shelley, but quickly dismissed the idea. It had been Mike, after all, who'd removed her from the Bruton Ellis case and ordered her to take some time off.

That left one other person. She groaned inwardly at the

idea of calling Frank. But she knew that if the crimes were connected, he would find the link.

"Damn you, Matrone."

She'd just reached for the phone when it chirped twice. Expecting Frank, she snatched it up on the first ring.

"You got a pen handy?"

Kate's heart began to pound at the sound of Jack Gamble's voice. He rarely called. When he did, it was invariably something important. "Do you have something for me?"

"I got an address on your man. Danny Lee Perkins."

A dozen emotions descended in a rush. Shock. Relief. Dread. And a surprising amount of fear. She hadn't expected to be afraid.

"Kate? You there?"

"I'm here." Putting her hand over the mouthpiece, she took a deep breath, mentally shifted gears. "What's the address?"

"It's 1421 Pioneer, Apartment 6, in Grand Prairie."

She turned to her laptop, pulled up a popular mapping website, and typed the address. "He live alone?"

"As far as I can tell."

Uneasiness swirled in her gut when she realized the cop parked in front of her house was going to be a problem. "I need you to rent a car. Something nondescript. Economy. Tie a ribbon or string to the antenna so I can identify it. Park it in the 3500 block of Beverly Drive."

"Kate . . ."

"I need you to do this, Jack. It's important."

He sighed. "Give me an hour."

She closed her eyes. "Thank you. I'll add five hundred dollars to your final payment."

She considered hanging up on him when he didn't respond. She hadn't told him what she had planned, but Jack Gamble was no dummy. He'd read between the lines. He knew. The last thing she wanted tonight was for him to try to talk her out of it.

"Kate, I ain't never asked you about your personal business."

"Don't."

"It ain't like you and I are strangers. We been working on this for a year now."

"You've been working on it for a year," she said. "I've been working on it for eleven years." It was the most she'd ever told him. The most she ever would. She didn't want to involve him any more than she already had. If things went south, she didn't want him getting into trouble. "The smartest thing you can do right now, Jack, is stop asking questions and forget I was ever a client."

He sighed. "Kate, don't do anything you're going to be sorry for."

"I never do," she said and hit the End button without saying good-bye.

TWENTY-THREE

Before becoming a private detective, Jack Gamble had been a police officer for twenty years. He'd spent four of those years working undercover in narcotics. Two as a tactical officer on the S.W.A.T. team. He'd been in plenty of dicey situations during those years. A couple of times he wasn't sure he was going to live to tell about it.

But none of those situations seemed as precarious as the one he found himself in tonight.

His wheelchair creaked when he leaned back, laced his hands behind his head, and stared at the phone on his desk. He hadn't bothered turning on the desk lamp, but he didn't need light to know he was in one hell of a pickle.

He'd had the name and address for days now, but hadn't been able to bring himself to call Kate. She hadn't told him what she was going to do, but Jack had been around the block enough times to know it wasn't good.

Growing up in a tough South Dallas neighborhood, Jack knew all about street justice. There had been times when he condoned it. A few times when he'd doled it out himself. He knew that sometimes it was the only justice served. Other times street justice wasn't justice at all, just another meaningless act of violence cloaked in self-righteousness and cruelty.

Street justice was a tricky thing. It didn't come without risks. It sure as hell didn't come without a price. Street justice forced a person to cross lines. One wrong move, one mistake, and that person could find herself on the wrong side of the law. Jack *wanted* Kate to have her justice. He just didn't want her to have to go to jail to get it.

He'd done his homework on Kate Megason. It hadn't been easy, but he'd finally learned what happened to her and her sister eleven years ago. He knew Kirsten Megason would never recover. He knew the two men who'd raped and brutalized the two girls had never been caught. He knew the statute of limitations had long since run out.

He'd never let on to Kate that he knew. He never would because he knew it would change the dynamics of their relationship. A relationship he'd grown fond of in the last year. He liked her grit. He admired her courage. He knew she was a decent person. But he knew that even decent people had their limits. Kate had endured the kind of physical and psychological anguish that would mark her forever. She might have survived, but she had not survived unscathed.

Jack had had the name and address for two days. Trying to decide whether or not to give it to her had kept him up nights. Now that he'd done the deed, the only question that remained was if he was going to let her ruin her life.

Cursing beneath his breath, he reached for the phone. He punched in four numbers before hanging up without placing the call. It was the third time he'd reached for the phone. The third time he'd hung up without completing the call.

Damn, he wished he knew what to do.

He wished he hadn't given her the name. He wished he'd tried to talk her out of whatever she was about to do. But Jack knew Kate well enough to know she couldn't be talked down. Not after she'd made up her mind.

The way he saw it he had two choices. He could sit here in the dark and kick himself for not stopping her. Or he could call the one man he could trust to do the right thing.

Jack had noticed the way Frank Matrone looked at her. The way a man looks at a woman when he cares. And he knew if he called Frank Matrone, the other man would keep her from getting hurt, either by someone else's hand—or her own.

Muttering a curse, Jack reached for the phone.

WEDNESDAY, FEBRUARY 8, 8:12 P.M.

Kate felt nothing but a low-grade anxiety as she changed into black jeans, a black turtleneck, and low-heeled boots. Tucking the latex gloves into her pocket, she entered the study, knelt at the credenza behind her desk, and unlocked the bottom drawer. Shoving the neatly labeled hanging folders aside, she withdrew the lockbox and set it on her desk.

She unlocked the box and found herself staring down at the blue steel of the Jennings .25 caliber pistol. It was a semiautomatic six-shooter with a two-and-a-half-inch barrel, black Teflon finish, and a wood grip. She wasn't proud of the way she'd obtained the weapon. It was the one and only time Kate had ever used her position with the DA's office to further her goal. But one snowy Saturday a year ago she'd been in the police evidence room preparing for a case. She'd overheard the officer on duty talking to another cop about four hundred and fifty confiscated guns. Guns that had been designated for destruction. These particular guns had been confiscated during busts. The striations had never been entered into the computer system. The opportunity had been too good to pass up.

It was as if someone else had been inside her body as she'd crossed to the wooden pallet. Someone else's hand that had reached inside and pulled out the deadly piece of steel that was now lying on her desk. By the time she'd walked out, her entire body had been shaking. But Kate had gotten what she'd wanted.

A gun that could never be traced back to her.

A few months later she'd asked Jack Gamble to help her buy a silencer. She'd told him it was her father's gun. That she would be taking lessons and didn't like the noise. She was pretty sure he hadn't believed her. But, as always, he'd come through.

Shoving the box back into the credenza, Kate rose and slid the Jennings into the waistband of her jeans. She turned off her cell phone and clipped it to her belt. She stuffed an old thrift store coat into her shoulder bag, and then slipped into her regular coat. Leaving on the front porch light, she locked the door and took the sidewalk to the street where the police cruiser was parked. The window rolled down as she approached.

"Hi," she said, offering a smile and her hand.

"Evening, Ms. Megason." He shook her hand gently. "Brian Kozloskow. Everything okay this evening?"

"Of course." She smiled. "Mike put you up to this?"

He nodded sheepishly. "Just getting in a little O.T."

She rolled her eyes. "I just wanted to let you know I'm going to drive over to the Turtle Creek Convalescent Home to visit a relative."

"Sure thing. I know where it's at. I'll just follow you."

"Thanks, I appreciate it."

Ten minutes later Kate pulled into the Turtle Creek Convalescent Home lot and parked near the door. She turned and saw Officer Kozloskow park a few spaces away and walked over to the car.

"I should only be an hour or so," she said.

"Take your time. I'll be with you until seven A.M. tomorrow morning, so you just follow your normal routine."

If her heart hadn't been pounding so hard, Kate would have laughed outright at the idea of any of this being routine.

The halls of the convalescent home had already been dimmed for the evening when Kate walked in. She'd been hoping to avoid being noticed by the head nurse, but the woman looked up as Kate turned down the hall where her sister's room was. Smiling, Kate raised her hand and waved, but she didn't stop to chat.

Once in Kirsten's room, Kate walked over to her sister's bed and looked into the face she knew so well. For an instant she saw her as the young girl she'd been, lovely and full of life and looking forward to a future that had wonderful things in store.

"It ends tonight, Kirs." Blinking back tears, Kate reached down and cupped her sister's face. "I'm going to get him. I'm going to make him pay for what he did to us. I'm going to make sure he never does it again."

She removed her coat and slipped into the thrift store coat. Crossing to the door, she turned left instead of right and went out the rear exit. The cars parked along the side street were cloaked in shadows from the live oaks that grew along the median. Kate spotted the string on the rental car's antenna immediately and jogged to it. Finding the keys in the visor, she started the engine and pulled onto the street.

WEDNESDAY, FEBRUARY 8, 8:29 P.M.

Frank's cell phone was beeping when he stepped out of the shower. Toweling his hair, he left the bathroom and limped to the bedroom where he'd left it charging. His heart did a weird little dip when he saw that the voice message icon was blinking, and for an instant he found he was hoping it was from Kate.

But Frank knew she wouldn't call. He was going to have to do some creative groveling if he wanted to get back to the place they'd been before he'd made his recommendation to Mike Shelley. Even then, he wasn't sure she would forgive him. The thought cut a lot deeper than he wanted it to.

He'd been thinking about her since the ugly scene in his office. Every time he closed his eyes he saw the way she'd looked at him when she told him she'd been removed from the Bruton Ellis case. As if he'd thrust a knife into her heart and then gleefully twisted it.

Cursing beneath his breath, he hit the voice message button and entered his password. An instant later a gravelly male voice came on the line. "This is Jack Gamble. Call me. It's urgent." He left a number and hung up.

Curious, Frank punched in the number. The PI answered on the first ring. "Gamble."

"This is Frank Matrone."

The silence that ensued made Frank crane his neck and hold the phone closer to his ear.

"We got a mutual friend and she's in trouble," Jack said.

"Are you talking about Kate?" Frank gripped the phone tighter. "What happened?"

"It's not what's happened. It's what's *going* to happen if someone doesn't stop her."

"Stop her from doing what?"

Gamble hesitated. "She's as good as gold, Matrone. As good as they come. I care about her like she was my own daughter. I'd do anything to keep something bad from happening to her."

"Maybe you ought to tell me what the hell is going on."

"Can I trust you to keep this under your hat? Because if you can't, I'll handle this myself. My way."

Frank didn't like the sound of that. "I'll do whatever I need to do to keep her safe," he said, not exactly sure what he was promising.

Gamble sighed. "She's about to ruin her life. I need for you to stop her. I'd do it myself, but you've probably realized by now my bullet-dodging days are over."

"Did you say bullet?"

"She's got a gun. I'm pretty sure she's going to take care of the son of a bitch who hurt her eleven years ago."

"Aw, man. Shit." Frank yanked jeans and a shirt off hangers. "Where?"

Gamble rattled off the Grand Prairie address. "You hurt her and I'll come after you."

"I'm not going to hurt her, goddamn it."

"I just pray to God we ain't too late."

"So do I," Frank said and sprinted toward the door.

WEDNESDAY, FEBRUARY 8, 8:33 P.M.

The apartment where Danny Lee Perkins lived was a single-story stucco dump with six apartments. It was located in a downtrodden neighborhood on a street laden with potholes and trash. A beat-up Dumpster squatted beneath a row of cedar trees on the west side of the gravel lot.

Kate drove past the place twice. She couldn't see Apartment 6 from the street, so she assumed it was at the rear, which suited her purposes just fine. Lights were on in two of the front apartments. The one on the end looked vacant.

She parked a block away beneath the shadows of a massive live oak tree and shut down the engine. Pulling her cell phone from her bag, she dialed Perkins's number from memory. He answered on the third ring with a hostile, "Yeah."

"Is Danny there?" she asked.

"This is Danny. Who the fuck wants to know?"

Kate disconnected, turned off her phone, and let out a long, shuddering breath as she clipped it to her belt. It registered somewhere in the back of her mind that she had recognized his voice. Even after eleven years she remembered the tinny belligerence. But she didn't let herself dwell on that too long. Tonight wasn't about thinking or feeling. It was about acting. Evening a score. Getting justice for her and her sister.

Danny Lee Perkins was home.

Kate was armed and on her way to see him.

The nightmare was going to end here and now.

She had visualized this moment a thousand times. She'd always thought she would be prepared. That she would be able to disconnect her intellect from the thin ribbon of darkness that ran through her soul. She hadn't counted on the edgy fear that had begun to slither along the back of her neck.

Her legs were shaking when she got out of the car. She could feel the press of the gun against the small of her back. Her heart pounding out of control in her chest. The night around her was so quiet she could hear her breaths hissing in and out of her throat.

It took a full minute for her to get herself calmed down enough so she could walk to the apartment. Her eyes had adjusted to the darkness, and she took the sidewalk to the rear of the building. She walked by Apartment 4. The windows glowed yellow. She could hear a television inside. A dog barking somewhere in the distance. The middle apartment was dark. No curtains hung in the windows and she assumed it was vacant. Just as well, she thought as she continued down the sidewalk to her destination.

Apartment 6 was dimly lit. The porch light was off. She could hear the base pound of music coming from inside. Kate was breathing heavily again. She could feel her entire body shaking, and she was angry with herself. How the hell was she supposed to finish this when her hands were shaking so violently she could barely hold the gun?

"Calm down, damn it," she whispered into the darkness.

She blew out several deep breaths. She wiped her hands on her jeans, then put on her gloves. Another deep breath and she rapped her knuckles hard against the door.

Her heart threatened to explode in the seconds she waited. This was the moment when a hundred things could go wrong. This was the moment when she had to stay cool. Keep her head. Concentrate on doing what she'd come here to do and forget about everything else.

The door swung open. Danny Lee Perkins stood before her, glaring at her with red-rimmed eyes and a hostile sneer. Eleven years ago he'd been thin with long hair. The man in front of her had gained fifty pounds. His hairline had receded. But the eyes were the same. Kate would never forget his eyes. The way he'd looked at her. The way he was looking at her now.

He was wearing a flannel shirt that was open down to his belly button. A gold chain glinted between his flat male breasts. Even from two feet away she could smell beer on his breath, the cigarette smoke on his clothes.

"Who the fuck 'r you?"

For several seconds Kate couldn't answer. All she could do was stare at him, the memories slamming into her like steel fists. She could feel the swell of hatred, like a pustule festering inside her, oozing poison until she thought she would burst.

Then it was as if she left her body and it was someone else standing at Danny Lee Perkins's door. His eyes widened when she brought up the pistol. Fear flickered in the depths of his gaze when she pulled back the slide and put a bullet in the chamber.

"What the fuck is up with this?" he asked, his voice rising.

Wanting to get out of the sight of potential witnesses, Kate leveled the gun at his chest. "Unless you want a bullet in your heart, you'll back into the apartment. Now."

His hands went up. "Whatever you say. Jesus!"

"Get inside. Keep your hands up."

Relief skittered through her when he complied and backed into the room. She closed the door behind her. Lynyrd Skynyrd belted out a song about That Smell from mismatched speakers. A hockey game was on the color television, but the sound was turned down low. From where she stood she could see into the dining room. On the dinner table was a scale, a pile of plastic bags, a convection oven, and a dinner plate piled high with white powder. The stench of marijuana hung in the air.

"Who the hell are you?" he snarled. "What the fuck are you doing here? Did John send you? Well, you can tell that motherfucker I'll pay when I get my money."

"Get on the floor," she said. "On your belly."

"What?"

"Get on the floor!" To make her point, she squeezed off a shot. The silencer *plunked!* and a bullet tore a hole in the wood floor just a few inches from his right foot.

"Okay! Fuck! You crazy bitch!" He dropped to his knees, then laid down on the floor, raising his head just enough to maintain eye contact with her. "If you want the dope, just fuckin' take it!"

"I don't want your drugs, you worthless son of a bitch."

He looked confused for an instant. "Well, then, why are you here?"

"I'm the girl you raped and left for dead eleven years ago, you piece of shit."

"I never raped no one, lady. You fuckin' got me confused with somebody else."

Kate saw red. Her finger jerked as if of its own accord. He screamed when a bullet tore through his foot. "Fuck! Fuck! You shot me! *God! Oh, God!*"

"Do you remember now?" she snapped.

"Yes! It was a long fuckin' time ago." He grasped his foot. "Fuck, it hurts!"

"My sister sustained permanent brain damage that night," she heard herself say. "You beat us and left us for dead. But guess what? You underestimated us, you filthy bastard, and now here I am."

"It wasn't my idea!" he shrieked. "It was all Eddie. He fuckin' made me do it."

"Eddie Calhoun is dead," she said calmly. "That leaves you and me."

She had visualized this moment going down a thousand different ways in the last eleven years. Shooting him in the forehead. Gouging his eyes with her nails. Slitting his throat. Severing his penis. But while the scenarios changed, the end result was always the same. She killed the evil son of a bitch responsible for devastating her and her sister's lives. She made him pay for what he'd done. She removed him from this earth so he couldn't hurt anyone else.

Kate wanted to hurt him. She wanted to kill him. She had him in her sights. Her finger was on the trigger. A bullet was ready in the chamber. It was the perfect scenario.

But this moment was nothing like she'd envisioned. She hadn't expected her stomach to go queasy. Her arms to quiver like taut bows. Or her legs to threaten to collapse.

Her vision tunneled on the man's face. Pale blue eyes. Greasy skin pitted with acne scars. Portwine-stain birthmark on his cheek. And for an instant she saw him as she'd seen him eleven years ago. An evil monster laughing at her pain and terror. Cruelty glinting in pale blue eyes as he grunted and sweated and made her feel so dirty she wanted to die. She saw the other man kick her sister with a booted foot. The sound of a steel-toed boot against flesh. Cries in the darkness. Sweet, innocent Kirsten who hadn't wanted to leave the house. Only Kate had cajoled and threatened and pouted until she'd agreed . . .

Her pulse was pounding so hard it drowned out all other sound. She raised the gun and aimed it at the bridge of his nose, where a bullet would kill him instantly and end her pain once and for all.

Or would it?

The question came at her out of nowhere. Kate stared at the man lying on the ground in his dirty clothes and greasy hair, and she hated him. He was a drug dealer and a rapist and a would-be murderer if things had gone differently that night eleven years ago. He was a wretched excuse for a human being and deserved to die.

Kate tightened her grip on the gun. Her palms were sweating. Her hands were shaking. Her finger squeezed the trigger. Tighter. Tighter . . .

Kill him.
Kill him.
Kill him!
"Kate! *Don't!*"

The earth tilted beneath her feet. She turned her head to see Frank Matrone come through the door. A hundred thoughts struck her brain at once. A split second to act because she knew he was going to stop her.

Turning back to Danny Lee Perkins, she pulled the trigger.

TWENTY-FOUR

The next instant passed in a blur. Kate felt the gun kick in her hands. She heard the *thwack!* of the silencer. Danny Lee Perkins screamed. In her peripheral vision she saw his body convulse. He clutched his thigh, a string of expletives spewing from his mouth. The bright red spurt of blood as it bloomed on his jeans.

Then Frank's hand was around her arm, tight as a vise and jerking her toward him. She felt the gun being pried from her grip.

He shook her with enough force to snap her head back. "What the *hell* do you think you're doing?"

Even through the haze of emotions, Kate saw the disbelief in his eyes. Dark brows riding low over eyes black with fury. She felt those same emotions screaming inside her, colliding and exploding until she was so overwhelmed she could do nothing but choke out a sob.

"I'm fuckin' shot, man!" Danny Lee Perkins's high-pitched wail sounded behind her. "She fuckin' shot me!"

Kate turned to see him sitting up with his right leg stretched out in front of him. His face had gone pale, but his cheeks were bright pink. His forehead was shiny with sweat. He leaned forward and his hands wrapped around his right thigh. She could see blood coming through his fingers.

"That fuckin' bitch tried to kill me!" he screamed.

Frank's eyes slid from Kate, to the man on the floor, to the drugs and paraphernalia on the table. "Damn," he muttered.

Kate felt as if she were watching the scene unfold from within a transparent plastic box. Her senses felt as if they'd been dulled by some mind-altering drug. Her thoughts were disjointed. Her vision had gone black and white.

"Did you touch anything?"

Frank's voice came to her as if from a great distance. Belatedly she realized he was gripping her biceps and shaking her gently. "Kate, damn it, did you touch anything?"

Danny Lee Perkins groaned. "I need a fuckin' doctor, man. I'm bleeding!"

"No," she heard herself say. "I wore gloves."

Frank looked down at her hands. "Okay." He shoved the pistol into the waistband of his jeans and looked around. Lynyrd Skynyrd had moved on to "Sweet Home Alabama." Danny Lee Perkins was lying on his side in a pool of blood the size of a turkey platter.

"Let's go."

The next thing she knew Frank was shoving her toward the door. She could feel his hands on her shoulders, pushing her out the door and into the night. Behind her she heard Danny Lee Perkins curse them. And then the door slammed.

On the sidewalk Kate stumbled and would have gone to her knees, but Frank caught her. "Easy, I've got you."

She didn't know how she made it to the parking lot. She was vaguely aware of their shoes crunching through gravel. Cold against her face. They entered the tree line and followed a darkened path that took them up a small hill and into an alley. Then Frank was hustling her toward the street. Beyond she could see the rental car parked curbside. Behind it was Frank's truck.

"Kate, what the hell were you thinking?" he said between clenched teeth.

"You should have let me kill him." She barely recognized the voice that squeezed from her throat.

They reached his truck. He opened the passenger side door and shoved her inside. She sat motionless and watched him jog around the front of the truck, then slide behind the wheel. Without speaking he started the engine and pulled onto the street.

He made a U-turn at the intersection, then sped east. It took several minutes of silence for Kate to realize what kind of shape she was in. She could feel her entire body trembling. She could hear her breaths coming too fast, too shallow, and she knew she was an inch away from hyperventilating. Cold sweat slicked the back of her neck and forehead.

"Put on your seat belt," came Frank's voice from beside her.

But Kate was working the coat from her body. She was burning up. At some point each breath had turned into a choking sob. She could hear them echoing inside the cab. Inside her head. Nausea churned in her stomach. She could feel the acid burn of vomit in her throat. The bitter taste of bile filling her mouth.

"I'm going to be sick," she said.

Frank turned onto a side street and pulled over. Kate threw open the door and stumbled from the truck. She made it three steps before vomiting. Another step and she went to her knees. She threw up again, then dry heaves racked her body. Weak and off balance, she fell forward. Her palms hit the gravel. Her arms were shaking. Her head drooping. She could see her hair hanging down. She spat and choked back sickness. But now it was the sobs choking her.

Vaguely she was aware of footsteps behind her. A gentle hand on her back. "You're going to be all right," Frank said gently.

Kate didn't think so. She didn't think she'd ever be okay. She couldn't stop crying. Couldn't seem to rally the strength to stand or raise her head. It was as if what had happened back at that apartment had zapped the last of the strength from her body.

After what seemed like an eternity, Frank slid his hands beneath her arms and helped her to her feet. Never letting her go, he guided her back to the truck, opened the door, and lifted her. Somehow, she made it onto the seat.

She was leaning back with her head against the rest when he climbed in. Without speaking, he pulled his cell phone from his belt and punched in numbers.

"I've got her," he said in a low voice. "I need for you to get someone over there to pick up the car. Yeah, but I don't want her alone. I'll give you ten minutes, then I need to call 911." A moment of silence. "She shot the son of a bitch, but I think he's going to be all right. Yeah. I'll take care of her."

Sighing, he closed the phone, clipped it to his belt, and turned to face her. "How did you lose the cop who was watching you?"

Kate had forgotten about the cop she'd left at the Turtle Creek Convalescent Home. She looked at the glowing numbers of the clock on the dash and was astounded to see that only twenty-five minutes had passed since she'd left Kirsten. It seemed like a lifetime.

"I left him at the convalescent home."

"You went out the back door?" Frank asked.

She nodded.

He put his hands on the wheel and stared straight ahead. "Here's what we're going to do. I'm going to drive you over there. You're going to walk in the back door. I'm going to go in the front. Then we're going to leave together and go back to your place. And we're going to fucking talk about this."

"Frank, you probably don't want to get involved in this."

"I'm already involved."

WEDNESDAY, FEBRUARY 8, 9:14 P.M.

Frank usually didn't have a problem figuring out his feelings. He was a black-and-white kind of guy. Cut-and-dried. He liked to keep things simple. But there was nothing simple about his feelings for Kate. Throw attempted murder into the mix and he had himself a real conflict.

He couldn't believe by-the-book Kate Megason had come within an inch of premeditatedly killing a man. Frank simply couldn't get his mind around the image of her holding that gun, her eyes wild, a very dark intent cemented in her expression. How the hell was he supposed to handle this?

But Frank knew what he had to do. He waited ten minutes then drove to a strip mall a few miles from Perkins's apartment and used a pay phone to call 911. "Someone's been shot. Fourteen twenty-one Pioneer, Apartment 6, in Grand Prairie." He hung up before the dispatcher could ask any questions.

Back in the car, he took Northwest Highway east to Bachman Lake Park. The park was in a tough neighborhood and deserted for the most part at this hour. Frank parked the truck in the shadows of an oak tree. Leaving Kate inside, he took the jogging path toward the lake, then cut over to the water's edge. He pulled the Jennings pistol from his pocket and threw it into the water.

"And now you're an accessory to attempted murder," he muttered. "Shit."

He jogged back to the truck. Kate was leaning forward with her face in her hands. Frank wanted to be angry with her. A part of him *was* angry with her. Furious, in fact. How could she do something so utterly self-destructive?

He'd always seen a big black dividing line between right and wrong. That was one of the things that had made him a good cop. There were no gray areas when it came to breaking the law. Until tonight, anyway, a nagging little voice pointed out.

Her actions clearly fell on the wrong side of the law. But as an ex-cop, Frank had a pretty good idea of what had happened to her and her sister eleven years ago. He'd seen the inhumanity of man against man up close and personal too many times not to have the images branded into his brain. He knew that sometimes bad things happened to good people. And he knew that sometimes good people did bad things.

Tonight Kate fell into the latter category. Frank had not only looked the other way, but he'd helped her cover it up. Now he was faced with the task of figuring out how the hell he was going to handle the rest of it.

Tense silence filled the cab as he drove to the Turtle Creek Convalescent Home. He parked at the rear of the complex. "Go to your sister's room and wait for me," he said.

Kate nodded and reached for the door handle.

But one look at her face and he wasn't sure she could make

it into the building, let alone fool the cop into thinking she'd been sitting next to her sister's bed for the last hour. Leaning over, Frank put his hand on her arm and squeezed gently. "We've got to make him believe you've been here, Kate."

Her eyes were large and fragile. "I can do it."

He watched her walk away and enter the building through the back door. He drove around to the front and parked in the lot, next to her car. The off-duty Dallas cop was parked a few cars over. He rolled down the window when Frank approached.

"How's it going?" Frank asked.

"Slow. The way we like it, I guess."

"Ain't that the truth." He glanced toward the building. "She been in there long?"

The cop looked at his watch. "A little over an hour."

"I gotta talk to her about a couple of things." Frank moved away from the cruiser and waved. "Have a nice evening."

He'd never told anyone to have a nice evening in his freaking life. If the man had known him, he would have known immediately that there was something terribly wrong. But he hadn't been able to think of anything else to say that would sound even remotely normal. He sure as hell couldn't say what was on his mind.

By the way, our friendly ADA tried to put a slug in some poor son-of-a-bitch's brain tonight.

He took the steps two at a time to the front entrance. The lights were dim, but there was a nurse at the station staring into a computer monitor.

"Can you tell me where Kirsten Megason's room is?"

"Down the hall on the right," said the nurse.

Realizing visiting hours were long past, he smiled sheepishly. "I'll only be a few minutes."

She smiled. "Oh, don't mind the rules. No one else does."

Frank forced a smile. He'd never liked places like this. Hospitals. Retirement homes. Funeral homes. They all made him uncomfortable as hell and in a hurry to get out.

He turned down the hall and walked quickly to Kirsten Megason's room. He knocked and entered without invitation. The room was small and homey with yellow curtains and stuffed animals lining the windowsill. A pink comforter covered the bed. An old Three Dog Night ballad floated from the radio on the sill. But none of the homey touches could change the fact that this was a hospital room or that the person in the bed was never going to get better.

Kate was standing next to the bed. She looked up when he walked in, and Frank was taken aback by her appearance. She'd cleaned up in the bathroom, but she still looked like the walking dead herself. Her face was the color of new snow. Her eyes seemed too dark and too large for her face. She was holding her sister's hand so tightly her fingers were white.

He looked at the woman lying in the bed. He knew she was Kate's sister, but there was no resemblance. The woman lying as still as death looked thirty years older. Her hair was lifeless and thin. Her face was sunken, her flesh slack over jutting facial bones. Her eyes were open, but sightless and utterly blank.

Jesus.

Worried that he wouldn't be able to conceal his revulsion, he quickly looked away.

"This is Kirsten," she said. "She's twenty-nine years old. She was prettier than me. Smarter than me." A sad smile touched her mouth when she looked at the woman lying in the bed. "This is what they did to her."

Frank didn't know what to say. He wasn't sure what to feel. The only thing he knew for certain was that he needed to get her out of there before she collapsed.

"Kate, we need to go," he said.

She'd changed into her regular coat, and it shocked him all over again that she'd had the foresight to wear a coat no one would recognize for her excursion to Danny Lee Perkins's apartment.

She didn't give him an argument, but rose on legs that didn't seem quite steady. She lifted her bag from the floor and put it over her shoulder.

"Can you drive?" he asked.

She nodded and started for the door.

TWENTY-FIVE

Frank knew his following Kate back to her place would probably start an avalanche of gossip that would start at the DPD
and stretch all the way to the DA's office. Cops were the worst
gossipmongers on the planet when it came to who was sleeping with whom. Even though he wasn't sleeping with her, the
off-duty cop was going to assume the worst.

But there was no way Frank could leave her alone tonight.
Not only was she on shaky ground emotionally, but they
needed to talk about what happened. About how they were going to handle it.

He parked behind her BMW and waved to the cop in the
cruiser who'd parked on the street. Kate had just opened the
front door when he caught up with her. She turned on the living room light and worked off her coat on her way to the coat
closet. Without looking at him, she hung it up, then walked
into the kitchen.

Frank removed his own coat, then draped it over the chair
in the living room. He found her in the kitchen, standing at the
sink, looking out the window as if the darkness beyond held

answers she desperately needed to know. Even from across the room he could see that she was still shaking. Her shoulders drooped slightly, as if the weight of the world were resting upon them.

She looked traumatized standing there in her black turtleneck and jeans, and for the first time it struck him that even her clothes had been chosen for what she'd attempted to do tonight. And still he couldn't reconcile Kate Megason the ADA and Kate Megason the woman who'd tried to kill a man.

"You look like you're going into shock," he said.

She didn't move, didn't even acknowledge his words, just stared through the window, her slender shoulders bowed.

Torn between impatience and sympathy, he crossed to her and edged her aside to get a glass from the cupboard. He filled the glass with ice then put it under the tap and handed it to her. "Sip this," he said. "It'll help."

She looked at him and took the glass. "I'm not going into shock."

Putting his hand over hers, he guided the glass to her mouth until she sipped. "We need to talk about what happened," he said.

"I don't know what I can say, Frank. I tried to kill a man." She lifted her shoulders, let them drop. "It was premeditated."

"I think this is a little more complicated than that," he said.

"I wish I'd succeeded."

"No, you don't."

Her mouth tightened. "How did you know?"

"Jack Gamble called me."

A mosaic of emotions fractured in her eyes. "He had no right. I'm . . . a client. The work he does for me is supposed to be confidential."

"You're a hell of a lot more than a client to him, Kate. He cares about you. So do I." The admittance made him flush. He hadn't intended to say that. But he'd been thinking it, feeling it.

Tears shimmered in her eyes when she looked at him. "I didn't mean to drag you into this."

"I'm here because I want to be here."

"I'm in trouble, aren't I?"

"Depends on how we handle it." It disturbed him that he'd

covered up a serious crime. Disturbed him even more that he would continue to do whatever he needed to do to protect her.

"The good news is that you have an alibi," he said. "The police won't find the gun. The bad news is that Danny Lee Perkins can ID you."

"He didn't remember me."

"Isn't he the one who's been stalking you?"

Kate blinked at him as if she'd forgotten about the stalker, a testament to just how horrific this night had been for her. "It's not him," she said.

"Are you sure? Maybe you didn't recognize—"

"Danny Lee Perkins has a speech impediment. He rounds his *r*'s. I'd forgotten about it until I was there and heard him speak. The person on the phone does not have a speech impediment."

"Are you sure?"

She nodded.

Frank let the thought bounce around in his brain for a moment. "If Danny Lee Perkins isn't the stalker, who is?"

"Whoever it is, they know about what happened eleven years ago." Her eyes were dark with an emotion he couldn't begin to fathom when she looked at him. "It's not common knowledge, Frank. My parents were part of Houston society. They went to great lengths to protect Kirsten and me. Our identities were never revealed. The police assigned us pseudonyms. We moved to Dallas just a few weeks after it happened so nobody would ever know. A new city. A fresh start."

But Frank had been certain the man who'd raped her was the stalker. "If the stalker isn't the man you shot tonight, then who is it?"

She wrapped her arms around herself as if the question had chilled her and walked to the dining room and sat at the table. Frank watched her, wishing he could find a way to reach her, to comfort her. But she was as distant and cold as the moon.

After a moment he followed her and sat across from her. "I think you need to talk to someone about what happened to you eleven years ago."

"I've talked to enough shrinks to fill the Dallas phone book."

Leaning forward, he took her hands in his, found them cold

to the touch. "Kate, you lost control tonight. You tried to kill a man."

"You're right on one count."

When he only continued to look at her, she sighed. "I didn't lose it, Frank. I knew exactly what I was doing."

He scrubbed a hand over his jaw, the sound of his palm scraping against his whiskers reminding him that it was late. "Kate, you're no killer. Whatever drove you . . ."

She stared at him, her eyes slowly filling. "Frank, what those men did to us that night—" Her voice broke with the last word, and for several excruciating seconds she struggled for composure. "We were only seventeen years old."

"Kate, I'm not inferring that he shouldn't be punished for what he did."

"The statute of limitations for sexual assault in the State of Texas is seven years."

"But this is an open case—"

"My parents wanted the whole thing to go away. They brought in the family lawyer; with some legal wrangling the whole thing was swept under the rug. They told me it had been done to protect Kirsten and me. But I always suspected they didn't want their society friends to know what had happened."

Realization dawned as cold and bitter as a winter storm. Frank stared at her and for the first time thought he understood some of what drove her. "I'm sorry."

She closed her eyes tightly, fat tears squeezing through her lashes. "I knew if those men were ever going to be made to pay, I would have to do it myself."

"That's a heavy load for a seventeen-year-old girl to bear."

"There was a lot driving me, Frank. This terrible guilt that just wouldn't go away."

"You had no reason to feel guilty about what happened." As an ex-cop, he knew that many times victims of sexual assault experienced feelings of guilt. He knew the emotion was common. And torturous. "You know it wasn't your fault, don't you?"

"Intellectually, yes. But on another level . . ." She looked at him, tears shimmering, her voice trailing. "It was my idea to sneak out of the house that night. Kirsten didn't want to go, but I made her."

"That doesn't make it your fault."

"If I hadn't insisted, she wouldn't be lying in that bed."

He was out of his chair and rounding the table before even realizing he was going to move. She looked startled when he took her hands in his. Frank wasn't sure what he was going to do; he'd never been good at giving comfort. He wasn't even sure if that was what she needed. The only thing he knew was that something inside him could not stand by and do nothing.

She made a sound when he pulled her to her feet. Only when he looked into the fathomless blue of her eyes did he realize there were tears on her cheeks. That there was more at the gate. That the gate was about to burst.

"Come here." He didn't wait for her to comply and pulled her to him.

A hundred sensations rushed his mind when her body fell against his. He was keenly aware of softness, of a woman's curves, and the coconut scent of her hair. A shudder moved through her when he wrapped his arms around her. "It wasn't your fault," he said.

She felt incredibly small and fragile cocooned in his arms. Her hair was like silk as he stroked the back of her head. He could feel her trembling and the urge to pull her closer was strong, but he didn't. She felt too good against him, and he didn't want the moment to change into something it wasn't.

"It wasn't your fault," he repeated. "You understand? You were seventeen years old. You were a kid. You were being a typical teenager. You didn't know predators existed."

A tremor went through her. Frank held her and tried to absorb it. He tried to absorb some of her pain. He wanted her to stop hurting. Wanted her to stop blaming herself for something she'd played no part in.

"My parents blame me," she whispered after a moment.

Frank eased her to arm's length and made eye contact. When she wouldn't look at him, he put his hand gently beneath her chin and forced her gaze to his. "What makes you think that?"

"My relationship with them changed after that night, especially with my mother. She . . . became distant and cold. She started drinking. And sometimes when she looks at me, I see it in her eyes."

"Kate, sometimes when we're traumatized, we read emotions and motives into things that aren't there. I'm no shrink, but you're probably suffering from survivor's guilt."

"I know about survivor's guilt. I know you're right. But I also know my mother. She blames me for what happened."

Anger surged through him at the thought of what that would have done to a seventeen-year-old girl who'd already been hurt so violently. "Why does she blame you?"

"Kirsten was always the good daughter. The one who followed the rules. She was studious and always on time. She was bright and pleasant and . . ." The smile she gave him broke his heart. "I was . . . well, I was me."

He smiled, but it felt sad on his face. "You were the hell-raiser, huh?"

She choked out a laugh. "A terror." She closed her eyes. "A few weeks after it happened, I took some of my mom's sleeping pills. I had to go to the hospital and have my stomach pumped."

"You tried to commit suicide?"

"Stupid, I know. But I really didn't want to die. I think it was more of a cry for help. After taking the pills, I called one of my friends. The paramedics got there in time. But I was a mess. I just couldn't live with what had happened to Kirsten. Not to mention what had happened to me."

"I'm sorry." It wasn't enough, but he didn't know what else to say.

"Don't get me wrong, Frank. My parents are not monsters by any stretch of the imagination. They're kind and generous, and they were good parents."

He wanted to point out that kind and generous parents didn't blame their child for being victimized, but he held his tongue, knowing she needed to get this out in the open.

He thumbed a tear from her cheek, and even though he was angry with her parents for what they had done, he moved to let them off the hook. "Sometimes people mourn the one who's lost more than the one who has survived. It's the way grief is."

"Thank you for saying that."

"I mean it."

They were facing each other, standing less than a foot apart. Even pale and with tears in her eyes, she was incredibly lovely. At some point the moment had become intimate, but Frank knew now was not the time for his thoughts to go there.

Never taking his eyes from hers, he took her hand and led her to the sofa. He sat down next to the arm, and she sat down beside him. He put his arm around her, and as if in unspoken agreement, she leaned into him and put her head on his shoulder.

They sat that way for so long he thought she'd fallen asleep. He was surprised when she spoke.

"We were going to a frat party." Her voice was hoarse and barely a whisper, but Frank was close enough to hear the words, and they broke his heart.

"I was so excited. I'd primped for hours. We had a six-pack of beer and a pack of cigarettes. My idea." The sound that squeezed from her throat was half laugh, half sob. "Kirsten had wanted to stay home and study. She had this big test coming up. So did I, but with me tests weren't a priority. I talked her into sneaking out of the house. I pouted and cajoled until she agreed. We took my mom's car. And we were on our way."

She paused for so long that Frank thought she wouldn't continue, but she did. "We were living in Houston at the time. I took a shortcut through a warehouse district. There were railroad tracks. We were stopped at a stop sign when the car hit us from behind.

"It never crossed my mind that it was anything but an accident," she said. "I didn't know that's how criminals got cars to stop. I got out of the car. I was wary of the driver, but he seemed normal. We were going to exchange insurance information. I told Kristen to stay in the car."

"You were looking out for her," Frank said.

"I've always had pretty good instincts. And even at the age of seventeen, I sensed we were vulnerable." She sighed. "I took my driver's license and my insurance card back to his car. I started getting nervous when I saw his passenger walk up to Kirsten's window. The next thing I know the guy has me against the car and—" Her voice broke.

Frank didn't know what to say or do. He wasn't sure if he was qualified to help her through this. The only thing he was certain of was that she'd finally lanced the wound that had festered inside her for so long.

"It's all right," Frank said.

She took a deep breath. "I tried to fight, but he was strong. I got away once and tried to run, but he was . . . incredibly violent. He struck me several times, and I must have passed out for a few seconds. When I came to, my hands were tied behind my back. He . . . he tore off my shirt. Pulled down my jeans. Made me feel so dirty I wanted to die." Another long pause. "The whole time he was raping me I could see the other man hurting Kristen. I could hear her screaming. I could see him hitting her and kicking her."

Outrage rose in a dangerous tide inside him. Frank could feel his heart beating hard and fast in his chest. He'd seen a lot of things in his lifetime. Back when he'd been a cop he'd seen the horrors that violent men were capable of. When he'd been in the Middle East, he'd seen things he could not let himself recall even now. But listening to Kate speak of what had happened to her that night filled him with such fury that he wanted to drive back to Perkins's apartment and finish the job she'd begun.

"It was dawn by the time we were found. A passing motorist, I think. My hands were still tied, but I'd managed to crawl on my belly over to Kirsten. I remember talking to her. Her eyes were open, but she wasn't there. I remember thinking she was dead and I felt so alone." Her voice broke with the last word.

Tightening his arm around her, he drew her close. "It's over, honey. You can put it behind you now. You did what you needed to do, and now you have to let it go."

"I almost killed a man tonight," she whispered.

"You didn't."

"I would have if you hadn't stopped me."

"You're no killer, goddamn it."

"Maybe I should turn myself in. Tell the police everything."

"Aw, Kate, don't do that." Frank pulled away and gazed into her eyes. "I don't know if you were in any frame of mind to notice, but there were drugs and paraphernalia in Perkins's apartment. Plastic bags. A scale. It looked like he was cutting cocaine. At the very least this guy is a drug dealer. You know he's a rapist capable of extreme violence. Is that the kind of guy who should be on the street?"

"No. But that doesn't change what I did."

"Yeah, it was wrong," he said, indignant. "But let me ask you this. How many other lives would he have ruined if you hadn't? How many seventeen-year-old girls would he rape? How many kids would get their hands on the drugs he sold? How many lives would be ruined?"

When she only continued to stare at him, he sat up straighter, a new anger spreading through him. "Don't give up your life for him a second time."

The dam broke in a rush. Her face crumpled. She closed her eyes against the onslaught of tears, but it was useless. Giant sobs choked from her throat. Violent tremors racked her body. "I'm sorry," she choked.

Frank held her tightly. "Don't be sorry," he said. "You have nothing to be sorry for."

And she went to pieces in his arms.

WEDNESDAY, FEBRUARY 8, 11:46 P.M.

It had been a long time since Kate cried. Once the gates were open, the tears had come in a violent, choking rush. All the while, Frank held her. He talked to her and caressed her and told her everything was going to be all right. And for the first time in what seemed like forever, Kate believed it would.

At some point complete mental and physical exhaustion overwhelmed her and she dozed. She had expected nightmares. The usual fare of that hot and violent summer night in Houston. The night she'd lost her innocence. Her faith in the goodness of people. Her conviction that good always prevailed over evil.

But the dreams that came to her had little to do with that blackest of nights. It was as if by holding her tightly, Frank was able to stave off the nightmares. And instead she dreamed of the man who held her in his arms.

* * *

She was seventeen years old and as wild and free as the South Texas wind. She and Kirsten were at the frat party. Kirsten was laughing and Kate was so happy her young heart was bursting.

"It's time for you to forgive yourself, Katie."

It was Kirsten's voice that came to her out of the shadows, but when Kate turned to look, it was Frank Matrone standing there. And then she wasn't seventeen years old anymore. She was a woman with a woman's needs, and she could feel those needs pounding through her body with a force that shocked her.

"She never blamed you." Frank held out his hand. Kate took his hand, and the next thing she knew she was in his arms. But it wasn't comfort she felt this time, but heat. The kind of heat she'd never felt before in her life. The kind of heat that could burn a woman alive if she wasn't careful.

It was as if her entire body had gone up in flames. She was aware of his mouth on hers. Flesh against flesh. His hands on her breasts. His body moving within hers. She'd expected pain. He gave her ecstasy like she'd never imagined and so much more. She could feel the crescendo building inside her, and she wanted to scream with the sheer joy of it.

Kate woke with a start, her heart pounding, her breaths coming short and fast. She was lying on her side, stretched out on the sofa. She could feel the solid warmth of Frank behind her. And for the first time she realized the heady pulse of arousal between her legs. The sensation of fullness in her breasts. The pleasant ache low in her belly as her womb contracted.

Around her the living room was dark. She could see into the kitchen where Frank had left the light on above the stove. She could hear rain hitting the roof. The hiss of heat coming through the furnace vents.

Snuggled behind her, Frank slept. His arm was around her. At some point during the night, he'd placed a pillow beneath her cheek and covered her with the afghan she'd draped over the back of the sofa. And for the first time in a long time, Kate felt completely safe and utterly content.

"You awake?"

She smiled at the sound of his voice. "Yeah." She wanted to make eye contact with him, but for the life of her she couldn't make herself turn around and face him.

"You cried out in your sleep," he said.

"I didn't mean to wake you."

"It's okay." He was silent for a moment. "You called out my name."

When she didn't respond, he sat up, gently pulling her up with him so that they were sitting side by side. "Bad dream?" he asked.

She shook her head. "No," she said, but she couldn't look at him.

"I just figured if you're calling out my name, it's got to be bad." He grinned.

Kate choked out a laugh, and it eased some of the tension inside her. It gave her the strength she needed to meet his gaze. His eyes were black in the darkness, and she got the uneasy sensation that he was looking right through her. She was keenly aware that her panties were damp against her skin. That her breasts were tingling.

"Are you okay with this?" he asked. Never taking his eyes from hers, he raised his hand and set his palm against her cheek. "With me being this close to you?"

"I'm okay." But her heart was pounding so hard she was breathless.

"You're shaking."

"I think it's a good kind of shaking."

"You know I'd never hurt you, don't you?"

"Yes," she said, and the truth of that warmed her.

She could tell he wanted to say something. Probably something inappropriate judging from his expression. But she knew Frank was an astute man. He knew that this moment was profound. He knew they had arrived at a crossroads, and he wasn't quite sure which direction to take.

His face was less than a foot from hers. His eyes searched her face, as if looking for some clue that would tell him what to do next. But Kate knew what he wanted to do. There was a small, reckless part of her that wanted him to. But in some small corner of her mind, she was terrified. Terrified that she wouldn't be able to respond. That she wouldn't feel anything. That she was cold inside, as she'd always believed.

"I've wanted to kiss you since the moment I laid eyes on you," he said.

Kate smiled, but she felt her lips tremble. "I wanted to fire you the first time I saw you."

They laughed together and she felt another notch of tension melt away.

"I wanted to do a hell of a lot more than kiss you," he admitted. "I still do."

Kate couldn't speak. The urge to pull back and run was strong. But the need to heal herself, free herself, was stronger. Until this moment she hadn't realized how desperately she wanted those things.

"Maybe we could start with something simple," she whispered.

"Like this?" Leaning close, he brushed his mouth against hers. It was a tentative kiss, a feather touch of his mouth to hers, but every nerve ending in her body zinged on contact. All she could think was that she'd never felt anything so powerful in her life.

When he pulled back an instant later, his nostrils flared. "On second thought, I don't think there's going to be anything simple about this."

"I'm good at complicated," she said.

"You're probably good at math, too."

"A whiz."

He kissed her again, and this time it wasn't gentle. Kate tasted hunger on his mouth. She could feel that same hunger coursing through her body. But it was tempered by the uneasy sensation that she was in over her head. That she'd bitten off more than she could chew.

Frank didn't give her a chance to think about it too long. His kisses were raw and urgent and demanding. Kate could do nothing but respond in kind. In some foggy corner of her mind it occurred to her that she didn't know how to do this. But for the first time in her adult life, she trusted her instincts to guide her. She trusted Frank to show her.

Vaguely she was aware of her breaths rushing in and out of

her lungs. The hard thump of her pulse in her ears. She could feel the heat of arousal barreling through her body, but this time she was not afraid and reveled in the wonder of it.

She was still wearing the turtleneck and jeans from earlier. She could feel Frank's hands on her face, sliding to her waist. A tremor ripped through her when he brushed his fingertips over her breasts. Even through the fabric the sensation was powerful enough to take her breath.

Kate was not a sexual being. For eleven long years she'd known there were certain parts of her psyche that would never heal. She'd accepted the reality of that and learned to live with it. Until recently, she'd never even questioned it. Never missed it.

And then came Frank with his troubled eyes and quicksilver grin and he changed everything she'd ever believed about herself.

She cried out when his hands closed over her breasts. A small part of her wanted to retreat. She needed time to think, to get herself under control. But the stronger part of her rejoiced in the sensation of being touched so intimately and with such utter gentleness.

She wanted to touch him, too. She wanted to explore his body. Discover his secrets. Give him pleasure the same way he was pleasuring her. But it was too much too soon, and Kate couldn't make herself do it.

"I want to touch your skin."

His whisper came to her on a sigh. Raising her arms, he pulled the turtleneck over her head. Cool air rushed over her heated skin. She wore only her bra. Embarrassment nudged her, but Kate was too caught up in the moment to care.

Pulling back slightly, he gazed directly into her eyes as he unlatched the front closure and eased the scrap of lace from her shoulders. Kate shivered when his eyes dipped to her breasts. His jaw flexed. When he raised his eyes back to hers, they were dark with desire.

"You're beautiful," he whispered.

A shudder moved through her when he brushed his palms over her nipples. The sensation raced through her body like electricity. She could feel her breasts swelling, her nipples puckering into tight buds. Low in her belly, her womb fluttered.

"Are you okay with this?" he whispered.

But Kate's heart was beating so hard she couldn't speak. He was looking at her strangely, and for an instant she felt awkward and foolish and light-years out of her league. But for the first time in her life she knew what it was to want with such desperation that she was willing to put her uncertainties and fears aside.

"I'm okay," she said.

His gaze went smoky. Never taking his eyes from hers, he unsnapped his slacks and lowered the zipper. He hooked his thumbs into the waistband of his boxers and tugged them down. She couldn't bring herself to look. She was terrified she'd lose her nerve and stop. She did not want to stop.

Gently he took her hand and brought it to his mouth. He kissed her fingertips. Her knuckles. He ran his tongue over her palm. "Look at me."

She stared at him an instant longer, then dropped her eyes. He was thickly built, with a long shaft that sent a pang of lust through her belly. Then he was lowering her hand, wrapping her fingers around the length of him. The skin was like velvet, but beneath the soft tip he was like steel, pulsing and hot to the touch.

A groan rumbled up from his throat. His breath quickened when she ran her fingertips over him, and he moved against her, sliding flesh against flesh. Abruptly he wrapped his fingers around her wrist and moved her hand away. He stood quickly and the next thing she was being swept into his arms.

"Matrone, what are you doing?" she whispered.

"Something both of us have wanted—" His words were interrupted when his shin thumped against the coffee table. "Ouch. Damn it."

Kate giggled.

Frank grinned down at her. "That wasn't supposed to be funny."

"I always laugh at the wrong things."

"One of a thousand things I like about you," he said and kissed her.

The bedroom stood in shadows. Frank carried her to the bed and let her slide to her feet next to it. She hoped he didn't notice the raw nerves slicing through her. She wore only her jeans now, and for several long seconds he stood there and looked at her as if she were a magnificent work of art and his eyes would never be able to take in every detail. Needing something to do with her hands, Kate reached out and began to unbutton his shirt. But her fingers were shaking so badly she couldn't manage a single one.

He took her hands in his, kissed both her knuckles, and then began unbuttoning his shirt himself. He made short work of the buttons. The world tilted beneath her feet when his wide chest came into view. It was covered with a thatch of black hair. All she could think was male animal. He was leanly built, but it wasn't for lack of muscle.

Kate felt overwhelmed. Intimidated by the power of his sexuality. She didn't know what to do next. But all of those uncertainties were tempered by the power of her own need.

She jolted when he reached for the snap of her jeans and was immediately embarrassed by her reaction. "I'm not used to doing this. I'm not sure I know how. I don't know what comes next. I mean, technically, I do, of course." Kate never babbled, but she was now and she couldn't seem to stop.

"You're overthinking this."

"I overthink everything."

He smiled. "Another thing I love about you." Lifting his finger, Frank set it gently against her lips. "Let me show you."

Her senses lit up when he kissed her. He used his tongue this time. She could feel her body heating and flexing. Her fears and uncertainties melting away like ice beneath a blowtorch. His hands were gentle and sure as they unsnapped her jeans. Kate didn't let herself think as she peeled them from her body and stepped out of them.

And then she stood before him, wearing nothing more than her panties, and she felt wonderful. Pulling back slightly, he stood naked before her. Arousal was like hot wax, burning between her legs. It was tortuous and sweet and like nothing she'd ever experienced in her life.

He kissed her mouth. Her temple. The point of her chin. Kate closed her eyes and let the pleasure rush over her, a waterfall of sensation that warmed her from the inside out. He trailed kisses down her throat, leaving a wet trail that cooled her heated flesh. She knew what he was going to do next and she braced. But the sensation of his mouth closing over her nipple was nothing like she'd imagined. The intensity wrenched a cry from her throat. Her back arched. Her arms went around his head. He suckled her hard, nipping at the sensitive bud with his teeth, first one breast and then the other. Need burgeoned, like a wildfire inside her, burning out of control.

He raised his head and kissed her hard on the mouth. Kate kissed him back hungrily now. He eased her onto the bed and lay down beside her. Her entire body quivered when he set his hand against her flat pelvis. Her legs opened as if of their own volition. The sight of his hand on her body shocked her, frightened her, thrilled her.

And Kate knew this moment would irrevocably change her. She knew Frank was going to break down barriers. That he was going to make her lose control.

"I'm going to touch you."

He didn't give her time to change her mind. He slid his hand over her mound and the crisp curls at her vee. Kate nearly came up off the bed when he slicked his finger over her, into her. She could feel her muscles clutching at him. Her hips moving to accept him. She closed her eyes and bright white stars exploded behind her lids.

Leaning close, he kissed her breasts, laving the engorged nipples with his tongue. Kate grasped the sheets in her fists to keep herself from writhing. She'd never wanted this way before. The need was greedy and edgy and would not wait.

He kissed the valley between her breasts. Her belly quivered when he kissed her there. Kate knew what would happen next. Anticipation warred with a thousand uncertainties and a thousand more fears. Then he moved between her legs and set his mouth against her most intimate place, and she couldn't think about anything except the pleasure.

Every nerve ending in her body exploded as he ran his tongue along her slit. He opened her slightly, and probed with his tongue, warm and wet and forbidden. Kate closed her eyes against the hot burst of sensation. She could feel her muscles trembling, powerful waves building low and deep. It was too much. It was not enough.

She wanted to cry out when the warmth of his mouth left her. She whispered his name as he kissed her belly, her breasts, and then he was kissing her mouth and she could taste the wetness of her body. She was keenly aware of his heated flesh against hers. The steel rod of his erection nudging her. He moved over her, keeping his weight off of her with his arms.

She looked into his eyes, and for the first time she realized this moment was as profound for him as it was for her. She saw the deep well of emotions in the depths of his gaze. The taut set of his jaw. The muscles corded at his neck. His arms quivered with restraint. He looked fierce, but his kiss was so gentle it brought tears to her eyes.

"Don't you dare cry," he whispered.

"I'm not."

He gave her a small smile. "Has anyone ever told you you're argumentative?"

"All the time."

They laughed together. A tension releasing laugh that Kate desperately needed at that moment. Frank leaned close, rested his weight on his elbows and kissed her forehead.

"Are you okay?" he whispered.

"Better than okay." She smiled.

"Nervous?"

"Terrified."

He looked at her as if she were a puzzle he hadn't quite figured out.

"I've never done this before," she blurted. "I mean . . . what happened . . . it just . . . ruined it for me."

He raised his hand and smoothed the hair back from her face. "It's okay." He kissed her gently, then started to ease away.

Realizing he thought she wanted to stop, she reached out and touched the side of his face. "Don't stop," she said. "I want this. With you. I'm ready."

She loved the way he was looking at her. As if she were the only person in the world. The only thing in his life that mattered. As if she were precious and rare and he would never get enough of her.

"Tell me what you want," he whispered.

"I want to feel," she said. "I want to feel you."

He kissed her hard on the mouth. When his tongue probed she accepted him. Vaguely she was aware of him easing his legs between hers. Her knees opening as he settled on top of her. She could feel the tip of his penis against her thigh. Her skin felt feverish, hot where he touched her. She couldn't seem to hold still.

Then his hands were on either side of her face, and he was staring down at her with an intensity that took her breath. She could feel him at her opening. The intimacy of the moment devastated her. She could feel her entire body shaking. Her heart bucking against her ribs.

He entered her with shattering slowness. Kate felt herself go rigid. She saw his expression go taut. He went into her deeply. Her body responded of its own volition and rose up to meet him. He began to move within her. Kate could feel the layers of control peeling away. Her body was not her own. She could feel herself thrusting up to meet him. She could hear herself crying out his name. Tidal waves of pleasure built higher and higher with every long stroke.

It was as if he became a part of her, as vital and life giving as her heart. And she found herself wondering how she had survived so many years without this. Without Frank.

The orgasm crashed over her with a power that stunned. Her control left her in a rush. It was as if every nerve ending in her body exploded. Every emotion she'd ever felt burst from her heart. She closed her eyes against the intensity. She could feel herself contracting around him. His name on her lips. The pleasure going on and on until she thought she would burst.

Frank didn't give her a reprieve. He brought her to peak a second time. No time to catch her breath. No time to think or regroup or gather her senses.

"Don't fight it," he whispered as he moved within her. "Let go."

Kate didn't know what he meant. The intensity of the sensations coursing through her was too much and brought tears to her eyes. She felt out of control. Physically. Emotionally. But for the first time in her life she didn't care. She trusted Frank, she trusted her own heart, and she let physical sensations sweep her away.

TWENTY-SIX

Bruton Ellis hadn't slept for six days, and he was feeling every minute of it. He was exhausted, but every time he closed his eyes he saw that needle sinking into his arm, pumping death into his veins. He imagined his lungs freezing, his heart giving a final surge. And he woke with his stomach in knots, his body bathed in cold sweat.

The jail was quiet at this hour, but he'd long since grown used to the silence. What he hadn't grown accustomed to was the fear. It crawled inside him like maggots on roadkill, burgeoning and festering until he thought he would scream.

He was lying in his bunk staring at the ceiling when the jangle of keys drew his attention. His heart leapt in his chest because he'd never given up hope that Mr. Corporate Executive would come for him and straighten things out. But when the door swung open Mr. Corporate Executive wasn't there. Just one of the jailers. A mean son of a bitch by the name of Skye.

"What's going on?" Ellis asked.

Without speaking the man entered his cell and closed and

locked the door behind him. Ellis knew immediately something wasn't right. No corrections officer or jailer entered a cell alone. Especially not in the middle of the night. The hairs on the back of his neck began to crawl.

"What the fuck is this?" Ellis asked.

"Put your hands up," the jailer said.

Ellis raised his hands. He noticed the small device in the other man's hand. It was about the size of a garage door opener, only it had two metal prongs on one end. His heart began to pound. "What the fuck is that?"

"Turn around."

Uneasiness trickled into fear. For an instant he considered not obeying the command. But the guy was big. Ellis had had his ass kicked by enough corrections officers to know what would happen if he got belligerent. Slowly he turned. "It's one o'clock in the fuckin' morning. What the hell are you—"

Five hundred thousand bolts of electricity hit him in the back like a baseball bat slamming in a homerun. Ellis heard an animalistic sound echo inside the cell. Then the floor rushed up and slammed into him.

For several seconds he lay on the cold tile floor, his thoughts disjointed, his body paralyzed. Vaguely he was aware of movement around him. The jailer placing something around his neck—some sort of soft fabric—and he wondered why he would do that.

Somewhere in the backwaters of his mind, it registered that this was not procedure. That whatever was being done to him was not supposed to happen. Convicts had rights, after all. You didn't just walk into a cell and hit someone with a fucking stun gun no matter what they'd done.

That was when he realized he was in very big trouble.

"What are you . . . doing?" he said in a voice that was much too weak to be his own.

"Shutting you up, I guess."

The fabric was jerked taut on the last word. On instinct, Ellis reached up to put his fingers around the noose to keep it from choking him. A second loud *crack!* split the air. Another five hundred thousand volts of electricity screamed through his body.

Ellis felt his body go rigid. He tried to get his fingers between his neck and the noose, but his arms refused the command. The next thing he knew he was being pulled upright by his neck. His feet left the floor. The pressure on his windpipe cut off his oxygen. A terrible sound ripped from his throat. He kicked his feet, and his body began to swing. He could feel his eyes bulging in their sockets. A freight train running through his head. At some point he'd wet himself.

He lifted his hands, dug his fingers between the noose and his throat, but his strength was waning. He couldn't breathe. Couldn't think. Oh, God, why were they doing this to him?

He looked at the man standing in the cell. At first he couldn't figure out why he had to look down to make eye contact. Then he realized the man had used a length of fabric to hoist him up and over the rail of the top bunk.

Ellis's face felt as if it would burst. He kicked but his feet found only air. He tried to scream, but when he opened his mouth no sound came. His tongue felt huge and dry and useless. His vision went black and white.

The cell began to spin.

His bowels let loose in a rush.

I'm dying, he thought.

And darkness closed over him like death.

THURSDAY, FEBRUARY 9, 12:59 A.M.

Frank lay in the darkness and listened to the whisper of Kate's breathing, trying not to think too much about what he'd done. They'd made love twice. The first time it had been awkward and fast and desperate. The second time had been slow and intimate. Eye contact had never been broken, and the experience had moved him in a way he'd never been moved before. Not even with Gittel, and that scared the hell out of him.

Even now, he couldn't get the sound of Kate's cries out of his head. The way she'd looked at him when he'd brought her to peak. The shock and joy and wonder he'd seen in her eyes. He couldn't quite get his mind around the fact that this was the first time she'd had intercourse.

Jesus.

He'd never thought of her as vulnerable. He wasn't sure how he felt about that. Kate Megason was one of the strongest, most headstrong, and maddening people he'd ever met. But she hadn't been any of those things tonight. They'd been intimate in a way that went beyond sex. He'd looked into her eyes and he'd seen the secrets of her soul.

Frank had liked what he saw. Too much, if he wanted to be honest about it. There was a part of him that wanted to help heal her. A part of him that wanted to protect her. From the pain of her past. From whomever was stalking her. From himself, maybe.

But he was in no position to protect anyone, let alone a woman as complicated as Kate. He suffered from chronic pain. There were days when he wasn't fit to be around another human being. There was a good possibility that he was addicted to narcotic painkillers. Not the kinds of problems he wanted to lay on her when she already had so much to deal with.

He was still hung up on Gittel. Beautiful. Laughing. Kind Gittel. He'd loved her more than his own life. He would have pulled his own heart from his chest if it would have kept her from dying. But Gittel had been intractable and reckless. She'd felt passionately about her cause. In the end, those things had killed her. Killed a part of him, too. A part he wasn't sure he wanted back. He couldn't bear the thought of caring for another woman and losing her.

He glanced at Kate, and the parallels between the two women struck him. Made a cold sweat break out on the back of his neck. Something akin to panic rose in his chest. He could hear his breathing quicken. His hands begin to shake.

Throwing off the comforter, he rose and walked naked to the bathroom. Closing the door, he flipped on the light and turned to the sink. The man staring back at him looked pale and shell-shocked, his eyes filled with a terrible realization.

He'd fallen in love with Kate.

He'd done the one thing he'd sworn he would not.

"Jesus."

Feeling the churn of nausea in his gut, Frank turned on the tap and bent to splash cold water on his face. He did it again and again until the shaking and nausea subsided. Then, with water dripping off his face, he looked into the mirror and whispered, "What the hell are you doing?"

Kate was awake when he walked back to the bedroom. He wanted to slide back into bed with her, but he didn't. He didn't want to dig this hole any deeper than it already was. But she looked incredibly lovely with her hair mussed and the comforter pulled up just high enough to cover her breasts. She looked happy and sated and slightly embarrassed. His response to that was instantaneous and instinctive. Standing there naked, he could no more hide it than he could hide one of his arms.

"Next time I want to know what you're thinking, I'll just take off your pants," she said.

Frank couldn't help it. He laughed. Leave it to Kate to say just the right thing at the wrong time. His heart was beating heavily in his chest when he crossed to the bed and slid beneath the comforter. For an instant they were both lying on their sides, facing each other. He could feel his need for her crawling inside him, but he couldn't make himself reach for her.

After a moment she slid toward him, just close enough to brush her mouth across his. "What's wrong?" she asked.

"Nothing." He hadn't meant for his voice to come out so rough.

She pulled back and studied his face for a moment. "You look . . . troubled."

It was difficult to have a conversation when he was hard and wanting her. That was the problem with women. Sex got in the way of doing the right thing most of the time.

Only this time, Frank didn't know what the right thing was. The sex had been good. It had been a hell of a lot more than just sex, even though he wouldn't dare admit it. The last thing he wanted to do was hurt Kate. But she was touching him in a place he didn't want touched. How the hell did he convey that to a woman who'd opened her heart and soul to him and not hurt her?

Sighing, he pulled her to him. She snuggled against him and put her head on his shoulder. "What's wrong, Frank?"

"I'm overthinking this."

Her expression went wary. "Overthinking what?"

He turned to face her. "Us. Kate, it was erotic and intense and . . . incredible." The words didn't begin to convey what he felt, but Frank had never been very good at putting his feelings into words. For Kate, he was going to try.

"I think there was a *but* in there somewhere," she said.

Reaching out, he put his hands on either side of her face. She was so lovely, it took every ounce of control he could muster not to pull her to him to devour her mouth. But while her gaze was level and direct, he sensed the fragility just beneath the surface.

"You know I suffer from chronic pain," he said. "I sustained an injury when I was overseas. I've been taking narcotic painkillers for the last year. I'm a functioning addict. That's why I've been late for work so much."

"I know," she said. "I'm sorry."

"Don't be. It happened. I'm dealing with it." *Yeah, right.* "I have a lot of pain, Kate, and I'm a son of a bitch when I'm hurting. I need the painkillers often. Almost every day. Sometimes it's bad. But even when I'm not hurting, I find myself wanting a pill. I find myself wanting to use these meds as a crutch. When something goes wrong. When life gets tough. I'm not proud of it, but I've done it. More than once." He sighed. "You saw it the night you came over to my place."

"That's a tough situation, Frank. To be on a highly addictive medication for a year and not become addicted." She hesitated. "OxyContin? OxyContin is a tough drug."

"Yeah."

She bit her lip. "Have you considered getting help?"

He hated the way that sounded. As if he had the willpower of some junkie. "I think I can kick it on my own, but I've got to deal with the injury first."

"What kind of injury?"

"Shrapnel from a bomb. I almost lost my right leg. Took about three hundred staples and four surgeries to save it. But the nerves were severely damaged. Weeks passed and the pain didn't go away. A couple of months later I was diagnosed with reflex dystrophy syndrome."

"A nerve disorder?"

"It's chronic and relatively rare. Happens with a high-impact injury." He shrugged. "We've tried everything except surgery."

"What kind of surgery?"

"It's called sympathectomy and basically entails cutting the nerves. It will alleviate the pain, but I'll lose all sensation in my leg."

He wasn't sure why he was telling her this. Trying to warn her off, maybe. Scare her away. But it wasn't what he really needed to tell her. While being addicted to narcotics was bad enough, what he really needed to tell her was that he was incapable of giving her the kind of love she deserved. That kind of love had been torn from his heart the day Gittel died in his arms. Kate deserved better. She deserved a man who could give her his whole heart.

For several minutes they were silent, the only sound coming from the branches of the live oak scraping against the window.

"Who's Gittel?"

Frank nearly started at the question and looked at her sharply. "How do you know about her?"

"You called me that the night I came over to your house."

For an instant he didn't know what to say. Words tangled in his throat, but none of them were right. "I met her when I was overseas. She was from Jerusalem. We were . . . together."

"You were in love with her?"

Frank smiled, but it felt false on his face. "I was going to ask her to marry me."

Kate blinked and he knew he had surprised her. "What happened?"

He hadn't wanted to get into the details. Not tonight. He should have known Kate would ask. "She was killed in the same explosion that injured me." *Not just killed,* he thought, *torn to pieces.*

"I have a feeling we're just now getting to that *but* part of *erotic and intense and . . . incredible.*"

Frank turned to her. She was smiling, but he didn't miss the skitter of nerves in her eyes. "I saw her die."

"I'm sorry."

"It fucked me up inside. It changed me."

"Witnessing something so horrific would change anyone. But people heal, Frank. So will you."

"Kate . . . what happened between us tonight reminded me of how good life can be. But I had no idea you hadn't . . . That I was—"

"My first?"

He didn't want to think of it that way, because it made him feel like a son of a bitch. "You deserve someone who can help you heal. A whole man who can give you his all. A man who can make you happy. You get tangled up with me, and I'll drag you down."

"What are you trying to tell me, Frank?"

"I'm telling you that I'm good at fucking things up. That I'll probably fuck this up. I'll fuck up what we have."

"How can you know that?"

"I'm tapped out," he said. "There's nothing left."

"You've been hurt, Frank. But you'll heal."

"I don't want to hurt you. If we get any closer I'm afraid that's exactly what I'm going to do."

THURSDAY, FEBRUARY 9, 1:23 A.M.

Kate stared at him, a hundred emotions rising and crashing inside her. She couldn't believe he was telling her this. That he was ducking and running. Not Frank, whose inner strength she had come to admire so much. Not after everything they'd just shared. But the truth in his eyes was unmistakable, and Kate felt it like a stake through her heart.

"It's okay to have sex, but add some emotional depth to the mix and you turn tail and run like a coward." The words were out before she realized she was going to speak. He reached for her, but Kate was faster and slid from the bed, taking the top comforter with her.

Wrapping the sheet around his hips, he rose and crossed to her. "I'm telling you this to protect you."

"Protect me from what?"

"Me. Goddamn it." He sighed. "I don't want to hurt you."

"Oh, that makes me feel a whole lot less used."

Anger flashed in his eyes. "I didn't use you, damn it. I didn't know—" He bit off the words, his eyes skittering away.

But Kate knew what he was going to say and it infuriated her. "You didn't know I'd never slept with anyone before? What's the matter? Not casual enough for you?"

"I'm trying to do the right thing."

"You're trying to take the easy way out."

"There's nothing easy about any of this. Damn it, I care about you."

She laughed, but even to her the sound had a bitter ring. She'd given him the power to hurt her. He'd taken that power and yanked out her heart. Whether he'd meant to or not didn't matter. "I want you to leave. Now."

Frank knew he should do exactly that. He could hear the voice in the back of his head screaming for him to take that first step toward the door. But the part of him that cared for her couldn't bear the thought of leaving her hurt and angry and with so many words between them left unsaid.

For several long seconds the only sound came from their heavy breathing. Indecision and raw emotions he didn't want to feel pulled him in different directions. His feelings for her terrified him. He knew just how quickly a loved one could be snatched away. He'd experienced the gut punch of grief. The black gaping hole of loss. Two things he never wanted to feel again as long as he lived.

But the primal side of him didn't give a damn about feelings or intellect or right and wrong. All that side of him knew was what he wanted. The need screamed through him with every beat of his heart.

"Goddamn it."

Crossing the distance between them in two resolute strides, he put her against the wall and crushed his mouth to hers.

Her body went rigid against his. He could feel the need clawing him, his control teetering on a dangerous edge, his intellect shouting for him to pull back and get the hell out of there. But when it came to Kate, Frank didn't have a rational bone in his body. He kissed her long and deep and hard, trying desperately to convey all the things he couldn't say. After several moments her body melted against his. He put his hands on either side of her face and feasted on her mouth, her neck. She didn't put her arms around him, but she didn't resist, either. It was all the encouragement he needed.

She gasped when he lowered his head and took a taut nipple into his mouth. She arched, giving him full access. Frank suckled her hard, wanting her deep in his mouth, needing her until he thought he would go mad with it. At some point he'd dropped the sheet. He could feel his cock against the smooth flesh of her belly. She was trembling. Choking back sobs. Breathing heavily. And he wanted her more than he wanted his next breath. More than he wanted to do the right thing.

Reaching between them, he tugged the comforter from her grip. He caught a glimpse of her surprised eyes. Her mouth opening to voice the protest he knew was there. He silenced her with a kiss. His hands were on her breasts. In her hair. The soft skin of her shoulders. He couldn't get enough. Had to have more.

In a single, smooth motion he swept her into his arms and swung her around. Two steps and they tumbled onto the bed in a tangle of arms and legs. Frank came down on top of her. In the back of his mind he worried that this was too rough for her, too fast, too intense. But he could no more keep himself from ravishing her than he could stop the wild beat of his heart.

He wedged himself between her legs. She opened to him and he thrust into her and went deep. A keening sound tore from her throat when he began to pump. Then she was raising up to meet him, taking him deeply into her body. She was wet and tight, her body already contracting around him, driving him toward release at a dangerous speed. Her head went back and an instant later she climaxed.

Frank held back as long as he could, but his control had long since left him. He ground his teeth against the impending orgasm. A guttural sound ground from his throat as he emptied his seed inside her. Closed his eyes against the barrage of emotions that followed, refusing to feel any of them.

For several breathless minutes he lay on top of her on the bed, unable to move. Guilt churned in his gut. He felt like hell for what he'd done. He'd had sex with her. He'd hurt her. And then he'd had sex with her again. What a great guy.

The chirp of his cell phone drilled into his brain with all the finesse of a chainsaw. He sat up, located the phone still clipped to his belt on the floor and slid from the bed.

"Matrone," he snapped.

"This is Detective Bates. Thought you might want to know Ellis is dead."

Shock slapped him like a bullwhip. "Dead? How?"

"M.E. will do an autopsy, but it looks like a suicide. Poor bastard hung himself in his cell."

"Are you sure?"

"Looks cut-and-dried. Officer found him in his cell, hanging from the top bunk. Looks like he used a blanket, tore it into strips, tied the strips together, and voilà: a makeshift noose." Bates snapped something to someone else, then came back on the line. "Look, I gotta work this. Just thought you might want to know."

Frank continued to grip the phone, even though the line was disconnected. He didn't give a damn one way or another that Ellis was dead. As far as he was concerned, the sooner Ellis got to hell the better off the rest of the world would be. What didn't sit well with him was that an egocentric sociopath like Ellis would commit suicide.

"What happened?"

He snapped his phone closed and looked at Kate. She was sitting on the bed, holding the comforter to her chest, her eyes sharp and questioning.

"Ellis is dead." Quickly he relayed everything the detective had told him.

"Do you believe it?"

"I don't know." He cursed. "No."

"It doesn't fit his profile." Taking the comforter with her, she crossed to the closet and opened the door. "Frank, I don't know if it means anything, but I found a connection between Ferguson and Rooks and a dozen or so similar crimes."

"What?" Frank caught a glimpse of pale flesh and titillating curves as she dropped the comforter and jammed her arms into the sleeves of a robe. "What are you talking about?" he asked.

He listened carefully as she told him about the string of fatal robberies spread over several states, several corporations, and several franchises. "Ferguson and Rooks is the only common denominator," she finished.

"The ratio of robberies to the number of stores is high."

"I can't figure motive."

"Money." His cop's mind spun into high gear.

"In most of the robberies, the cash taken was negligible."

"We're missing something." He bent to retrieve his slacks and stepped into them. "I'll take another look at everything when I get back."

"Where are you going?"

"The jail, to see what I can find out."

"I'm going with you."

Frank reached for her. But it wasn't to pull her to him the way he wanted. "No."

"Why the hell not?"

"Because it's not your case." He grimaced. "Because I don't want you there."

She looked at him as if he'd slapped her. "I'm on to something, damn it. I want to be involved."

"I have to go." Feeling like a jerk, he snagged his shirt from the floor, stepped into his shoes and socks.

"Wait a moment!"

He left the room without answering. He could hear her behind him, but he didn't look at her.

"Don't shut me out of this."

"I didn't. Mike Shelley did." He started for the door.

"Or maybe this is a convenient excuse for you to push me away."

He didn't let himself think about that as he shrugged into his jacket. He didn't let himself remember her face as he went through the front door. The one thing he couldn't do, however, was keep himself from feeling.

Frank hit the sidewalk running. The Dallas cop was parked at the curb with his engine running. The window slid down as Frank approached.

The cop's grin was a little too wide, a little too knowing, a little too smug. "Looks like we're going to get some weather tonight."

Frank hadn't even noticed the sleet. "Ms. Megason and I were working on the Bruton Ellis case. I slept on the sofa. You got that?"

"No problem."

"If any rumors start circulating, I'll know where they originated. And I'll make you sorry you opened your mouth."

"I got it."

Frank turned away and jogged toward his truck.

TWENTY-SEVEN

Kate stood beneath the shower and let the hot water wash away the tension, the bone-deep weariness, and the tears she didn't want to cry. Too much had happened in the last twenty-four hours, and she was so emotionally wrought all she wanted to do was crawl back into her bed and pull the covers over her head.

But Kate had never run away from problems, and she wasn't going to start now. She was going to have to deal with what she'd done to Danny Perkins. She was going to have to deal with her feelings for Frank.

It was ironic as hell that loving a man was so much more painful than shooting one.

She'd learned a long time ago that crying never helped. But she couldn't seem to stop. Now that the gates were open, the tears poured out in a violent rush. Frank had hurt her in a way she'd never been hurt before. In a way that cut her to the core.

Kate had never been in love before. Never even come close. But on an instinctive level she knew the emotions burgeoning in her heart—and twisting her into knots—was exactly that. She'd fallen in love with Frank Matrone. The thought terrified her. Thrilled her. Filled her with such despair that she could do nothing but stand beneath the spray and cry like an idiot.

"Oh, God, Megason, what have you done?" she whispered as she turned off the faucets.

Her cell phone was ringing when she stepped out of the shower. Kate reached it on the fourth ring, her only thought that Frank was calling to apologize and fill her in on the details of Ellis's untimely death.

"This is Belinda Ferguson. I need to meet with you." Her voice was breathless. "Tonight. It's important."

Shock rippled through Kate. Of all the people she would expect to hear from in the wee hours of the morning, Belinda Ferguson was not one of them. "Has something happened?"

A shuddering breath. "I'm in trouble. I'm scared. I didn't know who else to call."

"If you feel you're in danger, you need to call the police."

"I can't. I want to come clean, but I don't want to go to jail. I want to cut a deal with the DA."

Kate struggled to get her mind around the idea of the cool-headed lawyer being frightened and in need of help. "Belinda, have you broken the law?"

A hysterical laugh sounded. "Too many to count and I'm a goddamn lawyer."

"Who do you need protection from?"

"I can't get into this over the phone. All I can tell you is that it has to do with the Bruton Ellis case."

"The Bruton Ellis case?" Gooseflesh raced down Kate's arms. "What about it?"

A sound that was part frustration, part sob. "Corporate corruption on a scale like you've never seen. This is fucking huge. Makes Enron look like a company picnic. Worse than you could ever imagine."

"You're going to have to give me something."

The other woman made a sound of pure distress. "It has to do with life insurance policies. I think they call it dead-peasant insurance."

"You mean where corporations take out life insurance policies on employees?"

"That's exactly what I mean. Only he's taking it a step further, Ms. Megason. He's killing them in cold blood. Hourly employees. Clerks." Another sound of distress. "Please. I've said enough. *He knows what I'm going to do.* I need your help. Police protection. If he finds out I called you, he'll kill me."

Kate's mind was racing. "Are you talking about Jameson Rooks?"

"Look, I'm at home. We can meet here." She rattled off a prestigious Highland Park address. "Come alone. No cops. I'll tell you everything, but I want immunity. I'm not going to fucking prison. I want to cut a deal."

"I can't promise you a deal," Kate said.

"If you want to stop a mass murderer, you will."

The phone went dead.

Kate stood there for several seconds, Ferguson's voice echoing in her ears. *If he finds out I'm calling you, he'll kill me.*

"Who?" Kate whispered.

The only answer was the scratching of the live oak branch against her bedroom window.

"There's a minor emergency down at the convalescent home I need to take care of." Sleet pinged against the windshield of the police cruiser as Kate spoke to the officer stationed outside her house.

"No problem," he said. "I'll follow you."

"I appreciate it."

"Be careful. The roads are getting nasty."

Her nerves were stretched taut as she got into her BMW and backed from the driveway. She couldn't get Belinda Ferguson's words out of her mind.

If you want to stop a mass murderer, you will.

Sleet mixed with freezing rain was coming down in earnest when she pulled into the front lot of the Turtle Creek Convalescent Home. She left the car, watching as the police car slid into a spot a few cars from hers. The temperature had plummeted, and she could see her breath as she took the steps to the door. The doors were locked at this hour, so she used her proximity card and the lock snicked open.

The main hall was dimly lit and eerily quiet, the only sound coming from the television in the staff break room and the tinkle of sleet against the skylight.

Kate had called the taxi before leaving her house and asked him to meet her on the street behind the convalescent home. Making as little noise as possible, she jogged down the hall and ducked into Kirsten's room. The low hum of classical music floated from the radio. Kate walked to the bed and kissed her sister's cheek. "Hi sweetie. I can't stay, but I'll see you tomorrow." She crossed to the radio and changed the dial to a classic rock station, and left.

The rear exit was locked, but Kate used the release button on the wall and let herself out. Across the street a yellow cab idled curbside. She crossed the street and slid into the backseat. "Take me to 569 Lakeside."

"You got it."

Highland Park was a coveted neighborhood of multimillion-dollar homes, old money, and the bluest blood in the State of Texas. Belinda Ferguson lived in a gracious mansion on a quiet street just west of Lakeside Park. The neighborhood was quiet at this hour, the houses dark. The cabbie pulled up to the curb. Kate reached into her purse, ran her fingers along the cold steel of the mini-magnum as she withdrew money. She didn't expect trouble, but life had taught her that trouble usually came when you weren't expecting it.

"Can you wait for me?" She handed him a twenty-dollar bill. "I won't be long."

"Sure thing."

The house was an old Spanish-style with cream-colored stucco, mahogany shutters, and a red barrel-tile roof. The dual porch lights flickered merrily, and it looked as if at least one light was on inside.

If he finds out I called you, he'll kill me.

The words rang ominously in Kate's head as she took the sidewalk toward the house. Had Belinda Ferguson been referring to her partner, Jameson Rooks?

Was it possible someone high on the corporate food chain had hired Bruton Ellis to gun down those two women so the corporation could collect the life insurance money? Had it happened in other convenience stores? In coffee shops? In pizza parlors across the United States?

The questions taunted her as she crossed the porch and rang the bell. A minute ticked by. "Come on, damn it." She tried the bell a second time, then left the porch. For an instant she stood on the sidewalk that dissected the front yard. The cab idled on the street a few yards away. Behind her, a narrow stone walkway curved around to the rear of the house.

If he finds out I called you, he'll kill me.

For the first time it occurred to her that something might have happened to Belinda. The woman had sounded genuinely frightened when she'd called. Had someone hurt her in the minutes since she'd contacted Kate? Was Kate in danger, too?

Logic told her to walk away and call the police. If Ferguson and Rooks were involved in some kind of insurance scheme, who knew how far they would go to protect themselves. But Kate wanted answers; Belinda Ferguson seemed willing to give her those answers. Kate knew how slick some corporate executives could be, how very slick lawyers could be. And she knew it was possible that if she let this opportunity slide by, someone could cover up their crimes.

Mind made up, Kate slipped her cell phone from her belt and dialed Frank's number from memory. His voice mail picked up on the first ring, telling her he was on his phone.

"This is Kate," she said. "Belinda Ferguson called and asked for a meet. She sounded scared. I'm at her place now. Frank, she claims to know something about the Bruton Ellis case. Says it's part of an insurance scheme." Kate wanted to say more but the words jammed in her throat had nothing to do with the case. "Call me," she said and disconnected.

Clipping the phone onto her belt, she took the stone path to the rear of the house. A cedar privacy fence surrounded the backyard. Kate tried the gate and was surprised to find it unlocked. The hinges squeaked like arthritic bones as she went through.

The backyard was dark and so quiet she could hear sleet

hissing through the trees. A pool replete with a waterfall and Jacuzzi shimmered in the spill of light from a gas lamp. Kate walked past artfully arranged patio furniture and crossed to the double French doors. She was about to tap on the glass when she noticed one of the doors standing ajar.

She stared at the three-inch gap. The logical side of her brain told her this was not a good development; she knew better than to walk into a potentially dangerous situation alone. But the need to get to the bottom of a brutal and senseless double murder overrode the need for caution. Besides, Kate had covered her bases. She was armed. She'd let Frank know where she was and with whom she was meeting.

"Megason, you are so not being smart about this," she muttered.

Pulling the mini-magnum from her bag, she slid it into the waistband of her jeans, pushed open the door and stepped inside.

The interior of the house was lit only by the light slanting in through the French doors. The room was large and open. She could make out the dark shadows of furniture. She could feel her heart pounding too hard, too fast, as she crossed the room. "Hello? Belinda Ferguson? This is Kate Megason. Are you here?"

The click of her heels against the tile seemed loud in the utter silence of the house. She entered a wide hall. At the end of the hall, light spilled through an open door. Beyond, she could see into a kitchen with granite counters and stainless-steel appliances.

"Hello? Belinda? It's Kate Megason."

Kate didn't scare easily, but she could feel the hairs at her nape crawling. Sliding the mini-magnum from her waistband, she pulled back the hammer.

"Belinda, I'm armed, so don't do anything stupid."

Standing back and slightly to one side, she used the gun to push open the door. She caught a glimpse of bleached wood cabinets. Copper pots hanging from a rack above a butcher-block island.

Shock struck her like a bullet when she spotted Belinda Ferguson sprawled on the floor. "Oh my God."

The pool of blood seemed to cover the entire floor, an ocean that was stark and red against gleaming white tile. Kate could smell it. The stench of death. She could feel the terror of it seeping into her blood. The hard rush of adrenaline as the flight instinct kicked in.

"Oh, dear God. Oh, no."

It occurred to her that she was standing in the midst of a crime scene. That she was possibly destroying evidence that could impede the investigation. That she should get the hell out of there pronto. But for the span of several heartbeats Kate couldn't move. Couldn't take her eyes off the woman lying on the floor, her Neiman Marcus suit soaked with blood.

Her hands trembled violently as she fumbled for her cell. She could hear the blood rushing through her veins like a freight train. Punching numbers, she backed from the room. A scream poured from her throat when the dark silhouette of a man rushed her from the shadows. The phone was knocked violently from her hand. She brought up the gun, swung it toward her attacker.

Something slammed into her wrist. Pain zipped up her arm like a hot fuse. She heard a bone crack, and her hand went numb. She heard the gun clatter to the floor. Pain registered, tore a scream from her throat. She launched into a dead run toward the French doors. She'd throw herself through the glass if she had to. Kate had sworn a long time ago that she would never again be at anyone's mercy.

Two steps and the blow came out of nowhere. An electrical shock of pain at her right temple. The impact snapped her head to one side and sent her stumbling sideways. The second blow caught her squarely in the back. For an instant she thought her spine had shattered. Her legs went numb, tangled. The floor bucked beneath her feet. She reached out to break her fall.

Then the floor slammed her into darkness.

Awareness returned one sense at a time. Cold tile beneath her left cheek. The sound of sleet against glass. The metallic taste of blood in her mouth. The pain in her back throbbing with every wild beat of her heart. The knowledge that she'd made a very bad mistake. That she was probably going to pay for it with her life.

When she opened her eyes, she saw light and movement and shadows. But her brain couldn't seem to process any of those things into usable form.

She was lying on her side. She could see the ceiling above her. The slow spin of a fan. Nausea churning in her gut. Her arm hurt . . .

"Ah, Ms. Megason, how nice of you to join me this evening."

A groan was wrenched from her throat when she rolled onto her back. She looked up to see Jameson Rooks staring down at her, a cast-iron fire poker in his right hand.

"And in the midst of an ice storm, no less," he said. "Very impressive. You're a real tour de force, aren't you?"

She maintained eye contact with him as she pushed herself to a sitting position. She did a quick mental inventory of her injuries. Her arm felt as if it were broken. She could already feel the skin tightening as it swelled. She could move her legs. That was good. Her head hurt, but she wasn't dizzy. If she could get to the gun . . .

"I knew you were going to be a problem the moment I laid eyes on you," he said.

"I'm glad I didn't disappoint you."

"You have quite the reputation, you know." One side of his mouth curved. "I'm afraid this time it's going to cost you."

"Cost me what?"

"Your life."

"The same way it cost Belinda Ferguson hers?"

He tsked. "Come now. I couldn't have her talking to a prosecutor, now, could I?"

"I know what you did, Rooks. I documented everything. There's no way in hell you're going to get away with it, so why don't you just give it up?" Not a smart thing to say considering he was hovering over her with a fire poker in his hand and murder in his eyes. But Kate had never been one to pull punches and she wasn't going to start now.

"What is it you think you know, Ms. Megason?"

"I know you're behind the murder of those two clerks in east Dallas."

"Really?" He looked amused. "Do you have proof?"

"No, but it's there. There's a trail that leads right to you. You know it. I know it. It's only a matter of time."

He looked at her, the way a father might look at a dense child. "I don't think you're in a position to do anything about it."

"Frank Matrone knows everything. He's an ex-cop, Rooks. He hates corporate thugs like you. No matter what happens tonight, he's going to come after you."

"Or maybe you're just trying to save your life."

But Kate saw the flicker of apprehension in his eyes. "Come on," she said. "You're a lawyer. Think this through. I'm a prosecutor. If you kill me, the full fury of the criminal justice system will come down on you so hard you won't know what happened. Give it up now before things go too far. For God's sake, you'll probably get a deal. A good one."

He laughed, but it was an ugly sound. "I'm afraid things have already gone too far for deals, Ms. Megason."

Kate was sitting on the floor in the living room. Her back hurt, but she didn't think she was badly injured. Her arm was broken, but that didn't mean she couldn't use her left to get the gun. "It took me a while, but I think I've figured out how it works."

"Why don't you tell me?"

"You buy life insurance policies on your hourly employees. Upon their death—murder in this case—five thousand goes to the family. Three hundred thousand goes to the corporation. How am I doing so far?"

Something dark and unnerving flickered in his eyes. "You've drawn an interesting scenario, Ms. Megason. By all means continue."

Kate scanned the floor around her, but didn't see the gun. *Where the hell was the gun?* "How much do you pay the thug to murder your own employees? Do you always make it look like a robbery gone bad? Or do you kill them in different ways?"

"You get an A for effort."

"I think I should get an A plus because I'm right on the money, aren't I?"

He gave her that strange half smile again. "Your lack of vision disappoints me, Ms. Megason."

"What did I forget?"

"The scope of the plan." Intensity flashed in the depths of his gaze. "The ingenuity and talent it took to make it happen and pull it off."

The words sickened her, but Kate feigned interest. "I think you're giving yourself too much credit."

His gaze went diamond hard. "I'm operating in twenty-eight states. I have invested in life insurance policies with seven underwriters. I own six franchises with more than four hundred stores among them. Not to mention all of those layers of subsidiaries to cushion any suspicions that might be raised."

"How many people have you murdered?"

"In the last year?"

"Since the beginning."

He shrugged and feigned concentration, but Kate could tell he was enjoying himself. "Including the two in Dallas a month ago, about twenty-two."

Kate considered herself a strong person, both mentally and physically. But to think the man standing before her had murdered twenty-two innocent people so his company could collect life insurance sickened her. "At three hundred thousand a pop, that's quite a coup."

"Quite."

"Let me go, and I'll make sure you get a deal."

"Kate." His tone turned scolding. "You insult my intelligence."

"I know people," she said, surprised by the emotion rising in her voice. "Judges. I know the DA personally." The pain in her arm was wearing her down. The fear was taking hold. She could feel it leaching through her body, stealing her concentration, her calm.

He looked around. "If you hadn't been such a persistent little bitch, I wouldn't be in this position and neither would you. Why couldn't you just prosecute the case put before you and be done with it? Why did you have to keep digging?"

Grimacing, she shifted slightly so she could turn her head, look behind her. Her heart began to pound when she spotted the gun on the floor in front of the hearth ten feet away. Trying to appear nonchalant, Kate jerked her gaze back to Rooks.

"What are you going to do with me?" she asked.

"I'm considering my options."

"I don't think I can walk," she lied, trying to buy time. "My legs are numb."

"In that case, I'll kill you where you lie."

"And risk leaving DNA all over the place?"

Amusement flashed in his eyes. "You think you're so smart. So tough. I'm going to enjoy cutting you down to size."

Kate scrambled toward the gun on all fours. She heard Rooks behind her. His curse burning through the air. She saw movement in her peripheral vision. The black flash of the poker. She tried to get out of the way, but wasn't fast enough and steel slammed into her broken arm.

A scream of agony tore from her throat as she collapsed. A starburst of pain exploded in her brain. Her vision dimmed, and for an instant she feared she would black out.

"Stupid bitch! See what you've done?"

Vaguely she was aware of him crossing to the gun and picking it up. The pain came at her like a dangerous riptide, undulating and so powerful she feared it would pull her under. Kate tried to focus on what she could do to save herself, but the situation was bleak. She wasn't going to be able to talk him down. The only options left were to make a run for it.

Or kill him.

As she lay there at the mercy of a madman, both options seemed as distant as the moon.

TWENTY-EIGHT

Frank should have been in his element. Hanging out with cops. Drinking bad coffee by the gallon. A dead body hanging from the top rail of a bunk just twenty feet away. Hurry up and wait. Just like the good old days.

But tonight his mind wasn't on the job. Just when he thought he'd gotten his focus, thoughts of Kate would creep into his mind. He would remember something she'd said or a certain way she'd looked at him. And everything he felt for her would come rushing back. He hadn't intended to sleep with her. He hadn't intended for a lot of things to happen. But like plenty of other areas of his life, things hadn't worked out as planned.

He'd just poured his third cup of coffee when the cell phone clipped to his belt chirped. "Matrone."

"This is Mike Shelley. What do you have?"

"Detective thinks Ellis committed suicide."

"What do you think?"

"I haven't decided."

"Let me know when you do. I want a full report on my desk first thing in the morning."

Frank's phone beeped, telling him he had an incoming call. "M.E. will be able to tell us more once he does an autopsy."

Mike grunted. "You think there's anything to this, I want to know about it. All right?"

"Got it." Frank disconnected, then looked down at his phone, hating it that he'd been hoping for a message from Kate. He hit the code for voice mail.

The noise and hustle of the jail faded to babble when he heard her voice. "This is Kate. Belinda Ferguson called and asked for a meet. She sounded scared. I'm at her place now. Frank, she claims to know something about the Bruton Ellis case. Says it's part of an insurance scheme." A pause. "Call me."

Cursing, he dialed Kate's number from memory. Her voice mail picked up on the first ring, telling him she was on the phone. Or else her phone had been turned off . . .

Frank got a bad feeling in the pit of his stomach. "Goddamn it," he muttered and started toward the door. Someone called out his name, but he didn't stop. He didn't even look back. Suddenly the death of Bruton Ellis didn't matter. The only thing that mattered was finding Kate.

He dialed her number a second time as he jogged down the tiled corridor and out of the secure area. Once again he got her voice mail greeting. Growling, he punched the cell phone number of the cop who'd been assigned to protect her.

Bruins picked up on the second ring.

"Where the hell is Kate?" Frank snarled as he unlocked the truck and slid inside.

"She's at the convalescent home. Is there a problem?"

"Get your ass in there and check on her."

"What?"

"I think she went out the back door."

"Are you serious? Shit. Why would she do that?"

Frank could feel his heart drumming against his ribs. "I need an address on Belinda Ferguson. Get it for me. Right now."

He heard keys being punched. A moment later Bruins came back on the line. "I got a Belinda Ferguson in Dallas."

"What's the address?"

"Highland Park—569 Lakeside."

Frank put the address to memory. "Find Kate, damn it. See if she's inside. Check the back door. Call me back."

He disconnected, praying Officer Bruins found her inside. But Frank knew he wouldn't.

THURSDAY, FEBRUARY 9, 2:03 A.M.

Kate wasn't sure how badly she was injured. Her arm was by far the worst as far as pain. But the blow she'd taken to her temple was throbbing. She felt nauseated and dizzy and wondered if she'd sustained a concussion.

She lay motionless on the cold tile, taking physical inventory of her injuries, trying to gather her wits and decide what to do next. She was aware of Rooks pacing a few feet away. He was cursing. Talking to himself. A madman . . .

"Get up."

Kate struggled to a sitting position, and her head swam. Rooks was standing a few feet away. At some point he'd picked up her gun and had it trained at her chest. She looked around for her cell phone, but it was nowhere in sight.

"Did you kill Belinda Ferguson?" she asked.

That strange smile again. "Suicide, of course. She masterminded the entire scheme, you know. I would venture to say her conscience couldn't stomach the killing."

Kate didn't believe it for a second. "What are you going to do with me?"

"You're about to find out." He pulled back the hammer on the gun. "Get up. If you make me ask you again, I'll break your other arm."

Cradling her arm, Kate got to her knees, then slowly to her feet. The room gave a single wild dip and then leveled off.

"We're going to take a little ride. If you try anything, I'll tie your wrists behind your back." His eyes flicked to her broken arm. "The pain will be unbearable, I'm afraid."

Kate didn't relish the thought. Already, the pain was like a sledgehammer slamming into her brain with every beat of her heart. But she knew the pain of a broken bone was not the worse of what she would face tonight if she went with him.

She tensed when he started toward her. He smiled as he withdrew a kitchen towel from his pocket. It had been torn into two strips, the ends tied together. "Open your mouth."

He was going to gag her. Kate stared at him, her heart pounding. "Don't," she said.

"Move and I'll hurt you so bad you'll wish you were dead."

She closed her eyes. Tears squeezed between her lashes as he forced the towel into her mouth, then secured the ends at the back of her head. "We don't want to wake the neighbors, do we?"

When he was finished, he motioned toward the back door. "Don't touch anything. I've already wiped everything down. When the cops arrive, there will be no traces of either of us."

For an instant she considered making a mad dash, throwing herself through the French door, praying someone would hear. Before she could make her move, Rooks grasped her uninjured arm, opened the French door, and shoved her through it.

The cold air felt good on her face and helped clear her head. At some point the sleet had turned to snow. A thin layer covered the flagstone and patio furniture. She wondered if the roads would be bad. If that would work to her advantage . . .

He took her past the pool and gazebo toward the detached garage and opened the door. His Jaguar was parked next to Belinda's Mercedes. Kate stared at the vehicle, recalling that Bruton Ellis had mentioned that the man he'd met with drove a Jaguar. Only no one had believed him . . .

Rooks opened the passenger door. "Get in."

Fear tore through her with such violence that for a moment all she could do was stand there and shake. She knew if she got in that car, he would kill her.

"Get in," he repeated. "Now. Or I swear to Christ I'll kill you where you stand."

Her legs shook violently as she stepped toward the open door. In her peripheral vision she could see Rooks watching her closely, his expression wary. Keeping his distance.

She set her left foot on the passenger-side floor and leaned forward as if she were going to get in. An instant before sliding onto the seat, Kate pushed back, slamming her body into Rooks. She heard him grunt. Felt the whoosh of his breath against her ear. He grabbed for her even as he reeled backward, but she twisted in midair and his fingers clawed air. The garage door rattled as he careened into it, and then she was running for her life.

Around the Jag. Her boots slipping on concrete. Her hip brushing the hood. The front door to her right. Five feet away. She could hear Rooks behind her, cursing her, vowing to hurt her. Oh God. Oh *God!*

Kate's hand closed around the knob, twisted. The door opened, and she burst outside. Cold air on her face. Lurching into a sprint.

In the next instant Rooks hooked his hand in the collar of her coat and yanked her back. The gag muffled her scream. She stumbled, nearly lost her footing and turned to him swinging. Her first punch went wide. The second caught him in the throat. He made a strangled sound. Then his hand whipped out like a snake. His fist slammed into her broken arm.

Pain shocked her system. It was vivid and brutal and went through her like a thousand volts of electricity. She twisted away, but stumbled and went to her knees. She lashed out with her good arm, but her punch went wide. Before she could regroup, a second blow snapped her head back. She saw stars. Heard the roar of a freight train running through her head.

Then she was lying on her side, her face pressed against concrete that smelled of engine oil and dust.

You screwed up, Megason, she thought.

And then the world faded to gray.

THURSDAY, FEBRUARY 9, 2:25 A.M.

Frank drove like a madman to Belinda Ferguson's Highland Park home. The roads were treacherous and several times the truck fishtailed and nearly went into a spin. He parked at the curb, sprinted up the sidewalk and took the steps two at a time. He knew even before he hit the bell that no one was going to answer. He waited thirty seconds, then jogged to the rear of the property.

He peered through the French doors. The house looked deserted, but he could see a dim light coming from inside. "Kate!" he shouted. *"Kate!"*

On impulse he tried the door. Surprise shimmied through him when it opened. Drawing his pistol from its sheath, he stepped inside. "Kate! It's Frank."

The house smelled of eucalyptus and heated air. Listening, his weapon ready in his hand, he slowly made his way to the kitchen.

The light above the range was the only light. But it was plenty for him to see Belinda Ferguson lying in a large pool of blood. She was on her back, her arms and legs splayed. She was gripping a small, nickel plated revolver. *Dead,* he thought.

"Jesus." Holstering his weapon, Frank rushed to her and pressed his finger to her carotid. Her flesh was warm to the touch. The pulse was barely discernable.

Quickly he tugged his cell from his belt and hit 911. "I need an ambulance. There's been a shooting." He identified himself and recited the address. "Notify the Dallas PD and the DA ASAP."

He snapped his phone closed and looked around, a new fear gripping him. "Kate!"

A sound jerked his attention back to the woman lying on the floor. Her eyes were open and focused on him. She opened her mouth as if to speak, but all she managed was a gurgling sound.

"An ambulance is on the way," he said.

She blinked once, slowly, and he got the impression that she'd understood him.

"What happened?" he asked.

"Megason . . ." she croaked.

"Where is she?"

She seemed to be having difficulty focusing. She opened her mouth again. He saw blood on her teeth. But she didn't speak.

Urgency pushed him. *"Where, damn it?"*

Ferguson closed her eyes. Her body went slack. Frank cursed. He didn't know what to do or where to look for Kate. He knew Belinda Ferguson had had a partner. Jameson Rooks. And he wondered if Rooks had had a hand in this.

"Prov . . . dence."

The voice drew his attention back to the woman dying on the floor. Her eyes were open. Urgency burned in their depths. "What?" he asked.

"Kate . . ." she rasped. "Prov . . . dence Tow . . . er."

"Providence Tower?"

Belinda Ferguson blinked once. "Rooks. Bas . . . tard."

Frank reached out and squeezed her hand. "You're going to be all right," he said. "The ambulance is on the way."

Another blink.

"Hang tight. I'm going to find Kate," he said and sprinted toward the door."

THURSDAY, FEBRUARY 9, 2:57 A.M.

Kate woke to pain and the sensation of movement. She smelled leather and heated air and it dawned on her that she was in a moving car.

She opened her eyes to see Jameson Rooks behind the wheel. Her seat was partially reclined. The gag had been removed, but she could feel where it had bruised the corners of her mouth. She shifted, testing her strength. Pain shot up her arm, wrenching a groan from her.

Rooks looked away from his driving. "Your seat belt is fastened. Don't do anything stupid or I'll hurt you."

"You've already hurt me."

"Next time it will be worse."

She looked out the window, realized they were traveling North on Preston Road, heading toward the suburb of Plano. The clock on the dash told her it was 2:58 A.M. The dead of night. "Where are you taking me?"

He turned off of Preston Road without answering. In the distance the steel skeleton of Providence Tower was illuminated against the lights of residential Plano. Surprise rippled through her when he turned onto the street leading to the construction site.

"Are you familiar with Providence Tower?" he asked conversationally.

Kate looked at him, didn't answer.

"When construction is complete next year, the tower's

seventy-four stories will stand 945 feet. It will be the second tallest building in Texas. The sixteenth tallest building in the United States."

Everyone in Dallas had heard of Providence Tower. The high-rise office tower was the pride of mostly residential Plano. "I hate to put a damper on your fun, but at the moment I don't give a damn."

He smiled as if she'd amused him. "Ferguson and Rooks was instrumental in getting this immense project off the ground."

Kate said nothing. She could feel the fear and hopelessness pressing into her. She didn't know what he was going to do to her or why they were at Providence Tower. The only thing she knew for certain was that he meant to harm her.

"I'm glad I could be part of such a history-making project." He looked over at her. "Pretty impressive, don't you think?"

"I think you need to take a long hard look at what you're doing. I'm a prosecutor, Rooks. You don't murder a prosecutor and get away with it. You know that."

He stopped the car, turned off the engine, and turned to her. "I'm going to get out and unlock the gate. Don't do anything stupid." He stared hard at her for the span of several heartbeats, then opened the door and stepped into the night.

Her eyes darted to the ignition, but he'd taken the keys. "Damn it." She hit the locks. But Kate knew that wouldn't stop him. Through the window, she saw Rooks at the chain-link gate. The snow was coming down hard, coating the street and construction equipment. A ten-foot chain-link fence surrounded the construction site. Once they were inside, it would be difficult for her to escape.

She was about to reach for the door handle to make a run for it when the locks snapped. The driver's door opened. The overhead light blinked on as Rooks slid in with a swirl of snow.

"You weren't about to do something stupid, were you, Ms. Megason?"

Leaning against the seatback, Kate closed her eyes. She could feel the slick of sweat on her forehead. Her pulse beating like a drum. The pain was like a ricochet inside her bone, so intense she was dizzy and nauseous.

Rooks drove through the gate, then got out to close it. Kate thought about making a run for it, but with a broken arm and a concussion, she was in no condition to run.

Back in the car, Rooks put the Jag in gear and drove down a ramp and into the underground garage. There were no lights, and the place was very dark. Kate looked around, wondering if she could use the darkness to her advantage. She thought about the cop she'd left back at the convalescent home and wondered if he'd discovered she was gone. She thought about Frank and wondered if he knew she was missing. If he would come for her. If he would find her in time.

The thought sent tears to her eyes. Kate knew he would do everything in his power to find her. She prayed it was enough because she was certain Rooks was minutes away from killing her.

Rooks parked the Jag, got out of the car, and opened the passenger side door. "Get out."

Cradling her arm, Kate slid from the seat. "Where are you taking me?"

He motioned toward the construction site elevator, a steel grate platform surrounded by a chain-link safety cage. "I want to show you something."

Kate didn't want to get on the elevator. She envisioned herself making a wild dash for freedom. Rooks must have seen her thoughts in her eyes, because he abruptly reached out and squeezed her injured arm.

Kate cried out, the pain so intense her vision dimmed. "You bastard," she said, her voice breathless.

"I mean it," he warned. "Don't fuck with me."

Her head was swimming when she stepped onto the platform. Rooks stepped in beside her. The door clanged shut. He pressed the button for the seventy-fourth floor. The platform jolted, then began to hum upward.

"You're a fascinating young woman," he said after a moment. "Not many people interest me the way you do."

"Forgive me if I'm not flattered."

One side of his mouth curved. "I'm merely stating a fact. You've been a captivating study."

"You don't even know me."

"I know more about you than you could ever imagine. Including, shall we say, your history."

She looked at him, hating him, hoping that even if he killed her tonight, he would one day be made to pay for his sins.

"Your father protected your secrets well. But I've always been adept at obtaining information when I needed it."

"So you were the one stalking me," she said. "How brilliant."

He tsked. "Come now. While I found you interesting on a personal level, I consider such endeavors beneath me."

"I guess murder is more your style."

"When it's profitable."

"I think you're a sick fuck, Rooks."

His eyes lit with dark amusement. "I found your weak spot. I capitalized on it by hiring someone to frighten you." He smiled. "You don't frighten easily, though, do you, Ms. Megason?"

Kate said nothing.

He shrugged. "That particular endeavor was nothing more than a diversion, really."

"A diversion from what?"

"The case, of course. You were digging like the good little prosecutor you are. I wanted you to stop." He shrugged. "You pursued the matter, and now here we are. That's what happens to pit bulls when they don't know when to stop fighting. They get put down. Destroyed so they can't hurt anyone."

The elevator rattled and hummed upward. The wind grew stronger as they rode higher. Snow flew crazily. The building was only partially complete with ceilings and floors with intermittent support beams throughout, but few walls had been completed.

"You were raped and left for dead when you were seventeen years old," Rooks said.

Kate knew better than to let the words get to her, but the rise of temper, of hatred, was swift and powerful.

"Three weeks later you took a handful of your mother's sleeping pills."

"I know what I did," she snapped.

"Driven by guilt over your sister, no doubt. And, of course, the rape itself. That's a terrible thing for a seventeen-year-old girl to endure. I've always wondered, did your parents blame you?"

Kate said nothing, but she could feel the old guilt rising inside her. The unfairness of the blame she had shouldered. She hated it that he could do this to her. Reduce her to a powerless and hurting seventeen-year-old girl.

He contemplated her, and she had the oddest sense that in some sick, twisted way he felt something for her. Not sympathy so much as respect.

"In any case," he said, "you've handled all of this exceedingly well. Look at you. You have a broken arm. A head wound. You're standing there, knowing I'm going to kill you. And yet you haven't cried. You haven't begged." There was just enough light for her to see the chilling glint in his eyes. "Why not?"

"Because I want to kill you."

More than anything he could have said or done, the smile he gave her frightened her. Frightened her so badly that she began to shake all over. Her teeth began to chatter.

"There is one trait I admire over all others, Kate, and that is courage. You have that in ample supply. You're cool. Strong. I like that in a woman. Under different circumstances . . ." He let the words trail and shrugged. "Who knows?"

She looked away, but she could feel his eyes on her and the feeling was as vile as if he'd touched her bare flesh with his fingertips.

The elevator ground to a halt. The door grated as it opened. Rooks turned a key in a panel next to the door, withdrew it, and dropped it into his pocket. "The elevator is now locked. There is no way down or up without this key." He motioned forward. "Please."

A black and terrible sense of helplessness assailed her when she stepped out of the elevator. The floor was vast, dissected by sections of scaffolding, stepladders, and various construction equipment. There were few interior or exterior walls, and beyond the perimeter of the floor, Kate could see the lights of residential Plano.

"The vista is beautiful from up here, isn't it?"

Kate looked at him. He was standing with his back to her, staring out at the vast darkness beyond. His hands were on his hips. She wondered if she was strong enough to shove him off the edge. . . .

"Why did you bring me here?" she asked.

He turned and approached her, his expression grim. "I think you know."

He was right. Kate knew. She'd known the instant they'd pulled into the lot. Fear thrashed inside her. She did not want to die. She sure as hell didn't want to die at the hands of a bastard like Jameson Rooks.

"Let me go," she said.

"Ah, Kate . . . You know I can't do that."

"You have the resources to go anywhere in the world. There are countries that do not have extradition treaties with the United States."

He frowned at her, a teacher disappointed by a slow-witted child. "I have no desire to spend the rest of my life in some muddy hellhole." He shrugged. "I'm afraid this is the only way."

Her heart was pounding so hard she was dizzy. She could taste the metallic tang of fear at the back of her throat.

"You're going to jump to your death tonight." He said the words with all the passion of a man talking about the weather. "You have a history of suicidal behavior. You've been distraught over the Bruton Ellis case. You've been under a lot of pressure. And with your past . . ." He shrugged. "Even the strongest of people have been known to snap."

"No one will believe I committed suicide," she said.

"Ah, but that's where you're wrong. You see, I've been planning this for quite some time. Right down to the suicide note you sent your parents."

"I didn't," she choked.

"Just a simple apology for the pain your suicide will cause them. I think that will suffice."

"My parents won't believe it. Mike Shelley won't believe it. Neither will Frank Matrone."

But Kate could tell Rooks wasn't concerned. "I brought a

couple of Xanax for you." He reached into his pocket and retrieved two pills. "Please. Take them. It will make this easier
for both of us."

"Fuck you."

He smiled. "Strong to the bitter end. I respect that. But it's
not going to help you." He dropped the pills back in his
pocket. "If you change your mind, I have them right here."

He slid a sleek baton from beneath his London Fog. "I did
not want to use such a primitive instrument." A flick of the
wrist and the baton extended to three feet in length. "But for
obvious reasons a gun was out of the question. A knife would
raise questions. Physical trauma, on the other hand." He
shrugged. "Let's just say a nine-hundred-foot fall will leave
little for the medical examiner to work with."

"Stay away from me," Kate said.

He ran his hand along the deadly looking length of steel.
"The expandable baton is a law enforcement tool, when non-
lethal force is called for. It's illegal in some states." His eyes
landed upon hers. "One way or another, you will jump from
this building tonight."

Kate stepped back, looked wildly around for something,
anything to use as a weapon. The scaffolding was to her right.
A stepladder straight ahead. A plastic five-gallon bucket. A
toolbox, its padlock glinting in the dim light.

"This space where we're standing will eventually be the
penthouse," Rooks stated. "The rent will be outrageous. A filthy
rich law firm will claim it, I'm sure. Or perhaps a restaurant."
He circled her. "No one will think of the young woman who
jumped to her death months before. A month from now, no one
will remember you."

"I won't do it."

"Of course you will."

Kate could feel her eyes darting left and right. She felt like
a trapped animal, with a predator closing in to devour her. She
was trying to formulate a plan. Knock him out. Take the elevator key. Get the hell out of there. She wasn't expecting him to
lunge at her.

Air *whooshed* when he swung the bat. Kate reeled backward. All she could think about was protecting her broken

arm. She knew if he hit her there, she could black out. All he would have to do then was carry her to the edge and throw her off. . . .

The tip of the baton grazed her injured arm. The pain was like a supernova bursting in her brain.

An animal sound tore from her throat as she stumbled back. "No!" she screamed. "Get away from me!"

His lips peeled back, revealing perfect white teeth. Kate saw intent in his eyes. Cruelty. Self-preservation in its most primitive form.

He swung the baton again. She lunged sideways, but she wasn't fast enough. Steel slammed into her shoulder. Heat streaked down her arm. She snatched up the five-gallon bucket and threw it with all her might. He deflected the bucket and it bounced aside. Using her good arm, she grasped the six-foot stepladder and toppled it.

Cursing, he stepped toward her. "You can't get away, Kate. Give it up. Let's get this over with."

She knew she was out of time. Out of options. Out of luck. Kate did the only thing she could and ran.

TWENTY-NINE

Kate ran blindly through the darkness. She could hear her boots cracking against the concrete floor. Too loud. Giving away her location. She could hear her breaths tearing from her throat in ragged gasps. Her heart thundered in her ears. A storm of pain ripping through her arm.

She darted around a concrete support beam. A gust of wind hit her in the face, blew her back a step. Ten feet away she could see where the floor ended. Snow swirled crazily against the backdrop of light. The yellow safety netting flapped wildly.

Pressing her back to the concrete, she tried to catch her breath. If she could keep her head, she might be able to survive this. Surely the cop back at the convalescent home had realized by now that she wasn't there. Surely he would contact Mike Shelley. Mike would contact Frank.

"Frank," she whispered.

She closed her eyes against the tears. The thought of all that would be lost if she perished here tonight sent a sob to her throat. Using her good arm, Kate put her hand over her mouth, closed her eyes tightly, and fought hard for the control she needed to survive this.

"Kate!"

Every muscle in her body went taut at the sound of Rooks's voice. Taking a deep breath, she peered around the corner of the support beam. He was thirty feet away, turning in a slow circle, his head cocked as if listening.

When he turned in her direction, she sank against the support beam and looked for a place to run. A place to hide. But Kate had run out of options. There was no place left to run. Just a nine-hundred-foot drop and certain death.

"Frank," she whispered. "I need you. Come for me. . . ."

THURSDAY, FEBRUARY 9, 3:16 A.M.

Frank felt every second that ticked by as if it were the last beat of his heart. He sped north on Preston Road, pushing the Chevy to ninety miles an hour. He blew a traffic light at Park. In the distance Providence Tower loomed like a shadowy skeleton.

He whipped the cell phone from his belt. His hand shook as he hit the speed dial for Mike Shelley. The DA answered on the first ring.

"Jameson Rooks has Kate," Frank said. "He's taken her to Providence Tower. I think he's going to kill her."

"Where are you?"

"En route. I need the architect or the construction site manager on the horn. Now."

"Give me two minutes," Shelley said. "I'll notify Plano PD. You stay the hell out of the line of fire."

Frank disconnected, his mind torturing him with thoughts of all the terrible things that could be happening to Kate. He consoled himself with the fact that she was a fighter. A survivor. But he knew that not even Kate Megason was a match for a gun or knife or the savagery of a killer.

He swung the Chevy onto the street that would take him to Providence Tower. The construction site was massive with several outbuildings and a ramp to what looked like an underground parking garage. Too dark to see if there was a Jaguar parked in the lot. Knowing the gate would be padlocked, Frank hit the gas. The Chevy crashed through the chain link like a tank cutting through high weeds. Sparks shot high into the air as the truck dragged a length of fence into the parking garage. The truck skidded to a halt ten feet from Jameson's Jaguar.

Frank jammed the truck into Park and threw open the door. He darted toward the construction elevator and punched the Up button. The lighted sphere blinked, then went dark. "Damn it." He hit the button again and again, but the light that told him the elevator was operational remained dark. Rooks had somehow jammed it.

Desperation clawed at him as he left the underground garage and sprinted toward what would be the building's lobby. Toolboxes, coiled extension cords, and rolls of polyurethane sheeting lay scattered about. A forklift hulked in the corner like a sleeping beast. Huge slabs of marble that would comprise the walls were stacked twelve feet high.

He'd been hoping to find a stairwell or freight elevator, but found neither. He wished desperately for a flashlight, but he hadn't thought to bring one. He set his hand on his cell phone. "Come on, damn it."

The lighted dial told him four minutes had passed since he'd spoken to Mike Shelley. They were the longest four minutes of his life.

His cell phone chirped, and Frank snatched it up. "Yeah."

"This is Doug Johnson, construction manager of Providence."

"A woman is being held hostage on the top floor of the building. The suspect has jammed the construction elevator. Is there another way for me to get up there?"

"Shit, man, I don't think so."

"Think! Damn it, he's going to kill her if I don't stop him."

"Freight elevator might work. Company came out and installed the cables and electric motors last week. But it hasn't been tested or inspected or nothing."

"Where?"

"West side of the building."

"Stay on the line." Holding the phone to his ear, Frank

sprinted through the lobby toward the west side of the building. "I can't see shit," he muttered. "It's dark as hell. I'm in the main tower. Can you guide me?"

"Go straight west. Ten yards before you reach the end, go right. There will be an interior hall. Low ceilings. Freight elevator will be on your left."

Frank had already found the second hall. Halfway down he located the elevator. He punched the button. In the distance he could hear the wail of sirens. *Plano PD,* he thought. He knew he would probably pay dearly for not waiting. But in his heart he knew he was out of time. That Kate was out of time.

The elevator doors slid open. Frank stepped inside. There were no walls, just a plastic mesh safety net. Shit, he thought, and hit the button for the top floor.

The ride to the top seemed to take forever. The higher he went, the harder the wind blew. Every two seconds a concrete floor *whooshed* by. The occasional support beam. On several floors the walls were finished out. But as the elevator moved up the shaft, there were fewer walls. Just open floors, wind, and swirling snow. Frank stood with his feet braced in the center of the platform and tried hard not to look down.

An eternity later the elevator jolted to a halt. Drawing his weapon, he stepped out onto the concrete floor. His eyes had adjusted to the darkness and he could see that the top floor was little more than a concrete slab with a roof. Polyurethane sheets had been stapled to the west side of the building and whipped in the brisk wind, making it difficult to hear.

Dropping to a crouch, he ran to the nearest support beam. His heart stopped in his chest when he heard the scream. He spun, but it was too dark to see. His blood ran cold when he spotted the silhouettes against the night sky. Rooks and Kate were locked in a struggle just a few feet from the edge and a sheer nine-hundred-foot drop.

Terror swept through him, a violent tornado scattering his thoughts into chaos. Stepping out from behind the pillar, he drew down on Rooks. "Rooks! Stop! *Now!*"

Frank didn't need to see the other man's face to know his intentions. Rooks's arms were locked around Kate. Too close to her for him to get off a shot. Too close to the edge to charge.

Shifting his weapon slightly, he fired a warning shot. "Let go of her! *Now!*"

"Frank! He's armed!"

The terror in her voice ripped at him. He felt that same terror rampaging through his own body. The memory of Gittel's violent death had been imprinted on his brain, and those images paralyzed him with fear.

Arms locked around Kate, Rooks swung her closer to the edge. "Drop the gun, Matrone."

Kate fought him wildly, but Rooks outweighed her by eighty pounds. "Frank!"

"Rooks, don't do it!" Frank edged closer. He could feel his heart pounding. Fear whipping and coiling inside him. "I'll do whatever you want!" he screamed. "Just let her go."

Rooks's teeth flashed white in the semidarkness. He looked dangerous and evil and very insane. "What is she worth to you, Matrone?"

"Everything." But Frank didn't lower the pistol. He was close enough now so that even in the darkness he could see Kate was injured. She was cradling her arm. Choking back sobs. "Let her go, and I'll let you walk away from this."

"Liar." Rooks began to laugh.

A chill raced down Frank's spine.

Legs apart and braced, the lawyer heaved Kate toward the edge.

"Frank, kill him!" she screamed.

Two feet from the edge. Terror snarling inside him. Panic sinking into him like fangs. Knowing Rooks was seconds away from killing her, Frank risked the shot and pulled the trigger.

Rooks's body jolted, but he didn't release Kate. Another, stronger wave of terror. A beast galloping through him. The hard slam of panic in his heart. Frank wanted to kill the son of a bitch. He wanted to cut his throat, remove him from the face of the earth. "Let her go!" he shouted.

"That's exactly what I'm going to do."

Frank stared, his heart exploding, fear permeating his every cell.

Rooks shoved her violently. Kate stumbled over what looked like a rope, twisted in midair. Her arms flailed wildly. Her scream rent the air. As if in slow motion she went over the edge.

And then she was gone.

THIRTY

For the span of several heartbeats, Frank stood there, disbelief and rage coursing through him in a violent torrent. He couldn't believe Kate was gone. Couldn't believe God had taken her from him the same way he'd taken Gittel.

His vision tunneled on Rooks. Thoughts as black as death scrolled through his mind. He didn't remember closing the distance between them. He didn't feel it when the other man slammed the baton across his chest. He didn't remember raising the gun or pulling the trigger eleven times as he emptied the clip into the other man's body. The one thing he did remember was shoving Rooks's body off the edge of the building.

Alone on the twenty-seventh floor of Providence Tower, Frank Matrone went to his knees. "No! No! *Noooo!*"

He slammed his fists against the concrete with each word. An animal sound of rage and denial tore from his throat. The sense of loss overwhelmed him. Grief flowed through him like the black blood of the dead. He put his face in his hands as the thunderstorm of emotion doubled him over. "Oh, God, Kate."

"Frank!"

He raised his head, not sure if her voice was in his mind or if he'd really heard it. Then he heard it again. Kate. Hope burst through him, sent him staggering to his feet. He crossed to where she had gone off the edge on trembling legs. He spotted the orange extension cord running over the side. He walked to the edge and looked down. An instant of disbelief. Relief slammed into him when he saw Kate dangling ten feet down.

"Jesus!" Then, "I've got you!"

She must have known what Rooks had planned for her. She'd tied one end of the cord around the concrete pillar, the other end around her torso and beneath her arms.

"Sweet Jesus." Using the pillar for leverage, he wrapped the cord around his fist and pulled. "Hang on!"

A moment later a single hand reached up and grasped the edge of the concrete floor. Frank quickly secured the extension cord and ran to her. His entire body shook uncontrollably when he grasped her hand. "I've got you," he said.

She seemed weightless as he pulled her onto the floor, then to her feet. "Oh, God . . . Frank. Oh, God. I thought . . ."

She teetered for an instant, and then he pulled her into his arms. "Shh. Easy. I'm here, baby. I'm here."

"Rooks . . . He was going to . . ."

"I know. It's okay now. He's gone, honey. You're safe. It's just me."

"You came," she choked. "I knew you would."

Realizing she was favoring her arm, he pulled back slightly. "You're hurt."

"I think my arm is broken."

The thought of Rooks causing her that kind of pain filled him with rage. But it was short-lived. Rooks was dead. Kate was warm and alive against him. So close he could feel the warmth of her breath, the wetness of her tears. The softness of her hair. The scent of her perfume that had always driven him a little nuts. The vibrant force of her life.

"You saved my life," she whispered.

Setting his hands on either side of her face, he looked into her eyes. "I saw you fall. I thought . . ." His voice broke as the memory of the terror and grief pressed down on him. "If you had fallen, I would have died right along with you."

"I didn't know if the cord would hold. I couldn't see. My hands were shaking."

Closing his eyes against the rush of emotion, he set his forehead against hers. "That was smart, honey," he said. "That cord saved your life."

She pulled back, her gaze meeting his. Raising her uninjured arm, she set her palm against his face. "This is probably a bad time to say this. I'm not even sure you want to hear it. But I love you."

He grinned. "That could be the shock talking."

Choking out a sound that was part sob, part laugh, she hit him on the shoulder with her good hand. "I'm not in shock."

"In that case, I guess it's safe for me to tell you I love you, too. I've loved you since the moment I laid eyes on you."

"Liar."

"Okay, the second time I laid eyes on you."

He pulled her close. He could feel the tremors racking her body. He could feel his own body shaking. His emotions breaking free. He felt tears on his cheeks, and they stunned him. He couldn't remember the last time he'd cried. But he didn't care because Kate was alive. The future was theirs for the taking.

Holding her tightly, he bowed his head and vowed never to let her go.

EPILOGUE

For the first time in her career, Kate was late for a meeting. She tried not to notice the stares and whispers of the administrative staffers as she rushed toward Mike Shelley's office. At the doorway, she paused to take a deep breath in an effort to gather her composure, then opened the door.

Three heads turned, all eyes in the room landing on Kate. "Sorry I'm late," she said.

"No problem." Mike Shelley sat at his desk, his eyes steady on hers.

Kate wasn't sure she liked the compassion she saw in his expression. She was much more comfortable with annoyance or exasperation. She figured she was going to have to deal with that for a while.

"How's the arm?" Detective Bates asked.

He sat at the small conference table. Same bad suit. Same stained tie. Some things never changed.

"Better." Kate smiled. "Thank you."

"Everyone wants to sign your cast." Liz Gordon chuckled. "Totally inappropriate stuff, Kate. Don't let them."

Kate laughed, but her nerves were taut. She looked around the small conference room table. Frank was supposed to be here, but he was conspicuously absent. She didn't want to ask about him; she wasn't sure she would be able to keep a handle on her emotions. But she couldn't help but wonder if he was tied up with the legal problems that had arisen from the shooting death of Jameson Rooks.

As if reading her thoughts, Mike Shelley cleared his throat. "Matrone is on his way. Hopefully." Rising, he left his desk and walked to the conference table where he pulled out a chair for Kate. "You didn't have to be here today," he said.

"I'd like to stay apprised of what's happening with the case, if that's all right."

"That's fine," he said. "But I meant what I said about your taking some vacation time."

Kate tried not to wince as she lowered herself into the chair. She was still sore from the ordeal she'd gone through with Jameson Rooks atop Providence Tower four days ago. Her arm had been set and would heal with no lingering damage. But she knew the emotional wounds would take a bit more time.

Frank had stayed with her until the paramedics loaded her into the ambulance. He'd wanted to ride with her to the hospital, but the PD had had plenty of questions for him that kept him tied up the rest of the night. But he'd been in her room when she'd wakened the next day . . .

"Kate, I called this meeting to brief all of you on the Ferguson and Rooks investigation." Mike opened the folder in front of him. "I thought you might want to know what our investigation has uncovered so far."

Kate had already figured out most of how the insurance scheme worked. This morning, her overriding concern was for Frank. She'd found out late yesterday that a grand jury would convene to rule on the shooting death of Jameson Rooks. The process was routine, even for justifiable shooting deaths. But the legalities were never easy to go through.

Mike Shelley grimaced. "From what the Dallas PD and federal investigators have been able to find out, it looks like the law firm of Ferguson and Rooks created companies that purchased franchises for coffee shops, convenience stores, and pizza parlors. Nationwide, there were about four hundred and twenty-two units in twenty-eight states. The parent company took out life insurance policies on hourly employees. We believe Jameson Rooks then hired a hit man to go into the stores, murder the clerk on duty, and make it look like a robbery. The family of the deceased clerk usually received four or five thousand dollars, if anything. The corporation owned by the law firm of Ferguson and Rooks would receive between two hundred and three hundred thousand dollars."

Kate had done the math and the numbers astounded and sickened her. "Rooks told me they had murdered upward of twenty-two people."

Detective Bates sighed. "That's over six million dollars. Who says murder isn't lucrative?"

"A lot of families devastated," Liz said.

Mike Shelley grimaced. "The practice is known as dead-peasant insurance."

"Apt term," the detective said.

"What about the case?" Kate asked.

"We're still working out the details with the feds."

"And Belinda Ferguson?" she asked.

"She's going to make it." Mike's eyes glinted hard for a moment. "I've already told her attorney no deals. She'll do hard time."

Kate thought about that for a moment and asked the question that had been eating at her for four days now. "What about Frank?"

Mike's expression softened when he looked at Kate. "He's got some legal red tape to work through, but he'll be exonerated."

As if on cue, the door swung open. Kate looked up to see Frank standing inside the door. He looked as if he'd just stepped out of the shower. His hair was damp and mussed. A tiny piece of tissue paper clung to his chin. He was wearing a nicely cut charcoal suit, a crisp white shirt, a burgundy tie, and, of course, cowboy boots.

"We're glad you finally decided to grace us with your presence," Mike said.

"Sorry I'm late." Frank addressed the group, but his eyes were on Kate. "I had some things to take care of."

She hadn't seen him since the morning she'd wakened in the hospital. He'd called to check on her, but he hadn't come to see her. She didn't understand why. So much had happened in the last few days she wasn't sure she'd ever figure it out. The only thing she knew for certain was that it hurt not seeing him.

"Kate, I need to talk to you."

The utterance of her name jolted her from her reverie. She blinked, realized Frank was addressing her in front of the group. Uncertain, she looked at Shelley, who nodded. "Go," he said. "You're on vacation the rest of the week."

"What about my caseload?"

"We'll talk about that when you get back." Mike rose and helped her scoot back her chair. "I'll see you next week."

Then she was walking toward the door, toward Frank. She could feel her heart beginning to pound. Her emotions ebbing and flowing. His eyes burning into her as she crossed the distance between them. She was glad to see him. Too glad. But she didn't know what to expect. She didn't know where she stood with him. Where they stood. And it was driving her crazy.

He took her hand when she reached the door and ushered her into the hall, closing the door behind them.

"What do you think you're doing?" she asked.

"Getting something off my chest."

She was standing with her back to the wall. He was so close she could smell the tangy out-of-doors scent of his aftershave. His eyes were dark and level on hers.

"How are you feeling?" he asked.

"I'm . . . okay."

"Liar." But he softened the word with a smile. "I'm sorry I haven't come to see you."

"You have a lot to deal with." She pursed her lips, suddenly aware that she was inordinately nervous. "I've been worried. I mean, the grand jury."

"Grand jury is going to be a slam dunk." He grinned, but she saw the same nerves she was feeling in the depth of his eyes. "It's the other thing that's got me tied up in little knots."

"What other thing?"

"We said some things the other night . . ." He looked down, then met her gaze. "No matter how things play out between us, I just want you to know that I meant what I said."

Kate's mind was reeling. She hadn't known what to expect of this first meeting, but it wasn't this. "We said a lot of things. We were scared. The adrenaline was high—"

A smile whispered across his mouth. "You're a hard case, Kate."

"Habit, I guess."

Taking her face in his hands, he backed her to the wall, then gently lowered his mouth to hers. Kate knew that letting him kiss her right outside her boss's office was inappropriate and unprofessional. But the instant his mouth touched hers none of that seemed to matter. Nothing in her life had ever felt so right as being held in Frank Matrone's arms.

He pulled away and looked into her eyes. "I want you to know. I checked into a clinic. Outpatient. I'm going to get off the pain meds. Try some other things. Acupuncture. Surgery, maybe."

"Frank, that's wonderful. I know you can do it."

His gaze searched hers. "I know you may not want to hear this, Kate, but I'm crazy about you. I can't stop thinking about you. I want to be with you twenty-four hours a day."

"Frank . . ."

"I need you in my life." He let out a pent-up breath. "I love you. I didn't think I'd ever say those words to anyone ever again, but you proved me wrong. You turned my world upside down. You showed me I have a future. That it's as bright as I want it to be."

Kate knew it was stupid but suddenly she had to blink back tears. "Are you finished?"

His jaw flexed. "I think that just about covers it."

Raising her hand, she pressed it to his cheek. "You proved to me that even the deepest of wounds can be healed," she whispered. "You've healed me. Heart, body, and soul. I love you, too."

He blinked as if she'd stunned him, then a slow grin spread across his face. "In that case, why don't we blow this joint before the tongues start wagging?"

"The tongues are already wagging. Administrative staffers have a bet going."

"I put money in the pot."

"Did you win?"

"More than I ever imagined." Frank grinned and for the first time since she'd known him, Kate saw joy in his eyes.

*Turn the page for a special preview
of Linda Castillo's next novel*

A WHISPER AT MIDNIGHT

Coming soon from Berkley Sensation!

Julia Wainwright stood on the sidewalk in the chill morning air, a box of warm beignets balanced in her hand, a stack of books tucked beneath her arm. She stared through the storefront window, taking in the display of leather-bound tomes artfully arranged on a red and gold tapestry, not quite able to convince herself it was her creation.

"Not bad for a kid who flunked second grade art class," she murmured, unable to keep the silly grin off her face.

The sun rising over the French Quarter's St. Louis Cathedral warmed her back as she tugged the key from her coat pocket and stuck it in the lock. Hugging the books to her body, expertly balancing the beignets, she shoved open the door with her foot.

The aromas of old building, paper dust, and vanilla candles greeted her like an old friend as she stepped into The Book Merchant, the antique bookstore she owned and operated.

Julia had had a love affair with books even before she'd learned to read, which had occurred at the ripe age of four. Immersing herself in wonderful stories with characters who were every bit as real as her friends from preschool had transformed a rather lonely childhood into a world filled with enchantment and adventure. She had understood and appreciated the power of the written word long before most of her classmates had even read their first book.

As she'd grown older, her love of books burgeoned to include rare and old books. She could sit for hours with a battered volume, thinking about all the people who'd held it in their hands over the years, wondering if they'd wept or laughed at the passages within.

Two years ago The Book Merchant had been nothing more than a pipe dream. Then she'd discovered the derelict storefront in a historic building in the French Quarter—and known it was perfect. The space had been damaged by fire and water and had suffered years of neglect. But Julia had a gift for seeing potential—whether in people or old buildings—and she'd refused to listen to the naysayers telling her the place couldn't be saved. Risking her life savings, she'd procured a loan, purchased the narrow space, and begun the monumental task of transforming a dilapidated space into her dream. After months of backbreaking work and countless sleepless nights, The Book Merchant had been born.

Setting the books on the scarred surface of the old-fashioned counter, she worked off her coat. By the time she reached the coffeemaker, she'd already fished a beignet from the box and taken an enormous bite that would have sent her mother scrambling for her *Miss Manners Emergency Handbook*.

It was the one book Julia didn't carry.

She chose a dark roast with chicory, and while the coffeemaker ground beans she set her mind to the task of opening the shop. She lit the dozen or so scented candles she burned throughout the day. Yesterday had been vanilla. Today was hazelnut. Tomorrow maybe she'd try the café au lait she'd picked up at the candle shop on Magazine Street.

She'd just begun the task of counting petty cash when she spotted the envelope on the floor just inside the front door. Someone had slipped it through the old-fashioned mail slot, and she'd somehow missed it when she walked in. A chill that had nothing to do with the damp February weather ran the length of her.

Refusing to acknowledge that her heart was pounding, Julia

crossed to the envelope and picked it up. The absence of a post date indicated it hadn't come through the mail system. This one had been hand delivered. The others had been mailed. The realization that he knew where she worked raised gooseflesh on her arms.

She slit the envelope. Like the others before it, the letter was off a laser and printed on ivory linen stationery in an Olde English font. Hating that her hands weren't quite steady, Julia unfolded the letter and read the short passage.

> *Her tainted pen spills sin onto the page*
> *like the fevered blood from a sickle slash.*
> *Soon thine blood will be hers*
> *and vengeance will be mine.*

"Now what the hell is that supposed to mean?" she whispered.

But deep inside, Julia knew. And the realization chilled her almost as much as the letter itself.

She jumped when the bell on the front door jingled. Relief swept through her when she looked up to see her sister, Claudia, enter the shop.

"Hi," she said, tucking the letter into her pocket.

"Don't 'hi' me." Glaring at her, Claudia Wainwright crossed to the counter and hefted the cardboard box onto the scarred surface. "I can't believe you sent me to pick up these books without warning me," she said, brushing paper dust from her slacks.

"Would you like coffee to go with your bad mood? It's fresh." Unfazed by her younger sibling's wrath, her mind still on the newest letter she'd received, Julia crossed to the coffeemaker and poured French roast into a tall mug.

"Black," Claudia grumbled.

"What has you in such an uproar this morning?"

"Mr. Stocker is the rudest old codger I've ever had the misfortune of dealing with," Claudia said.

Julia withheld a smile. The accused Mr. Stocker was a fellow antiquarian who ran a bookstore near Tulane where Claudia attended law school. "He does have a knack for being difficult," she said diplomatically.

"He tried to charge me twice for these books."

Julia winced. She'd already paid fair market value for the books in question. "He's a little forgetful."

Claudia snorted. "He's a crude little man and uses his age to try and cheat people. I honestly don't know why you continue to do business with him."

"I deal with him because he has one of the most extensive collections in the city." More interested in the package her sister had brought her than her wily competitor, Julia tugged open the flaps and peered inside the box. "There are beignets next to the coffeemaker if you'd like one."

"I am not going to let you appease me with beignets," Claudia said, but her eyes were already drifting to the pastries. "Next time you can pick up your own books."

Anxious to see the gems her sister had brought from Mr. Stocker's shop, Julia pulled out one of the old tomes and her chest clenched with pride. "Oh, my. Victor Hugo," she whispered in reverence. "A first edition. I can't believe he parted with this."

Claudia grumbled something about grouchy old goats, but Julia wasn't listening. A flutter of excitement went through her when she slid the first book back into the box and pulled out the second. The redolence of aged leather and dust met her as the ancient volume in her hand came into view. "*Alice in Wonderland*," she murmured. "First English edition. London, 1865. Oh, Claudia, it's lovely."

Rolling her eyes, Claudia took a bite of beignet. "I don't think I've ever seen a book I would consider lovely. Especially one as dusty and old as that one. They make me sneeze."

Julia felt the burn of tears behind her lids at the thought of all the reading pleasure the book in her hand had brought to so many people in the century and a half since it had been published. Feeling foolish, she blinked rapidly and slid the book back into the box. "In any case, thank you for braving Mr. Stocker and picking them up for me. I would have had to open the shop late if you hadn't volunteered."

Claudia poured coffee and took it behind the counter. "Lunch at Arnaud's would probably make up for it . . ."

Thinking she might treat her sister to her favorite French

Quarter restaurant, Julia hefted the box and started for her desk. "I'd better get these books logged," she said over her shoulder.

"Julia?"

"Hmmm?"

"You didn't tell me you received another letter."

The words stopped her cold. Putting on her best smile, Julia turned to see her sister brandishing the envelope she'd inadvertently left on the counter. *Damn.*

"It was delivered before I arrived this morning," she said.

"I'm sure it hadn't crossed your mind to hide it from me, did it?"

"Why would I try to hide it?"

"Because you know I'm going to make you do something about it." When Julia didn't respond, Claudia raised the envelope and rattled it. "How many does this make? Seven? Eight?"

"Six." Julia set the box on her desk. "If you're counting."

"I'm counting. And you should be, too." Claudia put her hands on her hips. "Where's the letter? I want to read it."

Knowing she was busted, Julia slid the letter from her pocket and handed it to her. "It's the same as the others."

Claudia read the letter aloud. " 'Her tainted pen spills sin onto the page like the fevered blood from a sickle slash. Soon thine blood will be hers and vengeance will be mine.' " Her gaze met Julia's. "That is freaking creepy."

Hearing the passage spoken aloud made the hairs at Julia's nape prickle. "*Creepy* is a good word."

"Do you recognize the author?" Claudia asked.

"Not this one, but the one I received on Monday came to me last night." While she'd been lying awake, worrying about who might be sending her subtly threatening quotes from books.

"Which one?" Claudia bent and slid the manila folder containing five other letters from beneath the counter.

" 'The sins ye do by two and two ye must pay for one by one.' " Julia quoted the passage from memory. She walked halfway down one of the narrow aisles and paused to pull out a book. "Kipling, maybe." She carried the book to the counter, set it down, and both women began paging through it. "Let's see. Oh, here it is. Rudyard Kipling's *Tomlinson*."

Silence reigned for a moment while both women read the

poem. Then Claudia blew out a breath. "This guy is obviously some kind of nutcase, Julia."

"I'm getting that impression, too."

Claudia looked down at the letter in her hand. "What does it mean? Why would someone send letters like this?"

"I don't know." But after this latest letter, Julia had an idea as to the why, and it disturbed her almost as much as the letters themselves. She was going to have to do something about it. The question was what. "This one was hand delivered, Claudia."

Her sister's eyes widened. "He was *here*? He knows you run this shop? My God, I always thought he was, you know, in another state or something."

Julia nodded, resisting the urge to rub the gooseflesh that had come up on her arms. "No postmark."

Both women were silent for an instant, and then Claudia said, "I think it's time you reported this to the police."

"I'm not sure what the police can do. I mean, it's not against the law to send letters."

"These are more than just letters. They're . . . disturbing. Threatening. Julia, this creep could be dangerous."

More than anything, those were the words she hadn't wanted to hear. "He's quoting books, Claudia."

Her sister made a sound of annoyance. "He could be some kind of wacko stalker. He could be watching you. He could walk right into the bookstore and you wouldn't even know it." She looked at the letter and quoted. " 'Soon thine blood will be hers and vengeance will be mine?' It sounds like he wants to get back at you for something you've done."

Julia hoped her sister didn't notice the shiver that went through her. In the two weeks since she'd received the first letter, she'd found herself jumping at shadows, watching her customers more closely than normal. For the first time since opening The Book Merchant, she was uneasy working alone and staying late at night, both of which she did often.

She knew her sister was right. To ignore the situation any longer would be not only foolhardy, but potentially dangerous. The problem was, she wasn't sure how to address it without opening a can of worms she had absolutely no desire to deal with.

Julia chose her words carefully. "Do you have any idea the embarrassment this could cause Dad if the wrong person caught wind of this and decided to sensationalize it?"

"A few cryptic letters aren't exactly a scandal."

"For God's sake, Claudia, I'm not talking about the letters."

"Oh. *Oh.*" Understanding dawned in Claudia's eyes. "You think this is related to your book?"

Julia slid the letter from the folder. "Read the latest letter again." She tapped her nail against the ivory paper. " 'Her tainted pen spills sin onto the page like the fevered blood from a sickle slash.' " She sighed unhappily. "I think it's obvious."

Claudia bit her lip. "There's got to be a way to keep you safe and stop this guy without spilling the beans."

The beans her sister was referring to was the publication of Julia's first book, which had been released a month earlier under the pseudonym of Elisabeth de Haviland. Few people knew about Julia's writing. Certainly not her father, pillar of the community and New Orleans' religious icon Benjamin Wainwright. Julia wanted to keep it that way. "Dad has worked long and hard to get where he is. I would hate for my writing to affect him in any way."

"Or embarrass him."

"Thank you for stating the obvious," Julia said dryly.

"Maybe it's time you told him. I mean, come on, you're his daughter. He loves you."

Julia couldn't help it, she laughed even though the humor of the moment eluded her. "I don't think he's prepared for Elisabeth de Haviland."

"You don't have to tell him *what* you write."

"You know how Dad is. Once he finds out his daughter is an author, he'll tell all of his friends and rush out to buy the book." *And they'll all get the shock of their lives,* she thought with a shudder.

"Look, the fact of the matter is there's some weirdo out there sending you threatening letters. You can't ignore something like that these days."

Julia knew her sister was right. She should have done something when she'd received the first letter. "I hate it when you make more sense than I do," she muttered.

"At least file a report with the police. I'll check, but I think Louisiana has a stalking law."

"That will help. Thank you." Julia sighed. "If the police ask, I'll simply tell them the stalker must be referring to a book I carry here at the shop."

"I think it's a good compromise."

Taking the letter from her sister, Julia looked down at the cryptic words and felt a stir of anger. She'd finally found her place in the world, and now it seemed some warped individual had his sights set on disrupting her life. She wasn't going to let him do it.

"And in case you're wondering, there's nothing wrong with what you write." Sipping her coffee, Claudia looked at her over the rim.

Julia smiled. "Thanks. But I still don't want anyone to know about the book."

"You know your secret is safe with me."

"Is there a *but* coming?"

"I just hate for you to feel you have to keep such a big part of your life hidden."

"Come on, Claudia. Dad is about to become director of the Eternity Springs Ministries, the third largest church in Louisiana. There are people out there who think what I write is trash and would use that to hurt him. He's worked hard to get where he is. He's got so many wonderful ideas on how to help people and families in need. It would kill him to lose that." She shook her head. "Besides, I just don't think Dad is prepared to find out his daughter is writing something so . . ."

"Hot?" Claudia smiled.

"Misunderstood," Julia finished.

"Or maybe you're the one who's not prepared."

An unexpected quiver of emotion went through Julia at the wisdom of her younger sister's words, and she surprised herself by smiling. "Since when did you get so smart?"

"I have a really smart older sister." Claudia crossed to her and gave her a smacking kiss on the cheek. "My lips are sealed, Julia. But whenever you're ready to tell him, I want to be there because I have never seen Benjamin Wainwright speechless."